THE SUBSECTION

JAMES TARR

BOOKS

Vinci Books

vinci-books.com

Published by Vinci Books Ltd in 2025

1

Copyright © James Tarr 2024

The author has asserted their moral right to be identified as the author of this work in accordance with the Copyright, Designs and Patents Act 1988. This work is a work of fiction. Names, characters, places and incidents are the product of the author's imagination or are used fictitiously. Any resemblance to actual persons, living or dead, places and incidents is entirely coincidental.

All rights reserved. No part of this publication may be copied, reproduced, distributed, stored in any retrieval system, or transmitted in any form or by any means, including photocopying, recording, or other electronic or mechanical methods, nor used as a source for any form of machine learning including AI datasets, without the prior written permission of the publisher.

The publisher and the author have made every effort to obtain permissions for any third party material used in this book and to comply with copyright law. Any queries in this respect should be brought to the attention of the publisher and any omissions will be corrected in future editions.

A CIP catalogue record for this book is available from the British Library.

Paperback ISBN: 9781036707156

Printed and bound in Great Britain by Clays Ltd, Elcograf S.p.A.

By James Tarr

James Tarr Conspiracy Thrillers

Failure Drill
Splashback
Splits and Transitions
Whorl
Waiting for the Kick
Ghosts and Madmen
The Subsection

PART I
STOMACH AND TEETH

ONE

Playhouse Square

James Blinkenschaal yawned, took a long draw of coffee out of his flip-top insulated mug, and blinked with exaggerated care several times, trying to wake up. It had rained a little in the late morning hours, and the streets of downtown Cleveland were wet, reflecting the reds and greens of the traffic lights. It was peaceful, and he had the radio off. There wasn't much traffic—yet—and he enjoyed the hiss of the Durango's tires on the wet pavement, loud enough to be heard over the low rumble of the hemi. As he rolled into the downtown area the buildings around him grew taller. Depending on the district the towers were older and historic, with a lot of brick and stone, or more modern with steel and glass. Lights were starting to come on in some of the windows, but for the most part the towers were as dark and quiet as the streets.

But the wet traffic lanes and the smeared reflections of the lights triggered a memory. He'd landed an insurance case, years earlier, for a nationwide carrier he did a lot of work for, and their client was one of the big Hollywood movie studios. Someone had stolen some expensive electronic equipment from a location shoot, and the studio wanted it handled quietly, preferably without involving the police. Because the facts of the theft strongly indicated it was an employee, someone on the film crew. He'd figured out who was responsible pretty quickly, and turned his evidence over to the adjuster, but for a somewhat simple case it had been fascinating. He'd learned so much, talking to the movie industry people. Studios at the time were occasionally filming street scenes in Cleveland for big productions, having the modern downtown areas fill in for New York or other generic urban locales, just because it was so prohibitively expensive to film in NYC—in addition (apparently) to it being a giant pain in the ass due to all the permits and union bribes required to grease the wheels.

One assistant still photographer he'd interviewed had talked about "the water truck", and Blink—almost everybody called him Blink, Blinken, or Blinky—had thought he'd meant a truck that delivered drinking water. The guy—who'd gone on to some success on his own with his photographic "urban landscapes"—had shaken his head. "No, look at any TV show or any movie filmed outside on the street," he'd said. "Even ones that are filming under an overhang. The pavement—concrete, asphalt, whatever—has always been wet down. Almost always, ninety-eight times out of a hundred. Sometimes if it's a small space it's just a PA with a hose, but for a big area it's easier to use a water truck, especially if you're doing take after take. It drives down the street and sprays water. Enough to get it wet, but not to leave much standing water, maybe just a puddle or two out of the way."

"Why?" Blink had asked.

"Because it looks better, man," the skinny photog had

The Subsection

told him. "It looks *so* much better. Dry pavement is just flat. Doesn't give you anything. Might as well be standing on sand. *Ugly* sand. Wet, you get more saturated colors, blacker blacks, richer tans, but mostly it's due to the reflections. Wet pavement reflects lights, the reflections of your actors, clouds, movement, everything."

And damned if the guy hadn't been right. Blink couldn't watch a movie or TV show now without noticing the wet pavement under the feet of every single actor, even if there wasn't a cloud in the sky. Even if they were filming inside a damn parking garage with a roof over their heads.

Cleveland's Theater District was considered part of the city's downtown, but was on the south side of it, just over a mile southeast from the Rock & Roll Hall of Fame perched on the shore of Lake Erie. His destination was Playhouse Square, the beating heart of the theater district. It was the largest theater district in the US outside of New York City, not that anybody outside of Cleveland really knew that. But in-between the theaters and the businesses servicing those patrons of the arts—restaurants and hotels—were all sorts of mundane businesses.

He took several turns on streets that felt narrow from the buildings towering overhead, then pulled to the curb on 14th Street south of Euclid. The US Bank Centre was one of the largest buildings in Cleveland—not the tallest, but it spread over most of a block, a modern mirrored monstrosity in an area filled with old, beautiful, historic buildings.

Blink's focus was on the physical therapy center on the south side of the US Bank Centre building. It was part of the building, inside it on the ground floor, but it had a separate entrance. Mirrored glass double doors which could be opened with the push of a button, at the top of a long concrete handicap ramp. The ramp went up one direction, then turned and went the other before reaching the level of the door, the angle so gentle even someone rolling themselves up in a wheelchair would have no problem. There was a second door barely ten feet to the side, at the top of five steps. It fed into the US Bank Centre, although there was a door just inside which led into the therapy center's lobby.

Directly facing the south side of the building and the two entrances was a parking garage, and in-between the two was a small courtyard with a few steel tables and some decorative planters with low groundcover and small trees trimmed to provide the most shade.

Blink had scoped out the location the day before. There was no way to park a vehicle on the street long enough to do the job for which he'd been hired—the spots were metered. The first floor of the parking garage, directly across from the small courtyard, had no windows, and from the second floor (and up) the trees blocked the view of the entrances. So there was no way to park a vehicle with a stationary camera inside it where it would do the job. But those planters bordering the courtyard…they were perfect.

He looked around once more. There was very little traffic, foot or vehicle, at six in the morning. Humming to himself, he grabbed what looked like a big rock off the front passenger seat and climbed out.

His knee was a little stiff from just half an hour in the car, which told him there was likely a storm brewing. He stepped in front of his Dodge, walked across the sidewalk, and into the courtyard. It was empty, and badly lit by a few exterior lights. There were security cameras galore inside the US Bank Centre, but none covering the courtyard—at least that he'd been able to tell. So he was relaxed as he looked around.

Blink stepped into one of the planters, his shoes sinking slightly into the decomposing wood chips. The ground cover was bright green (more gray than anything in the cool pre-dawn light) and no more than ankle-high, which was perfect. He set the rock down into a small gap, then moved to stand behind it, looking back and forth between the rock and the two doors on the side of the building. He bent down and readjusted the rock, rotating it very slightly left. Then, satisfied, he strode back to his SUV, climbed in, and drove off.

TWO

Murph Takes A Trip

Murph squinted, and groaned. Something really, really bright was shining in his eyes. So bright he thought his eyes were open for a second. Until he cracked his eyelids, and took the full glare of the morning sun right in the retinas, like a razor sharp dagger.

He grimaced, clamped his eyelids shut again, and took inventory. It was not a quick process, but he wasn't in a hurry. Eventually he realized that unless gravity had reversed, he was lying on his back. The sun was warming his face and chest. He could smell dirt and water. Hear water, in fact, somewhere nearby. The rushing sound of it seemed all around him, burbling, swirling…

Abruptly he turned on his side, away from the glaring sun, and vomited. Just three heaves, his whole body jackknifing. Not much came up, although the stomach acid burned his lips and tongue. He knew not to eat much before taking peyote, as he almost always vomited after. Sometimes during. So he'd begun fasting beforehand, and hadn't actually eaten anything for a few days. The hallucinations from the mescaline were wild, and he felt bad for a few hours afterward, but the clarity that filled his mind for the next week was incredible. He'd done some of his best work during that post-peyote clarity. But the first few hours afterward…ugh.

This trip had been…he didn't even know how to describe it. Transcendent? Illuminating? He couldn't remember most of it, but the impact it had on his brain, on his subconscious thought processes, couldn't be understated. He had several new ideas, revolutionary avenues to explore to help solve his superconduction and scaling issues.

With his face shielded from the sun he opened his eyes again. His view was entirely Mother Earth—dirt and sand and a small tuft of slender, pale green grass. It was beautiful. He could feel the sun on his back. It was hot, but because the air around him was cool he could tell it still must be early in the morning.

Murph rolled onto his knees, then climbed to his feet, dizzy only for a second. He put his back to the sun, blinked his eyes a few times, and saw he was a dozen steps from the river. It was wide and placid here, and the riverbank sloped gradually down to the water, which was equal parts green and blue, with currently only a hint of mud clouding up the eddies and swirls. He looked down and saw he was dirty, caked with dust and grime like he'd been rolling around for hours. Mind still getting up to speed, it took him a few more seconds to realize he was naked under all the dirt.

His tongue felt swollen and dry, his lips hard and ready to crack. He swallowed a few times, licked his lips, then said, "Hunh." He heard a few birds, the clicks of something that could have been a lizard, a hard-shelled insect, or small rocks tumbling somewhere nearby, and over it all the soothing rush of the river. But no yells or screaming, which was good. Not that he looked that bad, clothed or naked, but people were weird when it came to nudity. Completely irrational. But then, people were irrational about almost everything. It was what made humanity both great and terrifying.

He looked left and right, but he was all alone. He headed into the river and spent a minute scrubbing off, dunking himself in the cold water. That woke him up the rest of the way, and when he popped his head up and swept his hair back he looked around carefully. He spotted the notch in the canyon wall he was looking for, maybe half a mile away across the valley floor, up a short gentle slope covered with grass and cacti. There was still nobody in sight either up- or downriver (which is why he'd chosen this part of the canyon), so he strode out of the water and slowly walked across the rocky, dusty ground, picking his steps carefully. There were low bushes to either side, sage and juniper and some small cottonwood trees. The banks to either side of the river were uniformly green with life, but get just a short distance away and the land became little more than dry earth and bare rock baking under an intense sun.

Ten minutes later he reached his tent, which was still in shadow. The cliff face rose steeply to either side—the spot he'd chosen was a narrow notch that was easy to miss unless you were walking right along the rock wall. The layers upon layers of rock had been laid down during the two billion years of the Proterozoic eon and Paleozoic era and eroded by the Colorado River over an estimated five million years—although there currently was a heated debate between geologists about that, some of which said the canyon had been formed over seventy million years. The steep rock walls stretched up to either side, stripes of orange and tan and brown and red in a dozen different hues. Sometimes—okay, usually—he went wandering when he took peyote, and so chose isolated campsites, nowhere near any of the usual tourist areas, but usually he never walked or crawled more than fifty feet during the night. Half a mile was a record, and he could feel it in his feet. In his knees. His soles were sore, and there were minor cuts and scratches on both his shins and abrasions on his knees.

He hooted and stomped his feet just to scare away any critters that might be nearby—rattlesnakes were the main worry—then crawled into his tent and pulled out his backpack. He had one one-liter bottle of distilled water remaining, and cracked the top on that and drank it down. It was still cold from the night before and tasted incredible, and seemed to fill dry cracks all through his body. That was it for the water he'd brought with him, but he had a water purifier. These weren't store-bought bottles but rather collapsible ones he brought with him whenever he went camping. He'd refill them before heading back out. The Colorado River water was full of minerals and didn't taste good, but he wasn't so much of a masochist that he'd backpack in days' worth of water when there was a river literally *right there*. The fifth longest river in the country.

Murph pulled a spare pair of boxers out of his backpack, tugged them on, then went looking for the clothes he'd been wearing the night before. He found his shirt twenty feet from the tent, draped over a small spiny bush. Fifty feet past that, out away from the cliffs, he found his left shoe atop a flat rock, a low-topped Merrell hiker that was light, comfortable, and had very aggressive tread. But that was it. He started a spiral search pattern, and after ten minutes had found his pants, socks, and underwear. But he couldn't find his damn right shoe. He couldn't hike out of the canyon with just one shoe. Well, he could, but it would be brutal.

He went back to where he'd found his left hiker, figuring he wouldn't have gone far before taking off his other shoe. He finally found it, well-hidden in the deep shade under a crucifixion thorn bush wrapped around a small cactus as if they were in a life-or-death struggle.

Immediate problem solved, he straightened and looked around him. As usual, the landscape was incredible, unbelievable. The peyote cleanse had sharpened his senses. His eyesight was clear, and he could hear the rustle and burble of the river as if it was just a few feet away, not half a mile.

He got his peyote from the locals, Hualapai indians, and it was the good stuff. He'd met a few of the younger braves during one of his first trips to the canyon, and they'd introduced him to a few of their friends in the Havasupai tribe, where he'd done a bit of business—some of it peyote-related, some of it computer/internet-related, for them and tribe. He often parked on reservation land if he wanted to hike in places he wasn't likely to meet another human soul. It depended on just how alone he needed to get with his thoughts. But he always got their permission first, the white man had already fucked them over enough. Then again, that was all of human history, a story of victors and the vanquished.

People sucked. That was why he preferred nature. Nature was bloodthirsty—'red in tooth and claw'—but not evil. Mother Nature might be trying to kill you, but it was nothing personal.

The canyon walls to either side were so tall that if the valley hadn't been so wide, the Arizona sun so high in the sky, it would have been dark and oppressive. Instead, but for the south rim wall still in shadow, the canyon floor was

The Subsection

bright and warm. Not hot, not yet, but it was liable to get there long before noon.

He appreciated that the National Park Service didn't try to sugarcoat it. It was a mile in elevation down to the river and another mile back up, which meant miles on switchback trails, and even the easiest trail wasn't so easy with that kind of elevation change. Most people simply couldn't make it down to the Colorado River and back in one day. The NPS's 'Introduction to Backcountry Hiking' brochure had warnings in red all over it, including "Know how to rescue yourself". And it was always ten or twenty degrees hotter down at the river than up at the rim, which mattered in the summer when it was in the eighties up top. Seven thousand feet of elevation along the South Rim, eight thousand at the North Rim, while the river flowed roughly two thousand feet above sea level. You'd see snow up on the rim through April while people down along the river were sweating and getting sunburned. All of which meant the people you were likely to meet at the bottom of the canyon were a different breed than those fat lazy NPCs lining the rims, looking down. Younger, in shape, more independent. Still, on average, over ten people a year died in the canyon. He didn't know the details, but he guessed most of them were from falls or heart attacks. But what a way to go. What *a place* to go.

At that thought Murph looked around again. It was gorgeous. Life—existence itself, just the fact of *being*—was wonderful, but there was something to be said for the natural wonders of the world still unfucked by humanity. For all of its tourists—and he doubted more than five percent of them ventured beyond the south rim between Grand Canyon Village and the Desert View Watchtower, a mere thirty-mile stretch in a park larger than the entire freaking state of Delaware—the Grand Canyon was definitely at the top of the list of nature's home runs. Unspoiled. He wouldn't have minded dying there. The Grand Canyon was one of the most beautiful places on earth, and maybe his favorite. His plan was to never die, and he was actually making some substantive progress on that front, but just in case that didn't work out he was compiling a list of places where he'd like his ashes to be scattered. Most of them were in the Grand Canyon. The Park Service, of course, would never allow it, but what they didn't know....

Humming to himself he walked back to his tent, broke it down, and strapped it to the outside of his pack. He policed his campsite, making sure he hadn't left any garbage, then walked down to the river and used his purifier to fill up three liter bottles of river water. It took a while, but he was in no hurry. He didn't have anywhere to be...well, ever, technically, but that's not to say he didn't have work to get back to. Responsibilities he'd taken on. Promises he'd made. And for that he needed a signal. He'd been out of contact, off the grid, for over three days, since he'd started the climb down from the south rim. No radio, and no cell phone—not that they really worked anywhere inside the canyon, or once you got more than a few miles away from the heavily-trafficked tourist areas. A satphone would have worked down in the canyon, most of the time, but the point was to be out of contact with everyone and everything but Mother Nature. He drank most of a liter as he stood beside the river, having learned long ago that the best place to store water in a desert was inside your own body, and then refilled the bottle and stuck it in his pack. Then he shouldered his pack and headed out.

The vast majority of tourists to the Grand Canyon only

The Subsection

visited a few spots that were easy access and provided great views. Ninety-five percent of them hung out at the southeast corner of the park, travelling along the South Rim between Hermit's Rest and the Desert View Watchtower which were just twenty miles apart in a straight line. Thick crowds of people, many with dogs, many of them not speaking English. When he did venture among the crowds he wished more of them didn't speak English, so he couldn't hear how stupid their comments were. Some did nothing but drive up to the visitor complex on the south rim, walk up to Mather Point a hundred yards past the idling tour buses, and jostle for space so they could take a selfie without anyone else in the picture. Then head toward the gift shop to buy some of the touristy memorabilia made in China. Which was a shame, because the park was huge. HUGE. The Grand Canyon was up to a mile deep in most places, often eighteen miles wide, and 277 miles long. 1900 square miles!

His first trip to the park he'd been standing at the Mather Point overlook, looking out at the enormity of the canyon, trying to spot the helicopter he could very faintly hear. And he finally did, off to the northwest, a dual-rotor machine tracing the course of the Colorado River—far, far below him. He'd never looked *down* on a helicopter before. At least one company did helicopter tours of the canyon.

Looking at the map they'd given him at the entrance he'd figured out the helicopter had been three miles away, and nearly three-quarters of a mile below him—and compared to the expanse of the canyon stretching in every direction, the helicopter had seemed close. Close enough to touch, like a green and white insect buzzing lazily along. It was that experience which had convinced him to get away from the tourists and do some real exploring. And he'd never regretted it.

There were well-known hiking trails, and of course you could book a horse-riding trip in the canyon, even mules, but if you weren't a big fat slob with a jiggling body full of preservatives and micro plastics and were willing to put in the work and maybe even sweat a little, and had some time, it was easy to hike through areas of the national park where you wouldn't see another person for hours or days at a time. Half the time he didn't even follow established trails, he just let his soul guide him. Although, over the years, he had hiked most of the well-known trails—Bright Angel, the North and South Kaibab Trails, and visited the Phantom Ranch. The Hermit and Grandview Trails. He'd skinny-dipped at Havasu Falls, ascended Mt. Trumbull, and walked across the Uinkaret volcanic field.

He checked his watch—just before eight a.m. Knowing the time he broke camp would tell him when he was getting close to his destination. He had a compass, but he wouldn't need it. The Colorado River was a known entity, running east to west through the canyon, although it did wind back and forth like a huge, sinuous snake. In a lot of places you couldn't walk close to the river, as it was rushing through deep rocky ravines, but you always knew where it was. He had about six hours of easy hiking east before it would be time to turn south and work his way up a trail the Hualapai had shown him. It was so narrow, and steep in some places, he wasn't sure it hadn't originally been a game trail—quite different from the maintained trails most of the tourists used that, while dirt, were nearly wide enough for a Jeep.

It was almost impossible to spot the end of his trail as it neared the river, but he knew to look for a promontory of rock in the distance shaped like a crooked nose. When he drew opposite that, it would be time to head away from the river, and he'd find the trail winding through the scrub on the narrow valley floor. Between where he was and the switchback trail up the rocks he expected to see very few people. Maybe none on land. Likely there'd be people floating down the river in kayaks or canoes, but that would be it. Whitewater rafting was a popular pastime, but not in this area of the Colorado.

Five hours later he stopped to refill his water bottles. He'd been stopping every hour for five minutes, to rest a bit and drink water, but was getting near to the point where he'd leave the river, and wanted a full complement of water, just in case. He'd been following one of the narrow trails that wound along the valley floor and stuck close to the river. They'd started out as game trails, but had been widened a bit over the years by human feet. He'd seen two people two hours into his journey, hikers, but they'd been on the opposite side of the river, which was fifty yards wide at that point. They'd exchanged waves, but that was it.

He drank half a liter, relieved himself in a bush, then set about using the purifier to refill the plastic bottles. The sun was bright and hot, the air dry. He hadn't seen anybody on the river all morning.

"Hello? Hey!" After so much quiet the human voices were strange. He looked up. Staggering around a rocky outcrop a hundred feet away were a handful of people who looked like they'd been dragged behind a car. Two girls and two guys who looked to be in their early twenties. "Can you help us?"

"With what?"

One of the guys was chubby and pale, the other was skinny. One young woman was a thick, pretty brunette, the other was a skinny blonde who seemed to have a great body but with a mannish, horsey face. They were all sweating and sunburned and covered in dust. And seemingly exhausted. They walked up.

"We're lost."

"You're in the Grand Canyon," Murph said. He jerked his thumb over his shoulder. "That's the Colorado River."

"Very funny, smartass," the skinny guy said. "We know we're in the fucking Grand Canyon." They crowded around him and looked up. Murph was tall and skinny, with a big mop of sun-bleached hair atop his head making him seem even taller.

"No, I mean," Murph said, "the river goes through the park from one end to the other. It's very tough to try to swim across it unless you're in one of the wide, slow moving areas, so most people stay on one side or the other unless you're rafting or kayaking. And there's cliffs all around. So how can you be lost? Follow the slope down until you find the water, then go upriver or down and go back out the canyon the way you came in."

"We got high last night, and couldn't find the trail," the blonde told him, embarrassed. "I think we passed it, and now we don't know which direction it is. We went back and forth for hours yesterday, until it got dark. We slept on the ground down here. We've been wandering around all morning, looking for something. Someone." She looked at what he was doing. "Is it okay to drink the river water? We weren't sure. We did, but…"

"Always better to use a purifier," he told them. "Here." He handed them a full bottle, and they passed it around. He looked back and forth between them. "Do you guys not have any backpacks? Any supplies?"

The chubby guy shook his head. "We thought we'd only be gone a few hours. Just down to the river and back up. It looked really close on the map."

The Subsection

Murph shook his head, dug into his backpack, and handed out two energy bars. All natural, no preservatives. "So where did you park up top?"

The skinny guy shrugged. "I don't know. We drove through a little town with a train and some cabins and a hotel."

"Maswik Lodge," one of the girls said around a mouthful of food.

"Grand Canyon Village," Murph told them.

"Yeah, whatever. But there were shit-tons of tourists there, so we kept going, found some side roads, and headed, um west. Like, half an hour? On dirt roads. Then the road we were on ended. But there was this awesome space to park on the side of the road, where we could see the canyon, and we followed this trail down here. But it took forever to get down. We went swimming, and got high, then we got lost, and couldn't find the trail that we came in on. We almost froze to death last night. I can't believe we haven't seen anybody, you're the first person we've seen."

Murph fought the urge to roll his eyes. "This park is huge. The closest place to here that tourists go is Supai Village, run by the Havasupai tribe. The Havasupai Lodge is very nice. But you can't even drive to it. You have to park and hike eight miles. Just to get to the hotel. I think you probably drove onto the reservation. But the canyon's no joke. You're lucky you didn't die. Seriously."

The brunette moaned. "Is that how far we have to walk? Eight miles? My feet are killing me." Murph looked at their feet. The whiner was wearing flat-bottomed Vans, a totally, completely horrible choice for hiking. The others were wearing various running shoes. Better, but still not good.

"To the Lodge?" He shook his head. "No, it's twenty miles from here, straight line. And there are no straight lines. It would take days to get there. I just mentioned it because it's the closest thing to civilization from here. But if you come with me, it's about an hour to the base of the trail I take up the south rim. There's this big spur of rock... Anyway, once we get to the top, which looking at you I'm guessing will take more than a few hours, my vehicle is another couple miles." On an unmarked reservation road that in many places was little better than a two-track. If the ground wasn't so hardpacked he never would have been able to get his RV down it, even with its all-season tires.

"Is that near our car?"

Murph shook his head. "I have no idea where your car is. But I know where the Village is, and from there you should be able to backtrack to your car."

"I can't believe there aren't police out here," the brunette said. "No cell service, and no police?" She looked around, then peered at him. It appeared she wasn't sure if they could trust him.

"Park Rangers," Murph told her. "And you're welcome to stay here. But considering all the dumb decisions y'all have made already, I'm guessing you'll end up dead before you get rescued. I'm Kelly. Come with me if you want to live." He smiled and cocked his head and waited. None of them seemed to get the reference, which was disappointing.

By the time they reached his vehicle the sun was down behind a ridge, the land in shadow but the sky still aglow. They'd spent hours working their way up the narrow switchback trail on the south rim, in shade almost the whole time, which was a blessing as three of the four of them were slow and out of shape. Laboring in the hot sun might have been too much for them. They still had to stop to take frequent breaks. Not quite halfway up the canyon wall was a flat-topped mesa that spread out for a hundred yards and could have been on Mars for as barren as it was, nothing but dirt and bare red rock. While they rested Murph walked out to the edge and enjoyed the view. The rest of them seemed to have lost their appetite for sight-seeing. By the time they reached the top of the south rim they'd gone through all the water and the remaining energy bars in his pack.

He'd learned they were college students and had just finished out the school year at ASU. Emily was the thick brunette—she'd just graduated, and would be going into nursing school after the summer. Rich was the chubby one, a junior getting a business degree. The skinny guy was Troy—more than a bit of a jerk, but his asshole tendencies seemed to be tempered by his physical exhaustion. His friends said he was really good with numbers, but he didn't know yet if he wanted to go into accounting or try something involving the stock market. All of them were smart, at least by normal standards.

The skinny blonde who'd caught his eye was Hannah. She handled the climb better than any of them, probably because she was in the best shape—she said she used to do track and field in high school, and still ran regularly. She had a plain, almost masculine face, but a pretty, shy smile.

"Where's your car?" Troy gasped, as they finally topped the rim. He looked around, then glared at Murph suspiciously. They all did. Their disappointment was palpable.

"I told you, it's another two miles," Murph said. He pointed. "But it's flat. At least, compared to that." He jabbed a thumb over his shoulder at the rim of the Grand Canyon. "No more climbing, just walking." The canyon behind them was sparse and arid as a desert. The south rim, on the other hand, was covered with a pine forest, and the temperature had dropped significantly. It wasn't cold, not yet, but it would be. "Anybody needs to go potty, pick a tree to hide behind, and if you see any elk, don't try to pet them." There seemed to be more elk than squirrels in the forests around the east end of the canyon.

Rich pulled out his phone, and lifted it into the air. He thought for sure he'd have a signal, now that they were out of the canyon. He frowned at the display. NO SERVICE "Seriously?"

Forty-five minutes later they came around the side of a small rise and saw his RV, the glass reflecting the glow in the sky. It was parked at the end of a narrow dirt road, little more than a two-track, running between two low hills.

"That's yours?" Rich said. He'd been expecting a shitty, thirty-year-old Winnebago. Their rescuer looked like a dude with no money, one of those spacey surfer/hiker types who'd be in-between jobs his whole life. And he sounded like one too, talking about nature and some of the wildest conspiracy theories ever as they'd trudged to the top of the canyon. But what squatted in front of them looked more like Dave Matthews' tour bus than an RV. And Rich said as much, as they walked up and stared at it.

"Yeah, well," Murph said, and shrugged. He glanced at his ride. It was a Prevost bus conversion by Marathon Coach with dual axles in the back and a bombproof diesel powertrain made by Volvo. Brand new it had probably been a million and a half, easy, maybe twice that, but it was fifteen years old, and he'd bought it from the Miami Police Department in an online property auction for a fraction of what it was worth. His stupidly-low bid had been the highest the department received, and they'd set no minimum price, so.... It looked brand new inside and out with leather-wrapped couches and chairs, all-new appliances, and cherry wood floors in the bedroom. Likely seized from a drug dealer who'd bought it and never used it. Murph had spent a decent amount of money and a lot of time customizing the interior, although most of his efforts weren't meant to be noticed by casual visitors.

"You rich, Kelly?" Troy asked him, eyeballing the motorcoach.

"What's rich?" Murph said. "Define rich. Hundred years ago, if you had a house with floors that weren't dirt, with running water, with electricity, with central heating, you'd be considered rich. And nobody had air conditioning back then, not even kings. Maybe servants, waving fans over you. Now everybody's got all that, in addition to cable TV, smart phones, cheap antibiotics…" He shrugged again.

Rich nodded at the RV. "That's rich, to me." He pulled out his phone again, checked the screen—his battery was almost dead—and silently swore. Still no signal.

"To me, if you can afford to fly private everywhere, not have to deal with TSA and commercial airports, if you've got enough money to do that, you're rich," Murph said. Not that he'd flown anywhere in years. He ran his hands over the big door which fit flush to the body, then reached under it casually and pressed a concealed button. Then he dug a remote out of his backpack and hit it. The door slid open with a hiss of hydraulics. He looked at his companions. "I don't have that kind of money. Which is why I've got this. I've got cold water and Gatorade in the refrigerator," he told them. "But more important than that, maybe, is the shower, if you're feeling grimy."

"Oh God yes," Emily said.

"Can she shower while you're driving?" Troy asked

Murph. He honestly didn't know, he'd never been in an RV before.

Murph shook his head. "I'm not driving anywhere until sunup. I'd break an axle or get stuck in the sand off the road, I tried to drive out of here tonight." There was a glow in the sky to the west, but the sky above them was black, the stars already coming out by the hundreds. Soon, there would be thousands of them. Too many to count. The sky at night was one of the best things about coming to the Grand Canyon.

"Are you kidding me?" Troy said, getting angry.

"Does this thing look off-road capable?" Murph asked. "Getting it to here, in daylight, is like threading a needle."

"We don't have to be anywhere until tomorrow anyway," Hannah said, looking back and forth between the two of them.

"You want to clean up, I can get the grill started. I've got steak, should be enough for all of us," Murph said.

"I'm a vegan," Emily told him.

Murph blinked at the chubby girl. "Then why are you here?" he asked, sounding confused.

"What?"

He waved his arm in the general direction of the Grand Canyon. "Out enjoying nature. A vegan diet is anything but natural. At least, for humans."

"What are you talking about?"

"Biology," he told her. "We don't have the stomach for it. Or the teeth."

"Humans don't have the teeth of carnivores," she said defiantly.

"Humans don't kill with their teeth," he pointed out. He raised his hands and wiggled his fingers. "Tool users."

The Subsection

"I am not having a debate with you," she said, hands on her hips.

"And it sounds like you're not having dinner, either," Murph said. "Because all I've got is steak. And weed," he added. "Marijuana is vegan. But I guess it only makes you hungrier, so…"

He put wood charcoal in the 12-inch Weber grill over a crumpled up tumbleweed he'd grabbed off the ground. It was dry as straw and made great tinder. He lit the fire and was giving the charcoal time to generate some heat before throwing the steaks on, rummaging around in the coach for another chair, so they could all sit outside, when the bathroom door opened and steam billowed out.

"Oh, I needed that," Hannah said, seeing his vague reflection in the foggy mirror. She had a big white towel wrapped around her. It reached from her collarbones to her thighs. "I've definitely got sunburn, though."

"Could be worse. Going to be throwing the steaks on in a few minutes," he told her, standing in the hallway. "I found some asparagus, and can grill that, if she's really not going to eat meat. I think I've got a few more energy bars in here…"

The blonde shook her head and rolled her eyes. "She just says she's vegan for attention. She'll eat whatever you give her. Ugh. I hate having to put back on dirty clothes, but…" She went to turn back into the bathroom, but she wasn't used to the tight spaces and banged her elbow on the door. She hissed, and grabbed at her elbow. The sudden move was enough, and the towel she'd wrapped around herself popped loose and fell straight to the floor.

Murph's eyes opened wide. "Wow," he said, looking her up and down. Then he realized that might not be the appropriate reaction. He looked away and moved down the corridor toward the front of the RV. "Sorry," he called back over his shoulder. Then he stopped, but didn't turn around. "Actually, not sorry," he said. "But...you know."

She stuck her head out the open door and called to him. "You don't think I'm too skinny? That I'm too flatchested?" It wasn't that her breasts were small, they were nonexistent.

He turned in place, and looked at her over his shoulder. "I did say 'Wow'."

She blinked once, then the corner of her mouth curled up. "Yes, you did." And it sounded like he'd meant it.

"No, seriously man, are you rich?" Rich was slumped deep in his folding chair. He took another hit and then passed the thick joint to Troy, then peered at Murph through the smoke. "How'd you afford this thing?" He stuck a thumb over his shoulder at the RV. "Looks like it costs as much as a house. Inside's nicer than my parents' house."

"Gravity," Murph told them. They stared at him stupidly. "I was working construction. A wall fell on me. On my head. Messed me up a little bit. But I got a lot of money out of it. Work comp."

"Cool," Troy said, nodding.

"Asshole," Hannah said to him, frowning. Emily tried to pass her the joint and she shook her head. They were arranged around the small grill, where a few embers still glowed. They'd eaten off paper plates, then fed them to the flames. A bit of heat radiated from the steel. The night air was growing crisp.

"What? What'd I say?" They were full of steak and exhausted, and the marijuana wasn't making them think any clearer. "Oh." He looked at Murph. Murph had a lot of sunbleached blonde hair above wide shoulders and a lean body. He was slouched in one of the cheap folding chairs he'd pulled out of the storage compartment on the underside of his bus-sized RV. "Not cool the wall fell on your head. Cool you got some cash out of it. You need a CDL to drive that thing?" He jerked his head at the bus-sized motorcoach.

Murph shook his head. "No, because it's a private vehicle."

"So you come here a lot?" The joint came back to Troy and he took a hit, then offered it to Murph. Murph shook his head. He had weed for guests, but rarely smoked it himself, and never right after doing peyote. It would completely mess with his clear head.

"At least once a year. I'm trying to hit all the national parks and monuments, but this is maybe my favorite."

"So you don't work? You just drive around?"

"I'm trying to teach myself to code."

"Code?" Emily was half-asleep, and having problems following the conversation.

"Computer code. Programming."

"Yeah, I saw that," Troy said. "You got a killer setup inside. I figured you were a hardcore gamer, all those monitors."

Murph shrugged. "I do some of that too." He leaned back in his chair and stared up at the sky. There was absolutely no light pollution—none—and there were too many stars to count. The night sky was so clear and bright he could see the Milky Way no problem. The stars looked close enough to reach up and touch. He raised his hand and grabbed at them. Emily watched him, frowning. Way off in the distance, likely several miles away, they heard a yip-yip-yipping.

"Did I just hear that?" Troy said. "Or am I that high?"

"The coyote? No, you heard it," Murph told him.

"Kelly your first or last name?" Troy peered at him with stoned eyes.

"First. Kelly Linklater."

"Kind of a girl's name."

"Don't be an asshole," Emily said.

Murph shrugged it off. "*Kelly's Heroes*. Machine Gun Kelly."

"The rapper?" Rich said.

"There's a rapper named Machine Gun Kelly?" Murph said.

"Who were you talking about, if not him?" Rich said, confused.

"The gangster. Used a machine gun. Back during Prohibition."

"Do you think that's where Machine Gun Kelly got his name?" Rich wondered aloud. "I mean, the rapper."

Hannah snorted. "You are so high."

"I need to go to sleep, and I don't want to fall asleep in this chair. I'll wake up paralyzed," Rich said.

"It is getting a little cold," Emily agreed.

Murph gestured at the RV. "That couch in there pulls out. And there's a foam mattress rolled up in that little closet next to the desk, you can put it on the floor. The chairs in front are nicely padded too, and the passenger seat reclines almost all the way. But the bedroom in back, the bed, that's mine."

Rich got up and staggered into the RV. Emily got to her feet and followed him inside. Murph was mellow, content and satisfied with a stomach full of steak and vegetables after a nearly four-day fast. He stared up at the sky. "You know, they say that if we ever do meet any aliens, they'll come from a planet that doesn't have complete cloud cover.

Like, they'd never come from a planet like Jupiter, which is always covered by clouds."

"Why?"

Hannah had asked the question. She was looking at him, her eyes glinting in the darkness. He glanced over. Troy was asleep in his chair. Murph gestured at the stars. "If there's never a break in the clouds, you'll never see what's up there. Out there. That there is a there there. You can't 'reach for the stars' if you don't know they exist."

She thought about it for a minute, then shook her head. "I think with any advanced civilization, eventually they'd wonder what was up there, in the clouds. Past the clouds. It might take them longer, but eventually…."

"Hmm. I guess that makes sense."

She pressed fingertips against the skin of her arm. "Man, did I get burnt. That shower hurt. I put on sunblock before we went down, but it wore off I guess. It's not supposed to last two days. What kind do you use?" He was very tan.

Murph shook his head. "I don't put that poison on my skin."

She blinked and frowned at him. "You've got to get your skin out of the sun, protect it, you'll get skin cancer."

"Horseshit," Murph told her. "Our bodies evolved to be out in sunlight as much as they were to breathe air, drink water, and eat meat. You ever hear of people in Africa getting skin cancer? The Middle East?" He peered at her.

"Uh, I guess not."

"Exactly." He sat quietly for a while, then added, "And if it is the sun giving people skin cancer, it's because it's interacting with something in them. I mean, it's the seed oils that are causing all the cellulite as much as overeating. So chemicals from food preservatives, maybe, interacting with the sunlight, the UV rays, to cause skin cancer. Maybe even fluoride. We are mostly water."

She blinked and sat up, wondering if she'd heard him right. "Fluoride? Like what they put in the water? To make your teeth strong?"

"Oh God." Murph sat up, and leaned forward. "They don't 'put it' in water," he told her. "Back eighty or whatever years ago when they first started treating city water to make it safe for drinking, they used all sorts of chemicals to kill the bugs. Including fluoride. But they discovered they couldn't get all the fluoride out of the water. At least, not cost effectively. It just would have cost too much money. So instead they began this huge PR campaign. Having doctors tell everyone that fluoride was good for you. Made your teeth stronger. Horseshit. Total horseshit. Fluoride's a carcinogen. Causes osteosarcoma, among other things."

"There's no way that's true," she said, frowning.

"Why not?"

"Doctors wouldn't go along with that."

He laughed, a short bark that echoed across the dry ground. Troy jerked awake and looked around. "Wha...?"

"Go into the RV," Hannah told him. "You fell asleep in the chair. You sleep out here all night you'll freeze to death."

The young man, still half-asleep, mumbled something, but then got to his feet and shuffled into the motorcoach. They watched him go. Then Murph turned back to Hannah.

"In the fifties, doctors were telling people cigarette smoking was good for them. Good for their lungs. Because the tobacco companies were paying them. Just like big pharma is paying them now to push pills for every little thing instead of exercise and eating right. Slightly irregular gut? There's a pill for that. Blood sugar not textbook perfect? There's a pill for that. Might cause your taint to fester and explode, but whatever. FDA started a massive campaign against ivermectin when it was shown to be a cheap cure for COVID, saying it was a horse dewormer and not fit for people. Except that was a flat-out lie, and doctors sued them, and won, and they had to take down all their bullshit lies. Didn't help the people who died because they couldn't get access to the drug, but whatever, right? They blame climate change for all the myocarditis, not the experimental gene therapy with spike proteins they were paid to push, and blame everything but the hundred vaccines they give to kids these days, for no good reason, for the sudden increase in autism."

"Ohhh," she said knowingly. She slowly nodded.

"Oh what?"

"Conspiracy theorist."

He smiled, his white teeth bright in the dark. "In the past five years, how many conspiracy theories have been proven right, versus how many have been disproven?"

Hannah shook her head. "I don't even...my brain is too fried to talk about this."

"I'll help—short answer, none have been disproven." He kept going. "And that's just the last five years. Then there's the classics. Operation Mockingbird, where the CIA infiltrated the news media. Cloud seeding. Operation Northwoods, a false flag plan to get us into a war with Cuba. TWA 800, which expert witnesses insisted was brought down by a surface-to-air missile. You want to talk conspiracies, how about the media's silence on what's happening in South Africa today, which is at least as bad as what went on during apartheid. South Africa is one bad day away from a Rwandan-style genocide. Directed energy weapons. Obama's missing student registration at Harvard Law

School. The non-existent plane that hit the Pentagon on Nine-Eleven. Area 51."

"Aliens?" she said dubiously.

He smiled and shrugged. "Maybe I just had one too many walls fall on my head." She grinned, and that turned into a yawn. He stood up. "Maybe we should go inside before we freeze. Find a place for you to sleep. I'd hate to have my rescue efforts all go to waste because of hypothermia." He smiled at her.

She stood up, and gave him a look. "You did say you had a bed in back," she said.

"Yeah. That's where I'm sleeping."

She stepped close to him. And was surprised how tall he was, she hadn't realized he was so tall. She was almost six feet, and he had her by at least four inches. She looked up into his face. "Maybe you saved our lives. Did you?"

He shrugged. "Maybe. I probably at least kept you guys from ending up in a hospital."

She bit her lip, staring him in the eyes. "Hmm. And you said wow."

He didn't say anything for a few seconds, then smiled. "I did, didn't I."

When he woke up the sun was shining in his eyes, again. He blinked, and saw Hannah was sitting upright on the bed, looking at him. It was the first time she'd gotten a good look at him in good light when she wasn't exhausted. "How old are you?" she asked.

"Thirty-five." She kept looking at him, her mouth twisted to the side. "Do I not look thirty-five?"

"You've got surfer hair, and a surfer bod, but you've got

a lot of wrinkles. Around your eyes. It's probably because you don't use sunblock," she said, one side of her mouth curling in a smile. "Your body is twenty-five. But you've got old eyes."

"I used to be fat," he told her. "Like, really fat. Four hundred pounds. Maybe more, but most scales only go up to three hundred, or three-fifty. When I lost the weight, I think it made my face look old."

She tilted her head. "I can see that, I guess."

They heard a groan through the closed bedroom door and looked that way. "Sounds like they're awake. I guess I better put some clothes on," she said.

"And that's a damn shame," he said. She turned away, smiling shyly, and reached for her shirt on the floor.

Once he carefully turned the motorcoach around at the end of the road it took just over half an hour of careful driving to reach the Maswik Lodge. From there he followed their (occasionally conflicting) directions, and backtracked along narrow dirt roads and forest service access routes for nearly an hour until their car appeared over a rise. It was dusty, but otherwise appeared unscathed.

The boys climbed down from the coach and checked the car out while Emily used the bathroom, leaving Murph with Hannah. "Where are you going to go from here?" she asked him, leaning an elbow on the front passenger seat. "Where do you live, Kelly? I never asked."

"I've got a place outside Columbia, Missouri," Murph told her. "I'm heading back there now."

She gave him another shy smile. "If you ever come down to Phoenix...you've got my number."

He smiled back. "I do. And you've got mine." They traded knowing grins. Emily came out of the bathroom and the two girls went down the steps into the sun. Murph gave them a final wave, closed the door, then drove past the car. He found a place to turn around a quarter mile on. When he came back, the car was gone. He stopped the coach in the middle of the road and stared down it, smiling. Eventually, his smile faded. He climbed out of the big driver's seat and looked around, out all the windows. He didn't see another vehicle, and wasn't likely to. They had wandered out of the national park onto tribal land. The Havasupai Reservation was the most isolated and thinly populated indian reservation in the country, entirely surrounded by the national park, and the road the quartet had found wasn't on the way to anywhere.

He pulled a set of replacement license plates out of one of the hidden cabinets and swapped out the ones on the vehicle. Then he woke up one of his computers and physically inserted a plug into the wall, connected his system to the hidden dishes on the roof, and thus to satellites. He waited five minutes, but he had no new messages—no emails, no texts, no voicemails on any of the accounts that were active. He pulled the plug again and got back behind the wheel. He drove out of the park, turned north, and not quite nine hours later pulled into a KOA outside Salt Lake City.

And got to work.

THREE

Hookers and Blow

"Okay, be honest," Dave Anderson said, staring at his face in the bathroom mirror. He turned his head to one side, then the other. "Is it better? I've been looking at myself so much that I can't tell anymore if it really looks better."

Lori was still in bed, propped up on her pillows, phone in hand and surfing Instagram. "Didn't they take 'before' photos? So you could compare it to the after?"

"Oh, yeah, right." He pulled out his phone. The doctor had taken a number of headshots and emailed them to him before starting the process three months earlier.

Technically, it wasn't "cosmetic surgery", it was scar revision, and, he'd learned, there were a lot of ways to reduce scarring, only one of which involved surgery. His scars were on his face, courtesy of a cartel soldier who'd pounded his head over and over with the receiver of his AK-47 while Dave hung on for dear life. For facial scarring the doctor felt skin resurfacing treatments were the best option, but did a bit of everything—one chemical peel, several sessions of dermabrasion, and laser treatments to stimulate skin cell growth. The doc had also done a tiny bit of surgery on Dave's left cheek, where the AK's bolt handle had done a real number on him. The "Z-plasty" involved cutting out the scar tissue in a Z-shaped incision, which when it healed was supposed to look more natural and provide more elasticity. The divot he'd had there was definitely gone.

Dave found the before photo and held it up, looking back and forth from it and his reflection. Lori got out of bed and walked up behind him. "I'm still a little swollen," he said. "And Doc Eisenstadt says the scars will fade even more over the next couple of weeks." His eyes darted left and right. "Okay," he said finally.

Lori smiled. "I didn't want to say anything until the end of the treatments. But they're less noticeable now with your face shaved than they were before when you had a beard. You don't really notice them unless you're up close, and looking for them. If you grow the beard out again, even short…"

"Yeah." Dave stared at his reflection, chewing his lip. He took a deep breath, and let it out. "So, out of the frying pan…"

She knew exactly what he was talking about. "Are you…are you nervous?" she asked him, incredulous. He shrugged. "After everything? How many gunfights have you been in? How many different people and groups have tried to kill you? I mean, you didn't get those scars on your face in the ball pit at Chuck E. Cheese's. You've got scars all over your body. Bullet holes. Burns. Fucking shrapnel from *grenades*. You're finally not limping after how many months?"

He shrugged again. "That was always just me against the world. Half the time I was just waiting for someone to

The Subsection

show up and kill me. And I wasn't afraid to die, so I wasn't scared or nervous."

"I know, I remember zombie boy very well." He'd clearly been nervous, he was back to practicing his draw an hour or more a day, and had bought a new AR-15 to replace the one taken as evidence by the police after the shootout at his trailer.

"But this is like…first day of school? Or at a new job? It's important." He looked at her, and gestured at the house around them. They'd been in it almost a month. "I don't want to fuck it up." He didn't mean the house.

"You haven't even done anything. They haven't asked you to do anything. Your phone hasn't even rung once. And they've been sending you checks. Which is typical tax-dollars-at-work kind of shit. When are they going to call? With all the government craziness and corruption, you'd think a secret—"

"No!" he said sharply, and shook his head, staring at her. "Never. Never around anything electronic connected to the internet. That's phones, smart TVs, laptops—basically anywhere indoors. Or outdoors, if you've got your phone, or someone else has one. I guess basically don't say anything anywhere."

She opened her mouth for a sharp reply, but saw the look on his face, and realized he was right. She nodded. Just then his phone rang. Her eyes went wide, and darted down to his pocket and back up to his face. "I didn't…" she mouthed at him.

He shook his head, reached into his pocket, and pulled out his iPhone. "It's Aaron," he said with relief, and laughed. He took the call and tapped the display with his thumb. "You're on speaker," he told his best friend. "Lori's here."

"S'up, you broke-ass bitches?" Aaron asked matter-of-factly. He was clearly in a great mood.

"Did my last skin treatment earlier this week," Dave told him. "Scars are way down."

"I don't know why you're doing that," Aaron said. "They weren't that bad. And chicks dig scars."

"Leave him alone," they heard.

"Hi Arlene!" Lori said. Arlene was Aaron's long-time live-in girlfriend.

Dave traded a look with Lori. For a number of reasons, Lori knew about his new job offer, but Aaron didn't, and Dave meant to keep it that way. For Aaron's own protection. They had a long history of protecting each other. "Then why'd you get those missing teeth replaced?" Dave asked him.

"Scars are good for snagging poon at the bar; missing teeth make you look like a meth head. Unless you're on the Red Wings. I got my payout!" he blurted.

"What?"

"They actually cut the check last week, almost two weeks ago, but I didn't want to say anything until I got my cut, and deposited it, and it actually cleared. But I'm a million-fucking-aire now baby!"

Dave had suffered all his most recent injuries at the hands of a Mexican drug cartel; Aaron, on the other hand, had been abducted and tortured by a West Bloomfield Township Michigan police officer working for the mafia. The detective had been sure Aaron had knowledge of Dave's involvement in the murder of Pietro Bufonte, head of the mob in Detroit, and the hit-and-run death of Bufonte's son years earlier. Dave was his prime suspect in the hit and run, but after years of investigation he had no evidence, and was getting desperate. He'd tied Aaron to a chair, shot him repeatedly with his department-issued taser, broke two of his fingers, and was using him as a punching bag when the FBI stormed in.

"What's the final number?" Dave asked.

"We settled on eight-point-nine million dollars," Aaron said proudly. "Biggest payout in the city's history, but they knew if we went to court and the jury saw those photos, listened to eyewitness testimony from FBI agents picking my teeth up off the fucking floor… Lawyers get their cut, forty percent, and the fucking feds and state get another forty percent or so in taxes, those fuckers, so my cut's only three-and a quarter million."

"Only," Dave said, rolling his eyes. "Only three million."

"Hey, inflation's a bitch," Aaron said, and laughed. "And it's three-and-a-quarter. Don't short-change me."

"Three point two two," Arlene corrected him.

"You talked to an investment guy, right?" Dave said.

"Yeah, yeah. We've got another meeting with him next week, got the money in a special account that's insured for the full amount. Meanwhile, it's all hookers and blow up here. Midget trannies and dancing dogs. Dancing midget tranny dogs."

"Stop it," Arlene chided him.

"Don't buy a Ferrari or anything stupid like that," Dave told him.

"Hey, I had to buy a few things just to make sure the numbers in my account were real," Aaron said. "But nothing too big," he added quickly. "TV was probably the most expensive thing. We're actually looking at buying a house. Moving out of the trailer."

"West of the city," Arlene said. "Maybe Canton."

"A house is a good investment," Dave said.

"You're just saying that because you burned yours down and Pork Snorkle had to buy you a new one," Aaron said.

"Hey, I'm working now, making a little money," Dave told him, feeling both guilty and defensive. His house had burned down, thanks to a few Molotovs tossed by cartel soldiers, and he'd had no insurance. Lori's house next door had suffered fire damage and taken more than a few bullets through the walls. The insurance company had paid out, and the day after the repairs were completed she told Dave she wanted to move. Too many bad memories. Her house was paid off, so even though the value was slightly diminished by the vacant lot next door (after Dave's house was torn down), it was all profit. They went house-hunting, and bought a place in a nice neighborhood northwest of downtown Prescott. Dave offered to help with the cost, but his savings had been seriously depleted as he waited for what he assumed was an inevitable ugly end. Lori's net worth, on the other hand, had skyrocketed thanks to heavily investing in the stock market right after it had tanked during Covid. With what she made selling her mother's house, the new place was completely paid off.

"Yeah? Doing what?" Aaron sounded genuinely curious.

"Some consulting. Shooting and…stuff." His bank account had finally started seeing some positive growth as checks, two months earlier, had started to come in every two weeks. They weren't made out to David Anderson or even Jack Burton, and were direct-deposited to a checking account he'd opened at a bank branch in Phoenix under the same name on the check. He—or rather, Henry Swanson, one of the several new identities he'd been issued—was getting paid nearly five thousand dollars every two weeks (before taxes) from Evergreen International. But he was feeling guilty about that too. He hadn't done anything to earn the money. Not yet.

"For the cops? That's not dumb, the sheriff knows you know a few things about that. I think you've been in more gunfights than the rest of his guys combined. Now that you're no longer the subject of an active FBI investigation—and you're welcome for that, by the way. My pain was your gain."

Dave changed the subject. "What about you? You still going to work for Absolute?" The two of them had met while working for Absolute Armored. They'd ridden around Detroit in an armored car together for almost two years before Dave's troubles had started.

"Fuck no. I quit as soon as the check cleared."

Dave wasn't surprised. But still... "Three million's probably not enough to retire on at your age, unless you start getting stock tips from a senator. You're eventually going to have to do something for money."

"Yeah, I know. I've never not had a job. It's been less than a week and I'm already getting antsy."

"Don't let him buy too much stupid expensive stuff," Lori said into the phone, talking to Arlene.

"I just bought a few guns," Aaron said defensively.

"Cars are horrible investments," Dave told him. "You want to buy one just to have a new car, that's fine, but don't think a car's a good place to store your cash."

"I know that. Jeez, it's like talking to ma, God rest her soul. I got enough cars already, I've got the fastback and the Taurus. That thing's faster than a SHO, now, the work I've done to it. I bought new wheels and tires for it right before Tiny Dick Dixon tazed my ass. Arlene's the one needs a new car."

"No I don't."

"You've been out shopping for airbags," Aaron said innocently.

"I swear to God," they heard Arlene growl. Lori put a hand over her mouth to keep from laughing.

Aaron did laugh at his own joke. "And she's still working."

"Well what am I going to do if I'm not working?" Arlene said. "Get facials and manicures all day?"

"I'll give you a facial," Aaron said.

"Aaaaand we're hanging up now," Dave said, smiling. "Talk to you later." He disconnected the call and looked at Lori.

"The rich *are* different," she said, deadpan. He laughed so hard his stomach was sore the next day.

FOUR

Daxpitcheeaasáao

Murph loved, absolutely loved, the Devils Tower National Monument. Of course, there was the thing itself, an awe-inspiring tower of igneous rock nearly one thousand feet high, with an improbably flat top and vertical hexagonal columns that looked completely unnatural. Even when you were there, in person, it looked fake, like a special effect. It towered above all of the surrounding land, visible for miles, completely unlike anything else in the area. Completely unlike anything else in Wyoming, Murph was pretty sure. It was the first national monument, established in 1906 by President Teddy Roosevelt himself. All the indian tribes in the area (including the Lakota, Cheyenne, Crow, and Kiowa) had names for it, usually involving bears. Probably because it looked like a bear had raked its claws down the sides of the tower. Murph's favorite, simply because the word itself was so crazy, was *Daxpitcheeaasáao*, Crow for "Home of Bears". The white man's name for the stone peak (somehow unsurprisingly) resulted from a mistranslation; "Bears' Tower" in the native Indian tongue into "Bad God's

Tower" in English. But you couldn't look at, even think of the Devils (no apostrophe) Tower, without thinking of *Close Encounters of the Third Kind*.

That 1977 classic was where most Americans had first seen or heard of the geologic oddity, and for a director who later went on to direct forgettable fluff and wildly inaccurate historical pieces (*Munich* was a factual disaster), *Close Encounters of the Third Kind* was a standout, and seemed to stand alone—it was Spielberg's embrace of all things conspiracy theorist. Aliens, of course, communicating telepathically with people, and visiting the earth, but also government malfeasance. A huge conspiracy, with the U.S. government slipping men and material into commercial semi-trucks and shipping them cross-country to set up a secret base, faking a nerve gas spill to force an evacuation of the area, gassing uncooperative people from the air (shades of chem trails, anyone?), roadblocks, barbed wire, loading people into box cars, gaslighting experiencers, even killing livestock to scare the doubters. The movie, narratively, artistically, in every way, still held up, nearly fifty years later.

Murph loved every tiny detail about the making of the movie. The latitude and longitude radioed in by the aliens were—in reality—nowhere near Devils Tower. The "dead" cows and horses lining the roads in the movie weren't props, that would have been too expensive and probably would have looked fake, given the prosthetic effects of the time— they were actual animals anesthetized by a veterinarian. The film was edited to match the completed John Williams score, not vice versa. The dog released by the aliens was Spielberg's Cocker Spaniel, Elmer. And Melinda Dillon, who played the mother of the little boy Gary abducted by the aliens, spent the entirety of the movie braless. Once you noticed that you couldn't un-see it, and it added an extra layer of enjoyment for any male out of adolescence watching the film.

Murph would have loved to spend a day or a week at the top of the tower, but there was no way he was climbing it. As climbs went it was reportedly pretty easy, but mountain climbers, especially free climbers, were nuts. Most of the climb was a seventy-degree slope, practically vertical—no fucking thank you. But he did walk and climb all around the base of the monument, had been everywhere on the thing other than up the insanely steep columns.

His vehicle was too big for the campground in the national park, so he always rented a spot at the Black Hills KOA, where they'd actually filmed a lot of *Close Encounters* in 1976. The military "decontamination" headquarters in the movie sat right where the KOA had been built, and they showed the movie every night at the campground. Perfect.

He would have stayed there forever, if there weren't so many other places to visit. In addition to the other projects he had going, that occasionally required his presence.

He rolled in late one afternoon. The KOA sat on the park's western border, less than a mile from the Tower itself, and unless there happened to be a tree or a Winnebago right in your face you could see the Tower, seemingly close enough to touch, no matter where you were standing in the campground. The tower dominated the landscape. Murph wandered through the fields of knee-high grass surrounding the campground for half an hour or so, staring out—and up—at the Tower—then headed back to his coach. He had a lot of work to do.

When he woke up early the next morning he saw an older Bounder RV had parked in the next site. From the bikes on the back and the stickers on the windows he could tell it was a family with kids. Not a sound from inside, but that wasn't a surprise at seven in the morning. It was still chilly, and he was wearing a light jacket over shorts when he headed out on a hike. He returned just before ten a.m., having done one slow circuit around the Tower, mostly avoiding the trails. And the people on them. The family next door was up, although he wasn't sure if "awake" was an accurate term from how bleary-eyed the parents were. They were both sipping from mugs, and Murph—who had a good nose—could smell both tea and coffee. They were sitting in folding chairs in the sun, ingesting caffeine and trying to wake up. Murph could hear the kids inside the Bounder. It sounded like they were playing video games.

"You our neighbor?" the man called out, as Murph strode up to his vehicle.

Murph stuck what he considered his "friendly normal" smile on his face and looked at them. "Yeah. Richard. Richie. Went out for a hike this morning."

"Getting up early doesn't sound like any kind of a vacation at all," the man said, his mouth twitching in a smile. "I'm Gene, this is Rosa."

"The earlier you go, the fewer people you run into on the trails," Murph told him.

"Yeah, well," the guy said. He shrugged, then glanced at the RV behind him where the video game was making a lot of noise. "We'll be going to the visitor's center later. Getting up close to that thing. It's even bigger in person than I thought it was going to be."

"It is something."

"I was worried we wouldn't be able to see it, but you can see it from…"

"Everywhere, yeah. Honestly, you can see it better from just outside the campground, near the park entrance on this side, than you can up by the visitor center. There are a lot of trees there. But you're a lot closer. You hike just a minute or two and you're at the base of the slope. Looking almost straight up. That slope, there's a lot of big boulders that fell off the sides of the tower, that your kids will probably enjoy climbing on, if they're not too little."

"Okay, thanks. Is it just you?" He was looking past Murph at his giant motorhome.

"At the moment."

The man glanced at his wife, then back at Murph. "Hey, when are you taking off? Are you going to be here tonight? We're going to be having a little picnic. Grilling burgers and dogs. You're welcome to join. Maybe…seven o'clock?"

"That sounds great, thanks. Hey, uh…when are *you* taking off?" Murph asked him. "Are you here tomorrow night?"

"Yeah, why?"

"You know about the movie, right? Every night at dusk they show *Close Encounters* on a big outdoor screen over by the Trading Post, with the Tower in the background. You can't come here and not do that."

Gene nodded. "We're going to do that tomorrow night. Weather's supposed to be even better. I think the kids are too young to really get the movie, I'm not even sure I like it, it's weird, but there's an ice cream shop right there." He smiled at Murph. "I appreciate the tip."

Murph emerged from his vehicle at five minutes after seven, blinking and working his neck. "That smells good."

Gene looked up from his small grill. He'd just put the first burgers on. "There you are. I was just about to knock. I heard the music, but then in-between songs I thought I heard typing." His wife Rosa was unfolding a table from the side of the RV.

Murph shrugged. "Yeah, well, just because you're on vacation doesn't mean there's no work to be done. But if you love what you do, you never work a day in your life, right?"

"I wouldn't know about that." Gene eyed the big shiny vehicle behind Murph. "What do you do, Richie, you don't mind me asking? Looks like you're doing okay."

"Marketing," Murph told him. "Mostly for smaller companies, ten, thirty employees, that can't afford their own in-house team. Google and Meta ad campaigns, SEO, stuff like that. You spend a lot of time on the computer. A lot. But," he said with a shrug, and gestured around them, "you can do it pretty much anywhere."

"You got Starlink or some kind of internet through satellite?" Gene asked him. He pulled his phone out of his pocket, looked at the display, and frowned. "My service is for shit."

"Something like that," Murph said agreeably.

"Language," his wife scolded him gently. Gene smiled as he flipped burgers.

"You had quite a drive. I saw the Connecticut plates."

Murph shrugged, and stuck a thumb at his vehicle. "I've got some condiments in the Landmaster. A can of corn, I think. And a big bag of Doritos that I'm never going to eat this side of the Apocalypse."

"We're going to be grilling corn on the cob, but the kids would kill for some Doritos," Rosa said. The children under discussion rode up on their bikes, an older boy and a younger girl. Somewhere between seven and ten, if Murph had to guess, but he didn't know anything about kids, or at least guessing their ages. They were old enough

The Subsection

to ride bikes without training wheels, but hadn't hit puberty yet.

"Is the food ready? We're hungry," the boy said.

Gene rolled his eyes, then pointed. "Richie, this is Antonio and Maria."

"Mary," the girl corrected him.

"You think you know your name better than the people who named you?" Rosa snapped at her daughter, an accent coloring her vowels for the first time.

"Maria is an old lady name," the girl complained. "I hate it."

"You were named after your grandmother, who was a saint," Rosa growled, and erupted in a torrent of Spanish. The girl hung her head. The boy drifted away from her, just in case any of it spilled toward him. Gene sent a rueful, apologetic smile Murph's way, but Murph just shrugged, unconcerned.

Ten minutes later they were sitting down at the small table attached to the side of the family's RV. Murph had a hamburger in front of him, no bun, as well as an ear of corn. It smelled great, having just come off the grill. "Do you want some butter for that?" Rosa asked him. She pushed a plastic tub his way.

"That's not butter," Murph said, trying to keep his voice neutral.

"It's got less fat in it," Rosa said. "We're trying to watch what we eat."

Murph had to bite his lip from shouting. "Fat's not bad for you," he said, a little too loudly. He shook his head and lowered his voice. "Not natural fat, like you get from butter or meat. It's all the processed fats and oils that are bad for you. Seed oils. Like what's in this." He poked the tub with his finger. "So much food in supermarkets is just flat-out poison. 'Processed food' barely has any food in it. Margarine was invented to fatten up turkeys. And it killed the turkeys. They couldn't just take the loss, so they added a little food coloring and salt and sold it to people as a butter substitute."

"I don't think that's right," Gene said.

"It's got less calories, less fat. And it spreads better," Rosa said defensively.

Through his teeth Murph said, "That's because it shares twenty-seven of the same ingredients as paint. It's one molecule away from plastic. It'll give you cancer. If you can't pronounce most of the ingredients, you think you should be eating it? It should be called 'I Can't Believe It's Not Cancer'. You've got a 45% greater chance of getting cancer, eating processed food. But Big Food tries to keep that a secret."

"Big Food? Like Big Tobacco or Big Oil?" Gene and Rosa traded a concerned look. "There's no such thing."

Murph took a deep breath. Then a second, and spread his hands out on the table in front of him. Flexed his fingers. "Sorry. Sorry about that. I used to be fat, really fat, and went on a health food kick, and, well, here I am your guest and I'm yelling at you."

"Health food kick?" Rosa said. She liked the apology, but wasn't quite ready to forgive him. "Didn't you bring Doritos?" She pointed at the open bag between them.

Murph reached into the bag, withdrew a chip, used it to scoop up a big dollop of the butter substitute, and shoved it into his mouth. "If I was perfect, my first name would be Jesus," he said around a mouthful of crunch, giving the name the Spanish pronunciation, *hay-soos*, and winking at the kids, who giggled.

The Subsection

After dinner, Antonio was staring up at Murph's ride. "Can I look inside?" the boy asked.

"I wouldn't mind a peek in there either," his father admitted.

"Sure." Murph led them inside.

Gene whistled, looking around. "*Madre dios*, this thing's nicer than our house. Is that a marble floor? It can't be."

"Tile. Polymer, meant to look like marble. Not really my style, at all but that's how it came. I bought it used. I think tile is more practical than carpet, at least out here, but red 'marble' is a lot more *Scarface* than I'd prefer."

Antonio ran over to the computer setup. "Wow," he said, looking at all the monitors. "Are you a gamer?" he asked Murph.

"Sometimes. Mostly I just use it for work."

Antonio grabbed the mouse on the table and moved it around. The screens before him lit up. His mouth opened, and he let go of the mouse quickly. "I didn't do it."

"What?"

"I think your computer's broken. I just touched the mouse. I didn't do anything."

Gene and Murph walked over. Gene squinted at the lines of code. On one of the monitors the small print was scrolling too fast to read. "Is that a computer program?" He didn't even recognize a lot of the symbols.

"Just running a systems check," Murph told him.

"It's just words," Antonio said. "Typing, like a book. Where's the…" The boy waved his hands. "Windows."

"Putting Windows on your computer is like putting screen doors on a submarine," Murph told him. "It doesn't keep the sharks out. It barely keeps anything out. I use Linux for a few things, but for the important stuff I use my own operating system. It's better than anything else on the market. Not simpler, but smarter. Infinitely more secure. I developed my own computer language, actually. Little bit of a hobby."

"Isn't computer language all binary? Ones and zeroes?" the boy said.

Murph looked at him approvingly. "Yes, you're right, but when you're coding you're not typing in endless series of ones and zeroes. Computer language is a kind of shorthand, and when you're working in the q realm, Java don't cut it. There's Qiskit, Cirq, and Q Sharp, but what I developed is better."

"There any money in that?" Gene asked.

"What?"

"The language. The OS. Did you sell it?"

"I would, if I wanted anyone else to have it." The sun had dropped below the horizon, and the sky was rapidly darkening. Murph looked out through the windows, then glanced at his watch. "Speaking of work, I've got to get back to it. I've got a project, and like you see that code scrolling in the background, I've got something similar going on in my brain, and I need to sit down and type a few things out."

"Absolutely," Gene said. "Not a problem. We'll see you tomorrow?"

Murph smiled. "You will. I can't leave before watching *Close Encounters* on the big screen. Maybe one day real aliens will show up and watch it with us." He gave the boy a wink. Antonio giggled.

After he got them off the coach he locked the door, then pulled the sliding panel shut behind the driver and passenger seats, so that anyone looking through the windshield couldn't see anything past the two empty seats. And he closed the curtains and blinds in all the other windows.

The Subsection

During the day the limo tint was enough to keep prying eyes at bay, but not so after dark. He sat back down at his monitoring station and woke the rest of his systems up. His fingers flew over the keyboard, sending out queries. An alert popped up on a side monitor. If it was off to the side it wasn't of primary importance, but it caught his eye.

Pursing his lips, he clicked over to it. A voicemail, left on one of the phone accounts he used, that the carrier wasn't even aware was active, in part because no physical phone had ever used that number. He recognized the incoming number. "Hi, it's Hannah," he heard in his speakers. "I just wanted to thank you again. Troy was being a jerk, but I realize you did probably save our lives. We were such idiots. Saved our lives, fed us, and then…afterward was nice. So…" She paused. "I guess I wanted to show you I gave you my real phone number. Maybe I'll never see you again. But if you come down to Arizona, seriously, give me a call. Maybe I can buy you dinner. Some…sunscreen." There was a pause as she considered saying something more, then the call ended.

Murph found himself grinning like an idiot. Then another alert was blinking, but this one was on the main screen, right in front of him, and the alert was a blinking bar of cerulean blue. "Hmm," he said. He leaned forward. "What do we have here?"

FIVE

Operation Turkey Sandwich

Bob Grinnand and his team—designation Colorado—had arrived a day and a half earlier, dressed in civilian clothes and loaded into the back of a C-130 along with the rest of the cargo. They'd sauntered down the ramp, and Bob had found a Senior Master Sergeant inside one of the hangars. Within the hour they were wearing the stained coveralls of contract maintenance workers and doing scut work on the airfield in and around one specific hangar—sweeping, emptying trash bins, even cleaning toilets. The enlisted troops working in the area had orders to ignore them.

The problem was Incirlik Air Base was located in Turkey, which meant it was operated by both the U.S. and Turkish governments. There were Turks—both military and civilian—all over the base. Turkey was a U.S. ally, and a member of NATO, but this operation was too sensitive for it to be run in standard fashion. So they were taking precautions. Arriving early. Watching and listening for any problems. They saw nothing.

With his unique condition—hearing music inside his

The Subsection

head ever since dying three times on an operation early in his career—every job had a soundtrack if he didn't tamp the music down, but he'd been enjoying the music his subconscious DJ had been playing while he did menial chores around the hangar. It was a bit like a vacation. Until it was time to go to work.

Bob was standing near the office at the back of a hangar when the jet touched down and taxied into view. He'd been acting lazy and bored since he arrived, and leaned on a broom as he watched the plane stop in front of the open hangar and the engines wind down. His brain was halfway through *Live At Red Rocks*, the epic album from the Dave Matthews Band, recorded live at the Red Rocks Amphitheater in Colorado in 1995. Once he'd heard something once his brain could recreate it perfectly.

The Gulfstream G550 was white over blue, with **UNITED STATES OF AMERICA** in big letters above the windows and an American flag on the tail. The Gulfstream was used for VIPs and operated by the U.S. Air Force's 89th Airlift Wing. Armored Humvees rolled up and parked around the jet at distance, and American soldiers in body armor and camouflage uniforms got out of the vehicles, rifles in hand, facing outward. Perimeter security. Four black Chevy Suburbans—also undoubtedly armored, from how low they were sitting over their tires—pulled up close to the jet, and men in suits climbed out.

The door in the jet opened, and stairs unfolded. There were more men in suits. Bob assumed some were Secret Service, and the ones on the ground were DSS, Diplomatic Security Service, part of the State Department. An older, shorter man stood in their midst, and it was clear that he was a local—Bob recognized him as the Vice President of Turkey. It was also clear he'd brought a few of his own men with him, to provide security—likely members of the General Directorate of Security, the Turkish National Police. They were wearing suits that bulged oddly, much like the Secret Service agents, their suitcoats covering firearms larger than mere handguns.

The U.S. Secretary of State appeared in the doorway of the Gulfstream, smiled, waved, then came down the stairs carefully. Tripping on stairs was a bad look even if there weren't members of the press around. A small entourage followed him.

The American Secretary of State and the Turkish Vice President greeted each other and shook hands, surrounded by assistants and security personnel. They exchanged a few words, then climbed into one of the Suburbans. All of the suits followed, filling the big SUVs. The convoy took off, heading for some local government offices. Bob knew their itinerary—after several low-level meetings, they'd be coming back to the air base and flying, together, in a Turkish Airlines jet, to an international economic conference in Cyprus, which was not quite three hundred kilometers southwest of Incirlik.

The soldiers clambered into their Humvees and drove off. The crew pulled the stairs up and closed the door on the Gulfstream, and then the ground crew hooked a boxy vehicle up to the front wheel of the small jet and towed it into the hangar where Bob stood. The jet door reopened and the stairs came back down. From his position Bob could see the pilot inside the cockpit, making notes on a clipboard and flicking overhead switches. There was a co-pilot moving around in the back of the plane, just a shape through the windows.

Bob leaned the broom against the wall and moved to the front of the hangar. He walked out onto the tarmac and

The Subsection

looked around. There was nobody nearby—the two adjoining hangars were quiet and empty, no moving vehicles or aircraft within half a mile. And there'd been no suspicious activity in or around the hangar since they'd arrived. He turned and gave a nod. His men went out the pedestrian door at the rear of the hangar, and a minute later they were driving around the side of the hangar, then through the big door in the front. There was a small parking lot behind the row of hangars where the ground crew parked when working in the area, and the three vehicles Bob's men were driving had deliberately been picked to not stand out—a Toyota Land Cruiser, an older Mercedes SUV, and a VW Caddy minivan. All of them had tinted windows but were dusty and unremarkable.

Bob strode back into the hangar. The three vehicles were parked beside the jet, pointing out toward the open door. He headed into the office and peeled off his coveralls, revealing nondescript civilian clothing. The Glock 19 on his hip had been there since he'd walked off the plane.

Bob carried a small duffel bag to the Land Cruiser, opened the front passenger door, and set the bag on the floor. He started gearing up. A tailored level IIIA soft body armor vest from Armor Express, which would only stop pistol bullets, but it would disappear under his t-shirt, which he put back on. Spare mags for the Glock on his left hip, and behind them a fixed-blade knife—currently an Acta Non Verba P250, big enough for serious work, including killing, but small enough to conceal. While being surprisingly light. He clipped his comm unit to his belt at the small of his back, and ran the wire up and stuck the earpiece in his right ear. Over everything went a button-down cotton canvas work shirt—not something khaki and tactical with a dozen pockets, but rather something he'd bought a few years before in Istanbul, brown with a little bit of modest embroidery at the cuffs and collar. Something no American would ever wear. He was a little pale and blonde for a Turk, but knew how to dress like a local. He left it unbuttoned in front. The end result left him looking quite thick. Unremarkable.

As a general rule he preferred big, powerful guns, and loved having air support—Apache gunships were nice, as were AC-130 Spectres—but this time around, due to the covert nature of the mission, it was just small arms for his team and an unarmed Northrop Grumman RQ-4 Global Hawk drone overhead providing ISR.

He was team lead, which meant he'd be taking on the protection of the principal if anything happened, including using his body as a shield—which was why he was wearing body armor. It also meant he might have to go hands on, so something smaller and lighter, that he could use one-handed if necessary, was what the covert protection/escort mission called for. He looked into the bag at the familiar lines of an HK MP5K PDW. He pulled it out, loaded it, and made sure the red dot mounted atop it—an Aimpoint ACRO P-2 in a quick detach ADM mount—was turned on. Finally he checked that the Omega 9K suppressor was firmly attached to the barrel's three-lug mount. It was short, light, and full-auto rated, half the length of the original KAC MP5 can. Both the Glock and the MP5K were loaded with black-tipped 9mm ammunition. The five other members of his team were doing the same thing—shedding their coveralls, and loading the weapons they'd brought in with them, various short-barreled suppressed 5.56 rifles, chosen by personal preference and mission needs.

Bob looked all around, eyeballing his team, and they gave him nods. He'd worked frequently with Fancy, and had

The Subsection

either worked with or had heard good things about the other guys, which is why he'd chosen them. Bob pointed at Fancy, and the man moved to the base of the jet's stairs. "We're clear," he called up.

The men who appeared were dressed in civilian clothing. The younger, thinner one was in a suit—he was Deputy Secretary of State Walter Derricks. With him was a thicker man in his fifties, the Commander of CENTCOM (U.S. Central Command, overseeing the middle east), General Erik Rasmussen. Each of the men had an aide with them. One of the aides looked vaguely familiar, but Bob couldn't remember where he'd seen the man before.

They climbed down the aircraft's steps and got into the cars. Bob did a comms check with his team, then they got into the vehicles and drove out of the hangar, heading for the front gate.

Bob was in the front passenger seat of the Toyota, with Fancy driving. General Rasmussen and his aide were in the back seat. Derricks and his aide were in the VW behind them, with two team members, and the Mercedes was in front.

"It's just over a three-hour drive, sir, provided there aren't any hiccups," Fancy said from behind the wheel.

The Commander of CENTCOM nodded. "Who are you boys with? DEVGRU? Delta?" he asked.

"DIA, sir," Bob told him. "DCS."

Rasmussen looked like he'd eaten something sour and just grunted in response. He seemed unimpressed. The Defense Intelligence Agency was the nation's second-largest intelligence agency behind the CIA, and the Defense Clandestine Service inside the DIA was full of experienced trigger-pullers harvested from various elite units, but it did not have the name recognition even with those in the business.

Which was fine, as far as Bob was concerned. Fancy, behind the wheel, frowned but didn't say anything.

They'd been heading east for over an hour without any issues other than occasional traffic. USSOCOM at MacDill AFB in Tampa was monitoring their progress with the drone, and Bob was checking in regularly. The Global Hawk was on station above them, being flown by a drone operator at Creech Air Force Base northwest of Las Vegas, and he reported no hostiles following their three-vehicle convoy and nothing of concern up ahead.

"Do you have any food in here?" the general abruptly asked. "I'm hungry as hell. There were a few snacks on the plane, but I haven't had an actual meal in…I don't know how many hours, with the time change."

"A few energy bars, sir, but that's it," Bob told him. "Bottled water."

"That gas station we passed back there had a restaurant attached. Next one of those you see, stop and grab something. Last thing I want for these negotiations is to show up hangry. They're going to be tense enough."

Fancy flicked his eyes at Bob, then at the general in the rearview mirror. "Um, general, I don't think that's quite a good idea…"

"We've got the time, we're ahead of schedule. And we're in civilian vehicles. If the opposition knows we're in-country, if they know where we are, we're already screwed. As much as I would prefer to be surrounded by a company of Rangers, the whole point of doing the operation this way was to keep the lowest of low profiles. Sending a guy in, wearing civvies, to buy some shawarma or whatever, while the rest of us wait in the cars, won't FUBAR operational security. I assume you have someone who knows the language and looks like a local."

"Yessir," Bob said, with a nod. "We'll keep an eye out for the next one."

Fancy glanced at him, and saw from his expression that he meant it. Which made him frown. "Pike…" he said, unhappily.

In the back seat the general looked up. "Pike?" he said to Bob. "You're Pike?" He snapped his fingers, trying to remember a name. "Grinnell? Robert Grinnell."

"Grinnand, yes sir. I'm Colorado One, team lead." They always used work names in the field. He'd been Pike forever.

"Well, why didn't you say so?" the general said warmly. "Former Delta, correct?"

"Yes sir. Among other things."

The general snorted. "Yes, I'm well aware of the other things. I didn't know you were with DCS now."

"For a few years. I like trying on new hats, and I'm not quite young enough anymore for Delta's operational tempo. All my team have similar backgrounds, sir. I picked them myself."

"Yeah? Good to know. So I trust you can keep me safe on a sandwich run."

Bob nodded, once. "Yessir. Operation Turkey Sandwich is a go."

Fancy's eyes went wide, but the general just barked out a belly laugh. "But not actually turkey, though," Rasmussen said. "Never been a fan of it."

"It'll be lamb, sir," Bob told him. "Everything's lamb in this country."

Their destination was just over the border in Syria, almost directly north of Aleppo. During the last hour of the trip Rasmussen and his aide were on satphones almost continuously, as was the Deputy Secretary of State from what Bob could discern from the few comments his team members made into their mics.

The tension ratcheted up as they approached the border on D850, Kilis-Öncüpinar-Suriye Road. Turkey shoved south into Syria like the tip of a fat spear. There were fields on the Turkish side of the border, and from satellite photos he knew there were fields on the Syrian side as well, but they were hidden from view by the twelve-foot wall running along the border.

From either direction the walls ran up to the road. A squat building sat a few meters on the Syrian side of the border, directly in the middle of the road, with swinging gates blocking the traffic lanes. Uniformed soldiers were visible inside the building, and as the convoy rolled up several of them exited the building.

The VW minivan was still in the lead, and it was fifty feet away from the border crossing, and slowing, when the soldiers swung the gate up and waved at the trio of vehicles to drive through. As they rolled by Bob saw one of the soldiers, who looked like an NCO, on the phone with someone. Likely announcing their arrival.

The small town of al-Salameh was a mile up. The convoy went around a traffic circle and turned east. It took less than a minute to drive through the paved streets of the small town, and then they were bouncing over a rutted dirt road. To either side were fields.

"What is that?" Fancy asked. His eyes were darting left and right, looking for threats, but he was talking about the crops to either side of them.

The Subsection

"Cotton," Bob told him tersely.

They made one turn, then another, the vehicles sending up a plume of dust, then they arrived at their destination. The compound was unmarked, several small buildings at the intersection of two dirt roads. On the far side stood a grove of olive trees. The three vehicles pulled into the dirt lot. There were no other vehicles present, and nothing moving nearby.

"Five minutes early," the general observed. "We'll see if they make us wait. No threats, no overt aggression," the general reminded Bob. "Just smile and stand there. Unless and until."

"Yes sir." Bob repeated the instructions to his team. He turned to address the CENTCOM commander. "Sir, I'd really like to check out these buildings. Make sure there aren't any surprises. Maybe post one of us in there."

Rasmussen shook his head. "Stay in the vehicles. We're guests."

Bob and Fancy traded a look, but Bob said, "Yes, sir."

The Global Hawk was still on mission, but staying over Turkish airspace. It was moving back and forth in a tight oval, at a high enough altitude for its camera to see to and past their meeting site. "Colorado, be advised you have three vehicles approaching your pos from the south," Bob heard in his ear ten minutes later. "ETA one mike."

"Sounds like they're inbound, sir," Bob told the general, casually unfolding the stock of his subgun. Fancy had a suppressed HK 416D in his lap and he adjusted it.

Two Range Rovers and a Toyota Land Cruiser arrived. Half a dozen men armed with AKs got out. Four stood by the vehicles, watching Bob's convoy, while two went inside one of the buildings. They reappeared a few minutes later and nodded.

One of the bodyguards opened the rear door of a Range Rover, and a casually-dressed slender man stepped out. He stood there, and stared at their vehicles. He was in expensive clothes, silk shirt and tailored slacks, and was pretty enough to be an actor.

"Okay, now," Rasmussen said. "Carefully."

Bob called it out to his team and they exited their vehicles. The men before them shifted their hands on their AKs, but kept them pointed at the ground. Colorado positioned itself around their three vehicles. Bob looked left and right, then gave a nod. Rasmussen climbed out, as did the Deputy Secretary of State, and their aides. The men walked over and greetings were exchanged. They quickly learned that Derricks spoke Arabic, and the sharp-dressed man spoke English. Bob and Fancy and several of the AK-toters moved as a group toward the building and went inside.

Bob quickly checked the interior, then gave Rasmussen a nod. Most of the building was one big room, with a table in the center. "Wait outside," Derricks told them flatly. Bob looked to the general, who nodded. Silk shirt muttered a few words to his security team, and then everyone with a gun was filing out the front door.

"Cover the perimeter," Bob said into his mic. "Call out anything moving." He paused, then added, "Be nice, until it's time to not be nice." He posted up near the front door of the meeting building, Fancy nearby, smiling neutrally at the three foreign security men. He kept his subgun on a sling, one hand on it loosely, and then stood still, only turning his head to scan from time to time and occasionally talking to his team. The guys with AKs talked amongst themselves, smoked, and generally scowled at the Americans, but they made no threatening moves.

Not quite half an hour later the door of the building

opened and the VIPs filed out. "We're done, let's go," Rasmussen said to Bob as he walked past.

Fifteen minutes later they were back in Turkey, and everyone breathed easier. Less than four hours after that Bob was standing in the same hangar, watching the G550 taxi down the runway at Incirlik, both the commander of CENTCOM and the Deputy Secretary of State aboard with their staff. Including the one familiar face Bob still hadn't been able to place. Fancy stood next to him. As the Gulfstream lifted off, Fancy pulled out his Glock and popped the magazine. "Okay, so what's this shit?" he asked. He meant the ammunition. The noses of the bullets weren't rounded but rather pointed, with black tips. "Black tips mean armor piercing, right?"

"Yeah. It's Federal EBR. 103 grains. Light, fast, and hard. The black tip is a penetrator. The base wraps around it, and then drops off and expands in the bad guy once it hits flesh. Detail like this, I figured there was a good chance the other security team might be wearing armor. This'll go through soft body armor like butter."

"Never heard of it."

Bob shrugged. "They don't advertise it. Only available to a select few, as they say, military and police, since armor piercing pistol ammo is illegal for commercial sale. B stands for ball or barrier, depending who they're marketing to."

Fancy grunted, stuck the magazine back in his pistol, and put it away. "Okay, so who was that guy?"

"That Rasmussen met with?"

"Yeah. The pretty boy. He looked familiar."

"That's because he's on our wanted posters." There weren't actually posters put up anywhere in their office, nobody had done that since the SEALs had been given credit for taking out Bin Laden, but there was a ranked list of most-wanted terrorists, generated by the DNI's office, distributed to any and all interested agencies, which included photos, if available. "Abu Ahmad al-Tunisi. At one point he was running Hurras al-Din, Al-Qaeda in Syria, then moved over to ISIL, Da'ish. They're all Salafi Jihadists, but maybe he saw more opportunity for growth with ISIL."

Fancy laughed. "What, like he's bouncing around between tech companies in Silicon Valley? Whoever has the better benefits package? A reserved parking spot close to the door?"

Bob shrugged. "Three months ago he was the number three guy in ISIL, and we were trying to kill him. Trying to bait him into one of the safehouses that we knew about, so we could send in JSOC or a cruise missile. Today he's the number two guy, and top-level members of the U.S. government and military are meeting with him in secret." He worked his neck, trying to loosen it up. For a mission where nothing had happened, there'd been a lot of stress. "How much do you want to bet in the next month or two the number one guy gets got by us, and ol' Tunisi moves up into a leadership role?"

"And what? Suddenly isn't a terrorist?"

Bob shot a look at Fancy, his eyes narrowed, then shrugged. "Better the devil you know, I guess," he said. If Fancy hadn't been paying attention on the drive back that was on him, but Rasmussen and Derricks had ridden together in the back seat of the Toyota. They'd barely spoken to each other, and had instead been on their satphones almost the entire time, reporting on their meeting to their superiors. They were careful not to say anything specific, remaining deliberately vague, but Bob could read between the lines: the United States government had entered into a secret arrangement with not just al-Tunisi but

ISIL itself. What that arrangement was, Bob wasn't quite clear on. Yet. But he'd figure it out.

Not quite thirty hours later he was back home at his townhouse in Virginia. He'd slept on the plane ride back—never pass up an opportunity to sleep—but his internal clock was completely scrambled. He pulled into the parking lot of his building just before noon, but it felt like the middle of the night to him.

He hadn't had the opportunity to work out at all while in Turkey, so he threw on his running gear—t-shirt, shorts, new Brooks Ghost Max running shoes with their extra-thick soles, as his knees weren't getting any younger, fanny pack loaded with a Glock—and did six slow nine-minute miles just to clear his head. The weather was cool, so he didn't even start to sweat until he'd done two miles.

You never knew exactly how long missions would last, and so he wasn't expected back in the office until the day after tomorrow. He took a leisurely shower, got dressed and armed, made himself a three-egg omelet with a bit of cheese and green onion, and only when he was ready to sit down and eat did he unplug his personal phone from the charger on the kitchen counter and check his messages. He never brought his personal phone or his wallet on missions.

Four and a half days gone meant two dozen emails had landed in the inbox of his Gmail account. All but two went right into the trash unread. There'd been several missed calls from random numbers—apparently one of the retailers from which he'd purchased something recently had sold his phone number. It happened several times a year. He welcomed it, it provided clutter and seeming normalcy to his life.

He'd also gotten half a dozen text messages. Two from politicians asking for money—he'd deliberately donated money to both the RNC and DNC several years earlier, and the amount of begging for cash they did was staggering. More chaff to distract. White noise. One text from a woman he knew, Lindsay, wondering if he was available for a meeting. Bob checked his watch, having to remind himself not just what time it was but what day it was. That message had come in two days before and was deliberately vague, as she was using her work phone. And married. He sent her a generic reply letting her know he was back in town and available to meet.

He saved what appeared to be a random text for last, from an unsaved number with a Washington DC 202 area code—YOUR ORDER IS READY ;-D NICK'S PIZZA

The text was a day old. Bob ate the last bite of omelet. He leaned back and crossed his arms, staring down at the letters on the screen. A hint of a smile touched his lips.

He walked through the huge complex of condo townhouses and apartments for a quarter mile. Some units, like his, had attached garages. Some had marked parking spaces. But there were also unmarked parking spots, for guests. His Subaru in his garage wasn't new, and wasn't hooked up to any satellite service which could track it, but it was registered to him, and there were license plate scanners everywhere. The eighteen-year-old Toyota Corolla he unlocked, on the other hand, had no wireless capability, and was registered to one of his cover identities. One the government knew nothing about.

The Subsection

Bob drove ten miles to a church. It was large enough—not a "megachurch", but getting there—that even in the middle of a weekday there were a number of cars in the lot, parked close to the building, and Bob parked amongst them. Then he popped the trunk, retrieved the backpack, and climbed back behind the wheel.

The problem—well, one of many problems—with most new smartphones and tablets was the onboard batteries—you couldn't take them out. And even if you could, those devices all had tiny back-up batteries hidden deep inside, to keep certain functions, like the clock, powered for days or weeks if the main battery died. There wasn't a smartphone or tablet connected to Wi-Fi or a cell provider that the government didn't have the ability to remotely turn on, even with the battery pulled. They could listen through the microphone, watch through the camera, and track via GPS, accurate to within a meter or two. There was facial recognition software in use by everyone, as well as voice recognition. And the government could use those devices to search out other active devices in the area. The Taliban had gone to hand-written notes and verbal orders, delivered in person, for a reason. You couldn't remotely hack a piece of paper. The government couldn't scan thoughts—yet. Although they were working on it….

It made things tougher, but not impossible. If you had to connect to the internet anonymously, and didn't know anything about hacking, you simply had to keep the device you planned to use physically separate from the rest of your life—completely and permanently. Never use it to connect to your wi-fi. Never turn it on near your other connected devices. Never use it to access your email or social media. Cover up the camera if you weren't using it. If you were up to no good—at least in the eyes of the government—never use it where you could be tracked by security cameras, which could then be used to tie your face to that phone.

A number of companies made sleeves and bags deliberately built to block electronic signals, to ensure your privacy and data security. Bob often used ones made by SLNT, and stored his burner phones and sterile tablet in a SLNT backpack that acted like a Faraday cage. You had to shut them off though, or if they were on put them in airplane mode, or they'd quickly burn out their batteries searching for a signal. He pulled the tablet out of the backpack, turned it on, saw he was at ten percent, plugged it in to charge it, and accessed the church's unsecured wi-fi signal. The signal only reached to the edges of the parking lot, but that was more than enough. He had three steady bars of service.

The internet was a vast sea, and there were ways to navigate it, to retrieve information, without drawing attention to yourself, but you had to be careful. Email was a last resort—it was common knowledge that Google scanned the contents of every Gmail account, every email, looking for information they could use and sell, just like every smartphone was listening to your conversations, picking up keywords, and tailoring the ads people saw on social media based on their declared interests. Bob presumed the other search engines/email providers like Bing, Babble, and Yahoo did the same. But there were all sorts of waystations, as he thought of them, throughout the ether, where you could park information anonymously and not have it automatically scanned. The winking smiley-face in the text—it hadn't been an emoji for a reason—had used a D for the mouth, and D stood for Discord.

Bob signed into the private Discord server, and saw a file —with a generic alphanumeric title—had been uploaded. 22 megabytes of data. He started the download, then

The Subsection

checked the progress. The church's signal wasn't especially strong, but apparently they had great bandwidth, because in less than a minute he had the entire file. He was out of the parking lot thirty seconds later. He drove ten minutes and parked in the lot of a strip mall that he knew wasn't covered by security cameras and opened the file. There were a lot of documents, but those took up very little space—most of the megabytes came from photos and a few short videos. He skimmed the case summary, watched the videos, and started to read the accompanying documents before realizing it would take him hours just to get through them once. There were hundreds of pages of reports, surveillance and otherwise. Packed with detail, which meant he couldn't simply skim them. And even then…

He sat for a while, visualizing what it would take to properly look into the case—that was what they'd decided to call them—before him. And realized that he really wasn't the right guy for the job. He checked his watch, swore, then put his car in gear. He needed to get somewhere with wi-fi he could access, because he needed to book a flight. And then do some shopping.

Even though it was a burner phone, and he was thirty thousand feet in the air, after he put it in airplane mode Bob stuck his phone in the Faraday backpack. All planes had wi-fi now. He couldn't strap a fake belly around his waist, not when he had to get through the body scanners at the airport, but he could wear bulky clothing, and there were ways to move, to stand, to sit, to totally change your appearance and demeanor. He slumped whether standing or sitting to make himself look shorter and fat. He took short, shuffling steps. He kept his head down and didn't make eye contact, his hair under a snap brim cap, his eyes hidden behind lightly tinted glasses, and his cheeks stuffed with foam to make his face much fatter, which matched the photos for this identity—Richard Kendall, resident of Elyria, Ohio, twenty miles west of Cleveland. Nothing about him stood out—he disappeared into crowds.

The Philadelphia Airport was only three hours away, and in a different state. He made it in plenty of time. Locker storage at airports was now a thing of the past, thanks to TSA regulations, so when flying on short notice he either had to go naked or check a gun like a regular civilian. But Kendall was an identity Bob had fully fleshed out and used regularly to keep it as real as possible. The driver license was real, not a forgery, and the pistol he had in a locked case in his checked luggage was actually legally registered to Kendall in Ohio.

Baggage containing firearms wasn't put on the carousel at his destination—at least, it wasn't supposed to be—and while Bob was waiting outside the Delta baggage office to claim his bag he turned on his burner phone. Somehow he wasn't surprised that it buzzed with a text message.

I WANT TO MEET HIM he read. NOON TOMORROW. Then a series of numbers that Bob knew were latitude and longitude.

SIX

Living Proof

Dave found that even when he had no problems reaching what he needed to paint, having the roller on the end of a long handle made it much easier. It extended your reach, but also lengthened each pass of the roller. He could do an entire wall from floor to ceiling in one swipe without even having to move his feet. As usual, it had taken him longer to tape off the trim than it had to paint the room. He looked around for any missed spots, any areas in need of another coat. He heard Lori somewhere nearby, through the open bedroom door, and called out to her. "I swear to God it seems like I just painted a bedroom."

She appeared in the doorway. Not frowning, not exactly. "You did just paint a bedroom. But then there were bullet holes. And smoke damage. And now we're in a new house. I very much do not want bullet holes or smoke damage in this one." She crossed her arms. "Should I put that in writing, or can you remember it?" He resisted the urge to sigh. He deserved that. "And stay out of the fucking hospital!" she said with sudden force.

He couldn't tell if she was being serious or not. "Three months, four, really, and I haven't even gotten a call," he pointed out. Just a package in the mail with new IDs—three of them, passports, driver licenses, and credit cards—not quite a month after his meeting in Michigan, which he'd put in separate and secure locations. He'd used one to set up a checking account, and two weeks later the checks had started dropping. What few doubts he'd still had that this was a real thing had disappeared when the IDs had shown up, but the paychecks cemented it.

"They've been working on your face," she said. "But now that that's all done…"

"I'm not sure they know about that. No direct contact, remember?"

"You are using your new employer's health care benefits to pay for the work, dummy."

"Oh, yeah."

"So…?" she said expectantly.

"I don't know," he said. "I haven't quite got a feel for the…organization. I've only met a few people. It's not that big. And it seems…compartmentalized. Which is good, but…" He shrugged. "Right now you know almost as much as I do. And how much do you know?"

She chewed at the inside of her lip. "I know they're not cutting you checks for nothing. Fixing those scars. You're going to be earning that money. Sooner or later."

"And definitely trying my best to stay out of the hospital," he told her, meaning it. She gave him a dirty look and walked away. He went back to painting.

It was late, almost ten p.m., when the doorbell sounded. They were on the couch having sex while Netflix played forgotten on the TV. Dave was off the couch and had his Glock—which had been on the end table—in hand almost before the chimes faded.

"What?" She was startled by his abrupt departure, and looked over her shoulder to see where he'd gone. It was only then that she realized she'd heard the doorbell too. "Bad guys aren't going to ring the doorbell," she told him, frowning, as he moved toward the front door, gun up. Both guns up.

"Yeah, who is it?" he asked, six feet from the door and off to one side. There was a peephole in the door, but anyone on the porch could see it darken when you put an eye to it.

"Time to earn that money you've been getting paid," he heard, the sound muffled.

Dave frowned. That voice.... He moved forward, and looked through the peephole. There was a fat old man standing on the porch, his face in shadow as he was wearing a snap-brim hat and the porch light was right over his head. But then he tilted his head back, and cocked it to the side. Dave was so surprised he opened the door, gun down along his thigh.

Bob Grinnand stepped through and Dave shut the door. "Who is it?" they both heard, and looked over to see Lori appear in the archway between the foyer and the living room. Naked. Lori put her hands on her hips, making no move to cover herself, and frowned at them.

Bob looked from her to Dave, noting the gun in his hand, and the other thing, then back to her. "Not the welcome I expected, but better than some I've had, and perhaps more than I deserve," he said drily. And he tipped his hat to her.

"Okay, I'm impressed," Bob said.

Dave had been lost in his thoughts, staring out the window at the passing scenery. He looked up, then over at Bob, sitting behind the wheel of the rental car. "What?"

"You haven't asked where we're going. Haven't asked anything." And they'd been in the car well over two hours. But before that, he hadn't asked much of anything. Bob had shown up late, slept the night on the couch, and they'd taken off early in the morning, and Dave'd just gone along quietly. It definitely wasn't because he was shy or cowardly.

"I don't know much about spy shit, but I'm not new to keeping my head down and my mouth shut," Dave said. "I figure you'll tell me what I need to know."

Bob nodded. He'd seen Dave in action, knew he could handle himself in stressful situations, *had* handled himself through some of the most intense combat Bob had seen in a few years. But seeing this side of him was good, too.

"But," Dave said, "speaking of spy shit, weren't you going to be getting me some training? High-speed tactical doorkicking moves, surveillance tech, whatever? I mean, all my wounds have healed and I'm back working out, but..." He'd spent most of two years working for a private investigator, but he figured tailing insurance scammers and adulterers around the streets of Detroit was far different than whatever intelligence spooks did. If nothing else, they had far superior gear. Bob had taken off the disguise he'd been wearing when he'd arrived the night before. Just a few small things and he'd been totally able to change his appearance and demeanor. That was something Dave needed to learn.

"Yeah, well, time and tide," Bob said, shrugging his big shoulders. "It's not going to be an issue, this time around. We get this one squared away, which seems right in your wheelhouse, I'll start sending you to some schools. Getting you some of that specialized instruction. Your gunhandling and shooting skills are excellent, and that's good if you're on your own, and you'll often be on your own, but when you're not, running with a team is an entirely different animal. Team tactics is on the class to-do list." He gave Dave a longer look. "You look good. Can't hardly see the scars."

"Get 'this one' squared away? What exactly is 'this one'?" Dave asked.

"Just wait 'til we get there," Bob said.

"Where?" Dave waved a hand out the window. There was nothing but sand and scrub and tumbleweeds as far as they could see, in every direction. They'd been heading northwest through Arizona for over two hours, and were now on State Route 377. It was a two-lane highway and Dave hadn't seen anything but desert, power lines, and passing cars for twenty minutes. He'd been trying to picture Arizona in his head, and there was nothing but more nothing between them and the state line with New Mexico. And a lot more nothing past that. Maybe a few indian reservations.

"To meet someone. And maybe give you a bit of an employee orientation."

Dave waited, but there was nothing more forthcoming. "That's it? That's all you're going to tell me?"

"I trust you," Bob said. "I trust you as much as anybody. But whatever you don't know they can't torture out of you." He cast a sidelong glance at Dave. "Not that it would be easy for them. Or quick. God knows both you and your buddy Aaron can take a beating. But everyone breaks, eventually. Look, our organization, we're in a unique position. An…internal affairs department, if you will. We're an officially sanctioned unit of the federal government, paid for by tax dollars, but we can't act like it, because our job is to not play by the rules. To hurt them when they step out of line. Doing what's right, for the good of the country. And to do it in such a way that they stay clueless about us. Because they'd crush us like a bug if they found out about us. Not just because the government hates competition, but because, comparatively, we're small and weak. We have to play by guerrilla rules. Asymmetric warfare. So the less you know the better."

"Are you the boss?"

"No, I'm…I guess you could call me a group supervisor. And you're in my group. You know I've got a day job. A lot of our people do. Even including us part-timers, our numbers are small. When I tell you, being a full-time employee with no other job, that you're part of a small, elite group, believe me."

"Are we going to meet the boss?"

"No more questions. Well, you can ask, but there aren't going to be any more answers."

"Can I ask how much longer it's going to be?"

"You can ask," Bob said, and only someone who knew him well would have seen the hint of a smile.

Not quite half an hour later Bob took an exit off I-40 eastbound, crossed over the interstate northbound, and coasted up a narrow access road. "You ever been here before?" he asked Dave.

Dave looked at the foot-tall metal letters on the low wall ahead of them. Petrified Forest National Park. "No."

"I think my parents took me here when I was a little kid," Bob said. "I remember climbing on stone logs." They

The Subsection

cruised north, reached a gatehouse, and Bob paid for an entrance pass. Just the daily rate, he declined an annual pass. Then he followed the drive north past the Visitor Center. It curved around in a big loop, past the Painted Desert Inn, ducked under I-40, then headed south through barren rocky desert landscape. Bare dirt and rock alternated with fields of sage and scrub grass.

The park employee had handed them a pamphlet and Dave had unfolded it on his lap. "This scenic drive is twenty-eight miles long," Dave said. "Petrified Forest Road. Puts us out on Highway 180 at the south end. If that's where we're going?" He looked at Bob, but Bob ignored him.

Frowning, Dave looked out the window. Bob was in no hurry, cruising along at a sedate 30 mph, even though the posted speed limit was 35. They passed three cars in the first ten minutes. Twenty minutes after starting their scenic tour the road crossed over what a sign indicated was the Santa Fe Railroad. Dave had no idea if it was a working railway or something historic, and figured asking Bob would be a waste of time.

Two minutes later they crossed over a narrow, muddy river, and there was a turnout on the left side with a parking lot and a small square building that was likely a public toilet. "I need to use the john," Bob announced.

Dave had had to go for quite some time but hadn't wanted to say anything. He nodded. The parking lot wasn't large and still it was nearly empty, with just three cars and one tour bus angled into a long space. Bob parked on the side of the lot furthest from the public bathrooms, away from the other cars. He got out, stretched, looked around, then he and Dave walked to the men's room. The public bathroom was a small building clad in fake adobe and they had the men's room to themselves.

When they were finished Dave followed Bob out. Bob seemed in no hurry to return to their car. He wandered around to the back of the building, onto a pathway. There were signs for Puerco Pueblo, and an informational sign covered by clear plastic designed to resist the elements and vandals. "Ooh, petroglyphs *and* pictographs," Bob said. He looked at Dave, and jerked his head. "It's only a third of a mile hike, round trip, you want to go?"

"Not really," Dave said, increasingly having trouble containing his impatience.

"C'mon," Bob said, and didn't wait for a response, he just strolled down the paved path. Up ahead they could see the remaining sandstone walls of the Puerco Pueblo. There were only a few wisps of cloud in the pale blue sky and the sun was hot on their faces. Dave caught up to Bob.

"Did you read that sign?" Bob asked him. "The tribe had to abandon this area because of climate change in the 1300s. Most people talking about climate change these days have probably never heard of the Medieval Warm Period or the Little Ice Age, but the transition between the two, in the thirteen hundreds, that's when things were wacky." He caught Dave's expression and shrugged. "Those ignorant of history are doomed to repeat it, blah blah blah. I read a lot."

"Me too, but mostly fiction." Dave took a breath and tried to relax. Tried to enjoy the ruins.

Twenty minutes later they'd completed a slow circuit of the site. Cars drove past on the road from time to time, but most of the people stopping did so only to use the bathroom. They'd seen just a few other people—one couple and one family—touring the site.

The Subsection

As they approached their car Dave saw the tour bus was still in the lot, two spaces over. And Dave realized that was weird—what was the bus doing there? There weren't any people at the site. No tour groups, anyway. Then the door of the vehicle hissed, and slid open right in front of them. "Bob!" Dave shouted, and his Glock cleared his holster before the door had finished sliding open. Bob grabbed his arm with both his hands, his grip steel.

"Man, you're fucking fast," Bob said admiringly. It was one thing being willing to kill. It was another thing entirely to be able to go from zero to *kill everybody* in a heartbeat. That was a rare gift, and Dave had it. "Put it away," he told Dave quietly, and let go of his arm. Bob looked around. Nobody had seen or heard anything. He looked toward the open door, and Dave followed his gaze. There was a tall man standing inside the big vehicle, looking down at them.

"Jeez, he doesn't disappoint, does he?" he said, looking from Dave to Bob and back. "What was your nickname, back in the day? Gunfighter? The man, the myth, the legend himself. Living proof that whatever government conspiracy theories you believe in…the truth is so much worse."

"Dave, this is…are we using your real name?" Bob asked him.

"With him? Yeah. I'm Murph," he said, stepping down toward them and holding out a hand to Dave. "I'm tech support."

"You want something to drink before we get started?" Murph asked them. "I've got water, soda, Gatorade." He pointed at the refrigerator. "Help yourself."

Bob leaned a shoulder against the wall. "I thought you didn't drink any of that due to the microplastics. Or fluoride. Or whatever."

"Doesn't mean I can't have it for guests. And I'll drink out of cans and glass bottles. You can filter out microplastics, you just need a filter or a purifier that removes anything 2.5 microns or larger. Fluoride is only in tap water."

Dave walked over to the small refrigerator and grabbed a can of Diet Coke. He cracked it open and took a sip. It was ice cold. He worked his neck, then looked at Murph, who was sitting in a big gaming chair in front of one hell of a computer setup. The man was tall with wide shoulders and looked like a surfer with a big mop of sun-bleached hair on his head. Older than he first appeared. And he was staring right back at Dave, a big smile on his face.

"Jeez," Murph said, shaking his head. "What was that, like a sub-one-second draw? From concealment." He traded a look with Bob, then peered at Dave. "Okay, so, how many times did they try to kill you?"

"Who?"

Murph laughed, and looked at Bob. "Fucking gold." He turned his big smile on Dave. "I don't give a shit about the mob or the cartels," Murph told Dave. "I'm talking about our lovely federal government. Because of your matching fingerprint problem."

Dave glanced at Bob, but the man didn't have an expression on his face. Which meant he was unsurprised Murph the Surf knew what he did. Dave looked down at his scarred fingers, then shrugged. "I don't know. Three, four? You tell me. You seem to know a lot about it."

Murph snorted, then leaned back in his chair and jabbed a finger at Bob. "You tell me you don't believe in destiny," he said accusingly. "That we're all just," he waved his hand around, "wandering around blindly, trying to figure shit out. Live our lives. That there's no prewritten plan. No order to the universe. You know how many times they came for him," he said, jabbing a finger at Dave. "The entire weight of the federal fucking government. Serious dudes, with serious skills. Plus the mob. Plus goddamn Mexican drug cartels." He threw his hands up in the air. "And he didn't just survive, he met you. Made it out of Mexico. You going to tell me that was chance? Random? Horseshit. We're all destiny's bitches. There's a reason we're here, together."

"Yeah," Bob said drily. "Because you texted me that you wanted to meet him."

Murph waved a dismissive hand at him, then pointed to the wall above his monitors, where he'd printed something out and taped up the paper. *You'll think you're going crazy, but you're not. You're going sane in a crazy world, and once destiny starts messing with your life you'll never be the same again.* It was from, of all unlikely sources, the short-run Amazon series *The Tick*, Season 2, Episode 6, *Categorically Speaking*.

Murph peered at Dave. "We're on the great adventure. Together."

"The great adventure?"

Murph's face split into a huge smile and he spread his arms wide. He had an impressive span. "Life, baby. Life! Don't you feel it? Coursing through your fucking veins. Every day is an adventure. Okay, so, what do you want to know?"

Dave threw a glance at Bob, but then focused on Murph. "Apparently what I want to know doesn't matter. It's only whether I have a need to know. Compartmentalization, or whatever. I don't know a damn thing about who I'm working for. Not even the name. Just the shell company listed on my checks. Does it have a name?"

"Our organization?" Murph shook his head. "It doesn't have a name. Not officially. Formally. Which might not be a bad thing."

Bob said, "The closest thing we have to a unit name or number is the subsection in the appropriations bill that originally established us."

Dave grunted, then looked at Murph. "How about you? Who are you? Simple 'tech support' doesn't seem to adequately describe why you're riding around in this drug kingpin tour bus. Marble floors, a fucking espresso machine, and a computer that looks like it could hack NORAD?"

Murph glanced at the computer. "Please. This thing's like an Atari 800 compared to what I've got at home. Anyway," he looked at Bob, "I checked the eyes in the sky while you were killing time, and you guys rolled in clean. No satellites looking down here—at least ours—and no drones in the air. This thing's impervious to any external surveillance, even lasers on the glass, so nobody knows we're here, and they can't hear anything we say. We've got all the time in the world." He looked back at Dave. "I could give you the long story, but I'm not sure you've got the background knowledge. What do you know about physics? Subatomic particles. Quantum information science, in particular."

"Whatever I picked up watching *The Big Bang Theory*."

Murph nodded. "Okay, that's what I thought." He pursed his lips. "Well…I could spend a few hours just giving you the basics on quantum mechanics…"

"Your idea of the 'basics' of quantum theory would blow out Richard Feynman's frontal lobe," Bob said drily. He looked at Dave. "Technically I've got a genius IQ, and

The Subsection

I'm fluent or close enough in five languages, not including English, and half the time I feel retarded talking to him. Murph was recruited by the NSA to work on quantum cryptography. When he was fifteen."

"You wouldn't have even recognized me," Murph told Dave cheerfully. "I was fat. Compulsive eater. I got up to four hundred pounds, I think. I loved the work, I just didn't like what it was being used for. Who it was being used by. Swallowed my feelings, in addition to four Whoppers every day for lunch, and a pizza for dinner, washed down with Coke. Pop-Tarts or Twinkies for dessert. God, I miss eating like that. But I don't miss being fat. It took me ten years to understand why I was unhappy. Once I did, and decided to do something about it, I was a different person.

"Edward Snowden, he was a comparatively low-level guy, subcontractor, and look what he exposed. I was there then, at the NSA, and the stuff I was working on was so secret most of the bigwigs weren't cleared for it. Didn't even know our team existed, or grasped what we were doing if they did. High level algorithms, early AI, quantum cryptanalysis, and that gave me access to everything. *Everything*. And if you think what Snowden exposed was bad, holy shit, that's nothing. It should give anyone nightmares. Unless you're one of those people who think government can do no wrong. Morons, or those ignorant of history, or those who are willing to sacrifice everything they have for that feeling of security. Honestly, distrusting your government shouldn't be a right-wing or left-wing thing, it should be a people thing. After all, the term 'Big Brother' was dreamed up by a Brit, not an American. The sky is up, water gets you wet, don't trust your government. Governments are the biggest mass murderers in the world, always have been, always will be—that's not an opinion, that's documented fact. Just read a history book. *Any* history book." Murph sighed. "Maybe it's not a right or left issue, maybe it's an IQ issue. Then again, I guess that's human nature. Scientific studies have shown that eighty percent of everybody will believe whatever someone in authority tells them, no matter how outrageous. We want to believe the people in charge have our best interests at heart. It takes a lot, *a lot*, to break us of that. Normally. I mean, this country was founded when we went to war with our own government over nothing, at least compared to the things they've been doing lately. A three-percent tax, and other piddly shit, all of which combined isn't as bad as a tenth of the shit the government did just during COVID.

"The U.S. government wholesale spying on its citizens without warrant or cause, the surveillance state, is just where the misbehavior starts, not where it ends. Once you get a peek behind that curtain, you'll never be the same. The heinous shit they've been doing would make anyone sick. The question isn't if you should believe in conspiracy theories, but rather whether any of them *aren't* true. Tower Seven, the Las Vegas shooting, Epstein Island being a honey-pot run by the CIA. They're not conspiracy theories after you've seen the evidence, they're just simple statements of fact. I didn't know what I was going to do, but I knew I had to do something. And I wanted to do it right. So I spent a few years setting things up before I left."

"*Years?*" Dave said. Murph nodded. "Back doors into their programs?" Dave asked.

Murph snorted. "When you designed the entire house, plumbing, electrical, carpet, and nailed the shingles to the roof, you don't need a 'back door'. I'm in the goddamn walls. And that was before I made a few advances that put me even further ahead of the game. When you're as big as they are, it's easy to do small shit that doesn't get noticed. Their server farms, which are recording all the data they're pulling off the web, look like something out of *The Matrix*. I guess they are, as they're powered by people in a way, which makes the comparison even better. Or worse, I guess." He shook his head. "Anyway, so then I went into the private sector, wrote a few algorithms for Cisco and HP that made me a stupid amount of money just so the government would stop paying attention to me. Set up a few algorithms that day-trade and generate a shit-ton of passive income. If the SEC got a look at them they'd make them illegal in a hot second. Well, once they figured out what they were looking at. It might take them a couple weeks. Anyway, now I'm just a rich eccentric who travels around the country off the grid. Which I am, but…okay, what do you know about computers?" he asked Dave.

"How to turn them on," Dave said. "Play video games. Watch porn."

"Why are you watching porn?" Murph asked, mystified. He gave a little wave. "Not, 'why are you watching porn, it's evil'. I'm not religious, and porn's been around longer than the three major religions combined times three. There's porn cave paintings from aboriginals in Australia that are thirty thousand years old. The Venus of Hohle Fels is forty thousand years old, and you should see the T&A on that thing. I mean, why are *you* watching porn. I know who your girlfriend is. Was. Is?" He wasn't sure of the proper tense when discussing a retired porn star.

"I'm not, not really, not any more. Lori does."

Murph sat up straight in his chair. "Waitaminute, that's her? I thought you were the freak, but it's her watching that stuff?"

"How do you know what she's watching?"

Murph pointed a finger at Bob. "You don't think I'd let him hire you for our little operation without doing a deep dive on you, do you? And my AI served you up and gutted you, all your secrets, that's what it does. That crooked detective that was all over you for so long about that hit and run, did he never clue to the fact that your buddy Aaron's girlfriend owned a vehicle which matched the description of the one involved in the incident?"

Dave blinked in surprise. "No."

"Idiot. The only question I had was whether you or your buddy was driving. I'm guessing you, since it was your parents Big Paulie killed. But I'm not asking. And not judging. But that's a hell of a friend, letting you borrow a car so you can run over someone, and then keeping his mouth shut about it."

"Acquaintances help you move, friends help you move a body," Bob said, sounding like he was speaking from personal experience.

"I guess," Murph said. He didn't really have any friends. Never had—too smart, too weird, maybe, and then, when all the work he was doing was secret…. "Anyway, you and your girlfriend, I'm in both your phones, your emails—not that there's many of those. You don't seem to use your computer much."

Dave shook his head. "I use her laptop, past few months. Mine burned up in my house and I haven't replaced it. Haven't much needed one of my own. I haven't had a social media account since I left Michigan. I barely email. I use hers when I need one."

"Well, I didn't activate the camera or microphone, I was only going to do that if it looked like there was a problem. If I had, I guess I would have known it wasn't you watching porn. Seriously, that was her? The fetish stuff? That's so hot."

"Murph, focus," Bob growled.

"Okay, right, sorry." He took a breath, tried to figure out where to pick up. "Ever hear of quantum computers?"

Dave thought. "I think I've heard of quantum supercomputers, but I don't know what that is."

Bob held out his hand like he was stopping traffic. "Murph, take a deep breath, and pretend who you're talking to isn't us but rather a couple third-graders. And not bright third-graders. The kind who eat glue. Then, maybe, we'll understand most of what you're saying."

Murph smiled, but nodded. He paused, then said, "Every quantum computer is a supercomputer, you consider the performance potential. Look, subatomic particles, things in the quantum realm, they don't always behave according to the rules of physics as we understand them. Quantum computers don't either. Or, at least, that is the plan. As far as the rest of the world knows, quantum computers are more an idea than an actuality. Sure, a few have been built, like IBM's stupid Q System One, but those have been more of a theoretical exercise than anything else. Barely proof of concept. Quantum computers look to take advantage of quantum superposition and entanglement, the qubits providing probabilistic, nondeterministic output that you have to know how to manage to get any meaningful data. But there are all sorts of issues. Hardware for one, but also scaling. I've been building one that's been working, on a limited basis, and it's far more advanced than anything else out there as far as I know. I think I'm on the verge of a breakthrough, too. The secret's expanding your mind to the whole of the possible."

"So what do they do better?" Dave asked. He'd barely

followed Murph's explanation. He thought qubit was a video game character. No, wait, that was Q*bert. "I'm assuming they're faster?"

"Yes, but it's not just that. Physics seems to break down at the quantum level. But so does time." He made a face. "I don't know any better way to explain it. We still don't quite understand why a lot of the stuff happens at the quantum level, but we are able to observe it. Affect it. Smash a few particles together at CERN like a three-year-old with blocks just to see what happens. When we finally do understand not just what's happening down there, but why, I believe we're going to see the face of God. Or the aliens who seeded this planet with life. Something like that. Anyway," Murph said, getting back on topic, "it's not just that the computer is faster, it's that its processing seems to occur independently of time constraints. Independent of time. So that, when it is working, it seems to be able to process things in no time at all. So fast you can't even measure the processing time in picoseconds. Once I, or anybody, develops a fully functional quantum computer, theoretically there is no type of encryption that it wouldn't be able to crack—instantly, or so it would seem. Which is why the government is pursuing the technology. And even though I'm not quite there yet, I'm really close. My computer, and the few programs I've written for it, algorithms, AI worm engines, allow us to get into any computer system that's hooked up to the internet and spread it open like a Penthouse centerfold. That includes everything the government owns and operates from DARPA to the NSA. They've got their own processing algorithms to go through all the data they're scooping up from social media, voice and facial recognition, but I wrote half of those for them ten years ago, and the ones I've made since are better. Much better. In fact, I was doing all this on my own, just keeping an eye on the government, because I don't trust them at all, compiling evidence of all their illegal shit, and my programs sniffed out the...the subsection. I guess that's a good name for it." He glanced at Bob, who shrugged. "Right when it was brand new. Before they'd really done anything, as an organization. Which showed them how much they needed me. And the rest, as they say, is history."

"Don't we have somebody in the NSA?" Dave asked, looking at Bob. One of the guys he'd met in Michigan. Steve. Supposedly high up with NSA.

Bob nodded. "He gives us a heads up if there's anything going on we need to know about that's not getting inputted into systems we can access. Air-gapped computers, or maybe old-fashioned paper files. Conversations held in SCIFs he's privy to. Lots of shit going on that doesn't get recorded. Provided we don't act on that intelligence in such a way that would expose him. Because we can't let them know they've been penetrated."

"So you can get into anything?" Dave asked. "The dark web?"

Murph snorted derisively. "The dark web," he said mockingly. "For most people, the dark web is anything that doesn't show up on the first page of Google search results. Look, there is no 'cloud', no internet that exists somewhere out there in the atmosphere." He waved a hand. "The internet is just servers. Computers. Some at the end of the equivalent of long, dusty corridors, behind locked doors. But if it's on a computer connected to the internet, if I can find it I can get into it. The problem isn't access, I've pretty much cracked that, the problem is the sheer volume of information out there. Sorting through it. Analyzing it. You need AI, algorithms, things like that." He smiled. He shrugged. "But I've cracked that, too."

"Babe Ruth?" Dave said to him.

Murph smiled, and pointed a finger at him. "Exactly."

"What?" Bob said.

"'It ain't bragging if you can do it,'" Dave said, quoting the famous baseball player.

Bob nodded. "Right." He looked at Murph. "Since I'm here, I can tell you in person—I need you to look into something for me. I need to know why the Deputy Secretary of State, the Commander of CENTCOM, and CIA's Chief of the Near East/South Asia Division were meeting with Abu Ahman al-Tunisi secretly in Syria two days ago." Bob knew he recognized the guy posing as Deputy Secretary of State Derricks' aide, and after sleeping on it finally remembered running into the guy in Kabul a decade earlier, where he'd been supervising one of the CIA's field ops.

"Abu who?"

"Number two guy in ISIL. Which means he's somebody we should be killing in a drone strike, or waterboarding, not meeting secretly."

"Where'd you get this intel? You sure about it?"

Bob shrugged. "Pretty sure. It was a short meeting, half an hour, northern Syria, just over the border from Turkey. Total low profile, civilian clothes, unmarked vehicles. The CIA guy was running incognito, but I recognized him." That admission got an interested look from Dave. "You got a piece of paper? I'll write down all their names and the details of the meet."

"Interesting. Certainly sounds like they're doing something they're not supposed to. Military, state department, and CIA? Maybe the CIA's trying to lock down new heroin suppliers now that the Taliban are burning all the poppy

The Subsection

fields in Afghanistan. Or maybe they're just trying to negotiate a ceasefire, put an end to hostilities in the area. Stranger things have happened. I'll look into it."

"Okay, so," Bob said to Murph. "Current case? What's so special about it that we needed to meet in person? Normally you're dead-set against that. 'Unnecessary risk.'"

"Oh, nothing," Murph said. "I just wanted to meet him." He nodded at Dave. Bob sighed. Murph grinned, then said, "Okay, so, we've got our dead private investigator."

Dave went cold. He glanced from Murph to Bob. "Not John. It's not John Phault, is it?"

Bob shook his head. "No, I would have told you." They both knew the Detroit-based PI.

"James Blinkenschaal," Murph said. "After high school he did eight years in the Marines, then joined the Cleveland Police Department. Worked there for thirteen years before a broken knee forced him to quit. Got tackled by a drunk. Technically a medical retirement, eighty percent disability, but was too young to sit on his ass, apparently, so for the last eleven years he's been working as a private investigator. And not quite three weeks ago he died of a heart attack. Fifty-three years old. Divorced, living alone, but found the next day by his maid who comes by once a week."

"And?" Dave said. "Fifty-three's not young. And even if he was, lots of people dying suddenly, unexpectedly these days from heart issues."

"Are they really 'sudden and unexpected' when you're undergoing experimental gene therapy?" Murph said. "That is the medically technically accurate term for what's in that injection, what it does. And the drug companies have finally started admitting there's a small chance of heart problems—and if they're coming out and saying that, it means they're trying to get out in front of the real data coming out, which basically was worldwide mass murder for fun and profit."

"Murph," Bob said.

"Right. Anyway, I did check, and there's no sign he was ever jabbed. But a simple natural death wouldn't have gotten the attention of my system."

"So what did?" Dave said, leaning forward, now interested. He'd always enjoyed the investigative aspect of PI work more than the simple surveillance, but surveillance was what paid the bills.

"Two emails," Murph said. He leaned forward, and his fingers flew over the keyboard. He pointed at one of the monitors before him. "If you don't recognize the name, or aren't familiar with dot-gov headers, this one was sent by Dr. Mason Phillips, who currently is the Deputy Director of the CIA for Operations. Which means he's a big fucking deal. There's the Director, then there are the deputies in charge of the five directorates. The email was sent to Daniel Kim, who appears to be a senior field man in Operations. A doer, not a desk guy. From how much detail I *couldn't* find on him, it seems he's one of the CIA's black bag guys. Not a trigger puller, not Ground Branch, but one of the gray men, guys that make things happen quietly. That make things look like accidents, that aren't."

Dave leaned close. The message was short. *James Blinkenschaal. Is this situation handled?*

"Kim responded four hours later," Murph said. "'Working on it.' That's it, no previous or subsequent mentions of that 'situation', but three days later Blinkenschaal was dead. Autopsy said it was natural causes. Heart attack. If his name was John Smith, my program never would have pinged it. But there are all of about three James

The Subsection

Blinkenschaals in the entire continental U.S. One of them was of interest to the DDO of the CIA. And dead three days later. You do the math."

Dave leaned back. "So you're in the CIA's emails? Their internal in-house communications, behind what I assume are hack-proof firewalls?"

"Yeah. I thought I said that."

"Shit. Wow. So, you ever decide to bring your computer to market, let me invest. I'll make a fortune."

"Until it becomes self-aware and nukes us all," Bob said drily. "I give the over/under on that three days." Murph barked out a laugh.

"Okay," Dave said. He pointed at the computer monitor. At the email. "Why?"

"That's the question," Bob said. "And that's where you come in. Even if we had somebody else available for this case, this is perfect for you, with your background. Not just because the dead man was a private investigator, but because it looks like it'll require some investigation."

Murph said, "Blink—that's what his friends called him—seemed to back up most of his files to that cloud we were just talking about. Maybe all of his files, but I don't know what might be on his laptop, as it is currently shut off. No idea if he's got actual paper files on anything that's not in digital form somewhere. The ex-wife was still his next-of-kin, and she's hired guys to pack up the house, with plans to put it on the market. He worked out of his house, so whatever he had is there. Unless Kim black-bagged the house while Blink was cooling on the bed, stole files, or the laptop, or wiped it. There's a lot we don't know with this one.

"If he was killed because of something he did as a PI—and that's the assumption—it was likely within a week or two of the DDO's email. Or maybe not, but you'd think there'd be a prominent note in his notes somewhere—'ran into some spooky government guys today on surveillance, pissed them off'. But there was nothing that my programs pinged, scanning all of his case files, his bank records, credit card receipts, emails. Nothing. He hadn't left the greater Cleveland area in months."

"I skimmed what you gave me, and didn't see anything either," Bob told Murph, then looked at Dave. "I'm guessing that whatever it was that brought him to their attention, it was not long before the DDO sent out that email. Blinkenschaal was working a few cases that week, but they were all generic insurance things. At least, that's how it looks. But the CIA doesn't give a shit about Cleveland work comp cases. They don't send one of their top ghosts out to unalive random people living their lives. If they did do it, and I think they did, they had a very specific reason. Find it. Because not only isn't the CIA supposed to be operating inside the U.S., they killed an American citizen."

Not quite twenty hours later Bob climbed out of his Toyota and yawned. He'd gotten a total six hours sleep between waiting at the airport and riding the red-eye back to Philly. When he was in his twenties, or even his thirties, that would have been enough, but he'd been on the go for most of a week between the mission to Syria and the field trip to Arizona, and he was dragging. And he was due at the office in two hours—which was just enough time to run through the 42-form *tai chi* once, maybe twice, to relax, stretch, and focus, then a long hot shower and a home-cooked breakfast. And a lot of coffee. Which hopefully would be enough to get him back on track. Dialed in.

The Subsection

He was in his own head as he trudged through the parking lot toward his townhouse, bobbing it slightly as he listened to *Brothers in Arms* by Dire Straits. It wasn't an excuse, but it was the reason he didn't notice the men sitting in the car in front of his building. Right as he passed by the car the driver's door opened and a man popped up. He reached a hand out to Bob as the passenger door of the car opened as well.

Bob reacted instinctively, kicking sideways at the man's legs, grabbing his outstretched arm with one hand and yanking downward as his foot connected, the man falling sideways, Bob palming the man's dropping head with his other hand and slamming it into, *through*, the side mirror of the adjacent car in a spray of plastic and glass. His hand swept back and in one smooth movement he drew his pistol and pointed it over the roof the car at the second man just rising to his feet.

"Pike!" the man shouted, eyes wide. His hands shot up. "Agency, we're agency! Friendlies! Jesus fuck, don't shoot me."

Scowling, Bob pulled his pistol back, but didn't lower the muzzle. "And you just come at me?"

"We thought you were inside, then you just came walking up before we could knock. The director sent us. He wants to talk to you."

"You can't call?"

"He's been trying to reach you for a day. Your phone's shut off."

"It's my day off."

"Yeah, well, the director needs to talk to you, and got tired of waiting, so here we are." He lowered his hands, then bent down and peered through the car windows. "Where the fuck is Tony?"

As Bob put his pistol away the man walked around the car and looked down at his partner on the pavement. He was semi-conscious, groaning, his head resting in a spreading pool of blood. "Shit," the man said, putting his hands on his hips.

"What's the director want?" Bob asked.

"Fuck if I know. He didn't say and I didn't ask. But I guess the he's going to have to wait a little longer while we go to the ER. Help me get him into the back seat. This is on you. Where the fuck you been, you're so tightly wrapped?"

PART II
DESTINY'S BITCHES

SEVEN

It's Always Better Not to Know

It was late morning when they arrived at the Defense Intelligence Agency's main headquarters inside Joint Base Anacostia-Bolling (JBAB), a 900-acre government facility in southwest Washington D.C. The DIA's headquarters was a huge office building, and yet only a third of the DIA employees worked there—there were a number of satellite offices, like the one Bob worked at, nearby in Virginia, left over from when the DIA consolidated a decade earlier.

The agent took him up to the executive floor. Bob knew where the Director's office was, and was striding down the corridor toward it when he was stopped by a hand on his arm. The agent nodded at a door in front of them. "This is where they want you."

It was one of the many conference rooms in the building. Bob kept any emotion off his face and went in. A middle-aged blonde man he recognized was sitting at the table, and looked up from his phone as Bob entered.

"Finally. You know who I am?"

Bob blinked, and nodded. "I do." Joe Clark. At least,

that was his work name. One of the senior supervisors on the doin-shit side of the DIA, as opposed to the talkin-about-shit side. That's how Bob thought of them in his head. Deeds, not words. Officially he was the same rank as Bob, but Clark had come up in the agency with the current Director, and was regularly put in charge of certain projects, so he was upper management in deed if not word. There was a folder and a legal pad on the table in front of him, but he was the only person in the room.

Clark nodded. "The director has tasked me with the inquiry into Gargoyle's last mission."

Bob took a seat across from him. "Good."

"Good?"

Bob nodded. "I'm glad someone is looking into it. They were my team. I want to know what happened to them as much as anyone else."

"Is that why you've been making inquiries?"

"Yes. And so far I've gotten no answers."

Clark leaned forward. "Walk me through your last contact with them. Assume I've been cleared on the mission details."

Bob shrugged. "Not much to tell. They had a package to deliver down south. I arranged transport, a small jet, one of ours, through a commercial cover. Small airstrip, south end of Arizona, near the border. They rolled up with the package right on time. I stood watch while they loaded it onto the plane. Then they took off. I took care of their vehicle, came back here. After three days, I think, they were considered overdue. And that was it, none of them ever returned, or surfaced, alive or dead. There was a big cartel incident right over the border about that time, and I wondered if they were somehow involved, but I've never gotten any answers to my inquiries."

The Subsection

"Why didn't you go down to Mexico with them? They're your team."

"If you've been cleared on the mission details, you know. Because I look like this." Bob waved a hand at himself. "I'm fluent, but I'm whiter than white, which is why I generally work in Russia, Europe, the Caucuses…. They wanted those going down there to look enough like locals to pass, at a distance at least, even if they didn't speak the language. So it was only three guys, half the team, who went down. That was Higgins' call, not mine." Hansford Higgins was his DIA section chief, and ran their field office.

Clark grunted, then peered at Bob. "What's your opinion on the package they were transporting?"

"At the time? I had none. I didn't know what it was. Who it was. That was their op, they planned and executed it while I was arranging transpo. I was not in on mission prep."

"You were at the airport. Did you get a look at the package there?"

Bob shook his head. "No, it was wrapped for the trip." The package being Dave Anderson. The plan had been to deliver him to the up-and-coming La Fuerza cartel in Mexico to make the DIA's undercover man embedded with them look like a rock star. Dave had killed a number of their people in Arizona, but more importantly had embarrassed the cartel. They'd planned to make an example out of him. At best he would have been tortured to death.

Clark tilted his head. "You sure about that? You didn't peek under the wrapping?"

Bob shook his head, firmly. "You know how long I've been doing this. It's better not to know. It's always better not to know. But I found out later."

"How did you do that?"

"I've got a few local law enforcement contacts. Phoenix PD. Tohono county. Two of my team were caught on nanny cam, making the snatch. No facial rec, so the cops couldn't ID them, but they were spun up about it, and that was enough to get me concerned. I brought it to the Director's attention. I was worried they'd grabbed the wrong package, as this seemed to be a citizen, not a cartel member. But I was straightened out. Chewed out, actually, for going out of pocket to the Director, skipping over Higgins, my supervisor."

"The Director's explanation satisfied you?"

"I was only worried for the company, and my men. Once he gave me assurances everything was proceeding according to plan, I dropped it. But then…nothing." Bob leaned back, frowning. "Do we have anything? Know anything? Right now I don't know if my guys are alive or dead. I mean, it's been months, I'm assuming they're dead, but I'd like to know. Like to know what happened. Some of them have families, and they should have closure. Once they were overdue I tried to contact them, cell phones, satphones, but nothing. I guess one or two of them pinged near Juarez before going dark, but that's literally the only intelligence I have. Did we receive any communication at all from them once they got down there? Did they complete their mission?"

Clark didn't answer. Instead, he looked at the file in front of him. "You ever hear the word tentpole?"

"Tentpole? No. Not in relation to this mission. Or any mission, that I recall."

"Weathervane?"

"No. I presume these are codenames? No."

"Nelson Santiago?"

"Not offhand, although it's a pretty common name."

"How about Martin Cabrera?"

Bob frowned. "Didn't he play for the Tigers? I'm not being a smartass," he said quickly. Bob snapped his fingers. "No, that was Miguel Cabrera. You said Martin? No, nothing."

"Chris Evenson, Doug Carr, and James Danner—do you know if they had contacts in Mexico?"

Bob blinked twice, then remembered those were the real names of his teammates who went by Cherry, Dog, and Boot when they were working. "I know some, maybe all of them have run missions in Central and South America over the years, but offhand I don't know about any assets, contacts, or friends they might have had or could have called if shit went sideways. If there are any, likely they'll be mentioned in those mission files. Do we not know anything about what happened to them?"

Clark frowned, then answered. "Evenson—Cherry—is dead. Confirmed. Shot to death on the streets of Juarez. Right in the middle of that firefight between the federales and the cartels."

Bob sighed. "Well, shit. I mean, I knew it, they wouldn't just disappear, not for this long, but still. And if he's dead, the others likely are too. Federales say what happened? Circumstances of his death?"

Clark didn't answer. He leaned forward, then casually asked, "You have a problem taking a polygraph about your role in all this?"

"Not at all," Bob told him. "Just tell me when and where. I think it'll be a waste of your time, though. I'm not even the last agency asset to see them. Have you talked to the pilots that flew them down?"

Clark grunted in non-answer. His phone, sitting on the table, buzzed, and he looked at the display. He frowned, and scrolled through a message. Then looked up at Bob. "Did you put one of the guys we sent to get you in the hospital?"

Bob offered a contrite expression. "He came at me in a parking lot. Didn't say who he was, didn't say anything, just reached for me. I...might have overreacted."

Clark snorted. "Concussion and seven stitches? Yeah, I'd say so. This might become something. You tell Higgins yet?"

Bob shook his head. "We came straight here. Well, after dropping him off at the hospital."

"Do that. Maybe he can keep this from becoming an official HR thing." He looked back down at the message, then up at Bob. "This makes me wonder if the rumor about how you got your work name is true. Cut off a guy's head in Afghanistan and stuck it on a pike as a warning? I've been given access to your file, including your record with JSOC, but shit, half of everything in there going back over twenty years is codeword compartmentalized. TS, SAP/SCI." Meaning Top Secret, Special Access Programs, Sensitive Compartmentalized Information, the highest/darkest/most secret level of classification in the United States government.

Bob's mouth spread in a smile that didn't reach his eyes. "If you're not cleared for that information I can't talk about it."

Clark pursed his lips in a half frown. "You know that's a yes, right?"

EIGHT

Idle Coffee

The government—the FBI in particular—no longer wanted him dead because two of his fingerprints matched those on two other people. And not just because he'd burned off his prints. They'd moved on. Murph had assured him of that, and if anybody had insight into the behind-the-scenes misbehavior of the government, it seemed to be Murph. But the government would renew their interest in him if they found out about his current job. Both Murph and Bob had impressed upon him the need to not be noticed, in the real world but more so online.

It hadn't been so long ago when Dave was watching every dollar he spent, trying to stretch his savings, make the dollars last until the government finally got around to killing him. He'd been accepting of his fate, but determined to take as many of them with him as possible. But things had changed.

Money was no longer an issue—the checks he was receiving from the government shell corporation were shockingly large. But he was technically employed by a private business, and Murph had assured him the government had no clue it was funding the shell corp, and if it ever did, it still would have no idea what the employees of that corp were actually doing....

So while he could have much more cheaply brewed a fresh cup of coffee at home, Dave was instead at his favorite local coffeehouse, The Aloha Snackbar in Prescott Valley, Arizona, run by two combat-wounded veterans, Matt and Mike. Matt was a redhead who moved with a slight limp as he'd left a foot in Iraq. Mike had scar tissue running up his left arm out of sight under his sleeve and reappearing again above his collar on the side of his neck. And Dave was at the coffeehouse because of the laptop sitting on the table in front of him.

It had been brand new when Murph had given it to him. Not new in the box, as Murph had installed more than a few of his programs on it, but there was nothing tying it to Murph or Dave, and Dave wanted to keep it that way. So he'd kept it in the backpack that had been provided for it, which supposedly blocked all wireless signals. Dave hadn't taken it out of the backpack until arriving at the coffee shop, and had left his phone in his car outside. He hadn't connected it to the wi-fi in the restaurant, had no plans to connect it to the wi-fi, at least today, but he was being as careful as possible.

He'd grabbed a big cup of coffee, sat facing the door, plugged the laptop into the wall, and gone to work.

What he was doing was going through the last month of James Blinkenschaal's life. At least, his recorded professional life. Dave was reading emails with clients—most of whom were insurance adjusters who'd farmed out cases to the PI

—and the reports that Blink had generated. A few investigations, but mostly surveillance.

He was two hours into the data, and a bit confused. Some PIs he'd known had a long list of insurance adjusters who would throw cases their way, usually surveillance jobs on people out on work comp claims. Others operated security guard services on the side to generate steady income if their case work was light. Blink Investigative Services was a one-man operation; he didn't have a security guard service on the side. As far as Dave could tell he didn't have anybody working for him other than an accountant that handled the business' taxes. So Dave was confused as to how the man, in the two weeks prior to his death, had been able to surveil so many locations—sometimes two or three on the same day, for extended lengths of time, twelve and sometimes sixteen hours at a time. Had he hired some guys to work under the table, for cash? But that really wasn't an option, with PI work—you could be asked to testify to your findings in court at any time, and testifying to a surveillance you personally didn't do would be just as bad as employing someone unqualified to do it for you. You'd get your license revoked instantly. When he'd been doing PI work for John Phault in Michigan, Dave hadn't been licensed, but he'd done the work covered by John's license—all perfectly legal.

All the reports and video were retrieved by Murph from the cloud storage service Blinkenschaal had used. Dave found video files from two different cases worked the same day. Both videos had been obtained by "DC". Dave had no idea who DC was, and assumed they were the initials of an employee. He started watching the first.

Normally, with a surveillance for an insurance company, investigating an injury claim or the like, you didn't film everything. Some clients wanted you to film the client's house when you arrived, and maybe for a minute every hour, just to prove you were there, but others only wanted to see video of the claimant when he or she was out and about. But the first video he pulled up was stationary continuous video of a house. Filmed from inside a car parked at the curb, if he had to guess, as the camera wasn't handheld, it was hardmounted on a tripod or something similar. And the video just ran and ran. Twelve solid hours of video, with no cuts. There was nothing special about the house, it was a bungalow, and just visible at the edges of the video were similar houses to either side, so it was in a neighborhood somewhere. The video was time- and date-stamped; Dave watched for ten minutes, then shut it off and pulled up the second video, taken elsewhere in Cleveland on the same day, at the same time. It showed a different house, and was again a stationary video that just recorded the front of a private residence non-stop. The video was almost eight hours long. He checked, but there was no audio with either video file. Both videos had been "obtained by DC", according to Blinkenschaal's notes. So who the hell was DC?

Dave was still trying to puzzle it out when the door of the coffee shop opened and the sheriff walked in. Sheriff "Shotgun John" Osterman was a larger-than-life figure who'd been the sheriff of Tohono County forever, a conservative firebrand well-known for his political views and friends in high places. Except he wasn't so "larger than life" anymore; he had never seemed to fully physically recover from the cartel attack where he'd been shot three times with an AK. And he wasn't going to be sheriff forever—he'd finally made it official, and announced that he wouldn't be seeking reelection. After almost forty years. "The end of an era," a lot of locals were calling it.

The Subsection

It was Sunday, and the sheriff, a devout Christian, never worked on Sunday unless there was an emergency. He was in a suit, and presumably had spent the morning at church with his wife. But it was also clear he wasn't stopping in for an idle coffee, as he gave Dave a look. The sheriff stopped at the counter and ordered a coffee—he wouldn't darken the doorstep of a local retailer without throwing some business their way, and always insisted on paying full price—then made a beeline for Dave's table. Dave closed the lid of his laptop and waited.

"Your better half thought you were here, when I stopped by, but there was no answer when I called," the sheriff said, lowering himself into a chair beside Dave. So they could both face the door.

"I guess I left my phone in the car."

"Hmm." The sheriff sat beside him for a time, sipping at his coffee. Dave waited. Dave could outwait anybody. After almost five minutes, the sheriff finally shifted in his seat and turned to look at Dave. "Since you returned from Mexico, it seems like you've been avoiding me," the older man said with a bit of a sigh. He peered closely at Dave.

Dave couldn't keep his mouth from looking like he'd eaten something sour. "Maybe. I guess. I don't believe I ever said I was in Mexico." He sighed. "You know I won't lie to you. But I hate to not answer questions, if you ask."

One of Osterman's eyebrows rose theatrically. "Have I been asking questions? Have I asked who the two men were who kidnapped you out of your house in the dead of night? Where they took you? Or what happened to them? Have I asked how you ended up, three days later, dumped on the curb outside the ER like a puppy hit by a car, except you had bullet and shrapnel wounds? Have I asked if you were in fact in Mexico during those missing few days, when they had the deadliest running gun battle between drug cartels and the Mexican authorities in history? Many of my men seem to think that a blurry figure seen shooting down a helicopter from the back of a speeding pickup, in the midst of that running gun battle, looks an awful lot like you. Which might concern them, being fellow law enforcement officers, were it not for your sterling reputation as an...anti-cartel activist, shall we say. The helicopter belonged to the federales, but then so did that pickup, leading one to wonder about collusion with a cartel. Calling the Mexican forces corrupt seems to be more statement of fact than opinion." He shrugged theatrically. "Have I asked who that gentleman was at the hospital, who spoke to Doc Brennan just before dumping you on the pavement like a bag of laundry?"

"It sure sounds like you're asking me questions," Dave said drily.

Osterman leaned back. "Hmm. Well, I have spent most of five decades as a police officer. I tend to ask questions. And be observant. I noticed that the man who delivered you to the ER was wearing a hat and seemed to deliberately avoid looking in the direction of the cameras, getting anywhere near them, thus remaining completely unidentifiable. Before arriving at the hospital someone provided you professional trauma care, including administering morphine, but yet no hospitals in the area admitted treating someone with gunshot wounds, which they are required to do by law. Running the plates of the car which dropped you off revealed that they were stolen." He took a sip of coffee, set the cup down, spread his arms, and smiled. "And here we are, three, four months later. You've had no problems. With anyone. There's been no serious cartel activity north of Phoenix. The FBI seem to have dropped their investigation of you related to Pietro Bufonte's death in Las Vegas. Fascinating." He lowered his arms. "And then I see you and your lovely girlfriend have moved into a new house off Jack Drive. Knowing what I do about Prescott property values, and that neighborhood, that's quite impressive. I see you seem to have had some cosmetic work done to your face, those scars are nigh invisible now. I see you sitting here, drinking a five-dollar cup of coffee, a brand-new laptop sitting in front of you."

"I got a job," Dave admitted.

"Excellent," the sheriff said. "Doing what?"

"Consulting." That was all Dave said.

"Putting Pima Jack's shooting skills toward turning a profit?" Locally Dave was known as Pima Jack, as the big shootout with the cartel soldiers had occurred at the Pima Motel, and he'd been living under the alias Jack Burton.

The sheriff said it with half a smile on his face, but Dave just shrugged nonchalantly. And the smile disappeared. Dave had said he wouldn't lie to the sheriff, and not only was that true, Osterman knew it. The sheriff digested that news for a bit, peering intently at Dave. Dave had no secrets from him, at least when it came to his background, and why various factions of the government had wanted him dead.

"Knowing you," Osterman said slowly, "I'm guessing I would approve of whatever you're doing, but…do I need to tell you to be careful? I feel like I do. I'm not sure if God has put a soul on this earth more prone to stumble into trouble…."

"I will be careful," Dave promised.

"Hmm." He stared thoughtfully at Dave for a long while. "Well," he said finally, "you've had your trial. Lord knows you've been tried. So now, maybe, it's time for you to find your place. Your purpose." He took a sip of coffee, then shrugged. Moved from pensive to cheerful. "But who am I to say? I'm just an old man finally heading into retirement. So let's change the subject. Let's talk about two young people who have been together for years, who have shared their bodies and known each other in a Biblical sense, been through stressful times together, have now bought a house, and seem to be in love. Doesn't it seem high time for them to get married? Perhaps bring some children into the world?" Osterman's smile was huge. "I asked Lori the same thing when I stopped by looking for you."

Dave groaned. "Of course you did." The truth was, for most of two years, he'd been expecting to die any day, so he'd never given any thought to tomorrow, much less the future. He was no longer so fatalistic, but it was still hard for him to think past the present. He changed the subject, and not just because he didn't want to talk about marriage or children. "You know the President. The former President. Were you more than just political acquaintances? I got the impression that you were."

"I consider him a friend," Osterman said.

"That's interesting," Dave said. "Because as much as you are a politician, I know you hate politicians."

"Because, as a general rule, they don't care about anything but power. They have no interest in doing right, only doing what gets them more might. As for him, the man is far from perfect, but he's honorable. The left wouldn't hate him so much if he didn't actually believe what he says. Or, more importantly, do, or at least try to do, what he said he was going to do. I wouldn't be his friend if I couldn't trust him. Which makes him different from just about every other politician I've met. What makes you ask?"

Dave shrugged. "You can't turn on the news without

The Subsection

seeing something about him, in power or not. And you never know what someone's like just by watching them on the news. Especially when the media hates you. I was...curious. A lot of things seem to be pivoting around him."

Osterman nodded, paused, licked his lips, then his mouth opened in surprise. He blinked rapidly, then turned to Dave. "I got a call. Months ago now. Concerned about all the violence that had been happening down here. Involving me. Involving you. He knew your name. And he'd heard some rumors that he needed clarification on. That was how he put it. He had some information. I added a bit more, avoiding details. Nothing that he didn't seem to know already...but the man is one hell of a poker player. I knew he could be trusted with the information, and wasn't sure if it was personal curiosity or something else."

"Who?"

"Exactly who you were asking about."

"You gave him information. About me. Did you tell him about...?" Dave waved his burned fingertips in the air.

Osterman shook his head. "I wouldn't tell anyone about that without your permission."

Dave nodded, thinking. So Bob had lied, during their recruitment meeting. The President had reached out to Osterman about Dave, but the fingerprint info hadn't come from him. It had come from Murph, clearly, but telling Dave they had a hacker on staff didn't quite have the same gravitas as casually mentioning a President. And he hadn't lied about that, Presidential involvement in their operation. If the man himself had called up Osterman, asking questions about Dave...

Osterman watched the expressions on Dave face and shook his head at the wonder of it all. "You clearly met some new friends with connections. And now you're sitting here with half a new face, an all-new laptop, living in a brand-new house, doing 'consulting'? The detective in me wonders if there's some kind of connection. Especially thinking back to that phone call."

"I'm just a guy, sitting here, drinking coffee," Dave said.

"Mmm-hmm," Osterman said.

NINE

The Antithesis of Oatmeal

"So, what do you think?" the realtor asked, as they followed her out to the driveway.

"I don't hate it," Aaron told her.

Arlene rolled her eyes at him, and looked at the chunky blonde realtor who was squeezed into a blazer. "It's very nice," Arlene assured her. "I'm not sure if it's our style. Maybe we haven't quite figured out what our style is."

"Well, it's got everything you were looking for. And it won't last long on the market. I'd be surprised if it lasts the week. Seriously. If you think you want it, you need to pull the trigger on it today. And if this isn't the one for you…let me know what you liked about it, and what you didn't. I'll find something perfect." With a wave she got into her BMW parked at the curb, did a careful U-turn, then drove out of the subdivision.

Aaron leaned his butt against his Taurus parked in the driveway, crossed his arms, and stared at the house. "Four hundred fucking thousand dollars," he marveled. "That house should be a hundred grand."

"No, it shouldn't," Arlene said, frowning at him. "Two thousand square feet, not including the basement, which is half-finished. Two-and-a-half-car garage. Built less than fifteen years ago, so we wouldn't have to replace any of the appliances or do more than paint. On a quarter-acre lot. In a great neighborhood. I doubt there's any crime around here. Kids stealing bikes out of garages, maybe."

"You think the people that owned it were color blind?" he asked. "I mean, bright red walls in the dining room, Air Force blue walls in the kitchen. Mustard yellow in that one bedroom, looked like Big Bird threw up."

"It's a Detroit thing," she said with a shrug. "They love bright primary colors. You go up to Rochester Hills with all the wine moms, every wall in every house is painted off-white, and they've got twenty-seven different names for it. Eggshell. Ecru. Oatmeal. We can paint the walls, easy."

"All the houses look the same on this street," he grumbled.

"We live in a goddamned trailer park right now," she nearly shouted at him. "Where all the trailers look the same." The subdivision was on Ecorse Road near Morton Taylor Road in Van Buren Township, ten miles almost directly west of the trailer park where they lived. But those ten miles made all the difference in the world. It practically felt like being out in the country. There was an actual farmer's field across Ecorse from the subdivision entrance. They were only five miles from the airport, but they weren't under any flight paths and so shouldn't even notice the planes. "We're a mile from I-275," she said. "I can jump on there and be at work in half an hour, if the traffic's bad. Probably only twenty minutes."

Frowning, Aaron dug in his pockets for his Marlboros,

The Subsection

then remembered he'd quit smoking. He muttered, shaking his head.

"You don't like this one, fine," she said. "Tell me what you don't like. I'll tell Tammy, and she'll find us something. But don't be a dick."

"I'm just...worried about making the wrong decision. You sure you still want to work?"

"What the hell else am I going to do all day?"

"Whatever you want. That's the great thing about being rich."

"We're not rich. Almost, but not quite. And *we're* not rich, *I'm* not rich, you're rich. We're not married, remember?"

"We can fix that this afternoon," he told her. He checked his watch. "County clerk's open for another three hours."

She waved a hand at his suggestion. "Let's settle on a house first, one thing at a time. Then we can get married. And have the reception somewhere nice, not some Knights of Columbus that smells of cigarettes and grease, a real, fancy banquet hall. Doesn't have to be big, but it needs to be nice."

"I know, you told me."

She smiled, and looked around at the other houses. It was a nice neighborhood. "Peanut will like the yard."

"No fence."

She rolled her eyes. "We don't have a fence now. Hell, we barely have a yard, just a patch of grass barely big enough to park a car on. You let her out the door and she doesn't go anywhere, just does her business and comes right back. You could walk her without a leash, she's a good dog." She looked between the houses. "Although there might be possums or whatever around here she might want to chase.

Did I tell you I was heading out to visit my cousin Leonard next month? Mindy and Carl are going to be there. I'm taking Sachelle, she's never met them."

"You know I have no idea who any of these people are, right?"

"You never listen. It's going to be a great trip. Long drive, but she's never been."

Aaron stared at her, waiting for her to finish. But apparently she was done. "And?" he said.

"And what?"

"You're going on a trip. To visit a cousin. Long drive. She's never been."

"Yeah, and?"

"So where the fuck are you going?" Aaron almost shouted, throwing his hands up in exasperation. "That's like the most important part of this fucking story, telling me where you're going. Is Leonard in prison?"

"What? Why would he—"

"Is he in prison? For killing kids? Killing and eating kids and having sex with their corpses? Is he sitting on a mountain of kiddie skulls in a Russian gulag, spanking his monkey while doing that Mongolian throat singing? I can't believe you're related to someone who killed and ate kids."

"No! I'm— Why would you—he lives in Maryland."

He jabbed a finger at her. "Alex, I'll take 'Information That Should Have Been Included in the Original Story' for five hundred."

She put her hands on her hips and glared at him. "It's not the house that has you all pissy," she told him. "You need to get a job, or a fucking hobby, or something."

"Don't start shrinking me," he told her.

TEN

You Can't Stop the Signal

"John Phault."

"Hey John, it's Dave Anderson."

"I thought I recognized the number," his former employer said. They were closer to friends than acquaintances, but the space between them was filled with shadows neither could shine a light into. The Detroit-based private investigator seemed to have as many secrets he couldn't talk about in his past as Dave.

"You don't have me saved as a contact?"

"You have called on a burner a time or two. Should I save this number? Things calming down for you?"

"They seem to be. I've got a couple questions. Some PI questions."

"You back to doing investigative work?"

"Ummm…not officially. Just trying to help a buddy out."

"Okay, shoot."

"I feel like I'm missing something. Something obvious. So these might be stupid questions. Anyway, say you're a PI.

No employees, just you. And you're generating surveillance reports for clients like you've got a whole team working for you. Surveilling different addresses…at the same time. And billing for it."

"I believe that's called fraud," Phault said drily. "We investigate that."

"But you've got the video to back it up," Dave said. "That's what I don't understand. Video of the claimant's house, or whatever. Hours and hours of it. Meanwhile, you're getting video of another location. Same day, same time. I suppose you could change the date and time on the camera, but…"

"It sounds like you haven't had your coffee yet. What time is it out there? Early. Okay." Phault chuckled. "That's stationary cameras, sounds like."

"Like cameras, set up in a car?"

"No, don't you—oh, I see. It's been a few years since you were doing this stuff. And I was never that big into it. Cases I took, it was you and other guys set up on claimants, filming them whenever they went anywhere or did anything. Or domestic stuff, husband/wife, boyfriend/girlfriend, waiting for one of them to hook up while the other was out of town. But say there's a house you can't set up on without immediately getting spotted. What would you do?"

"Back off and sit somewhere you'll see him leaving the area. I worked a few cases like that. Small subdivision or trailer park where there's nowhere to park where you can see the house, so you sit at the exit, and wait for their car to head out. Maybe do occasional drive-bys of the house, in case they're out in the yard, working, or someone comes to visit."

"Glad to see you haven't forgotten everything I've taught you. But you're forgetting the miracles of modern technology. How things keep getting better and smaller. Back when I started I was using actual full-size VHS cameras. I even did a case where I recorded on 8mm film. Extended batteries lasted maybe an hour. And they had, at most, a 4X zoom. Now, I've got a camera in a fake watch that will record at 1080p for four hours onto an SD card. My camcorder fits in the palm of my hand, has a twenty-five-power optical zoom, can record a hundred hours onto the memory card, and has a battery that lasts for days. And that's if I'm not using my phone, which is often better if I'm up close, following the claimant through a CVS or something, pretending to FaceTime or whatever. Or just have it stuck in my shirt pocket. It's so easy now. Anyway, these stationary cameras, you buy a digital camera that's small, hide it in something, and set it out. A lot of them have wireless capability, so you can be sitting in your car half a mile away, watching the feed from the camera you put in front of the claimant's house. So you know if he's in the yard, if he's heading out in his car."

Dave frowned. "What do they look like?"

"What, the cameras? They look like cameras."

"I would think they'd get stolen, you set them out in the hood."

Phault laughed again. "You been living in a cave? You ever hear of 3D printers?"

"I've heard of them, but…"

"You can print out all sorts of fun stuff with them. Out of plastic. There are thousands of programs out there, and you just plug them into your printer, and it spits them out, like a Xerox copier, only 3D objects, not words on paper. But it takes six or eighteen hours, not two minutes. Toys, tools, even guns."

"3D printing guns?"

"Absolutely. And suppressors. It's driving the feds nuts. But you can't stop the signal. Anyway, I don't do it nearly as often as some guys who specialize in them, but I've used those stationary cameras. They're powered by lithium batteries, so they'll last days. Some are controlled by an app on your phone like a GoPro, some have wireless capability, like you could connect them to a wi-fi hotspot, some are just turn on and walk away. With a 64-gig memory card they'll run for close to three days, recording at 720 or 1080p. The ones you can turn on and off remotely, you shut them off at night, and they'll last an entire week, five days, before the card is full."

"Really? Wow."

"Rocks are the most common prop, and I've printed out a few rocks to hide dropcams in. You hit 'em with a little spray paint, rub them with dirt, you can't tell they're not actual rocks. Set them under a bush or next to something else if possible, so they're not sitting out in the open. Some of them do pretty well in low-light too. Digital cameras have always been better in low light."

Dave was sitting up. "Dropcam?" he said.

"Yeah. There was a company that trademarked the name, but they made home security cameras. I think they're out of business now. I use the term because it's a camera that you drop off. Although in reports I use the term 'stationary camera', or 'egress camera', depending on what I'm using it for. Mostly what I use them for is keeping an eye on a claimant's house during a live surveillance when we can't sit on the address. Mine are just simple rocks, but I've seen some printing programs that allow you to hide a camera in all sorts of things, depending on where you've got to set it up. This one, it looks like a section of gray PVC tubing you'd attach to the side of a light post or a telephone pole.

The Subsection

Inch and a half in diameter, maybe. Looks very industrial, like it's supposed to be there, full of wiring, maybe. You can barely find the hole for the camera if you're looking."

"Really."

"If you want to record everyone going in and out of an address, there's no better way than to run continuous video, and a dropcam is cheaper and far less likely to be spotted than an investigator sitting in a vehicle." Phault laughed. "Here, let me text you a photo. I was dropping off a camera in front of an IME site. Um, okay, here it is, sending now. Let me know when you get it." IMEs were Independent Medical Evaluation centers where doctors examined claimants to determine just how injured they were. If they'd been off work for a while, the doctor evaluated whether the claimant would be able to return to work. The only problem with the system, Dave saw, was that the IMEs were paid for by the insurance companies, so the doctors had a motivation to take the employer or insurance company side over that of the claimant. Dave's phone buzzed and he clicked on the photo.

"Okay, I'm looking at a landscaping bed. Rock garden and bushes."

Phault laughed again, like a little kid. "Yeah, okay, so which of those rocks there do you think holds a camera?"

There was a bed of pea gravel, but scattered around the low bushes were larger rocks, maybe six or eight inches in diameter and various shades of gray. "Um, I don't know, the one in the middle?" It was pretty convincing.

Phault snorted. "So I get there before they open, because I've got two claimants with IMEs that day and you can't sit where you can get any video of the front door, at least from a car, and I see all these rocks in this planting bed. So I start checking them out. Three of them, not including mine, *three of them*, were dropcams. Every big rock you see in that photo. Every single goddamned one. That place is under more surveillance than the Pentagon."

"Other PIs?"

"I'm assuming. I don't know. But you see, they look just like real rocks. Can't see the camera lens, it's darn near a pinhole. And you can hide the cameras in all sorts of 3D-printable objects. Those rectangular electrical junction boxes are everywhere, and you can print out a matching plastic box for your camera and just stick it on the side with glue. No one will even notice."

"And a lot of PIs are using these?"

"Oh yeah. I need to do more of it, it's like printing cash. Does that help?"

"Absolutely."

He went back to reading. He'd answered one question, but there was something else bugging him. Something in the files that was tugging at his brain, but hadn't risen to the conscious level yet. Two hours later he finally spotted it. He doublechecked, did some more digging, then put the laptop into the Faraday backpack, and took it out to his car. He pulled his burner phone out of the backpack, walked a hundred yards through the parking lot before turning it on, then texted Bob. I NEED TO TALK. GIVE ME A TIME. He assumed he'd have to wait to get a response, but still he gave Bob five minutes. Nothing.

The next day he drove five miles from his house, leaving his personal phone home, and turned on the burner. There was a message from Bob, specifying a time to call the next day. When the time came, Dave was on the north side of Phoenix when he made the call. He didn't know if he needed to be so far away from home, but figured it couldn't hurt.

"It's a burner, but assume it's not secure, so watch what you say," Bob told him as he answered, before Dave could even say hello.

"Okay. I think I found it. It took me a while, going through all the reports and his notes. And it's not what I found, it's what I didn't find. There's no report, and no video. But there's an assignment from an adjuster, and a reference in his notes that he was scheduling the case, then an email to her, the adjuster, that he was working the case. But there's no indication that he did anything. No notes, no report, no video. This was five, maybe six days before he died. Plenty of time to have at least put down notes, if not started a report. Most of his cases he had the reports to the adjuster five business days after he finished. So if he did work it, I think someone went into his file storage, his computer, and deleted all evidence from the case. Probably that dude from the…company, but I'm sure we'll never know." Dave figured "company" was far safer than saying "CIA".

"What kind of case? Bob asked.

"Insurance fraud. Suspected. And not against a person, against a physical therapy clinic. Some sort of billing scam, they were charging for people they weren't treating. Allegedly."

"Why the fuck would the company care about that?" Bob said after a pause.

"You tell me, you're the expert," Dave said. "But I can't imagine they would. Not that. And I suspect he set up a stationary, covert camera to record everybody going in and out. He seemed to be doing a lot of that, and it makes perfect sense for this case. So it's...what? The camera recorded something it wasn't supposed to see?"

Bob thought about that for a while. "That sounds like a plausible theory. See, I knew this case was right for you."

"I checked local news reports. Looking for anything unusual happening where the clinic is. I found nothing. I looked the clinic up online, and looked at it on Google Street View. But it's just in a regular office building, in downtown Cleveland."

"Then it sounds like you've got more work to do. You've got the what, probably, but you need the why."

"Yeah."

"Email tech support with all the info on the physical therapy place. He can do a background, see if there's something hinky with the business. Maybe it's a joint venture owned by the company and Al Qaeda. Stranger things have happened."

"If he doesn't find anything, I might need to go there. In person."

"Do what you need to do. You understand that you're going to be on your own for a lot of this stuff. Out in the wild. And I might not be reachable. So you're going to have to make the call yourself. I know you can do it, you've been doing it. Use your cover ID. That credit card will work for expenses. Driving as a general rule is better than flying—the less they can track the movement of even a fake ID the better—but that's a call you'll have to make. Because that is not a short drive. Use a rental car. And..."

"Swap out the plates?"

"If you think it wise. Number one rule is not get noticed. 'Leave no trace', as the fruits, nuts, and flakes crowd likes to say."

"Yeah. Hey, um, I called our mutual friend. John. To ask

him some general questions about this. Nothing specific, but he is a bit of an expert. Didn't tell him why or where or anything. Just making sure that's okay."

"Absolutely. I told you, we've got a lot of people doing work for us that have no idea it's for us. You call that a force multiplier. As long as you're not giving them details they shouldn't have, putting them in positions where they can compromise us or the mission, that's fine."

ELEVEN

Due Diligence

Joe Clark sat down in the chair. "I don't know that we're ever going to find out exactly what happened with Gargoyle," he announced. "And it pisses me off. Because *something* fucking happened."

Winston Elliott, Director of the Defense Intelligence Agency, leaned back in his padded leather chair. He looked across his desk at a man who probably would have counted as a friend, if anyone in the intelligence field could truly have friends. They'd known each other for most of two decades. "Tell me."

"They grabbed the package in Arizona. Drove him down to the airport. Flew him into Mexico. They had a satphone on them, but never used it to make a call. They went down to do the exchange, and as near as I can tell everything was fine up to that point. Then the next thing I know Weathervane, Marty, is calling me, saying the cartel just tried to have him killed, and they were making a run for the border."

The Subsection

"And we let that play out. Deliberately. Because whatever happened, we'd have an angle."

Clark nodded his head. "I know, but I'm not just going through the motions here. It's more than a show of due diligence. First, Marty says they need a helicopter big enough for six guys. When there should have only been five of them. The three members of Gargoyle, Weathervane, and the package."

"People make mistakes under stress."

"Evenson dies in the middle of the street in Juarez, surrounded by two dozen *federale* and cartel bodies. Part of that running gun battle between the *federales* and at least two cartels that stretched for over a mile and left as many dead as the battle for Hamburger Hill. We find Danner's body, of all places, in the house in El Paso where Gargoyle nabbed the Chinese team coming through the cartel tunnel. Dead. The tunnel blown. And then the package shows up at the goddamn hospital twelve hours later, badly injured, dropped off by someone who knew to keep his distance from the security cameras. I've tried IDing him from the footage, but it's impossible, he was too far away and kept his head turned."

"You think it was the third member of Gargoyle?"

"I don't know. If it was, it doesn't make sense. Doug Carr—Dog—was number two man on the team, team lead since Grinnand wasn't there. If it wasn't Dog, who the fuck was it? If that wasn't Dog, where is he? If that was him… why? Did he suddenly develop a conscience?"

"You tell me, you've been interviewing everyone."

Clark made a face. "I talked to the air crew, pilot and co-pilot. They say they never got a look at the package, didn't know who it was. That Gargoyle rolled up on time, he was loaded in, they took off, landed in Mexico without any hassle, and watched the team climb into two vehicles with the package and take off. They said the package appeared to be unconscious the entire flight. Grinnand wasn't involved in the mission planning at all, I confirmed that. He was only responsible for arranging the flight and says he didn't notice anything strange when they rolled up. They loaded the package and took off without any problems."

"So whatever happened, if Anderson somehow turned Dog, Doug Carr, it happened in Mexico?"

"Whatever happened happened in Mexico. Losing a team on a mission sucks, but it happens. You try and figure out what went wrong, if anything. Learn from it. But Anderson ending up back home is what's wrong with this picture. That makes no sense. And I still want to know how Marty got burned. He was in solid with La Fuerza. Did he get sloppy? Did someone on our side sell him out? I've been reviewing the signal intercepts we have of the cartel's phones and internet, but I haven't seen anything yet which explains it."

"Anderson probably knows who dropped him off. What happened in Mexico."

"Probably. Whatever happened, he was in the middle of it. But he looked out of it at the hospital, he arrived doped up on morphine. And he hasn't said anything to anyone. He says he got shot vacationing in Detroit. So he's protecting someone."

"Maybe just protecting himself."

"I can go talk to him…" Clark said.

The Director shook his head. "This investigation was a formality. Evenson and Danner, Cherry and Boot, were killed in combat. Dog could have died in Mexico as well. Maybe in that blown tunnel. Anderson might have been dropped off at the hospital by a good Samaritan that didn't want his name known because of the cartel being involved, and I honestly think that's the most likely scenario. Which is why I don't trust it, so if you want to put signal intercepts on Anderson's phone and computer, fine. Maybe they'll turn something up. Have you found any evidence that Doug Carr, Dog, is still alive?"

Clark shook his head. "No phone calls, no visits to his ex-wife, no activity on his email, nothing."

"What would he have to gain, bringing Anderson back?" Elliott asked.

Clark shrugged. "I haven't been able to think of a good reason. People turn traitor for three reasons, sex, money, or politics. Anderson wasn't fucking him, and there's no political angle here. Which leaves money, but Anderson didn't have any money. He didn't even have a job. Or a house, it burned down when the cartel made a run at him."

"Well, unless Dog found Jesus, or a conscience..." The Director shook his head. "Man with his experience? I don't see that happening. He's dead. If he's not buried in the tunnel he's one of those badly burned bodies from the gas station or chopper crash or whatever it was in Juarez. You know, Grinnand came to me, when the mission was still ongoing. With concerns."

"He told me."

"He take a polygraph?"

"I haven't put anybody on the box for this."

"Well, we had a team go dark, and two out of three men confirmed dead. That, unfortunately, is not so unusual, but their package mysteriously ending up back home is.

Monitor Anderson's communications. Polygraph the pilot, co-pilot, Grinnand, and whoever else was involved in mission planning."

"Higgins, their section chief?"

"Absolutely. And let me know if you turn up anything."

TWELVE

The Onion

Bob sank into one of the leather-clad chairs with a sigh and worked his neck. "You know, you'd think a smart guy like you would be able to design an encrypted cell phone or satphone so we could talk securely."

Murph smiled and shrugged. "I could, and I'm working on something, but you should just assume that everything wireless can be compromised. So even if I design something, somebody smarter would eventually come along and find a weakness I missed." He gestured at the luxurious motor coach around them. "In here, I know we're secure. And if I've got any doubt, one simple yank and we're air-gapped inside a giant Faraday cage."

"Yeah, well, I've just been running around non-stop for two weeks. The most rest I've had this month was pushing a broom around a warehouse in Turkey, and sleeping on a cot. Well, that and taking a polygraph."

"Scheduled, or…?"

"Regarding my team's last mission to Mexico. That I wasn't on."

"And I assume you passed? One of these days you're going to have to tell me how you do that."

"The 'lie detector' measures various physical reactions when you tell the truth or lie. The theory being that when you lie, when you know you're lying, your body will react. Change in heart rate, blood pressure, breathing, perspiration. Because you're scared, worried about being found out. Polygraphs work, usually, because most people are just a mess. But my body doesn't do anything my brain doesn't tell it to do, and I'm in charge of both of those. There's a reason polygraphs aren't admitted into evidence in most courts."

"I'll take your word for it. I'm sweaty just thinking about it." Murph paused, then frowned. "Wait a minute. You're in charge of your brain? I thought your brain played music non-stop because of you coding out a few times after your thing in Maryland, back in the day. Dying on the table for a few minutes. So now you've got an internal DJ."

Bob's brain was, in fact, currently playing *Ride Across the River* by Dire Straits, a wonderful, nicely mellow tune from a criminally-underrated band. Mark Knopfler was the best guitar player most people had never heard of. "Yeah, well, that's the one exception. Although, whatever dying in the street and on the table a few times did to my brain, all that practice turning down and tuning out that music has helped my focus. I can drop my pulse below forty when I'm taking a poly, you give me a minute to focus. And jump it up whenever I need to. You didn't have to take any, working for the NSA?"

Murph shook his head. "Contractor. And, funny enough, the stuff we were working on was so sensitive, none of the polygraph examiners were cleared to even ask us questions about it."

Bob snorted. "Oops. You said you found some information? You couldn't have loaded it onto a flash drive and mailed to one of the generic mailboxes we rent? Contact increases chance of compromise, isn't that what you like to say?"

"I do have a copy of everything on a flash drive, but I was in the area, and I don't think it'll take you long to read through what I found. And we might need to talk, and it's quicker and easier this way. It wasn't too long of a drive for you, was it?"

Bob frowned, and looked through a gap in the blinds out one of the tinted windows at the parking lot of the Harry F. Byrd Sr. Visitor's Center of the Shenandoah National Park in Virginia. "Two hours, with traffic." He didn't need a day off to travel to the meet, so that was good. "I've never been here."

"Me either. Park runs along the Blue Ridge mountains south/southwest for a hundred miles like a snake. Looking to get in some good hiking. Parking's a bit limited, with all these winding roads."

"Especially when you're driving something the size of a 737," Bob said drily. "Okay, what do you have for me?"

"Okay, well, first, as of two days ago, your employer is monitoring Dave's cell phone."

Bob blinked at that. "Really. The DIA? Hmm."

"Just hmm?"

Bob shrugged. "He was kidnapped and taken down to Mexico to be turned over to a cartel. The team that did it ended up dead, but he ends up back home? Of course they're going to want to know why. They've been doing an internal investigation into it, that's why I had to take the poly. I'm honestly surprised they haven't snatched him to ask a few pointed questions about that. If he still mattered it would already have happened, but with their embedded cartel guy dead Dave is no longer of any value to them. But they're curious. That's why I wanted you to keep an eye on him. Let me know if it becomes anything more than just his phone."

"Will do. Now this." Murph handed him a sterile Samsung tablet with one hand, and a flash drive with the other. "The answer to your question about that secret meeting in Syria. I don't know the players without a score card, so I had to do a lot of research to figure out a few things. You probably already know who's who. And I think I figured out what they're doing, kinda, but I wanted you to look at it all, get your opinion. Honestly, this one made me feel dumb, because I think I see the what, but the why completely mystifies me. It's mostly emails, but there's also an unclassified position paper I tracked down, news reports out of Russia, the Baltic, etcetera, and a few other things," Murph told him, as Bob stuck the drive into the USB port on the side of the tablet. "No one thing by itself is incriminating, or a smoking gun, but my A.I.-gorithm—you like that name? I'm trying it out—put most of it together, and I think it'll show you what's going on. You want something to drink?"

"Diet Coke, if you've got it. Water, otherwise."

Half an hour later Bob looked up for the first time. "Wow," he said, and worked his neck. He'd just done a rough read through of all the information Murph—or rather his quantum programs—had collected. Murph had been sitting in front of his computer, quietly typing the entire time. He stopped and turned when Bob spoke. Bob pointed at the tablet in his hands. "This thing connected to the internet?

The Subsection

I'd like to check on a few things. Just general background information, to refresh my memory. Sky News, Moscow Times, maybe—God forbid—Wikipedia."

Murph rolled his chair sideways to a second keyboard, and his fingers flew over it for twenty seconds. "It is now," he said. "But don't use it to access anything connected to you, me, or the group."

Bob nodded. "But before I do that…" He set the tablet aside, used the bathroom, grabbed a bottle of water, then sat back down in the chair. He looked up at Murph. "You got coffee?"

"I can make some. Fresh grind some for an espresso?"

Bob smiled. "Stay golden, Ponyboy."

Murph frowned. "I assume that's a yes."

Almost exactly ninety minutes later Bob set down the tablet and used both hands on his head to crack his neck so loudly and abruptly it looked like an attempted suicide. "Well, first off, well done," he told Murph. "How long did it take you to put all this stuff together?"

"I've been working on it since you brought it to me. So, a week. In addition to all the other stuff I'm working on. My system found a few things, like that email between Paul Irving, the CIA Chief of Station at the meeting in Syria, and Walter Derricks, the Deputy Secretary of State. After that it was a matter of pulling threads, and figuring out what to look for. What to look at. Who traveled where, when. Who's talking to who. Who? Or is it whom?"

"It's whom. Yeah, we're all wearing three hats these days." Bob gestured at the tablet. "I normally have analysts do this kind of stuff. Okay, so Abu Ahmad al-Tunisi is a guy who has murdered American servicemen, probably started his career setting off IEDs in Baghdad, and who should be eating a Hellfire missile for dinner, or getting waterboarded with kerosene. Instead, we're secretly bankrolling him. We're—they're—setting up a whole operation around him. Shit, not just one, they're setting up an onion."

"Onion?"

"Operation inside an operation inside an operation. Layers, like an onion. And it starts with a local, a guy in the region, who already has some pull. Because we can't do it. Our fingerprints can't be on it."

"Did they pick him because he's already got some power and recognition? Street cred?" Murph asked.

"I'm sure that's part of it. But I saw the guy, he's got expensive tastes. Silk shirt. Range Rover. Hating the Great Satan is well and good, but it doesn't put cash in your pocket, which apparently he likes. We're giving him an opportunity to do things he wouldn't otherwise have the pull to do, so, the enemy of my enemy kind of thing. Offering him a little fame, as much as fortune, to go after people who aren't us, because our goals temporarily align. The CIA's got a loooong history of that. As I'm sure you know."

"Oh yeah."

"Okay, so, the American government, through cutouts, is giving al-Tunisi cash and guns to re-form the short-lived Islamic State—Caucasus Province, *ad-Dawlah al-Islāmiyah – Wilayah al-Qawqaz*, which operated in Russia, Georgia, Armenia, and Azerbaijan for a few years. Until the Russians defeated it in 2017 by killing off the head and most of the senior leadership in raids. We're giving him cash and arms to resume terror attacks. Which is bad enough, that's real fucking bad, but nobody in the U.S. not the Congress, the military, the public, give much of a shit about what happens in that region unless it involves Israel. Shit, terror attacks occur against Christian schools all the time around the world and the U.S. media doesn't even cover them because they don't fit their narrative. Same with what's happening now in South Africa. Hell, in most of the world. So that's the first layer, setting him up, getting him operating.

"Second layer is a false-flag attack. It looks like they're still spit-balling, and they're being careful not to put much in writing, so much of this is supposition and inference. I'm guessing most of the planning of this is being done face-to-face, in SCIFs. The favored plan they're considering seems to be to attack the country of Georgia and make it look like the Russians did it. Most likely Tbilisi, the capital. Most likely something noteworthy there, a government building or a school. Dead kids always make for good TV."

"To what end? That's what I don't get. The media doesn't have people hating Russia enough?"

"No. Honestly, other than some of them, maybe a minority, being upset about their tax dollars going to fight the war in Ukraine, most Americans don't give a shit about what's going on over there. And I don't think this will really change their mind. Neither do the assholes planning this." He pointed at the tablet. "Hell, I bet most Americans don't even know there's a country named Georgia, much less where it is. 60 Minutes did that big story on Havana Syndrome, basically laid out the case that Russia has declared war on our spooks, using sonic weapons to take something like two hundred of them out of the game, FBI, DHS, State, you name it, and…crickets. But this false-flag attack, that's just the middle layer of the onion. To make Russia look bad. To prime the pump of public consciousness. Get them thinking about Russia perpetrating attacks outside the Ukraine theater."

"For what? To get more funding for the war?"

"Like I said, the American public doesn't care about that part of the world, and even video of collapsed buildings and dead kids will only move that needle a little bit. But that is just a stepping stone. For what they're calling ABLE."

"I saw that. Is that a codeword? Or does it stand for something? They capitalized it."

"Probably short for Operation ABLE. And it's clear what it is. An attack, a big attack, on the BTC, the Baku-Tbilisi-Ceyhan pipeline. Again, as a false-flag op, making it look like Russia's behind the attack."

"But why?" Murph asked. "It doesn't make sense."

"That's because you're used to thinking in straight lines," Bob told him. "If you have a problem, you go straight at it. You solve it. Or you write a program that solves it. This gray-game spy bullshit, I hate it, but I've learned to understand it. Everything happens in a web, everything's interconnected. You pull on one string, and it affects eight other strings somewhere else, and maybe not for a month or a year—half of them not the strings you expected, but if even one thing out of ten you were hoping for happens, they consider that a win. You never go straight at something.

"Anyway, the BTC, that's the biggest oil pipeline in the region, outside of Russia," Bob said. "Runs from Baku in Azerbaijan on the Caspian Sea through Georgia and Turkey and ends at the Mediterranean. All those oil and gas fields around the Caspian Sea are land-locked, so getting product out of there is a pain. When the Soviet Union was in charge, all oil went through them. When the wall came down those countries went looking for new routes. Russia initially insisted that all the oil and gas that came out of that region had to go through them, but they backed off. Probably because they knew they no longer had the might to enforce that demand. But they're still pissed about that, even now. That pipeline moves a million barrels a day. Its very existence has weakened Russian power in the region, and that's more important, well, at least as important to them as the money.

"Some of it is guarded, and almost all of the pipeline is buried, so that makes it harder to attack, but when your jihadis are armed with the very best toys, and given help under the table by the CIA, your chances of a successful terror attack skyrocket. If that pipeline is damaged so bad it is out of commission for months or more, it will force Turkey and maybe even southeastern Europe back onto the Kremlin tit. Russian oil, Russian influence. Russia is still pissed about Nordstream, so attacking that pipeline is a completely believable move for them, which makes this a great op for a false flag. Everyone would assume it was the Russians even if they produced evidence that it was al-Tunisi's group, not them."

"Isn't Turkey an ally? They're in NATO."

"Yeah, but the deep state is currently pissed at Erdogan, for a number of reasons. And they've never really liked Turkey being in NATO, and they're currently being romanced in D.C. by the Armenian lobby in the U.S. You want to talk about hate, it doesn't get much worse than between the Armenians and the Turks. They invented the term genocide for what the Turks did to the Armenians." Murph was blinking at him, trying to follow. Bob smiled. "Like I said, a web. So, you blow that pipeline, the American public still doesn't care. We only get a fraction of a percent of our oil from it, so it won't affect our gas prices. But you know who would be affected? NATO countries. Turkey, of course, but two-thirds of that oil, two-thirds, goes to EU countries. You damage that pipeline, shut it down for an extended period, that's huge. Especially considering the current embargoes on Russian oil. Taking out that pipeline would be a massive blow to a lot of European economies. You're going to have politicians shouting that it's an act of war. An attack on their national security. Politicians who, up til now, likely haven't given a shit about the Ukraine war. It suddenly elevates that Russia/Ukraine war into something more than it was. Suddenly a war between two countries now involves the whole region. Far more than it did before."

"Okay, but why? Why would they do it?" Murph said. "Who wants war?"

Bob leaned back, a wry smile on his face. "You're looking at war like a normal person. War is death and destruction and misery. But if you're in the government, our government, war is big business. War is huge profits if you're a defense contractor. I don't know that they actually want war, Russia is positioned so awkwardly at the moment I'd be worried about them lobbing a few tactical nukes. But Europe, the Baltic states, simply preparing for war, buying more tanks and planes and guns, is trillions of dollars moving that weren't before. And that increased worry about war, I think, will finally trickle down to the American voters. The government and the media have been trying to get them to care, and something like this would probably finally do it. Which does two things." He raised a hand, and stuck a thumb up in the air. "With half of Europe now pissed at Russia, scared of war, their energy prices skyrocketing, our politicians and media beating the war drums, public opinion will change, and the money we've been sending to Ukraine will suddenly seem like spare change. This will finally get the majority of taxpayers on board supporting Ukraine in the war. Happy and eager for their Senators and congressmen to send ever more billions of cash to Ukraine, after all the billions they've already sent. Most of which is coming back here, to buy tanks and planes and guns."

The Subsection

"And senators."

"Yeah. Most Ukraine war funding ends up being money laundering or bribes. Ukraine is a washing machine for the American political class and military contractors. Meanwhile, people are dying…" He sighed and shook his head.

"So what's number two?"

Bob looked at his raised hand, and stuck a second finger in the air. "Number two. War, or the threat of war, always makes Americans more patriotic. More supportive of their government. Less likely to want to change administrations." He paused, and gave Murph a look. "It is an election year."

"Jeez, that's…cold-blooded. You really think that's one of the reasons behind this?"

"You're the big fan of conspiracy theories, you tell me. Governments have done far worse things. Our government has done far worse things." Murph frowned, but he didn't argue. Because Bob was right.

"Honestly, this just seems like they're throwing a wrench into the machinery of state, and they've got no idea what's going to happen," Murph said.

Bob nodded. "You're not totally wrong. But if *they* throw that wrench, no matter what happens, that's their mess. They made it. They controlled what happened. They can take credit for what happened, if they want. That's been their modus operandi for generations, replacing one dictator with another who's even worse, but because the new guy is *their* guy it's considered a win."

Bob shook his head, a look on his face like he'd eaten something sour. "Your programs are great," he told Murph. "AI, algorithms, coding, Skynet, whatever the hell it is. But we shouldn't have a tenth of this," he said, gesturing at the tablet in his lap. "We should barely have an outline, and instead we've got nearly the entire picture. Because they are beyond sloppy. Referring to 'BTC' in the clear, for fuck's sake. Now, if you didn't know what we know you'd think that they were referring to Bitcoin, but still. They're being cute. Their tradecraft is shit. It's insulting, is what it is. They don't think they're going to ever get caught. And they know that nothing will ever happen to them if they do."

The two men traded a long look. After a while Murph said, "You know, I could never do what you do."

"What?"

"Kick down doors. Kill people."

"You've got guns in here, don't you?"

Murph glanced off to the side, then back. "Yeah, but…"

Bob shrugged. "Having fun looking for trouble is something else, I'll admit, but you'd be surprised what even the most timid person is capable of when their life is in danger. And you don't strike me as timid, just…self-contained. You are your own private Idaho. Like most of us."

"I guess."

Bob tilted his head back, thinking. "You know," he said. "This is pretty smart." He stuck a thumb at the tablet's screen. "There's very little downside to it for them."

"What do you mean?"

"If things don't go the way they want. Say IS-CP takes out the pipeline, but al-Tunisi can't help but take credit for it. Which, honestly, is half likely to happen. They exist on credit for what they do. Shit, ISIS, ISIL, Al Qaeda, all of them, they take credit for things they don't do. That terror attack in Russia on the Crocus opera house was almost certainly a false flag op by Spetsnaz to blame Ukraine, but practically before the last body hit the floor ISIS was taking credit for it, fucking up all of Putin's plans." Bob shrugged. "In our case, if al-Tunisi can't keep his mouth shut, so

The Subsection

what? Pipeline is still blown. All the EU will be nervous, nobody will be cutting defense spending, and you just know Russia is going to try and take advantage of the situation. And now we've got a major new terrorist in play—perfect excuse for the CIA to ask for more funding. Job security. Other possibility—say al-Tunisi completely fucks up somewhere along the way. Our hands are clean. And we go to the number two guy in his organization, or whoever the next powerful guy in the region is, and offer him the same deal. Second verse same as the first."

"What if Al-Tunaboat tells everybody that the Americans tried to bribe him, are trying to get him to do these attacks?"

Bob shook his head. "First off, nobody would believe him, even if they probably should. Second, it looks like he's already received a shipment—don't know what it was, weapons or tech or cash. I'm sure it's sterile and can't be traced back to us. He can't tell any of his guys who it's really from, or they'd likely kill him for collaborating with the infidels. Al-Tunisi seems to care as much about the money as he does the intifada, but he's got a lot of true believers in his camp. So he has to keep his mouth shut about that. No matter what happens, there's almost zero chance of blowback on the guys behind this." Bob frowned, thinking. "It's going to be months before they can position him where he can go after the pipeline, but in the meantime they'll be arming him, giving him material support. He probably won't take any of their advice, and won't trust their intelligence. At least at first. Meanwhile, he'll be attacking civilian targets, schools…."

"So what do we do about it? What can we do about it?"

Bob chewed at his lip. "That is the question."

THIRTEEN

Blink's Requiem

Dave was surprised. Pleasantly so. He stood on the sidewalk and looked at the buildings towering around him. They were either modern with mirrored glass, or historic, with fancy brick- and stonework. Everything was neat, and clean. The historic buildings had businesses on their ground floors —tailor, barbershop, restaurant, bank branch, Starbucks, etc.—windows looking out onto the sidewalk, and there were colorful awnings shading most of the windows.

The sidewalks weren't ugly slabs of gray concrete, they were carefully-laid patterns of black and brown bricks. There were planters of flowers outside many building entrances. The light posts up and down the block were hung with colorful posters advertising the latest performances at the many theaters.

It wasn't quite New York City, but it sure wasn't what he'd expected out of Cleveland.

With typical urban efficiency, the business he was looking for had an address on Euclid Avenue but was actually located on E. 14th Street. E. 14th Street ran north and dead-ended at Euclid Avenue, running east and west. The US Bank Centre was a modern skyscraper on the southwest corner of Euclid Avenue and E. 14th Street, sixteen stories of black/brown reflective glass. Its main entrance was on Euclid, facing a clearly historic five-story building which housed the United Way of Cleveland, among a host of other businesses. There was another entrance on the side of the US Bank building, on E. 14th Street. But what Dave was interested in was the Playhouse Physical Therapy Center.

It was physically located inside the US Bank Centre, at the rear of the building on the south side. Even though the business was inside the US Bank building, 1350 Euclid Avenue, it had a separate address, 2040 E. 14th Street. That confused him for a bit, and he'd had to park and walk around for a bit, actually go into the skyscraper's lobby, before he figured things out.

Playhouse Physical Therapy Center was suspected of billing several insurance carriers for patients they hadn't actually treated. James Blinkenschaal had been hired to document the foot traffic going in and out of the site. Which seemed problematic, now that Dave was there and checking it out.

The physical therapy center was on the ground floor, and Dave soon learned that there was an entrance to the facility off the lobby. The main entrance to the clinic was on the opposite side. There was a small courtyard on the south side of the bank building with a few tables and decorative landscaping in small enclosed beds. There were two entrances to the building there—one set of double doors led straight into a short hallway leading to the US Bank Centre's lobby, and the other, atop a switchback handicap ramp, led into the physical therapy clinic's waiting room.

The small courtyard was nestled between the big office

building and a parking garage. The parking garage seemed to be the most likely place for clinic patients to park, and doors at the top of the concrete handicap ramp seemed the quickest and most convenient place to enter the physical therapy clinic. If Blink had set up a dropcam to cover that door—which seemed the smartest play—it would have to be nearby. Close. There were both space and line of sight issues.

Dave stepped up into the landscaped areas and nudged at the bushes with the toe of his shoe, but didn't find any rocks hiding cameras. He looked around, then checked the side of the parking garage, and the bodies of the light posts, but found nothing. But he hadn't expected to. If the camera was what had gotten the Cleveland PI killed, someone had either seen him emplace it or found it and tracked it back to him. Either way, they wouldn't have left it there.

Murph had dug deep into the physical therapy clinic and found nothing of interest. It was one of a chain, owned by a corporation, and neither the corporation nor any of the employees had ties to law enforcement, the military, intelligence agencies, terrorists, convicted criminals, anything. The only thing he'd found was a drunk driving conviction for one of the clinic employees.

But Dave, eyeing the side of the building, saw immediately what likely had happened. Any camera positioned to catch traffic going in and out of the PT clinic's main door would have also captured the traffic going in and out of the other door, the side entrance to the US Bank Centre's lobby.

Dave couldn't imagine the CIA or any other part of the US intelligence community giving a shit about a Cleveland physical therapy clinic. But, apparently, there was something else of note going on in the building. Or there'd been someone of note visiting….

He went back inside the main lobby. It had recently been refinished and looked gorgeous. The floor was polished stone, reflecting the light coming in through the many windows. The walls and furniture in the lobby were colorful pastels. There was a small café in the northeast corner. He was one of a few people walking through the echoing lobby, which was full of life. He found the building directory and looked through it. Sixteen floors of businesses. Dozens of them. There were a number of names he recognized, and a lot he didn't. Based on the titles, "last name & last name", a number of them had to be law firms. Maybe accountants.

U.S. Army Cleveland Battalion HQ. Interesting, and he made a note. A district office for the U.S. Housing and Urban Development Department. A regional office for Babble, the new search engine competitor to Google, which he didn't think had much of a chance, seeing how huge Google had gotten…but then again you never knew when the government was going to file an antitrust lawsuit against them, alleging a monopoly. He was pretty sure he'd read that Babble executives were testifying in front of congress about online security issues. Probably trying to make allies among the politicians. GCA Services caught his eye. He frowned. Didn't that have something to do with the federal government? He pulled out his burner smart phone and looked them up. Nope, GCA was a janitorial service. He'd been thinking of the GSA, the General Services Administration, which, if he remembered correctly, was a kind of maintenance and janitorial service for the U.S. government. He took a photo of the directory, sighed, then headed for the elevators.

Ohio was now a permitless, "constitutional carry" state, which meant you didn't need a permit to legally carry a concealed weapon. A majority of US states had legalized constitutional carry, which was not something he ever would have suspected would happen. It seemed to be in response to riots, crime, and the perceived deliberate failure of the federal government to do their job. But it meant that Dave didn't have to worry that there was no concealed weapon permit attached to the name on the driver license and credit cards currently on his person. And it was a concern, as he thought he might have drawn some suspicion, spending close to two hours checking out every suite, every hallway, on every floor of the building.

He started at the top and worked his way downward. There were a lot of lawyers in the building, as he'd suspected, as well as a lot of state and city offices and contractors. He rode the elevators, he trod the stairs, he poked his head into every bathroom he found that wasn't locked. But at the end of his efforts, he had nothing. Maybe one of the law firms was engaged in some nefarious shit involving the CIA. Whatever was going on wasn't obvious to someone just wandering around. Not that he'd thought it would be, but hope springs eternal.

The lobby was just as busy as it had been before, and he took a seat and watched people come and go for a while. Half of them were dressed in standard modern business attire, somewhere between suits and sloppy business casual. For part of the time he pretended to be on his phone. After twenty minutes he frowned, stood up, and walked outside the main entrance onto Euclid.

He walked a block west, then turned and walked a block east of the US Bank building. There were signs everywhere for theaters, and performances. He couldn't turn his head without seeing colorful posters advertising Cleveland's Classic Company performing King Lear at the Hanna Theater. Who knew Cleveland had a theater district? The Playhouse Square. There were illuminated signs, posters hanging and taped to windows.

There was a Starbucks on the ground floor of what he learned was the historic Hanna Building, built in 1921—there was a brass plaque he'd stopped to read. The Hanna Building—sixteen stories of apartments—was as tall as the US Bank Centre, and it sat directly across 14th Street from the US Bank building. Windows in the Starbucks looked out on both 14th Street and Euclid. Dave went in, noting the hours posted on the door—the restaurant closed at 6 PM.

It was a very artsy area, and the people he'd seen walking around had either been dressed for business or like they worked in theater. He slowly walked up to the counter, dredging his mind for something pretentious enough that would make him utterly forgettable to the employees. The arresting display of colored hair, piercings, and fabric masks was unsurprising—Starbucks employees were like their own tribe, with similar ceremonial plumage no matter the state. Dave ordered a Venti Misto with heavy cream, doctored it with Splenda, then sat down at a table near the west windows where he could see the side entrance to the US Bank Centre.

14th Street there was two lanes north, one lane south, with metered parking on both sides. He was maybe forty yards from the east entrance of the building, but he couldn't see the main entrance on Euclid, and could only see the bottom half of the handicap ramp leading in/out of the physical therapy clinic. But there didn't seem to be any better place to sit and watch, at least for an extended period.

He sat there for twenty minutes, sipping occasionally at his coffee, watching people walk in and out. He hadn't done surveillance in years, and felt a bit of nostalgia. Sitting in a Starbucks was definitely better than sitting in his Cherokee in the summer heat, sweating through his shorts, peeing in a bottle. However, he didn't know what he was looking for, much less who, so in that way it was more difficult—he had to study everyone going in and out.

After an hour, he texted the photo he'd taken of the directory to a number he had for Murph, along with the address of the building. Ten minutes later he got a one-word response. AND?

PRETTY SURE THIS IS THE PLACE, NOT THE CLINIC, Dave texted him. BUT IT'S HUGE, CAN YOU HELP ME NARROW IT DOWN?

ON IT, he received, thirty seconds later. Then a minute after that, THAT'S A LOT. GIVE ME A DAY OR TWO. Dave responded with a thumbs up emoji. Then he sat. Watching and thinking.

They had no idea what Blinkenschaal's covert camera had captured. Someone or something, likely going in or out of the building via the door by the physical therapy clinic, but...was it a regular thing that would happen again with Dave sitting right there? If it did, would he even spot it/him/her? Was it a one-time occurrence? Was this a complete waste of his time? There was no way to know. But he'd learned one thing—

When in doubt, sit and wait and watch.

The Subsection

"I can't get hold of…my group supervisor," Dave told Murph around noon the next day, sitting inside the same Starbucks, at the next table over, staring out the window. He'd shown up when the Starbucks opened, at 6:30 a.m., sat behind his laptop, and watched hundreds of people arrive for work inside the US Bank Centre building. He'd made sure to buy something every hour—coffee, bottle of water, sandwich—then, four hours in, the employee behind the counter, whose nametag read MAR, gave him a look.

Dave's shoulders slumped, and he launched into the sad story of how he and his boyfriend had had a huge fight, and he was sort of kicked out of his own apartment, on top of being unemployed, and….

Mar in his green apron had said, "Oh, honey," patted him on the hand, given him a commiserating nod, and apparently passed the word, as none of the employees bothered him again.

"That's not an emergency worthy of a phone call," Murph said in his ear. "You are aware he has another job."

"Yeah, it's just…this thing, I don't know if I'm wasting my time or not, sitting here."

"I can't answer that for you, I've literally never done what you're doing. Aren't you supposed to be experienced? Isn't that how you got the job?"

Dave took a breath. "I suppose. I know enough to see that I can't do this alone. Not properly. There's too much to watch for just one guy. You can't see it all from one position. Add to that the fact that I don't even know what I'm looking for, and if there is anything to see it might not pop for a week…you find anything that could help?"

"If I did I would tell you. I'm still working on it."

"Can I get any help? Any backup? I need at least one other set of eyes here to do this thing right."

"I do know that, currently, there is nobody else available from the group to help. They're all busy doing other things. You're there. You're the guy. You have to make the call."

FOURTEEN

Fashion and Fine Dining

Aaron was chopping vegetables for a homemade sauce that was somewhere between a traditional spaghetti sauce and marinara. It had a few personal touches, including some diced carrots. Peanut was sitting patiently nearby. From time to time he was tossing her an odd carrot tip, which she crunched very noisily. Arlene was putting together ingredients to throw into the bread machine for homemade garlic bread later. Having the machine knead the dough for you still counted as homemade, as far as Aaron was concerned —it was working smarter, not harder.

"I'm just saying," he said, finishing a thought. "Women mostly don't want to watch sports, but if they do, most of the time they want to watch guys playing. So if you want the WNBA ratings to climb out of the toilet, they need to get guys watching it. If they want men to watch women's basketball, then have them dump the baggy outfits and dress like women volleyball players. Women *beach* volleyball players." He heard Arlene sigh, and looked over at her.

"You know I'm right. Don't hate a man for speaking the truth."

"Is that what you're doing?"

He tossed the dog another carrot piece. "You know," he said, eyeing Peanut, "I think she likes the crunch more than the taste."

Arlene glanced over her shoulder at Peanut. "I don't know," she said with a shrug. "Carrots taste good. They're sweet…"

Aaron shook his head. "They taste good to *you*. Dogs have different taste buds. Dogs eat ass. Literally."

"You eat ass too, but you still care about the taste," Arlene said nonchalantly.

One eyebrow going up, Aaron slowly turned to look at her. She was smirking at him. He opened and closed his mouth, and for once had nothing to say.

His phone rang. He pulled it out of his pocket and looked at the display. He didn't recognize the number, and it wasn't one of his contacts, so he set the phone on the counter and let the call go to voicemail, assuming they wouldn't leave a message. He was surprised when it beeped only a few seconds later.

"Who's that?" Arlene asked.

"I don't know," he said. "If I knew who it was I would have answered the fuckin' call." He hit the button for voicemail, then put it on speaker as he was still working.

"Hey, it's me," he heard. Aaron traded a look with Arlene. They both recognized Dave's voice. "I'm not too far from you, and I could use your help with a thing for a few days. If you're not too busy."

FIFTEEN

Seems Like Old Times

"Grand prize, one trip to Cleveland," Aaron said, sitting down next to Dave at the table beside the window. "Second prize, two trips to Cleveland." He turned and looked around the crowded Starbucks, then peered out the windows. "Although this looks a lot better than I was expecting."

"Turns out Cleveland has a theater district. Who knew?" Dave eyed his friend. Aaron's hair was a bit long, especially in back, his moustache shaggy, but he looked good. He had a dark work shirt unbuttoned and loose over jeans. Dave spotted the expected bulge of a gun on his hip. Dave lowered his voice. "You got a burner?"

"Yeah. My phone's wrapped in three layers of aluminum foil in the car. The rental. Parked next block down. I need to swap the plates on it?"

Dave shook his head. "I don't know. I don't think so. Everything should be happening right here." He nodded out the window.

"You look good," Aaron said, looking at him. Smiling. "Your face doesn't look fucked up at all anymore."

"You know just how to sweet-talk a guy."

"It's a gift," Aaron said, just as someone stepped up to their table, between them. Dave looked up. It was Mar, in his green apron.

"Is this him?" he asked Dave, in a flat tone of disapproval.

"No, this is just a friend," Dave assured the barista. Dave reached over and patted Aaron's hand. Aaron frowned. Dave leaned toward Mar. "He's still on a river in Egypt," he said confidentially, his voice low, almost a whisper.

Mar nodded knowingly. "Honey," he told Aaron, "I see you're trying to butch it up, but, and I say this with love, that haircut's just not working for you. It's *soooo* 1982." He patted Aaron on the shoulder, spun, and then headed back toward the counter.

Aaron turned and watched him leave, then looked at Dave. "The fuck was that about?"

"Just trying to fit in with all the artsy types and sensitive caffeine slingers."

Aaron shook his head and leaned back in his chair. "So you're pretending to pitch for the other team. When they say, 'You're only gay for the stay' I thought they meant prison, not Cleveland, but maybe I repeat myself. But why am *I* here?"

"You're just a guy helping a buddy," Dave said. "I can pay you, but it's got to be cash under the table. I was never here. Neither were you."

"I shouldn't have to pay taxes the rest of my life, with what I just forked over out of my settlement," Aaron said. "My plan is to live the rest of my life cash under the table.

The Subsection

But I'm not here for the money, I'm here for you. So what the fuck are we doing? You helping Phault with a case?"

Dave made a face. "Okay, so, I won't lie to you, but… you remember that scene in *The Godfather*? Michael tells his wife, 'Never ask me about my business'?"

"You giving me a *Godfather* reference because I'm Italian? That's just prejudice and bigotry. Profiling. And stereotyping."

"You did get tortured by a guy working for the mob…" Dave said.

Aaron hid a smile. "Yeah, asking questions about *you*. You got more ties to the mob than I do, I was just an innocent bystander."

Dave snorted. "So assume I'm Michael Corleone here."

Aaron chewed on that for a while. He glanced around, making sure nobody was close enough to hear, then said, "This have something to do with you getting kidnapped out of your bed in the middle of the night and showing up three days later with fresh bullet holes and shrapnel in your ass? And everything's fine and nobody knows shit?" He frowned. "What kind of juice does that take? Government juice?"

Dave sighed. "Dude, I love you, but if you need answers, you might as well head home right now. And it's not because I don't trust you. You're here *because* I trust you."

Aaron shook his head. "I'm just bustin' your balls. Secret squirrel Dave is definitely better than borderline suicidal Dave. Just as long as I'm not Fredo in this. No boat rides. And you go into the bathroom, I'm checking behind the toilet tank. So, what do you need me for?"

Dave jerked his head. "Go buy a coffee. And then let's take a walk."

Ten minutes later they were standing on the sidewalk, south of the Starbucks on 14th Street, across from the courtyard outside the physical therapy clinic. They'd done a slow lap around the area, and walked through the lobby of the US Bank Centre building. It was just before 8:30 in the morning, and the lobby had been very busy. Aaron took a sip of his coffee. He liked it with a lot of cream and sugar. Real cream, and real sugar. "So you can't tell me what you're looking for?"

Dave rolled his eyes. Again. "Seriously, dude, I'm not lying to you. *I don't know.* That's why you're here. I don't know if it's a person, or a thing, was here and gone and never to return. Maybe we're staring right at it right now. I've got somebody doing a background check on all the companies in the building, but I'm not confident anything's going to turn up. But something bad happened about a month ago because of something somebody saw here, right here. Probably somebody going in or out of that door right there." He nodded his head, trying to be subtle. "I'm trying to figure out who. Or what. So I've been watching for anything suspicious, anything out of the ordinary, anything weird. But you see, this place has public entrances on three sides, not including the walkway from the parking garage, the loading dock around the corner, maybe something else. Even with two of us it's going to be tough to watch them. Without being obvious. And that's important, too. To not be noticed. I'm not here. We're not here. Not in any official capacity. Which means we can't have anybody calling the cops on us."

"So I'm not here, you're not here, I drove a rental down, I'm using a burner phone…so should I be using an alias? How about Darrin?"

Dave rolled his eyes. "Are you kidding me right now?"

The Subsection

Aaron took a swig of coffee and from behind the cup said, "You know I'm not much for fucking subtle, right?"

"You can try."

They changed position every hour or so—sitting in the Starbucks, inside the Vietnamese café inside the US Bank Centre on the ground floor, in the lobby of the target building, loitering around on Euclid where they could see the front door, or on 14th Street where they could see the side entrance.

"I've never had Vietnamese food before," Aaron said to Dave in the lobby, after having a late lunch in the café. They were standing a bit apart, and looking in opposite directions.

"You like it?"

"Fuck no," Aaron spat. "Sad, shitty noodles soaked in Dumpster juice. No wonder they went commie. But at least I'm getting reimbursed, right? I need to save receipts for that and all the overpriced five-dollar coffees I'm going to be drinking?"

"No, just let me know what I owe you."

"It's just stupid," Aaron said.

"What?"

"If you're going to translate it, the Vietcong chicken-scratch symbols into English letters, why the fuck wouldn't you do it right? If it's pronounced *fuh*, why is it spelled P-H-O? That's fucking *fo*. Then they act like *I'm* the asshole, can't read the menu."

Dave fought back a laugh. Aaron hadn't changed a bit from when they were riding around Detroit in an armored car together. "Well, I'm going to go try some. Maybe I'll like it."

"Then I guess I'll go sip a latte with the pole-smoking peacocks."

"The what?"

"You saw their hair. Hey, that would make a great name for a gay bowling team," Aaron said enthusiastically. And he walked off, leaving Dave with his mouth open, shaking his head in wonder.

The Starbucks closed its doors at 6 PM. By that time most of the US Bank Centre building had emptied out. Dave had previously observed people leaving well into evening, and security locked the lobby doors at 9 PM. The two of them met just after six outside Green Rooster Farms, a small restaurant on the ground floor of the Hanna Building, across the street from the target building, that was only open for lunch.

"One of us can come in here and have lunch tomorrow," Dave observed.

"How the fuck do you stay profitable when you're only open for lunch, and only serving sandwiches and salads?" Aaron said, reading a menu taped to the inside of a window, while Dave, trying not to be too obvious, watched the building.

"Lot of people work in the area," Dave said. He nodded at the US Bank Centre across the street. "How many people just work there? A thousand?"

"Too many."

"There are a lot of restaurants around the corner on Euclid," Dave said. "Let's give it a little bit. Then eat there. I want to sit on this place after dark, but I don't know how that'll work. None of the restaurants are open, and I don't want to loiter on the sidewalk like a comic book bad guy."

"Sit in your car?" Aaron said, glancing at the metered spaces. "Some of these spots will be open."

"I think that's a real quick way to get the cops called on me," Dave said, speaking from years of surveillance experience. He glanced over at the parking garage. "I think I might be able to stand up there, second or third floor, and see those doors."

"And loitering around a parking garage won't get the cops called on you?" Dave sighed, because Aaron was right. Aaron asked him, "Do we know that what happened here happened in the middle of the day, during business hours, and not the middle of the night?"

"Nope."

"Well, it gets dark, maybe nobody will notice you hiding in the shadows like a kiddie snatcher. C'mon, let's go get something to eat, I'm starving after my lunch of Dumpster juice noodles."

"I had them, I ordered that. It was good." They started walking up 14th Street toward Euclid, surreptitiously keeping an eye on the office building to their left.

Aaron tsked and shook his head in disappointment. "All that getting punched in the face must have damaged your taste buds. I saw an Italian place around the corner. Let's go there, I'll show you what real pasta is. You're buying."

Dave laughed out loud and glanced at his friend as they walked along. "Man, I've missed you."

SIXTEEN

Ohio, But With Better Cars

Bob stood with his back to the narrow equipment lockers, arms folded, and tried to make himself smaller. There was only so much room inside the high-roofed Mercedes van. In addition to him there was the commander of the Bundespolizei (BPOL) BFE+ unit currently en route to their location, a BPOL subordinate in charge of the electronics in the surveillance van, an American Army CID major from Rammstein AB, and a female special investigator from the DISA. The van was running, the air conditioning on full blast, but it was barely holding its own against the five bodies and the warm electronics.

Bob felt his phone buzzing in his pocket. He pulled it out and saw it was Hansford Higgins, his DIA section chief. "Sir?" He had a separate work phone when in Europe, that worked off the local cell networks. It was simpler (and smaller) than toting around a satphone.

"The raid go off yet?"

"Ten minutes, maybe less. Tac team's en route. Guys are still inside the target location, near as we can determine."

The Subsection

"And the hardware?"

"We're assuming it's in there with them. I'm currently in a surveillance van with a number of people, so…"

"You can't really talk freely. Well, keep me updated. I'm glad you're there," Higgins said warmly.

"And why is that?" Bob asked.

"Why am I glad?"

"No, think more existential. Why am I here? I had nothing to do with this investigation." He glanced at the major with the U.S. Army's Criminal Investigation Division. He'd been the man spearheading the investigation, and the guy whose hard work had developed an address.

Higgins chuckled. "No one from the DIA did, but that's still our mission, to support the Department of Defense whenever and wherever we can. The equipment that went missing is about as sensitive as sensitive gets. Having a representative there when this all goes down can only make us look good. And you speak German, so…"

"Higgins, you've been to Germany. Everyone here speaks English. I think it's a mandatory class in their schools."

"Yeah, well, just in case. And you get a lovely trip to exotic Germany."

"Where are you going when you come to Germany, Berlin bondage clubs?" Bob asked in wonder. He waved a hand. "Exotic? Germany looks like Ohio. With better cars and worse food."

The BPOL officer turned and frowned at him. "What is wrong with German food?"

"Nothing, if you like sausage and potatoes. Great fuel for your body if you're erecting a barn or stomping around the Maginot Line, *aber ich bin schon fett wie ein Bär im Winterschlaf.*"

"What was that?" Higgins asked.

"Fat as a bear in winter," the DISA liaison said, leaning toward Bob, having heard the question. Elisa Matthews. The Defense Information Systems Agency was involved due to the tech inside the stolen items. She flashed a quick smile at him, but didn't say anything further. She was slender and in a black suitcoat over a white silk blouse and black slacks. She was petite and pretty and smelled nice. Bob was in generic "business casual" attire, a polo shirt over khakis, both of which were a little snug around his muscles.

"Yes, well, having you out of the country for a few days didn't seem a bad idea given your misstep," Higgins said into his ear, referring to the injury he'd done to the DIA employee in the parking lot.

Bob fought the urge to sigh. "Is that really going to have legs?"

"Probably not, but better safe than sorry. Out of sight out of mind, a stitch in time saves nine, all that. If you'd done it in the field, in a combat zone, that'd be one thing, but in CONUS.... We are part of the kinder, gentler, modern federal government, with diversity and equity and, um..." The buzzwords failed him.

"Yes, we kill with kindness and microaggressions," Bob said drily.

The BPOL commander's radio crackled. He held it up to his ear, said a few words into it, then turned and announced, "Two minutes," to the other people inside the van.

The action would be taking place most of a block away. The only way it would come anywhere close to their van was if the bad guys somehow turned the raid into a pursuit or a running gun battle through the streets for Frankfort, and if that happened Bob was still out of it—he didn't have a vehicle or a firearm. He was there simply as an observer, representing the Defense Intelligence Agency. He would have preferred being in the stack that went through the door, but there was a reason—a lot of reasons, most of them political—why it was the BPOL doing the raid and not some unholy combination of FBI agents, CIA officers, U.S. Army MPs and CID operatives. Truth be told, this was probably better, from a safety standpoint. Multi-jurisdictional raid teams were accidents waiting to happen.

"I've got to go. I'll call with an AAR," Bob told him.

The van rocked as two racing engines passed by. Twenty seconds later the two black Mercedes SUVs appeared on the monitors in front of them. The surveillance cameras were set up in an empty apartment across the street from the target building, and Bob watched the BFE+ arrest team, in black tactical gear and balaclavas, jump out of the vehicles. HK G36c rifles up they moved up the steps of the building, breached the front door, and were inside.

The apartment in question was on the second floor, and Bob knew they wouldn't have long to wait. Still, the minute they were all waiting, staring at the screens, seemed to last ten minutes. Then the radio sprang to life. "*Zwei in Untersuchungshaft. Keine Probleme.*" Two in custody. No problems. "*Schicken Sie den Experten hoch.*" Send up the expert.

Bob turned to the DISA liaison. "They're playing your tune," he told her.

She flashed a thin smile, then looked at the BPOL commander. "Sir, I'll need a ride."

Two minutes later she and Bob were climbing out of the back seat of an Audi sedan. He opened the door of the target building, then followed her up the stairs toward the apartment. He very definitely noticed her backside in those tight slacks marching up the stairs, but kept the expression on his face neutral.

The apartment door had been breached with a ram, and Bob could smell the unique odor of a flash-bang in the air. There were two men face-down on the floor, wrists zip-tied behind their backs. U.S. servicemen, one Army, one Air Force. Drinking buddies, reportedly. Who'd stolen laptops and spare drone electronics and had tried to sell it all to the highest bidder. Unfortunately for them, the "Chechen terrorists" with whom they'd arranged a deal were undercover CID investigators. Both the laptops and drone motherboards contained highly classified software and hardware, so this was a little more than just a simple theft case. Now that they were in custody, there would need to be an interrogation to make sure nobody else examined the stolen materials.

Matthews goggled at the apartment, turned an incredulous eye on Bob, then glared at the two men on the floor. She put her hands on her hips. "You just leave it all sitting on the kitchen table? Just out on the table. Idiots."

"Is that all of it?" Bob asked.

"It looks like it, but let me check," she said. "Get these jokers out of here," she told the black-clad tac team members, jerking a thumb at the fractured doorway behind her. Bob pressed his lips tight to avoid smiling and watched as she unfolded a sheaf of papers. The bulky German policemen hoisted the prisoners to their feet and marched them out of the apartment. The CID major would be waiting outside.

"You want me to search the place?" Bob asked her.

She shook her head. "It looks like I've got everything right here. I'll let you know."

Bob looked around, then shook his head as they were

left alone in the room. "Then I guess I'll just stand over here and look pretty," he said, frowning, and crossed his arms. As far as he could see, the entire trip to Germany had been a waste of time for him.

The DISA liaison looked at him out of the corner of her eye and smirked. He was thinking about searching the apartment anyway—for guns, for drugs, for other intelligence, for something to do—when his phone buzzed in his pocket. He didn't recognize the number, but he did recognize the country code. Turkey. "Hello? *Merhaba?*" He only had a smattering of Turkish.

"It's tech support," he heard in his ear, but he didn't recognize the voice. It was a neutral American voice. Sounded like a white guy, Midwesterner, in his thirties. But he didn't sound anything like Murph.

"I think you have the wrong number," Bob said pleasantly, but inside he was frowning.

"Hold on," he heard. Then, "Typing. This is a text…to voice…program," he heard, with short, almost imperceptible pauses between some of the words. "Trying something new. No voice recognition possible this way. Amazon calls theirs, which uses AI, 'virtual voice'."

"I still think you've got the wrong man," Bob said.

"Last time we net," the smooth, apparently computer-generated voice said in his ear, "sorry, typo, met, you asked me to make coffee. I ground it flesh. Flesh. Fuck, FRESH. Maybe…I…should…type…slower. And I Googled what 'Stay golden, Ponyboy' meant. Watched that movie. How have I never heard of that movie before? Everybody was in it."

"You're a little young. But it's like the Rosetta Stone of eighties movies. So what's up?" Bob asked him, confident he was now talking to Murph. "I am working currently. In the field."

"I know what you're doing. And where you are," the smooth voice said slowly. "And maybe that's better."

"Better for what?" The pretty DISA operative glanced over at him and he flashed her an apologetic smile.

"I think I found a solution to your Bitcoin problem," the generic voice said into his ear.

Bob connected the dots in his head. Bitcoin equaled BTC, which meant the operation to covertly spin up Abu al-Tunisi. "Really."

"It's the kind of solution you seem to like."

"Hmm." Bob sighed.

"What?" Murph asked/typed

"I was in the planning stages of another mission," Bob said, eyeing Elisa Matthews' backside as she squatted beside the kitchen table, looking for a serial number on a motherboard.

"Something serious?"

"Aren't they all."

SEVENTEEN

Optisizing Search Parameters

Intermittent surveillance of the building after dark, until past midnight—from inside the garage, from cars parked briefly nearby, from drivebys—yielded no results. They were back inside the Starbucks the next morning, not long after it opened, and truly needed the caffeine.

"I'm going to go try the parking garage," Dave told Aaron, after they got coffee. He was thinking he wouldn't stick out with all the people arriving for work. There were several spots where he could look directly down upon the courtyard, and the two exterior doors.

Aaron grunted and hoisted his coffee in salute. He was at a small table near the window. "I will be here until this kicks in. It might be a while."

There were at least eight people behind the counter working hard and fast, spinning in random patterns around each other like green-aproned dervishes, filling online orders and servicing walk-in customers. Coffee grinders, milk steamers, espresso machines, and blenders were a pulsating wall of mechanical noise behind the shouts of names read off cups. There was no drive-through, but that didn't seem to have affected the store's work load at all. A lot of customers walked up to the counter to place an order, but at least half the orders seemed to be from people who put in online orders and then picked them up on their way to work.

Aaron finished his coffee, but it hadn't quite kicked in yet. He would have lit up a Marlboro if he was still smoking, and the nicotine would have opened his eyes the rest of the way, but that wasn't an option. He glanced at the line at the counter. It was short at the moment, just six people, and he was thinking about joining it when he noticed group of four guys coming in the front door. They were talking and smiling. He watched them walk up to the "pick-up" counter and the lead guy grabbed cups of coffee and handed them out.

All four of them had a look. Khaki pants and blue polo shirts, although the polos didn't match—there were a few different styles and colors. Same with the pants, there were shade and style variations. They had ID badges clipped to their belts. Aaron stood up as they headed out, letting them pass by. The last one held the door open for him and Aaron nodded politely to the man. Aaron pretend-sipped at his cup as he followed the group across the street and into the lobby of the US Bank Centre. It was just before eight, and the lobby was crowded with people arriving for work.

Aaron joined the flow of people heading for the elevators. He tried to look both bored and pissed off at having to work, which seemed to be the predominant expression on most of the faces around him. When he got onto the elevator he moved to the side, then the back as more people got on, and he kept his face pointed at the floor.

Two women got off the elevator on the fourth floor, leaving just him and the quartet. He listened to their small talk, but it was about people and things which seemed unimportant. But it wasn't the words that had Aaron's attention. The four got off together on the seventh floor without a look back. Aaron stayed in the elevator, and when the doors closed he waited until the last possible second, then stuck his hand out. The doors slid back open. He leaned forward, and stuck his head out. Halfway down the hallway the group of men were clustered around a door. One of them unclipped his badge from his belt and held it to a reader. The door beeped and unlocked, and the four of them headed in.

Aaron exited the elevator and walked down the hallway, in no hurry, coffee cup in hand. He passed the doorway and continued on to the stairwell door. He pushed that open and headed down to the lobby. He found Dave on the second floor of the parking garage, leaning a shoulder against a wall, looking down at the courtyard.

"You get lonely?" Dave asked.

"I finally saw something," Aaron told him. "I don't know if it's what you're looking for, but..."

"What?"

"Four dudes. Came in and grabbed coffee off the counter that somebody had pre-ordered. Blue polos over khakis."

"I think that's the Babble uniform," Dave said. He'd seen a number of people going in and out of the building similarly attired.

"Yeah, I figured that out. They had keycards, IDs, on their belts, but I couldn't get close enough to read them at first. Followed them over, and they swiped into one of the offices on the seventh floor."

"Seventh floor is all Babble. A regional office or something. It's just a search engine and email provider, I don't know why you couldn't do everything in California or wherever the headquarters is located, but whatever. Is that it? You just saw four guys together?"

Aaron shook his head. "These were not computer nerds," he said firmly. "These were not Zuckerbots. They didn't act like it, and they didn't look like it. These guys were all in shape, with muscle. Maybe late twenties, early thirties. All white guys, short hair. One guy, maybe I wouldn't have noticed, but four? They might as well have had signs around their neck, 'COPS'. And it wasn't just a look, it was an attitude."

"You sure?"

Aaron nodded. "Probably federal, if I was a betting man. I haven't seen anything like it since the last Patriot Front demonstration."

"I don't know what that is."

"Supposedly a right-wing group that marches and protests. But there's like fifty of them at a time, all dressed identically, carrying plastic shields and flags, wearing masks. These days the only people wearing masks are old people, the lunatic virtue signalers, and federal agents trying to hide their identities. The only time real right-wingers would be wearing masks is if they were planning violent anti-government shenanigans. And when do they ever do that? These guys get all dressed up, march around, and don't do shit other than make the news. Which, I think, is the point. Give the talking heads more to talk about."

"I don't know, it's not like there's not a lot of anti-government feeling these days…"

"Those Patriot Front guys? They're all white, and they're all in shape. Not one fucking beer belly. How many actual real right-wing groups you know where not one guy has a gut? No long hair, no beards? Not one guy is over

The Subsection

thirty-five years old? Please. And whenever they do get taken into custody, the cops let them keep their masks on. Feds. Total fucking feds, and that's what I was seeing here. I don't know who they are or what they're doing, but they're not optisizing search parameters or whatever the fuck internet people do."

Dave chewed at his lip. "Okay." He didn't know what that information meant.

"Interesting thing I noticed, there's security cameras up, covering that floor. Seventh floor. But I double-checked, there aren't any covering any of the other floors. Just the lobby, and the exterior doors."

"Hmm. Maybe Babble put them up. Might be required to have additional security because their servers contain personal information, credit card numbers, whatever."

"I didn't see where they came from, but most everybody working in the building parks in here, right?" Aaron said, looking into the parking garage.

"Yeah."

"And there's a second-floor walkway. These guys got to work at eight a.m. Figure at least a half-hour lunch. I'll post myself on this end of that walkway a little before four-thirty, spot at least one of them coming out after work. Follow them, get a license plate. You didn't see them, so it's got to be me."

Just before five-thirty Aaron found Dave in the lobby of the US Bank Centre, which was filled with people filing off the elevators and heading home. Aaron held up his phone. On the screen Dave saw his friend had typed out two license plate numbers.

"You have luck?"

"Yeah," Aaron said. "Two plates, which should be better than one, right? A bunch of them came out just after five. All Babble people, in the same getup. And the same four guys, hanging together. Followed them into the garage, got the plates. The way they were hanging together I was wondering if they'd all get into the same vehicle, but no. Then I went back. Eyeballed the other Babble employees heading home. And except for those four, they're all regular people. The kind you'd expect working for an internet company, low-T dudes, fat women, and they are appropriately ethnically diverse, like a bag of Skittles."

"So you're saying these four dudes stand out."

"That's exactly what I'm saying. So what now?"

"Now I see if I can get those plates run," Dave told him. "Meanwhile, we keep watching. Just in case."

"But I did good?"

Dave nodded. "You did good. Tomorrow morning, you point these guys out, if you see them. I want to get a look at them.

"So, who is 'tech support'?" Aaron asked as they sat at a small table, sipping coffee, the next morning. Dave just sat there, not answering. Aaron waited, then said, "Okay, fine. But how long does it take to get back a couple of plates?" Dave had sent the plates to one of the generic email addresses he had for Murph, along with a note that they belonged to a couple of suspicious guys working for Babble.

"Not long, but the plates get you names and addresses, and I know he's going to look into those too. That could

The Subsection

take a while. And we're not even sure this is anything." Aaron grunted.

The Starbucks was busy as usual. That early in the morning very few people were sitting at the tables, they were just grabbing their orders and heading off to work. Dave looked around. He'd been doing surveillance in the area long enough that some of the people were starting to look familiar.

"Is this the kind of stuff you were doing when you weren't riding around in the armored car with me?" Aaron asked. "This is boring as shit."

"Honestly, this is better than the average day doing surveillance out of a car in Detroit," Dave said. "You're not freezing or roasting, you're not pissing in a bottle, you can get up and walk around, there's coffee…"

"Hey," Aaron said quietly, with a nod out the window. Dave looked over, and saw four guys walking across the street toward them. Dave tilted his head down toward his coffee, but watched them as they came into the coffee shop and got in line at the register. Apparently nobody had phoned in their order ahead of time.

"You see what I mean?" Aaron asked, deliberately looking out the window, in the opposite direction.

"Yeah," Dave said. They had a definite air of…something about them. Authority? Confidence? Superiority? They didn't carry themselves like IT guys. Short haircuts. And they were all in shape. None of them were armed, that he could see, but they wore the polos and khakis like a formal uniform. He casually pulled out his phone, waited, and when he saw them walking toward the door his thumb tapped repeatedly on the screen, discreetly taking half a dozen photos.

"Think that'll help?" Aaron asked quietly, as the men filed out the door.

"Couldn't hurt."

Aaron grunted. "I'll go wander over there, see if they get off at the seventh floor again, then maybe hang out in the lobby." And he was up and out the door, jogging across the street.

"Do you mind if I sit here?"

Dave looked up. There was a woman standing beside his table. She wore glasses with thick black frames, had shaggy, shoulder-length light brown hair, and was wearing a baggy summer dress. Before he had a chance to respond she added, "I like sitting by the window. I just love people watching, you know?" She sat across the small table from him, and peered at him through the glasses. "Do you live around here? You look familiar." She flashed a smile at him, and took a sip from her cup.

"I just moved in."

"Oh, really? Where?" She leaned across the table.

"Upstairs."

"The Hanna? I don't know if that's where I've seen you."

Dave shrugged. "It's a big building." He was hoping that by not engaging too much with her that she'd go away, but he didn't want to be rude and draw attention to himself. He thought that she was younger than she first appeared, maybe not even thirty, but she dressed and made herself up like a middle-aged woman. He wondered if she had a cat. Or three. She looked the type.

"It's a piece of Cleveland history. I love that it's an anagram."

"What is?"

The Subsection

"The Hanna. Spelled the same backwards and forwards."

Dave shook his head. "An anagram is a word or phrase made by rearranging the letters of it. Tom Marvolo Riddle spells I Am Lord Voldemort." It was the first one that popped into his head. He'd recently read the entire series. "You mean palindrome. And Hanna doesn't have an H on the end, so it's almost a palindrome, but not quite." 'Palindrome' had always sounded like a word out of science fiction to him. A Doctor Who villain, maybe.

She leaned back, smiling, almost smirking. Then she gave a little nod. "Okay," she said. Her eyes ran over him. "So you're not dumb. But you could do with something more than just a baseball cap. Who's Mullet Man?"

"Excuse me?"

"Your friend. How does he fit in?"

Dave frowned at her. "Into what?" His phone, lying face down on the table, buzzed with a text message. He flipped it over. SHE'S WITH US. He frowned at the screen, then looked up at her. She gave him an innocent smile. It took him a minute to process the change in situation. She waited. "How do *you* fit in?" he finally asked her.

"You wanted help. I was busy. Then I wasn't. So I'm here. Who's he?" She tilted her head toward the window.

"I needed help, so I got help. Another set of eyes. An old friend. He doesn't know what this is for."

"So he's just helping out, and he doesn't know why?" She sounded dubious.

"Yeah," he said flatly.

"I guess he is a friend, then. What exactly are we doing, and where do you need me? Tech support gave me a thumbnail sketch, but that's it."

"Tech is running down a lead, but until he gets back to

me we're still keeping an eye on the building, looking for anything unusual. And no, I don't know exactly what that might look like."

"Like those Babble guys who look like fresh police academy graduates?"

"You saw that, huh?"

"I saw you taking pictures. Not too subtle. And tell me you haven't been here for days, with just a cover for camouflage."

"Cover?"

"Hat."

"We've been moving around," he said defensively. "I didn't know how long we'd be here. I've been making it up as I go along."

She frowned. "I thought that was a wig, but that's your friend's actual hair, isn't it. And moustache."

Dave peered at her. "Is *that* a wig?" He looked at her hair, and her glasses, and the baggy dress, with new eyes. She just smiled, and took a sip of what smelled like tea. It hadn't occurred to him that there might be women in the subsection, working in the field. But maybe that was just sexism. He knew women had a long successful track record, historically, as spies. And snipers.

"You're a couple of amateurs," she said. "Him especially. Why'd they bring you on board?"

"You'd have to ask them."

"Military?" she asked. Her eyes ran over him again. He didn't have the look. And he shook his head. "Police?" she said, with visible distaste. He shook his head again. "Intelligence community?" she asked dubiously. He didn't have that look either. Again, a head shake. Her frown grew deeper, but then turned thoughtful. So he was an out-of-the-box acquisition. That might be a good thing. "What happened to your fingers?" she asked. She'd noticed the bad scarring on the insides of his fingers. All his fingers.

"Boating accident. What's your...what do I call you?" he asked.

She didn't answer, and instead asked, "What's *your* name?"

"They didn't tell you?" he asked. She shook her head. "Wow, they do keep things tightly wrapped. Well, then, the name on the ID in my pocket is Henry."

She smiled. "The name on my ID is Rebecca."

Dave made a face. "Ugh. Hank and Becky?"

A smile pulled at the corner of her mouth. She set her tea down, pulled out a phone, and tapped at it with her thumbs. Five seconds later Dave's burner phone lit up with an incoming call. That was immediately disconnected. "That's me," she told him. "Where do you want me?"

"I thought I was an amateur."

"You're still team lead."

Dave hadn't been expecting that. And he had all sorts of questions about not-Becky. Not the least of which was what she really looked like under the baggy clothes and big hair. He thought he detected muscles under the dress. "How much training or experience do you have doing surveillance?" Her coming up on him inside the Starbucks didn't necessarily mean anything.

She gave a little tiny nod that he'd asked the question. "Training and experience," she said simply.

"Okay, well, all we've got are phones, not radios, so things could be better. Are you armed?"

Her mouth twitched again in what might have been a smile. "You do not have to worry about my physical safety. I am not an office worker."

Which wasn't, technically, an answer, but she'd said it

with calm confidence. "Okay. He said he'd be hanging out in the lobby. Why don't you take Euclid, and keep an eye on the front door. If he rotates in your direction, you move too. Euclid, 14th, here, the restaurant on this side of the street, the café in the lobby across the street, the lobby itself, the courtyard on the south side of the building, and the parking garage. We've been bouncing around."

"You going to tell him about me?"

Dave smiled. "Let's see if he spots you."

"So who the fuck is she?" Aaron asked. He turned to the woman going by 'Becky'. "Who the fuck are you?" He eyed her as they sat in a booth inside the bar area of a Texas Roadhouse. The restaurant was busy, and noisy, and there were TV screens above their heads tuned to various sports channels and The Chive, which ran non-stop viral clips of people and animals doing stupid or funny things, serving as a hamster wheel for the human brain. The restaurant was miles from the surveillance location, and they could barely hear each other, so Dave figured they were safe from eavesdropping, electronic or otherwise. It was after seven p.m., and the bank building was closed for the day. They'd seen nothing out of the ordinary. Aaron had obtained another license plate, following one of the tightly-wrapped Babble employees into the parking garage, and Dave had texted it in, but Murph still hadn't gotten back to them with any information.

"She's helping out too," Dave told him.

Aaron gave both of them a dirty look. "You could have told me. Here I think I've got something, someone doing surveillance on the same building, just the kind of suspicious shit you're looking for, and she's with us?"

"I didn't know she'd be coming," Dave said with a shrug.

Aaron shot him a dirty look, then glanced around. "You couldn't get a table away from the bar?" He wasn't happy.

"It was this or wait twenty minutes," Dave told him.

"You know," Aaron said, making no attempt to keep his voice down, staring at the crowded bar, "I've never looked at the people sitting around a bar and thought, 'Man, those people look smart.'"

"Don't be a pissy bitch," Dave told him.

Their companion glanced over her shoulder at the crowded bar. "Yeah, they're all idiots, but they're why we're doing this. So they have the freedom to be idiots."

Aaron didn't quite understand what she was talking about. He was still looking at the bar. "I miss smoking," he said with a sigh.

"You just quit?" she asked him. He looked like a smoker.

Aaron nodded. "Just at the right time."

"Before COVID?"

"Fuck no," he said. "After. Smoking's what kept me healthy during that bullshit."

"What?" She goggled at him.

"My lungs are coated in tar, used to fourteen hundred chemicals and carcinogens. What do you think that fucking little virus was going to do to me? I'm self-inoculated. My lungs are like superheroes." He beamed at her.

She wasn't sure if he was being serious. "When did you spot me?" she asked Aaron, cocking her head.

Aaron said, "I don't know. Morning. Late morning. Saw you on the sidewalk, and in the building. But you weren't moving right, didn't go up in the elevators, just through the lobby. Then when I saw you near the parking garage I knew."

"What do you mean, I wasn't moving right?" She was honestly curious.

Aaron glanced between her and Dave. Dave seemed interested too. "Running an armored car," Aaron said, "you're always dealing with traffic. Both when you're moving and stationary. Cars and people. But there's a natural flow to it, to all of it. What the fuck do they call it... organic." He glanced at Dave, then back at her. "You pull up to a place, you eyeball the fuck out of it. If you've never been there before, you eyeball everything. But if you've been there before, once, twice, and you pay attention, you get a feel for how cars and people move through the space. Streets, sidewalks, alleys, lobbies, parking lots, all that shit. At that point, you look for the things that aren't flowing right. That are...stuck, I guess, or moving in the wrong direction. Cars idling where cars shouldn't be idling, that kind of shit. I'd been here long enough, eyeballing everybody and everything, you stood out."

She was interested. "How?"

Aaron told her, "People coming out of that building, they go every-which-fucking way. But the people going in, they head for the elevators, and the few that don't, they're heading for the restaurant or the physical therapy place. You came in off Euclid, went through the lobby, right past the elevators, and kept going. Didn't stop at the directory or anything. Nobody does that. Maybe I saw you before that, but that's when I really noticed you. Then I saw you again, over by the parking garage, but not sitting at one of those tables in the courtyard. Just...hanging out, but not where anybody hangs out. Later you went back through the lobby in the other direction, but you didn't stop at the elevators, or the directory. You went to that shitty Vietnamese restaurant, and sat where you could see the elevators. That's when I told Dave about you." He shrugged. "Keeping my head on a swivel kept me alive on the mean streets of Detroit. Both of us." He nodded at Dave.

"Detroit, huh." She gave Dave a look. He didn't respond.

"What's with the getup?" Aaron asked her.

"Getup?" She peered at him from behind the thick-rimmed glasses.

"You look like a crazy cat lady. But you don't act like one. Or sound like one. And you're younger than I thought. You wearing a disguise? Because looking like that, you should smell like cat piss." She barked out a laugh. Aaron told her, "Normally I can't smell a damn thing, but since I stopped smoking I can actually smell stuff, and there is no Chanel Litterbox No. 9 around you."

"Maybe I just let myself go," she said.

Aaron shook his head. "If you really were who you're trying to look like, you'd have ordered something vegan, not an eight-ounce sirloin." He frowned, and his eyes roamed around her. "Baggy dress, but one thing that's tough to hide is shoulders, and you've got shoulders. If a chick has shoulders, she's in fucking *shape*. Or she's a tranny."

"Chick?"

"Broad. Babe. Bitch. Dame. Split-tail?" Aaron was fighting back a smile.

"Keep going, assclown," she snapped. "Maybe I just got tired of guys hitting on me. Neither of you did," she pointed out. Aaron barked out a laugh and rocked in the booth. It seemed a weird reaction to her. "What?"

His face split in a wide smile. "Sure, me, maybe I'm into hairballs and Wookieebush, crotch cobwebs and cat piss, maybe not, you don't know, but you know who he's with, right?" He jerked a thumb at Dave. She followed the thumb and looked at Dave. "You don't?" Aaron said, reading her expression. "Hold on." He pulled out his phone.

"Aaron..." Dave said.

"Hold *on*," Aaron said, thumbs flying. Then he tapped the screen, and turned the phone around. There was a movie playing.

She leaned in, squinting. Then she jerked back. "Why are you showing me porn?" she said, a near-shout turning into a hiss. She looked around the crowded restaurant to see if anyone had noticed, then back at Aaron. "What is wrong with you?"

Aaron jerked his head toward Dave. "That's his girlfriend. Or was, she's retired. The Pork Snorkle herself." He kept the phone up. "Been with her a couple years now, so I guess it's serious?" He gave Dave a questioning look, which Dave ignored. "There is literally nothing you can offer him that he doesn't already have at home, at Olympic gold medal levels. Unless you *are* a tranny."

"What?" she said. She looked at Dave, but then her eye was caught by something. She glanced back at the phone, then squinted again. Tilted her head nearly sideways, trying to decipher what she was seeing. When she did her eyes went wide. "Holy shit." She looked from the phone to Dave and back to the phone.

"I do a lot of cardio," Dave told her, deadpan. Aaron almost slid to the floor under the table laughing.

The next morning, Dave and Aaron showed up at the Starbucks at six-thirty, and 'Becky' was already sitting at a table by the window, sipping at a cup of tea. She was in a loose sweatshirt over baggy jeans, her big mop of brown hair pulled back by a tie, and she'd changed her glasses to ones with much thinner frames. She looked the same, and yet very different. He was impressed. They ignored her, pretended they didn't know her, and stood in line to get coffee, looking around just in case they spotted anything unusual.

The willowy male in front of Aaron stepped up to the counter. "Hi, Mar," he said, his voice a singsong. "The usual, a venti white mocha, quad shot, two shots on bottom, two on top, almond milk, extra hot, caramel drizzle inside the cup, and extra whip cream." He held up his phone to the credit card reader to pay.

Aaron opened and closed his mouth, blinking in disbelief. As Mar stepped away from the register to prep the drink, Aaron leaned close to the young man. "You know nuts don't have nipples, right?"

The man turned and looked at Aaron in confusion. "What?"

Aaron went on without pause. "But I suppose almond milk sounds better than ordering nut juice. Two spurts of nut juice. Although some people might like that." He looked at the guy. "You look like you'd like that."

Dave leaned in. "We're supposed to be keeping a low profile," he growled in his ear.

Aaron looked back over his shoulder. "I am," he said amiably. "I'm just talking with Hufflepuff here about the semen milkshake he ordered." He turned back around, but the man had fled, standing over by the opposite counter, waiting for his order to arrive. Glancing nervously at Aaron. Mar was back at the register.

"Coffee," Aaron told him. "Black. Large."

"You mean venti?" Mar said, frowning, obviously displeased with him.

"Venti means winds in Italian," Aaron told him. "Or twenty. *Un grande non è né venti né venti, finocchio.*"

Mar blinked at the fluent Italian, a total counterpoint to Aaron's shaggy moustache and mini-mullet. "Ooh, aren't you full of surprises," he said.

After they had their coffees in hand and stepped away from the counter, Aaron glanced at their female partner sitting by the window. "I'm going to go hang out in the lobby across the street," Aaron told Dave. "You can sit with clam chowder if you want."

Frowning, Dave watched him go, then saw Becky twitch her head, just a little jerk toward her. He sat down at the small table beside hers, both of them sipping from their cups and looking out the window at Aaron as he crossed the street.

"Okay. I get it," she said, not looking at him but rather down at her phone in her hand, resting on the table. "First gig with us, right? Didn't think you'd be sitting on it this long, so you just went right in, bare-faced. But you always have to assume someone's after you, and that they'll have incredible resources. Moscow Rules. Don't know what that means, look it up. You fucked up, bringing him in, but I get it, this is too big a site for one person to cover. But now I know your name's Dave, you're from Detroit, and you're dating a, um…"

A line appeared between Dave's eyes. Across the street, Aaron disappeared into the US Bank Centre. "We're on the same team."

"Still. If they'd wanted me to know who you were, or wanted you to know who I was…"

"Right. Got it."

A small frown touched her lips. "So what the fuck is your skill set?"

The Subsection

Dave fought back a smile as he said, "If they'd wanted you to know..." He looked at her out of the corner of his eye, saw she had a wry smile on her face. The screen of her phone reflected off her glasses. She was flicking through Instagram with her thumb. He was pretty sure she wasn't even looking at the display, it was just part of her cover.

At a quarter to eight the quartet of in-shape young men showed up, grabbed their venti cups off the counter—obviously someone had remembered to phone in the order this time—and headed back across the street. TO YOU Dave texted to Aaron's burner phone. The men walked across the street and entered the office building. Five minutes later Dave got a text back. NOTHING NEW, SAME PLACE.

"They went into the same Babble office," Dave said quietly, looking down at his phone.

"Whatever they're doing, it's a regular nine-to-five job," she observed, talking to her own phone. "Eight to four-thirty, whatever."

"If they're even related to the reason we're here," Dave said. "For all we know they're part of a Babble weightlifting club. Or something else, that's got nothing to do with what happened."

She gave a little shrug. "Sometimes you never know. Get used to disappointment." She looked at the time on her phone. "In ten minutes that little café down the street opens for lunch, I'll head over there," she said. "Green Table?"

"Green Rooster. I'll head over to the pho place. I drink any more coffee and I'm going to get arrythmia." He made a face. She saw it.

"What?"

He shrugged. "I have no idea if I'm wasting your time. Our time. I—" He got distracted as his phone buzzed with an incoming text. Hers did as well, at the same time. He tapped it with his thumb and it opened.

OKAY, I THINK I'VE FIGURED OUT WHAT'S GOING ON OVER THERE. MOST OF THE WHY AND WHO. NEED TO HAVE A GROUP MEETING TO DISCUSS HOW TO PROCEED. YOUR GROUP SUPERVISOR IS CURRENTLY BUSY, SO THAT WILL HAVE TO WAIT. I WILL CONTACT YOU.

Dave stared at the message for a while, then glanced at 'Becky'. She had a neutral expression on her face. He looked back at his phone. "That's it?" he said.

"Apparently. For now. I told you to get used to disappointment," she murmured.

Dave frowned and sighed, looked out at the building across the street, then down at his phone as he typed a response with his thumbs. SO...WE'RE DONE HERE FOR NOW?

He waited. Thirty seconds later he got a text. UNLESS YOU REALLY LOVE CLEVELAND. His frown grew deeper, and he looked over to ask her a question, but she was gone. Nowhere to be seen.

Dave got up and walked across the street. He found Aaron in the lobby, and jerked his head for him to follow. Dave headed across the courtyard and into the parking garage, only because he hadn't spotted any security cameras in the parking garage. Which seemed completely dumb to him, a dark parking garage seemed the exact kind of place you'd want under surveillance. "S'up?" Aaron asked him.

"We're done," Dave said.

"What?"

"Gig's over, we're done."

"Why, what happened?" Dave just looked at him, until

Aaron figured out that was his answer. "Fuck, really? Was it those guys I spotted?"

"We get out of here, I'll give you the money I owe you. Cash."

Aaron waved the suggestion away. "I don't give a shit about the money. I'd just like to know if I was right about those guys. You tell Harriet the Spy?"

"Yeah."

"Well…shit." Aaron looked around, tried to take a sip of his coffee, and discovered the cup was empty. He tossed it to the concrete floor. "So what are you doing now?" he asked Dave. "You got something going? This, or something else?"

"Not at the moment."

"You want to drive back to Michigan with me? We can hang out. I told you I bought some new guns, we could go shooting…" He looked at Dave hopefully.

Dave had bought a round-trip ticket, but the return flight wasn't for several days, he'd given himself a week, and figured he could rebook the return leg if he needed to. The same with the rental car, he'd reserved it for a week. He glanced over his shoulder at the US Bank Centre building, but it gave him no guidance. And he had no idea if Murph would be getting back to him with information in a few days or a few weeks.

"Sure," he told Aaron. "Sounds like fun." Aaron's face split into a big smile.

EIGHTEEN

Tactical Sauna

He could taste the dust and the stink of his own body after four days away from soap as he sat cross-legged behind the crumbling wall in the dark, hearing the vehicles, finally, approach. He'd been waiting seemingly forever, eating beef jerky and PowerBars, and was just about out of water. He'd filled only a third of the empty water bottles with piss, sure sign of just how fucking hot it was even inside, in the dark and out of the sun. Waiting had been an exercise, not in frustration but rather meditation. And not just for him.

"We've got four vehicles," he heard in his ear. "Thank fucking God. Finally. Two Range Rovers bracketed by Hi-Luxes. Lot of tint but multiple tangos inside each. This could get interesting."

Bob clicked his throat mike in response and stretched his legs out. He'd arrived at the location, an abandoned homestead, eighteen hours before the scheduled meeting. The house, after being empty for years, was little more than a dusty shack, the windows long gone. He'd checked it over, looking for a suitable place to hole up, and found one wall was crumbling—some sort of dry rot. He punched through a foot above the floor and discovered the dark dusty space behind it, perhaps a closet that had been closed off years before. He enlarged the opening until it was big enough he could fit through quickly. There was a small bookshelf against another wall, and he moved that over. It covered the hole completely. But he'd made all sorts of fresh bootprints in the dust, and had to sweep the entire floor with a rag to get rid of the prints and all signs of his work. His only hope was that nobody would notice the floor was too clean. Then he climbed into his hole, pulled the wooden bookshelf across the opening, and waited.

He'd tried to stay limber, but his hideyhole was small, and he'd been in there over thirty-three hours. Hot, stuffy, and tight as a closet. He touched his toes, swung his arms around, and worked the kinks out of his neck as the sound of engines grew louder. He wore body armor and mag pouches, but not so many they got in his way. He had a pack, but it was wedged behind him, and he shouldn't need it…not in a hurry, in any case.

He heard car doors slam, maybe three, but it was hard to tell because the thick walls muffled sound oddly. Then he heard movement inside the building, coming closer to him. Bodyguards, he was sure, checking the building. The man on the other end of the radio could have told him, if he'd asked, but Bob was observing radio silence until he went loud, because who knew what kind of electronic monitoring equipment these guys had in their vehicles. Or might bring into the building. And on that note…he reached down, and shut his comm off. Just in case.

The suppressed MP5K PDW sat in his lap, and he put his hands on it, very slowly clicking off the safety—one click to semi-automatic, one more click to full-automatic. The sub machinegun was not a true German HK product but rather a licensed copy produced by MKE in Turkey, which was better if he had to ditch it. He was wearing gloves, and had been since he'd entered the house, so he'd left no prints. The footsteps drew closer, and he heard talking in Arabic, too muffled for him to make out. He pointed the weapon at the back of the bookcase, but the steps and the voices moved away from him as he did so, and he relaxed as much as he could. The red dot reticle in his optic seemed too bright, but he didn't adjust it.

His cell, for that's almost what it was, wasn't completely dark, as some light seeped in through a crack in the roof above his head. His eyes had long since adjusted to the dimness, but he mostly worked by feel as he reached down and verified the Glock was clicked into his thigh holster and the magazine was firmly seated. If he needed the pistol things had turned to shit, but better to have it and not need it….

After days with no sound other than skittering lizards and desert songbirds, the noise the men made as they came into the adjoining room seemed huge, but he supposed it wasn't. The two principals, with a few commanders acting as aides, plus likely four to six bodyguards. Not as many as the men would have liked, Bob was sure, but they were already running a risk with four vehicles. There were always eyes in the sky, and convoys and caravans drew attention very quickly. He guessed they had joined up nearby and then made a quick run to this location, where several vehicles could park out of sight under the dilapidated roof jutting out from one side of the unremarkable dirt-colored edifice. Two vehicles were nothing of note to drones or satellites.

The noise inside died down, and changed. The bodyguards had been sent outside, as the two important men had important things to discuss. Bob heard chairs being moved around, and soft voices. Game time. He turned his comm back on and waited if that set off any alarm, but there were no shouts or running feet. He clicked his throat mike once, then settled his helmet onto his head and secured the chin strap. He hated the fucking thing, but the Kevlar would stop a pistol bullet and, sometimes, AK rounds. Some of the meeting attendees were sure to be armed with pistols, and maybe one or two might have an AK sitting nearby, but if he did everything right the only person who got a shot off inside the room would be him. He slid his clear eye protection into place, rated to stop most projectiles short of actual bullets.

Very carefully he climbed into a crouch, breathing deliberately, and tucked the SMG's buttstock into his shoulder. He had thirty rounds in the magazine, and another full one clamped to the first, but if he needed more than a full magazine then the shit had truly hit the fan, and it would be far quicker to grab the Glock. He clicked his throat mike twice.

Bob reached up carefully with his left hand and stuck a finger through the pull ring. It was attached to a wire that ran up the wall and across the rafters to the 'flash-bang', the concussion grenade whose pin was already pulled. It was wedged into place, lever still down and keeping the grenade from detonating. He visualized the action in his head one more time, knowing that these things never went exactly according to plan, then pulled the ring.

He heard the grenade hit the table, and there was just enough time for several shouted exclamations and the frantic scuff of chairs before the grenade went off with a huge boom that shook dust off every wall and made his head hurt even in the next room. At the blast he shoved the bookshelf over and popped out right behind it like a tactical leprechaun, taking out a part of the soft wall with his shoulder. Then the world slowed down.

Someone coming into the room from outside would have found it dim, but after days in his near-dark room the scene before him seemed bright as a sunny afternoon. The air was filled with smoke and dust and random particles, and he could see every one of them with supernatural clarity. The men, he instantly saw there were six, were around the old table and floundering, some on hands and knees, some on their backs, one struggling to find his feet. All but one in traditional Arabic robes, most with dark complexions and a lot of facial hair. Bob shot the one on his feet first, a short burst in the upper chest, then moved his muzzle just a little right and down and hit a man on his knees with a longer burst, running it up the side of his neck into his temple. The SMG wiggled in his hands, but with the blood rushing in his ears he couldn't even hear it going off, not that it was that loud anyway with the suppressor.

Both men were dead before they hit the ground. The man closest to Bob was on his hands and knees and had just laid his hand on the pistol he'd dropped when Bob put two rounds into the back of his head.

The table blocked his view of the remaining men, and he sidestepped in slow-motion to his right as one of the others came up, his eyes squinted shut from the grenade, pointing his pistol where Bob had been. Instinct, maybe. Bob shot him in the chest, then again, still sliding sideways. The man didn't realize he was dead yet, and Bob finally had to put a burst into the center of his face to sit him down. By that time Bob was most of the way around the table and could see the two remaining men.

The Subsection

One man was on his hands and knees, shaking his head, stunned from the flash-bang. Bob pressed the SMG's muzzle against this man's head and killed him with two rounds, then side-stepped and planted a boot on the distinctive AKS-74u on the floor. The man trying to lift it was on his back, squinting and blinking from the grenade.

Abu Ahmad al-Tunisi. In a dusty suitcoat and white silk shirt over slacks and loafers. No socks. Showing off a lot of gold jewelry on his fingers and at his throat. The man the U.S. government—or at least high-ranking members of it, just how high up the conspiracy went they weren't sure—was apparently now working with in secret, to arrange false-flag operations. The man who was known to have killed dozens of Americans during the war on terror. "*Min 'anti?*" he shouted at Bob, his hearing wrecked from the concussion grenade. Who are you?

Bob smiled. "*Alshaytan al'akbar.*" The Great Satan.

"American?" the man said in accented English. His confusion was clear. "CIA? But we are having a deal."

"Not with me," Bob said, and fired a burst into the man's face. Three rounds, right between his eyes. Then he stepped back and swept the room with his weapon once more, to make sure there was no longer a threat. The shooting had lasted maybe five seconds, the talking another five. Everyone was dead.

Bob keyed his mike. "Clear," he announced, aiming his SMG in the general direction of the front door, which appeared to have taken a number of incoming rounds. He was glad he hadn't been in the line of fire as his partner engaged the bodyguards outside the building, that could have ruined his whole day.

"Exterior clear," he heard in his ear.

"Thirty seconds," Bob said. He darted back to his hole,

shoved his piss bottles into his backpack, checked around for any other trash, then crawled back out. He stood the bookshelf back up, covering the hole. The spent flash-bang was on the floor under the table, and he left it there where it would be easy to find. A US-made M84 stun grenade. He pulled the magazine out of his subgun and cycled the cartridge out of the chamber. It landed on the wood floor and bounced around. There were still a few rounds left in the magazine, and Bob dropped it onto the wooden floor and reloaded with a fresh one. Lastly he shouldered his pack.

"Coming out," he announced, then opened the door.

The desert sun was nearly blinding, and he squinted against the glare and held a hand up to block it. The Subsection—Dave Anderson's name for it had stuck—was always running lean. He would have had a six-man team with air support if this was a sanctioned op, but it was just him and Jerry Phillips. They'd been friends since high school, along with a few other guys, and when Jerry was still in college they met John Phault and got involved in several serious misadventures. The last one actually killed Bob, if only for a few minutes, and the details of that incident, and the NDA they'd all had to sign, was still classified at the highest levels. Jerry had spent the better part of twenty years working for the DEA. He'd done multiple tours in Afghanistan during the War on Terror and was fluent in Arabic. Jerry had been baking in the thin shade under a camo cover beneath an olive tree across the street for two days, behind a suppressed rifle, and looked exhausted. He'd thrown his gear into one of the Hi-Luxes and was standing beside the truck, facing out, waiting for him. The bodyguards were dead on the ground around the vehicles, blood soaking into the sand, most of them sniped where they

The Subsection

stood before they had a chance to react. One of them had made it to the door, and was dead at Bob's feet. "We good?" Bob asked him.

"So far."

"Then time to go," Bob said, and got behind the wheel of the Toyota. They sped away from the scene.

"There were a lot easier ways to do that," Jerry grumbled. He twisted the top off a bottle of water and chugged half of it down.

Bob used his upper arm to wipe sweat off his forehead. "Easy wasn't the point."

The men would be discovered within a day, most likely. And from the evidence left behind—the US-issue stun grenade, the specialty American-made armor-piercing ammunition only available to police and military, on the floor and in the discarded MP5 magazine—it would seem obvious the American government was behind the assassination. Maybe ISIL would publicly accuse them of the assassination, which the U.S. government would then of course deny. But any hopes the shadowy bureaucrats inside America's government had of working with anyone in the region were as dead as Abu Ahmad al-Tunisi.

PART III
BALL SO HARD

NINETEEN

The Right Kind of People

Robert MacGregor finished tying his necktie, a silk Turnbull & Asser in his usual half Windsor knot, and checked himself in the antique mirror. He'd thickened up a bit with age, but he'd avoided becoming fat—at least, so far—and the suit made him look nearly trim. The bespoke suit was simple 400g Birkdale Twill Weave from Huddersfield Cloth, purchased and tailored at Norton & Sons on Savile Row in London. It was a deep blue that in lesser light would look black, offset today by a bright red tie. He checked the knot at his throat, shot his cuffs, nodded once, then glanced out the window.

The morning sun was bright against the faces of the townhouses lining the opposite side of the street, and the mature trees spaced evenly down the length of the block. Calm. Beautiful. Old Town was one of the pricier neighborhoods in Alexandria, and looked it. Not that he worried about money, but it helped to keep out the wrong kind of people. Not that he had to worry about them, either.

The townhouse was three and a half stories, nearly

seventy years old (although it had been remodeled at least four times) and yet the hardwood stairs and floors were remarkably solid, barely creaking under his soles as he headed downstairs. He found his wife in the spacious, tiled kitchen, the air thick with the scent of freshly brewed coffee. Something exotic his wife had picked up, from Sumatra or somewhere similar. She'd been into coffee for the last few months, buying bags of small batch beans from roasters he'd never heard of all around the country. He liked some more than others, but all of it was better than anything he could find at work. And, unlike most people, he'd actually been to Sumatra.

"How much did you say this place is worth now?" he asked her. He opened a cupboard and pulled down a stainless steel insulated travel mug, one of a dozen he had. The travel mug didn't offer the same panache and style as his clothes, but fine china cups were not suitable for sipping from in the back of a moving vehicle.

"Based on what a few others on the block have sold for, two point five, maybe two point six, and that's before you add in the security upgrades. I don't even know what they add to the price."

"And what did we pay? Seven?" He gave a little snort and shook his head.

"Six hundred and ninety-five thousand. Why?" She gave him a suspicious look. He didn't read anything into it. She was always giving him suspicious looks. Mostly when he didn't deserve them.

"Just thinking how right Will Rogers was when he said to buy land, because they aren't making any more of it." It was just over three thousand square feet, with four bedrooms—far larger than what they needed, they'd been empty nesters for over a decade, but he doubted if they'd ever move from the place. He filled the insulated container with piping hot coffee, screwed the lid on, then moved toward the front of the townhouse. He stood before one of the windows in front, looking out at the quiet neighborhood, staring at nothing at all, really, just thinking, sipping at his coffee. His security team hated when he did that, but what was the point of having bulletproof windows if you weren't ever going to look out of them? He glanced at his watch, and as he did so the armored Suburban pulled up out front.

Two members of his security team exited the vehicle and looked around. One of them talked into the cuff of his suitcoat, checking in with the team positioned in the townhouse almost directly across the street. Apparently he liked what he heard in his earpiece, because the two men moved toward the front of his townhouse.

MacGregor moved to the front door but resisted opening it before they gave the all clear—they hated when he did that too. At the brusque knock he opened the heavy, lacquered door built to withstand a direct hit from an RPG—or so he'd been told—and stepped out.

"Morning, gentlemen," he said, and strode briskly toward the waiting vehicle, not waiting for their replies.

Gerald, his personal assistant, was in his usual spot in the back seat. "Good morning, sir," he said to MacGregor. MacGregor nodded to him as the other men climbed in.

"Heading to the White House this morning, Jeremy," MacGregor called out to his usual driver.

"Yes sir, I've been informed," he said, glancing in the rearview mirror. Then the vehicle pulled away from the curb.

"If the Speaker is going to be at this meeting, you know it's going to be a waste of time," Gerald said, opening his briefcase. "Every meeting which includes her ends up being a waste of time."

"Well, until she has the good grace to retire or die, we're stuck with her," MacGregor said. He was a fatalist. And a realist.

Gerald handed him a file folder whose very thickness made MacGregor frown. "Looks like traffic's bad this morning, so you'll have more time to get through all that," Gerald said, trying to make the best of a bad situation.

MacGregor grunted, leaned back in the leather seat, opened the folder, and began reading. Twenty-two minutes later he frowned and re-read a paragraph. Then read it again. His frown grew deeper. "Gerald, get me Mason Phillips on the phone."

"Yes, sir." A minute later he was handing his cell phone over. It was encrypted, but MacGregor knew all that meant was it was unlikely any of their enemies would be able to eavesdrop—the NSA would have no problems untangling the digital spaghetti, which is how he thought of it.

"Mason."

"Yes, Director?" Dr. Mason Phillips, the Deputy Director of the CIA for Operations, was quite competent. He'd been with the agency for over twenty years, and in his current position for three.

"Have you read your copy of the PDB yet this morning?" The Presidential Daily Brief is a classified daily summary of all high-level all-source information and analysis on national security issues produced for the President and key cabinet members and select advisors. For decades it was a printed document, but President Obama indicated he wanted it in digital form, and that is how it continued to be issued, as a password-protected digital document produced and delivered by the Office of the

The Subsection

Director of National Intelligence. As Director of the CIA, one of the agencies responsible for providing intelligence which went into the PDB, MacGregor was of course provided a copy, but he didn't want to perch a laptop on his thighs in the car, and so Gerald printed out the PDB, among many other things, for him every morning.

"I have not."

"The Islamic State—in Syria—is claiming that America, specifically the CIA, assassinated Abu al-Tunisi the day before yesterday."

"I think I'd heard some chatter about someone of rank being taken out, but I didn't realize it was him. Or that they were claiming we did it. Where is this coming from?"

"It looks like the original source was sigint harvested by the NSA. Cell phone intercepts. They say they have hard evidence directly implicating America in the strike. But it's more than backchannel chatter now, they've reached out to Al Jazeera and the BBC." MacGregor paused, and glanced at Gerald out of the corner of his eye before continuing. "Al-Tunisi, if I remember correctly, was an up-and-comer in the region. You know how I hate to ask direct questions of you, but…"

"We didn't take him out, Director," Phillips said. "As far as I know," he added quickly. "I didn't order it. I'm not aware of any JSOC operations in the region where he might have been hit as collateral. But I will look into this, and confirm that."

"You do that," MacGregor said. "I want a face-to-face on this, soonest."

TWENTY

A Dirty Game of Lies

"So how was it?" Lori asked him, when he got back home from Cleveland.

Dave thought about how to answer. "Good," he said. "Frustrating. Really frustrating, in the end. But…it was good to get out there. To be doing something." He nodded to himself at that. "Really good."

"Not dangerous, then?"

He snorted. "Only to my heart. I spent most of the time sitting in a Starbucks. Getting hit on by the cashier."

"Oh yeah?" One of her eyebrows slid up half an inch. "Was she hot?"

"He had a lovely personality."

She smiled at that. "So what next?"

He shrugged. "I don't know. I'm waiting to hear back on something, but…"

She made a face. "They don't seem to tell you much."

"That's kinda the deal. And you already know more about it than you should, so…"

"Don't ask you any questions."

"Right."

She nodded, and then gave him a look. "What?" he said.

"Nothing," she said with a shrug. But in truth she was glad that he was working. Even if what he was doing seemed like it ultimately could be just as dangerous as some of the other things he'd been involved in that had gotten him shot. And abducted. And his house burned down—twice, if you counted his grandfather's cabin. That had been before she'd known him, but she'd learned all about it.

And while, like most men, he didn't talk about his feelings, maybe he felt the same way. Since he'd been back he'd worked out twice, hard, now almost fully healed from his injuries, and was back to practicing his draw every day for half an hour or more at a time.

But if he was in danger, at least this time it was his choice.

Three days later Dave was doing a little repair on the back corner of their house when his phone chimed in his pocket. He pulled it out and saw he'd gotten a text. ANSWER THE PHONE. He was still frowning when Lori's phone rang. Lori was ten feet away, trimming some dead bits off a succulent. She reached into her pocket for her phone, then looked at Dave as he snapped his fingers at her. When she looked up he just gestured for the phone. She opened her mouth, closed it, frowned, then handed it over. He didn't recognize the incoming number. It had a 202 area code, which he was pretty sure was Washington D.C.

He thumbed the screen and held the phone up to his ear. "Hello?"

"The planning committee requests your presence at a

strategy meeting regarding your current project," he heard in his ear.

Dave frowned. He didn't recognize the voice at all—a woman, maybe in her thirties, with a lovely warm British accent. "I think you've got the wrong number," he said.

"I do not," she told him.

He blinked. "You do not?"

"I very definitely do not."

His burner phone was shut off and hidden away in a faraday bag, and he wasn't scheduled to turn it back on to check for messages for thirty-six hours. "You sound different," he said. "Less…generic."

"Sexy? I thought I sounded sexy."

"It's hard to go wrong with a British accent. As long as it's not cockney, or whatever it was that Eliza Doolittle had." Lori had been staring at him the whole time, and at that comment gave him a quizzical look. "So…?"

"Same place as before. Noon tomorrow."

"Which same place? The…coffee shop?"

"Was I there?"

"No."

"So there you go." There was a pause. "Do I make you horny, baby? Fancy a shag?" The words had a very different feel when spoken by a woman with a gentle accent.

Dave shook his head. "Don't do that. It's just creepy." But he was talking to a dead line.

"Who was that?" Lori asked him.

"Prank call," he told her, looking pointedly at the phone, then back at her, before handing it over.

"The Subsection" seemed to be a more informal operation than he'd expected, although maybe his limited exposure to them and their people wasn't typical. Still, he was having to fly solo, and make more decisions, than he'd thought he would. And he didn't want to make the wrong decisions, so he was putting a lot of thought into them.

Last time, he'd been in a rental Bob had secured, presumably using a cover identity. Dave could do that for this meet, obtain a rental car using the provided credit card for his Henry Swanson ID (the bills of which were paid by a corporate cutout) …but that still involved using a credit card. And even if the satellite radio/navigation system in the rental didn't have an active subscription, the GPS unit inside the vehicle would be live, making it trackable. His Jeep, on the other hand, was over fifteen years old and had no navigation, no GPS. And six months earlier he'd secured a second license plate for it, lifted off a totaled Jeep sitting inside a junkyard. Not because he'd had a specific need for it, but you never knew….

The drive took him a few hours. He was careful never to go more than five miles over the speed limit, which didn't look out of character for the age of his vehicle. The plastic cover for the driver's side mirror was more than a little droopy after getting slightly melted in his house fire, although the Jeep hadn't taken as much damage in that fight as he had.

He pulled into the lot ten minutes before noon. There wasn't a cloud in the sky, which was a brilliant crystalline blue. Murph's giant RV was parked where it was before. There were a few cars in the lot, parked near the restrooms and the walkway to the petroglyphs, but he saw no movement.

Dave parked four spaces away from the RV, looked around as he got out, then walked toward the big vehicle. He couldn't see anything through the tinted glass, but as he approached, the door slid open with a hiss of hydraulics. Murph was there in a vintage Ocean Pacific t-shirt and board shorts, looking hugely tall as he stood on the step. "There he is," he said with a big smile. "Come on up." He beckoned with a hand.

Inside, Dave found he was far from the first to arrive. Bob was there, along with a woman he didn't recognize. She had short black hair spiked up. She wore a racerback tank top and tights over running shoes, and her outfit displayed a world-class athletic body laced with muscle—she looked ready to compete in the CrossFit Games. If it wasn't for the muscle she would have had no chest at all, but she didn't look masculine, just uber-fit, and was wearing a bit of makeup.

"You drove your own car?" Bob asked, looking out the tinted glass.

"I put different plates on it," Dave told him. After a second Bob nodded, so Dave figured he'd made a good call on that.

"What happened to your mirror?" the woman asked.

"Molotovs," Dave told her. He blinked twice. He recognized her voice, and stared at her. "Becky?"

"Becky?" Murph said, looking back and forth between the two of them.

"My cover name, when I was on mission," she said.

"You do not look like a Becky, Dimi," Murph said.

"She did when she was there," Dave said. He kept staring at her, shocked at how different she looked. Which, he realized, had been the point of the disguise. Under the wig and glasses and baggy dress she'd almost seemed chubby. She was not chubby, she had defined abs. And prominent delts. Impressive quads. He guessed she probably ran about 150 pounds, with maybe fifteen percent body fat

—which for a woman was very low. Hell, for a guy it was low. "What's Dimi short for? Dimitra?" That was the only girl's name he could think of. Maybe Dimi was a nickname unrelated to her actual name.

"Don't ask don't tell," she told him. "Molotovs?" she asked, one perfectly curved eyebrow rising up.

Bob sighed and told her, "Since we all know you're going to Google his name in conjunction with 'molotovs' I'll just save you the trouble and tell you to search 'Pima Jack' when you've got a few minutes. There's even a video," he said drily. Bob looked at Dave. "Don't bother trying to find any information on her. You won't. Now, can we get to why we're here?" He looked from them to Murph.

"Right," Murph said. He walked toward his computer setup, and waved for them to follow him. "Okay, so, to start off, I was bored, so—"

"You were *bored*?" Bob said incredulously. "I know how much you're doing for us, and there are three other full-time teams. Plus your transcendental SkyNet quantum computer project on the side that will probably end humanity. Do you even sleep?"

Murph shrugged. "Kinda sorta. Anyway, I got bored, and decided to see if I really could put Daniel Kim in Cleveland when we thought he was there, doing the deed on Blinkenschaal." Bob gave him half a frown, and in response Murph said, "We're making our own way with this thing," he waved a hand at the assembled group. "I always want to dot the I's and cross the Ts before we get to the life or death or ruin-someone's-life-forever part." And he gave Bob a direct look.

Bob nodded. "Fair enough."

Murph continued, "He would have been travelling low key, maybe under cover, but Cleveland is far enough from

D.C. that I figured there was a good chance he flew, rather than drove. And, he wouldn't have taken a company jet, or one registered to one of their shell companies, not for a black op like this. So I did a brute force attack on the likely commercial airports."

"Um..." Dave said, raising his hand like he was in class.

"Hacked into their systems," Murph told him. "Specifically their camera footage. Just about everything inside an airport, outside the bathrooms, is caught on camera. And the video is stored digitally, so the feds can review it at their leisure. I started with Cleveland first, as there's really only one airport, and it's small. Well, comparatively. Smallest commercial airport I've ever been in was Manhattan, Kansas, you can throw a rock over the terminal. Anyway, you run facial recognition on the arrivals—I used my own recog software for that, the government's is shit in comparison—and then if you get a hit you figure out what flight he was on, backtrack it. I had a good time window, with the far end the date of Blink's death and the near end a day this side of that email he sent, saying he was on it. That's a ninety-six-hour window or so. Kim could have already been in Cleveland at the time he sent that email, but I don't think so."

"How do you know what he looks like?" Dave asked. "Isn't this guy a super spook or something? You get into his personnel file in the CIA?"

Murph held a finger up. "Ah, now that's where things get fun. You know he's going to be using a cover identity... but, my hope was, not a disguise, at least not en route, since nobody knows who he is, where he is, what he's doing, and he's in the U.S., where his bosses control everything, not a hostile country. So, first off, I got into the passenger manifests from any flights that came into Cleveland from any airport in or around D.C. Which, unfortunately, is too many. Then I checked to see which of those names flew back to the D.C. area before the coroner's report said Blink died."

"How many is that? Wouldn't that be a lot of people?" Dave said.

Murph nodded. "Hundreds. But you eliminate the women, and run the rest through all the databases to get profiles. Some are too young, some are too old, some have health problems that would eliminate them. Kim is likely an Asian, so we can cross off the black guys. Then I dove into raw surveillance footage from the Cleveland Hopkins International Airport in that time frame I was talking about. Even with all the cameras some people don't look up, so facial recognition can't get a full scan on a certain percentage of people, but it gets most of them, and you can use that to thin the herd, so to speak. So I just let my system loose on all that footage and it crunched along and gave me three possibles. Asian males of the right age, who flew from D.C. to Cleveland and back in the right time frame. I ran the names my search produced through everything I could, but it was his face that gave him away."

"Let me guess," Bob said. "Social media."

"Bingo!" Murph said.

"No way a black bag guy is on social media," Dimi said, her arms crossed.

"But his sister is," Murph said with a smile. "One of those faces in the airport turned up in the background of three family photos she's posted in the last five years to Facebook. Birthday, Christmas and something else. And very helpfully, after what sounds like an ugly divorce, she's gone back to using her maiden name, Kim. It's just about the most common Korean surname, but, still, that eliminated any doubt I had this was the guy." His fingers flew over his keyboard, and then he clicked his mouse twice. Stills, obviously culled from the airport security footage, popped up on his monitors. Daniel Kim was an Asian male with a medium build. He had bland, unremarkable looks, and was probably in his thirties, but with bone structure that would hide his age well. Murph typed some more, and the mentioned Facebook posts appeared on a different monitor.

"He flew under the name James Lee. Unfortunately, that's even more common than Daniel Kim, but it appears that he's used that cover at least twice before in the last three years for travel. Once to fly to Seattle—and from there I'm guessing he went either to Asia or Canada, covertly. And he flew to Mexico City nine months ago."

"Two trips in three years?" Dave said.

Bob knew what he meant. "I'm sure it's just one of half a dozen cover identities he's got." He looked at Murph. "Were you able to confirm his employment?"

"His sister's life is an open book spread messily all over social media, so finding out his age and hometown was easy. As for confirming employment…no, not exactly. I did find his original federal job application to the State Department, almost twenty years ago. Not sure how he got from there to where he is now…."

"Someone, probably in the field, downrange, noticed he had the right aptitude for wet work," Bob observed. "For guys who do what he does, there is not a traditional hiring process. Okay, so we've verified that a guy tasked with doing the deed in an email from the DDO was in fact in Cleveland at the time, using a cover identity. So," he looked around at their faces, "that is all the confirmation I need that James Blinkenschaal was murdered by the CIA.

Anyone disagree?" Nobody did. Then Bob looked at Murph. "So, you figure out why?"

"I don't know."

"You don't know?" Dave said. He looked from Murph to Bob and back. "You pulled us off surveillance."

"I don't know *exactly* why," Murph clarified. "But it has to do with what I found. What you found. And when I pulled on it, that thread…" Murph looked at Dave and Dimi. "You saw four people working at Babble who didn't fit in. Got me three license plates. You know, before that, I ran down everyone I could determine was working in that building, every business, and nothing popped. The reason why is because those guys you spotted, they're not listed as employees of Babble. Because they aren't employees of Babble."

Bob said, "Babble, the search engine company, right? That's who we're talking about?"

"Yeah. They've also got their own Twitter clone that's not doing so well."

"We got them going in and out of the Babble offices several times. Wearing the uniform. And ID badges," Dave said.

"They're working at Babble, but not *for* Babble. Because they are employees of the U.S. Department of Justice."

"They…what?" Dave said.

"Oh," Bob said, blinking. "I know what this is. FBI, DOJ set up their own crew inside Babble."

"Exactly," Murph said.

"Why?" Dave asked.

"To monitor social media posts. Monitor, and censor. Once I figured out what was going on I got into the Babble servers at that site. Saw what that team was doing. Content suppression, shadow bans so nobody sees your posts, flagging some posts so the users could be visited by federal agents at their houses. And that includes scanning any private messages sent or received using the Babble messaging app, and all travel data harvested by the Babble navigation app. And none of it, that I saw, for criminal activity, it was only for posts that had political content that went against the official government/media narrative. They also maintain the real-time link between the Babble servers and an off-site facility run by the NSA, so everything anyone types into Babble is immediately scanned and evaluated."

"Not metadata, actual data?" Dimi asked. Murph nodded.

"This is all a clear violation of the Fourth Amendment, right?" Dave said, looking around for confirmation. "Protection against unreasonable search and seizure. It's why you need a search warrant just to get into somebody's phone. Warrants for wiretaps. Not even mentioning the clear First Amendment violation you get when the government is censoring political free speech. And Babble is just… hosting these guys?"

"You don't need a warrant if they're handing over the information voluntarily," Bob said. "If they're a willing co-conspirator. No warrants, subpoenas, or formal requests necessary. Have to keep a lid on that disinformation and misinformation after all. You can't let just anyone criticize the government or question the official narrative." He shrugged, then crossed his arms across his chest. "This is well-known. People know the FBI has agents stationed at Facebook and Google, combing through posts they deem dangerous, worrisome, or offensive. Several mainstream media outlets have written about Facebook, and Twitter before it was bought by Elon, being riddled with FBI and CIA. Supposedly ex, but saying you're ex-CIA is like saying you're only a little bit pregnant. Hell, the FBI actually has an office at the Facebook headquarters. This isn't anything new, most of the telecommunication corporations had in-house offices for alphabet agencies for decades. It's been going on since before the fed broke up Ma Bell."

"Again, fourth amendment? Search warrants?" Dave said. "Am I being naïve?"

Bob nodded. "Yes. When you're the federal government and you can shut them down or make it impossible for them to be profitable, you do what you're told. You cooperate fully. Even if it is in clear violation of the constitution and federal law. And if you're Google, Babble, whoever, you keep your fucking mouth shut if you know what's good for you. It was bad before, but after the Patriot Act, and the FISA court, warrantless surveillance became the norm. Everybody knows it, but no politician on either side in Washington does more than grumble about it, and then only when they're running for reelection. The CIA is specifically prohibited, by law, from operating in the U.S. When it came out recently that they were involved in January 6, spinning up people, even the FBI, you know what happened?"

"Nothing?"

Bob nodded. "Nothing. There's a reason we're here, doing what we're doing."

"So once I was in," Murph said, "I started tracking their communications, and it's not just them. Not just those four guys. They're just one cell of a whole system, a web of federal government teams in every Babble regional office, in every Google and Facebook office. They don't directly communicate much, everything goes to a central hub, but when alerts go out from Big Brother to be on the lookout for certain key words, they all get the same notice. Tracking them all wasn't hard, although it took a bit of time. I've mapped out all of the FBI/DOJ observation posts, listening posts, whatever you want to call them. I mean, I knew that the government was monitoring everything on the internet in real time, and America is still amateurs compared to the Great British Surveillance State, but still, this kinda sucks. These are hundreds of guys, federal employees, being paid with tax dollars to spy on and censor the American people, people who are doing nothing but exercising their First Amendment rights."

Murph looked around at them. "You know, Google began as a DARPA grant. They got their funding as part of a joint CIA/NSA program to see how people gather online, to chart that through search engine aggregation. One year later they launched Google, became a military contractor. They got Google Maps basically by purchasing a CIA satellite, or the product and software to use it." He shook his head. "Shit like this used to be done out of CIA station houses, embassies, and consulates, officially, pursuing known bad guys. Overseas. Now the government doesn't seem to give a shit about actual terrorists, because they're not a threat to their power. Now it's all being done by agents working in-house at Google, at Facebook, at Babble, and it's not just that they're turning over the information without warrants, the information is going straight to government agents stationed at these companies, and they're using their algorithms right there to process people for their potential threat level to the powers that be. Political posts. Plus running all the images through facial recognition software, the videos through voice recognition software, generating digital profiles of everyone. Shit, it was less than a year ago when word leaked out that the FBI was running DSAC, their secret portal for building profiles on problematic people who dared to post things on social media opposed to the COVID lockdowns, gun control, vaccine mandates, or who were for border security. Labelling them domestic extremists. Any government that tells you sugary breakfast cereal is better for you than red meat, well, they hate you and want you dead."

"Nothing surprises me anymore," Dimi said. "If you expect disappointment, you'll never be disappointed." Dave glanced at her. He was pretty sure the quote had originated in a Spider-Man movie.

Bob looked up at the ceiling, thinking. "If I remember correctly, during a congressional hearing with the FBI Director, it came out that over a twenty-year period the government had engaged in over a quarter million illegal FISA 702 searches. And nobody was ever charged with a crime. So, it's not news, not really." He gestured at Murph's monitors. "We didn't discover who really killed JFK here. But this landed in our lap. In our faces. We now know about a discrete U.S. government organization specifically tasked with doing something that is in clear violation of at least the First *and* Fourth Amendments to the Constitution, at best exploiting a loophole in federal law. In addition to it being just plain wrong. And I feel we've got an obligation to do something about it." He looked around. Nobody disagreed. He looked at Murph. "And you're in their computer systems?"

Murph nodded. "I'm in all their shit. They're running different, better security protocols, because of who they are, where they come from, but yeah. In addition to the personal and government cell phones they've got, at least for these four guys in Cleveland. Give me a few days and I can be in every phone and laptop any of these guys use at work or home."

"You mean all of them?" Bob said. "All the dot-gov guys posted in Babble or Facebook offices around the country?"

"Yeah. Babble, not Facebook, that's a whole other web that I'm not specifically hooked in to. There's a hundred of them, more, just at Babble, so it would take me at least a few days."

"This is horrible, it makes me want to scream, but it still doesn't tell us why Blinkenschaal was murdered," Dave said. "Or did I miss something?"

Murph jabbed a finger at Dave a few times, agreeing with him. "Right. So I put in a query to my system. You've just got to ask the right questions. On one of the days that we, that you, think Blink had his camera set up, covering the doors of the building in Cleveland, Thomas Hutton, Deputy Director of the NSA, and Olathe Granderson, the Deputy Director for the CIA's Directorate of Digital Innovation, were in Cleveland for a meeting about internet security. With several high-ranking executives of telecom and media firms, according to a news blurb I saw on a tech site, that was only posted days after the fact. The meeting took place at a hotel downtown. But my guess is, after they finished their meeting, either Hutton or Granderson, or both, stopped by the Babble regional office you were surveilling. Where Blink had his camera set up. Maybe to give the team there an attaboy for their work spying on their fellow Americans."

Dimi said, "Thereby tying the NSA and the CIA in to their operation there. But would they really care enough to kill someone over that? After all, what they're doing is kind of public knowledge."

"Who else but people doing security for an NSA executive would have even noticed a camera like that?" Murph asked. "And what do they care about some Cleveland PI's life? Better safe than sorry, right?"

"I hate this," Dave said. "There are no straight lines in this bullshit."

Dimi nodded. "Shadows and snakes," she said in agreement. She'd made her peace with it.

"It would be very embarrassing if that video came out," Bob observed. "Not enough to get them to stop them doing what they're doing, of course, it would take open warfare to make that happen, but if someone rolled out that footage during a congressional inquiry it might be enough to end a career, especially if the congresscritter was smart enough to get them to deny it before he rolled tape and proved them a liar." He looked at their faces. "So, the question is, what do we do about it? My background, I much prefer problems that can be solved by shooting them in the face. It's quite cathartic. That's not going to work here. What we do, generally, is the very definition of asymmetrical warfare. It has to be, since we don't have the numbers or hardware to take on the government straight on. Our greatest strength is that they don't know we exist. So, with that in mind… anyone got any ideas?"

"I feel dirty," Dave said, not quite an hour later, as their meeting broke up and they prepared to depart.

"You feel dirty?" Murph said from in front of his screens. "*You* feel dirty?" He gestured at his monitors. Dave glanced at them, then quickly away. Murph went back to typing, his fingers tapping the keys almost angrily.

"We all voted," Bob said. "It was unanimous."

Dave nodded, and looked around. Dimi was using the bathroom in the RV. "I know. It's just…"

Bob nodded. "You tend to shoot all of your problems in the face too. No gray area in a gunfight. And this is dirty, I won't lie. But it's a dirty game we're playing. A dirty game of lies. Doing something ugly for the right reasons is exactly our specialty. And I can't think of any better way to expose this entire federal monitoring network and shut it down. It will only be temporary, I have to be honest, but...small victories."

"Yeah, I suppose."

"They're going to know somebody fucked 'em. Hopefully they'll blame the Chinese or something." That thought made him turn. "Murph, you want to give them a false trail to follow, for blame?"

"Sure," Murph said, his fingers a blur as he typed, not looking away from the monitor directly in front of him. "You care where it leads?"

"I like China," Bob said. He looked at Dave, who shrugged. "China," he told Murph. "Let the head shed try and figure out their motives."

"On it. This is going to take me at least a few days to set up, maybe more, and then we've got to throw out the baited hook. Hooks. I don't know how long the staties might take to do something. How long their investigation will take. But, I guess, we're giving them something they just can't ignore."

"Make sure you do. We're not on a clock," Bob told him. "It takes however long it takes. Anyway," Bob said, to Dave. "Moving on. I will email you a link to a covert entry class. Sign up for it. It's not just lockpicking, he has an excellent, well-rounded approach to getting into places other people don't want you to be. It's not a government or military school either, although he does teach cops and firefighters. He also teaches urban surveillance, and you can sign up for one of those courses as well. I don't know if it will include anything you don't already know how to do, or have done, but in that case just treat it like a refresher. And I'm going to arrange a tactical school for you, maybe next month, depending on when Cracker's got an opening. It won't be just you, there will be a few familiar faces there. For them it'll be a refresher."

"Cracker?"

"Former teams guy, makes a living training interesting groups of people from around the world. Probably have you do a five-day course to dip your toe in, combatives, room clearing, and team tactics. Good job in Cleveland, if I didn't say that already."

Dave shrugged. "I barely did anything. My friend's actually the one who spotted those guys."

Bob nodded. He knew that. "But you were the one who brought him in. We do a lot of that, using whatever resources we have available to us. I'll be in touch."

Dave nodded, opened the RV's big door, and stepped down. Behind Bob, Dimi came out of the bathroom. Together they watched Dave through the windows as he headed toward his car. She'd been on her sterile smartphone as she'd sat on the toilet. Googling 'Pima Jack' and the other name which had come up, 'David Anderson', connected to the internet through the RV's untraceable satellite uplink.

"I was curious just what the hell he brought to the table," she said. "To our table. But he's a straight-out old-fashioned gunfighter. I didn't even know people like him existed anymore, outside of Special Forces."

"They don't."

"SWAT cops, bank robbers, mob thugs, and cartel soldiers…unless the news stories are bullshit?"

"They aren't. Add a GRS team to that list."

"What?" she blurted, jerking her head in surprise. GRS was like the CIA's private Blackwater. It was GRS operators who'd been involved in the "13 Hours in Benghazi" incident. Most everyone GRS employed were former SF operators with combat experience.

"Although you won't find that detail anywhere on the web," he told her.

"Seriously?"

"In addition to a few other things that never made the press."

"Why? I mean..." She shrugged and waved her hands. Anderson didn't seem like anyone special.

Bob told her, "We've all got our secrets. He's got more than his share of luck, good and bad. He's got a few things to learn about *this* world, but if shit goes kinetic he's a good guy to have by your side. And that's from personal experience."

"Yeah?" She looked at him, but he provided no further details, just smiled and shrugged enigmatically. Together they watched Dave drive off in his Jeep.

TWENTY-ONE

The Quiet Room

"I'm not sure why you consider this a big deal," his assistant said as they walked down the corridor. "Or any deal at all. We get accused of things we didn't do all the time. We get accused of things we did do all the time. And we simply deny them."

"When they say they have evidence, when they go to the press, that makes it something completely different," CIA Director Robert MacGregor said, as they stopped outside the SCIF. He pulled his phone out of his suitcoat pocket and stuck it in one of the clear plastic slots. As Gerald was about to do the same, MacGregor shook his head at him. "This won't take long. You can just wait out here."

That gave Gerald pause, but only someone very familiar with his mannerisms would have caught the half-second hitch in his movements. "Of course." He kept his phone in his hand—he always had emails and texts to follow up on—and took a step to the side. MacGregor opened the door and went inside.

The interesting thing about SCIFs wasn't the rooms

themselves but rather what was discussed inside them. Sensitive Compartmented Information Facilities—pronounced "skiffs"—were generally bland windowless rooms shielded from any sort of outside monitoring, electronic or otherwise. There were a number of them at Langley.

He was the last to arrive. Seated at the table was Mason Phillips, Deputy Director of the CIA for Operations, and Paul Irving, the CIA's Chief of the Near East/South Asia Division, based in Amman, Jordan. Neither man looked happy.

MacGregor sat at the head of the table and looked down it. "So what do we know?"

The two men traded a look, then Phillips said, "Abu al-Tunisi was definitely taken out. Him and his whole team—two lieutenants, maybe three, and the entire security team."

"How?"

"Ambush."

MacGregor shook his head. "No, I mean, don't these guys usually use car bombs? IEDs? And this wasn't that, correct?"

Irving leaned forward. "Correct. They were hit by a team, inside a building. Shot."

MacGregor turned his attention on the division chief. "You pushed back this meeting so you could look into this."

Irving nodded. "There were U.S.-issued concussion grenades and specialty ammunition recovered at the scene. They had it on display during that interview with the BBC." Also during the interview with Al Jazeera, but he didn't care about them.

Mason Phillips got MacGregor's attention and shrugged. "They could have gotten that anywhere."

The Subsection

"I was told it's hard to come by," Irving said, in defense. "The ammunition in particular."

"Apparently not hard enough," MacGregor said, "because we didn't do this raid. Or am I missing something?"

The DDO leaned forward, a sour look on his face. "I'm still looking into it," Phillips said. "But no American government or military forces were involved in this incident. Officially or off the books."

"What about private contractors? American private contractors?"

Phillips shook his head. "Not that I've been able to determine. As for the incident itself, there wasn't satellite coverage of the area at the time in question, and we didn't know about the hit for at least a day afterward, and had to play a bit of catch-up. We've since gone over the sigint harvested in the area and are busy analyzing it, as well as flight manifests, running facial recognition on any feeds from public cameras in any cities in the area, the usual, in hopes we spy a familiar face that will give us a lead."

Irving shook his head. "If I had to guess, ISIS took him out themselves in an internal power struggle."

"Do we have any evidence to back up that theory?" MacGregor asked, looking between the two men. They shook their heads.

"But it makes more sense than a team of American operators taking him out," Irving said.

MacGregor nodded and jabbed a finger at the man. "Now you're getting to the meat of it. Forget the who for a moment, look at the why. The why will tell you the who. So…why would somebody want to take al-Tunisi out?"

"Power struggle in the organization," Irving repeated.

"Maybe his people found out he was working with the Americans," MacGregor said.

"If they had, I'm pretty sure they would have taken credit for taking out a traitor, a lackey of the Great Satan, rather than blaming the assassination on us," Phillips said.

"Well, needless to say, the chances of us being able to recruit anybody in the region to fill Tunisi's shoes are fucked. Nobody there will trust us now no matter how much cash we promise. ABLE seems to be in a holding pattern. At least until we come up with an alternate avenue."

"The press secretary was asked about this at the White House daily briefing today," Phillips told the Director.

"By the BBC?" Irving asked.

Phillips shook his head, and looked from Irving to MacGregor. "No, AP, apparently they've picked up the story. The press secretary issued a generic denial, as she's been instructed. This story doesn't have legs," he assured the Director. "It's not going anywhere."

"That's not the point," MacGregor said. "Somebody took out al-Tunisi and we got the blame. Deliberately, or so it seems. I want to know who did the deed. The who will tell us the why, the why will tell us the who. Find me answers."

The two men at the other end of the table traded a look, and they both nodded at MacGregor. Phillips took the lead, because he was the senior man. "We'll keep digging."

TWENTY-TWO

The Wheeled Confessional

He'd barely brought the RV to a stop when he saw Hannah jogging across the parking lot, a big smile on her face. He moved to the side door and opened it. She looked up at him. "I wondered if it was as big as I remembered," she said.

"That's what a guy likes to hear," Murph said, and she burst into snorting laughter, holding a hand up in front of her mouth. When she lowered it she was smiling shyly.

"Permission to come aboard?" she said.

"That's for ships," he said. "It's not quite *that* big." He stepped to the side and she came up the steps, carrying a backpack. She was in a baggy t-shirt over tights. And looked even better than he remembered.

She took a quick glance around the RV, then moved close and gave him a kiss. "Hi," she said, looking up at him.

"Hi yourself."

"Where did you want to go?" she asked him, as he closed the door with a hydraulic hiss.

"You've got all weekend, right? Three day weekend?" It was just after noon on a Friday.

"Yeah, I don't have to be back until Monday night."

"I was thinking Lake Mead," he told her. "Unless you want to try hiking the Grand Canyon again."

"No," she said firmly.

He smiled. "It'll take about five hours," he told her. "We can stop for dinner along the way." He headed toward the driver's seat. "You want to come up here, help me navigate out of this parking lot?"

She sat down in the passenger seat. "Aren't the Lake Mead campgrounds booked weeks or months in advance?"

"Yep. But I know a guy," he said.

As she settled in, and buckled the seat belt, she told him, "I brought sunblock. Since I know you won't have any. My neck hurt for a week last time. And peeled in sheets, it was gross." She glanced over. "You look tired," she said, studying him.

He sighed. "You ever see something that makes you seriously consider humanity's value as a species, whether we have anything left to offer the planet, or whether Bill Gates is right in thinking the world would be better off with most of us dead?"

"Geez," she said.

"Yeah, sorry." He glanced over at her. "It's really great to see you. You look amazing."

She rolled her eyes. "I look like a slob."

Murph was staring out into traffic as he piloted the RV around a turn. Without looking at her he said, "You're fucking beautiful, inside and out, and don't let anyone tell you different. Not even you."

The Subsection

Devils Tower was America's first National Monument, and Lake Mead was the first designated "National Recreation Area". It was formed by the Hoover Dam on the Colorado River, just west of the Grand Canyon. As it wasn't a natural lake but rather an artificial reservoir formed along the lake bed, it was both oddly-shaped and very large, over 100 miles long when at maximum capacity. That created a lot of available space for recreation, and there were fifteen official camping sites along the shores of the lake.

"This looks a lot like the Grand Canyon," Hannah had said, as they'd pulled into the park. She was peering out the big windshield, and they sat up high enough to see over the other vehicles.

"But flatter," Murph said. "We are at the ass end of the Grand Canyon. It's the same river, the Colorado. But no climbing. We're in civilization. Kind of."

The size of his RV limited Murph a bit, but only a bit. He secured a campsite at the Temple Bar Marina RV Park, which was in Arizona about twenty miles due east of the Hoover Dam which sat just on the edge of the Nevada state line. The campsites had full electrical hookups, and there was a coin laundry, public restrooms, and coin operated showers if your RV didn't have one or you wanted more room to move. The park was a bit run down, but Murph didn't care about that as he only needed a parking spot and a hook-up, he had everything else he needed inside his vehicle. He wasn't sure if Hannah wanted to do a bunch of things or a whole lot of nothing, but there was hiking in the area, beaches, boats for rent, and beautiful desert scenery in every direction.

"How far are we from Vegas?" she asked. She knew the Hoover Dam was close to Las Vegas.

"From here it's about an hour drive."

She looked at him. "You don't like Vegas?" It seemed clear from his tone.

He liked the spectacle of Vegas. What he didn't like was all the surveillance cameras. He shrugged. "I don't hate it, it's just not my scene. I'm more of a natural wonders rather than man-made wonders fan."

"Oh." She sounded disappointed.

"You like Las Vegas?"

She shrugged. "I don't know. I've never been."

Murph looked at her. He forgot how much younger she was. She probably hadn't done a lot of things. "We'll have to fix that," he told her. "But not this weekend, please, I need some quiet time."

He slept straight through the night on Friday, something he rarely did. It wasn't the sex—well, it wasn't just the sex, which was just as nice with her as he'd remembered. Maybe it was because he was more relaxed with her there.

But Saturday night, even after a day of hiking and swimming, a good dinner, and more good sex—hell, great sex—he still woke up after a few hours. Just after midnight, according to his watch. And it didn't feel like he was going to be able to fall back asleep any time soon.

He extricated himself from her long limbs, pulled on his boxers, and padded out into the RV. There were faint night lights down low, to keep you from stubbing your toe, but the brightest source of illumination was the nearly-full moon flooding the area with cool light. Murph wasn't sure what he should do—grab a book and a beverage and sit in one of the chairs, or maybe camp himself down in front of the computer and do a little work? But he knew that if he got in front of the computer he'd be at it until dawn, and that wouldn't do. He was still standing there, undecided, when he spotted some movement outside the RV. He watched for a few seconds, then moved to the door and opened it with a hiss. The sudden sound made the two men outside jump.

"Something I can help you with?" Murph said. Standing on the step, combined with his height, likely made him look even bigger than he was to the two scummy, homeless-looking young men who'd been eyeing the twelve-inch Weber grill and folding plastic table they'd left outside after dinner.

They froze, one of them uttered an unintelligible sound, and then they took off. Murph watched them go until they were out of sight. Outwardly he was calm, but his heartbeat was pounding in his ears. He didn't like conflict, or confrontation. Sweat popped out on his forehead, and under his arms. He waited until his heart rate slowed, then stepped outside and collected the table. He was bringing in the grill when he got another shock.

"What are you doing?"

He jumped and nearly dropped the grill. Hannah was standing in the open door of the bedroom, hair tousled with sleep. Naked and squinting. "Holy crap," he blurted.

"What?"

He stared at her standing there naked for three long seconds, then shook his head. "Girls have no idea sometimes. Wars fought, kingdoms lost…looking at you, it all makes sense."

"What?" She was still half asleep.

"I woke up, couldn't sleep, decided to bring in the stuff we'd left outside."

"Come back to bed."

He liked the idea of that. He hadn't looked away from

her toned, tanned body, but it was clear she was ready to go back to sleep. "I'm not really sleepy, I was going to read."

She yawned. "You can read in bed, it won't bother me."

"You're sure?"

"Yeah." She gave him a small smile. "You wore me out."

"I think it was the hiking and swimming, but I'll take partial credit."

He closed the door and locked it, reactivated the security system, grabbed a book, and followed her into the bedroom. He turned on a small light he had for reading. He propped his head up on two pillows, and she snuggled in next to him. "What are you reading?"

He showed her the cover. *Economic Policy: Thoughts for Today and Tomorrow*, by Ludwig von Mises. "If you've ever heard of Mises' 'Six Lessons', this is what they're talking about," he told her.

She frowned. "You sure you're a construction worker?"

"Why, don't I look like a construction worker?"

She huffed into his chest. "During dinner, you just casually used the word vertiginous. Correctly."

"Did I? Maybe I heard it in an episode of *Phineas and Ferb*. And who says construction workers can't be smart?"

"Yeah, but a wall fell on *your* head." She was smiling.

He snorted. "Maybe it gave me superpowers." He smiled, then said, "I can read it to you. It'll help you fall asleep faster. He opened the book, and began reading from the introduction, penned by Bettina Bien Greaves in 1995:

"The ideal economic policy, both for today and tomorrow, is very simple. Government should protect and defend against domestic and foreign aggression the lives and property of the persons under its jurisdiction, settle disputes that arise, and leave the people otherwise free to

pursue their various goals and ends in life. This is a radical idea in our interventionist age."

When he looked down, she was already fast asleep, one arm draped across his chest.

Saturday was great—they slept in, then rented a canoe and paddled to various landing sites around the lake, hiking around a few. Then they had a great dinner cooked on the grill. Which he remembered to bring in when they headed to bed. He assumed there wouldn't be any sex, she was falling asleep in the lawn chair after dinner, staring up at the stars, but getting into bed seemed to wake her up a bit and…and every time it was just as good as the time before, if not better.

Afterward, they both fell asleep, exhausted. And after the day he'd had, a normal person would have slept through until morning. But he'd never slept much, or very well, and woke up an hour after falling asleep, feeling like he'd gotten eight hours of shuteye. His brain racing. Full of thoughts, ideas.

Murph extricated himself from her, pulled on a t-shirt and shorts, and padded out of the room. He didn't have to boot anything up, his computer was always running, there were always things that needed doing for the various teams, or for himself, but he did have to wiggle a mouse and hit a few keys to wake up some dormant screens. He didn't turn on any lights, and just the glow of the monitors lit up his face as he was typing.

Ten minutes later he heard a tapping. Then a pounding. He looked around, thinking that it was Hannah. But the noise was in the wrong direction. He got up and moved over to the door. The blinds there were angled halfway open, and through the tint he saw two figures outside the RV's door. The same two guys he'd run off the night before. The window tint was dark, but there was almost no light outside the RV, and he was lit up by the glow of the various monitors, so they could see him.

"Open up, man," the more scruffy of the two said to him, looking up at him through the glass.

"Yeah," the guy in back said, bouncing on his feet.

The two of them looked like veteran homeless, with deep tans and dirty faces. They probably weren't as old as they looked, but the life aged a person quickly.

"Go away," Murph said, just loud enough to be heard. He didn't want to wake Hannah, and he'd left the door to the bedroom open.

"Open up man, we're taking your shit," the man at his door said. He thumped it down low, then lifted his hand. Murph's heart pounded in his chest as he saw the pistol in the man's grimy fist. A battered revolver.

"Yeah, man," his backup vocalist said. "We knows you got to have some nice shit, this is the nicest RV I evah seen."

Murph tried to get his heartrate under control. "Go away," he said, even more firmly.

The scruffy armed robber almost looked offended. He lifted the revolver up higher and waved it between them. "Do you not see this? Open the goddamn door." His voice was a bit muffled through the glass.

"No. Go away."

"What? You—I will shoot you! I will shoot you right through this fucking window and climb in there," he said, pointing the small revolver at Murph. Murph's heartrate jumped again, he couldn't help it. He felt himself getting sweaty. He really didn't like confrontation.

"No you won't. The windows are bulletproof."

"The fuck they are." The man banged the muzzle of the revolver against the glass. It made a dull thud. "Open the fucking door."

Murph sighed and shook his head. "Just go away. I'm not even going to call the cops, you can't get in."

The man was getting more agitated. "I swear to fucking God I'm going to shoot you. Right in the fucking face." He waved both his hands around, then pointed the gun back at Murph.

"Go ahead," Murph told him, sounding calm even as sweat popped out all over his body. "I don't know if the bullet will get stuck in the glass or bounce off and hit you, I really don't."

"Fuck you man, I'm going to kill you!"

"Either shoot, or don't, but I've got to get back to work."

There was a rushed, whispered conversation outside his door. "You got to come out sometime, man. Gotta open the door sometime," he said, as if he was announcing the cure for cancer. He seemed very proud of his conclusion.

"I could just drive off," Murph said. "But I don't want to. How about this—if you're still here when I want to come out, I'm coming out with a shotgun."

"What?"

"What do you think the chances are I've got an RV like this and I don't have a gun in here? Go bother someone else." He stared at them. There was another whispered conference, then they called him names, flipped him off, and stomped away into the darkness.

He found he was shaking. He leaned against the door a few seconds, then walked back to his chair and sat down. He let out a shuddering breath he hadn't known he was holding in.

"Is that window really bulletproof?"

"Jesus Christ!" He jerked so hard he nearly fell out of his chair. Hannah was standing in the open doorway, the sheet wrapped around her naked body. "What?"

"Is it? Bulletproof?"

"Yeah, yeah. You don't think I'd bluff him, do you, standing out there waving a gun in my face?"

Her face scrunched in a small frown. "Do you even have a shotgun?"

"Yeah." He decided not to lie to her. He didn't want to lie to her.

"Yeah?" She peered at him. "Show me."

"Why?"

"Just show me."

He looked at her for a few long seconds, then reached far underneath the desk with his long arm, past where his knees would be if he scooted the chair all the way in, grabbed, and pulled. Her eyes went wide when she saw the shotgun.

"What's that?"

"It's a shotgun."

"Is it?"

He looked from her to the long black gun in his hand, then back to her. "Yeah. It's a Beretta." A Beretta A300 Ultima Patrol, to be specific, but he rightly assumed she didn't care about the exact model. "The kind of shotgun SWAT guys would use. I don't know anything about guns, but I know someone who does. He recommended this for protection. It doesn't look like a duck gun, because it's not for ducks." He didn't want to keep holding it, so he laid it across his thighs. Which felt weird too, but he wasn't sure what the right move was.

She frowned, and chewed at her lip. Her eyes moved

from the shotgun to the screens behind him. "You know, I've got a minor in computer science," she said. "And I don't even recognize that language." Her eyes darted back and forth, trying to make sense of the code he'd been typing, then came back to him. He opened his mouth, then closed it. He didn't know what to say.

"Are you a drug dealer?" she asked.

"What? No!" He fought the urge to laugh.

"A…money launderer for a drug dealer?"

He did laugh then. "No. I do computer stuff. No drugs, no cash. Just…tilting at windmills. I have done, am doing nothing wrong." He scooted his chair back, then crawled under his desk. He stuck the shotgun back in the spring loaded, padded clamps hidden in the shadows back near the wall. When he came back out she was back to chewing her lip. She'd noticed his word choice.

"Wrong? What about illegal?"

Murph opened his mouth, closed it, then said, "Jaywalking is illegal. Driving one mile an hour over the speed limit is illegal. There are so many laws on the books that there's nobody in this country old enough to be out of diapers that hasn't broken a law, mostly unintentionally. But am I doing anything wrong? Am I a bad guy? No. Definitely not. I am a good guy. I'm one of the good guys."

"Nobody thinks they're the bad guy," she told him. "Not even the bad guys."

He thought about that for a bit. "I guess you're right. And I worry about it every day."

"Just computer stuff? Are you a hacker?"

"Yeah. Kinda."

"But you don't steal money?"

He shook his head. "I've got all the money I need."

"From what? And don't tell me a wall fell on your head."

"I wrote some programs back in the day. Software for some companies, like Cisco, that made me a stupid amount of money."

"Then why the lies?"

"Before I wrote code for the private sector, I wrote it for the federal government. For the NSA. Doing some really secret stuff. And I…still dip my toe into that world. Once you're in, it's hard to get out." He knew he shouldn't be telling her any of it. He had a cover story all ready, if and when he had to explain anything, but when the time came he told her the truth. Or most of it. He didn't want to lie to her. Yes, he'd practically just met her. Barely knew her. And she was ten years younger than him. But she seemed older than her age. It felt like he'd known her for years. There was definitely something between them, something other than sex. Although there was also the sex, which was great. He didn't have a lot of experience with girls, he sometimes still thought of himself as fat, and it often affected his confidence with the opposite sex, but when their clothes came off he and Hannah always seemed to be on the same wavelength. Hell, clothes off or on, he loved talking with her. Loved being around her, even if they were just sitting in silence. He'd never experienced that before. He didn't want to lose it.

She frowned and thought for a bit. "Is that why you're all with the conspiracy theories?" She was never quite sure how serious he was about that.

"Yeah. I know how many of them aren't theories. It's… well, honestly, you don't want to know. And I can't tell you."

She chewed at her lower lips again. She probably had no idea just how sexy it was. Her eyes roamed over the monitors behind him. "What's that?" she asked, nodding at lines of scrolling text.

He glanced at it. "I'm networking some cell phone numbers, and cross-checking them against other associated data, trying to track down everything on the phones, and everything I can find about a quarry in Illinois. Using, basically, an AI program, that I wrote."

"Why do you care? What's so important about a quarry?"

He shook his head. "It's not for me. And I don't know, that's the point. Burner cellphones associated with at least one known terrorist have done internet searches on a quarry that's the second largest quarry of its type in the world."

"Diamond? Silver? Lithium or something like that?"

He shook his head. "Bulk stone and sand and aggregates, that are priced by the ton. It doesn't make sense, and it's weird, so it pinged my system." Every word out of his mouth dug him in deeper, gave her more information she shouldn't have. And yet he couldn't stop himself.

"Terrorists? Like in the middle east?"

"Wouldn't that be nice. No. They're middle eastern, but the FBI started tracking them after they crossed the border a week ago. They were in Texas, and now Arkansas."

She frowned. "The FBI knows about them? Why are they tracking them, why aren't they arresting them?"

"And that's another reason it pinged my system. It notices patterns. And things that don't fit into the patterns they should, that don't make sense. Like this. The FBI letting a known Syrian terrorist, and maybe a few accomplices, wander around inside the U.S." Possibly buying guns. That was another thing Murph was looking into, but he didn't want to mention it to Hannah. "It's a...a watchdog program, I guess you could say."

"And what happens when you find something out?"

"Then I give the information to somebody else. To the guys who actually do stuff. Like I said, I'm just the computer guy."

Hannah thought about that for a long while. Finally she said, "So the program will keep running until it finds what it's looking for? What you're looking for?"

"Yeah."

She nodded. "So come to bed."

"I couldn't sleep," he said apologetically, with a shrug.

"Who said anything about sleeping?" she said, and let the sheet around her nude body fall to the floor as she headed back into the bedroom.

"Wow," he said, blinking at the afterimage, then was out of his chair and after her.

He'd been worried, but the two scruffians never reappeared. He started driving back late Monday morning, in no rush. Things seemed to be better than ever with Hannah. Not just the sex—but definitely the sex too—but everything. Maybe it was just because he was more relaxed around her. He didn't have to hide so much. And maybe she was happier that she knew some of his secrets. He wasn't sure. Girls had always been most of a mystery to him. But she still thought his name was Kelly. He wasn't sure what to do about that, if anything. He should tell her his real name if they were going to have a future together. But who knew if that was going to happen? He had no idea what was going on in her head most of the time. He still didn't know what she saw in him. The fact that she hadn't run off when she found out he'd been keeping some pretty important secrets from her mystified him.

The Subsection

She had her bare feet up on the dash as he motored south, the tinted shade rolled halfway down the big windshield to protect him from the sun. After ignoring it for most of the weekend, she was on her phone, scrolling.

He kept glancing over at her. She was in a t-shirt and shorts. Eighties-style short shorts were back in fashion, and her legs went on forever. He could see just the bottom curve of her butt cheek. He didn't know who was in charge of women's fashion, but men everywhere owed them a favor—first it was yoga pants, where panty lines were discouraged, and now short shorts were back in fashion.

She saw him looking at her. "What are you smiling about? Keep your eyes on the road, buddy."

She was going to be graduating in less than two months. They hadn't talked much about her plans after that. He was afraid to. Especially after all the revelations this trip. "Yes ma'am, sorry."

"Ugh. Don't call me ma'am. Makes me feel old." She kept scrolling through her phone. "Wow." She shook her head. "Have you seen the news today? I guess the shit really hit the fan over the weekend."

"Really," he said, his voice neutral. "About what?"

TWENTY-THREE

CQB and Gators

Dave exited baggage claim, looked around, then pulled his phone out and sent a text. While he waited, he set down his checked bag and pulled a "tactical pen" out of his carry on. It had a thick aluminum body, meant to hold together if you had to use it as a striking implement. Better than nothing, if you were on an airplane.

He slid the pen through the thick zip-tie the Delta baggage handlers had put through the zippers of his checked bag, twisted it twice, and the zip-tie snapped. He left it on the concrete deliberately. Ever since a guy had pulled a gun out of his checked bag at a baggage carousel, loaded it, and shot a few people, the baggage crews at Delta zip-tied shut any checked bag containing a firearm before handing it over to the owner. It was a pain in the ass, and no other airline did it.

He heard a beep and looked up. A battered tan sedan idled in the traffic nearby. He peered through the glass and recognized Dimi, but just barely. She was wearing a curly-haired wig and a baggy t-shirt which hid her shape. He

The Subsection

tossed his bags into the back seat, but pulled his gun case out and brought it with him into the front seat. Dimi glanced at it but didn't say anything as he used a key to unlock the small plastic case. His unloaded pistol was inside, along with three magazines and a fifty-round box of ammo.

"It's about an hour drive," Dimi told him, as he started loading his magazines. "This week, you're Buck, I'm Peggy, and we'll be meeting Steve there."

"Okay." He'd booked the flight using his Henry Swanson ID, and worn a baseball cap and glasses in the terminals and on the plane. He'd also let his beard grow out for the past couple weeks. "Have I met Steve? Is it ?" He tried to think of any aliases Bob had used, and couldn't.

"No."

Dave looked around the interior of the car. "This yours, or a rental?" It was a Honda, but seemed to old to be a rental.

"Neither."

Dimi didn't seem to be in any mood to talk, which was fine. Dave filled his first magazine, loaded his gun, shoved it in the holster, and threaded the holster onto his belt. He started loading the other magazines. Then he paused.

"Steve, Buck, and Peggy?" he said, looking at her.

"Yeah. Why?"

"You come up with those?"

"No. Tech support booked this for us. Another old lady name for me, I guess. Which is why I chose this wig. Why?"

"Steve, Bucky, and Peggy." He could see she didn't get it. "Captain Steve Rogers, Bucky Barnes, and Agent Peggy Carter." Which was pretty funny, actually.

It took her a few seconds. Then she squinted at him. "So there's a nerd underneath all those scars?"

For a retired Navy SEAL, "Cracker" didn't look so imposing, just a middle-aged guy, medium height, medium build, with graying hair. Far more interesting was his assistant, a six-foot-eight Guatemalan, also a former SEAL, nicknamed "Pebbles", with a faint but exotic accent. And while Dave hadn't been sure what to expect from another member of the subsection, "Steve" wasn't it. Steve was about thirty, five-ten and lean, with a gymnast's build. He had good cheekbones, a strong jaw, bright blue eyes, and a big head of great jet black hair. Dave guessed if he had a profile on any dating apps very few women swiped him away. He clearly knew Dimi, and gave Dave a long look up and down, but didn't say anything.

"We're starting late so we'll take it easy today," Cracker said, as he showed them around the facility. "I've got thirty-five acres here, but it's surrounded by state forest, so my closest neighbor is almost half a mile away. Hasn't stopped them from filing complaints with the county about the noise, but I made sure I was legal on everything before I opened up, so they can go fuck themselves."

Cracker's training facility was an hour almost due west from Orlando, and there were as many palm trees as there were pines. It wasn't quite jungle in appearance, but the humidity sure wasn't what Dave was used to, coming from the high desert. "We can shoot out to a thousand meters, I've got a Simunition shoothouse, a short live-fire driving course, three obstacle courses, a bunch of handgun ranges. Oh, for those of you who've never been to Florida, you see a puddle bigger than you can jump across anywhere in this state you should assume there's a gator in it. On land even the big ones aren't a problem for a full-grown adult, especially if you're armed, but don't go swimming. You guys will be sleeping in the bunkhouse on site while you're here,

The Subsection

which means we can get started early in the morning. You've got four and a half days of close-quarters fun ahead of you—ground combatives, weapon retention, CQB, and maybe a few other surprises." CQB meant close quarters battle, which included house clearing and fighting at indoor distances.

"You train SEALs here?" Dave asked.

"A few. Mostly I train NGOs and private groups," Cracker said. "Like you. Just an FYI, if you plan to run into Deland for anything, for six months last year I had guys camping in tents on the public land right outside my gate. I haven't seen anybody for a while, but that doesn't mean they're not there."

"Camping, for six months?" Dimi said. She shook her head. "Idiots. Let me guess, FBI."

Cracker shrugged. "I presume so. Everybody on the outside listens to the PR the FBI puts out, that they're so great, but apart from HRT they're generally just a bunch of accountants and lawyers who happen to have guns. I don't know a street cop who has a good opinion of the FBI. FBI barely shoots ten people a year, I think Daytona Beach PD gets into more gunfights."

"Occasionally they can be trouble," Dave muttered, but nobody heard him.

"Just go ahead and warm up over there, we'll do a little bit of shooting before lunch," Cracker told the three of them. They put on eye and ear protection and moved to a row of plastic barrels set up about fifteen yards from an array of steel targets. There were the usual plates and silhouettes painted various colors, plus interesting targets, including a pink flamingo, a baby T. rex, and Bigfoot.

Dave loaded up from the fresh case of ammo atop one of the barrels, dumping his hollowpoints into his pocket, and alongside Dimi and Steve (whatever his real name was) shooting at the steel while Cracker and his team were running errands back and forth, setting things up for the afternoon. Steve was shooting an unremarkable Glock 19. Dimi was using a Walther PDP-F Compact, which was an interesting choice. She'd ditched the wig in the Florida humidity. Then Cracker and Pebbles walked up.

"Okay, come on this way," Cracker said. He led them over to the side and downrange, stopping in front of a plate rack. Six falling steel plates, eight inches in diameter, lined up in a row, about four feet off the ground on a metal frame. Dave had shot a lot of plate racks during his competition days. His experienced eyes told him they were about seven yards from the plate rack, minimum safe distance when shooting steel targets, unless you were using frangible ammunition.

"This isn't a shooting school, it's a tactics school, but we do a lot of shooting, and because I prefer 'big boy rules', I like to see where people are with their skill set," Cracker said. "Running a plate rack, on a timer, will do just that. At the beep you draw and keep going until you knock down all the plates or you run out of ammo. Who's first?"

"New guy," Steve said.

Dave had no problem going first, and he *was* the new guy, so he stepped up. "You loaded up?" Pebbles asked him.

"Yeah," Dave said, eyes on the plate rack, focusing.

"Okay, this is a simple drill, but doing it with people watching, on a timer, really messes with you. I think—" he heard Cracker saying somewhere behind him, as Pebbles, right in his ear, said, "Shooter ready?", and a second later the electronic beep of the timer sounded.

The Subsection

Dave had a good draw and punched out. He rode the recoil from one plate to the next, working left to right, trying to be smooth and quick, but not go so fast he'd have to fire makeup shots. He went one-for-one on the plates, then holstered. He turned and saw Cracker frowning.

"What the fuck was that?" Cracker said.

"A 3.21," Pebbles told him. "Three two one. Bingo."

"What was his first shot?"

Pebbles hit the button on the timer, working the display backward. "One oh three."

"I was trying to go slow, guarantee my hits," Dave said in explanation. "You let me run it a few more times, at this range I know I can keep it under three. If I push it I know I can do two and a halfs."

Cracker shook his head, then turned to Steve and Dimi. "As I was *saying*," he said, "as far as I'm concerned, if at this distance you can draw and knock down all six head-sized plates in five or six seconds, that's pretty damn solid. I consider that par. And if you can't do that, you need to work on your shooting." He looked at Dave, and glanced at his holster. "What are you using? A Glock? Shit. Okay, next!"

Dimi wasn't very fast, but she was accurate, and could run the plate rack in five seconds or less every time, and didn't seem to get rattled by shooting on the clock, or spectators. Dave wasn't surprised at all. Steve was faster but a little wilder—he'd have a smoking three-second run without a miss, followed up by a seven-second run where he missed more than he hit. He seemed to be trying to beat Dave, and the more he wasn't able to, the angrier he got, and the worse he shot.

Lunch was subs from Subway, brought in by Cracker's wife, who had a fat toddler on one hip and a huge German Shepherd at the other wherever she went. They ate in a covered open area big enough for twenty or more people, with a dark flat-screen on one wall, then followed Cracker and Pebbles into the big warehouse building fifty yards away.

"First rule is safety, so all real guns and ammunition and mags over there, on the table," Cracker pointed. The three of them walked off, then came back, holsters empty. Cracker nodded. He had an inert plastic blue gun in the shape of a Glock in his holster. "When I was on the teams, for every training cycle, between dedicated CQB, MOUT, shipboard operations, and everything else, we'd do two and a half months of nothing but CQB. And the DevGru guys would still say we didn't know our asses from a hole in the ground." Dave knew DevGru was Seal Team Six, who were considered the best of the best, equivalent to Delta Force, and who specialized in counterterrorism and hostage rescue. "We're going to be doing two and a half days of CQB this week, which is basically just enough for you to learn what you don't know. But I'll have you working in teams, which is very different than going solo. The main thing, you'll see, isn't movement so much as it is communication, whether it's verbal or hand signals. Okay, so who here's done CQB?"

"Um," Dave said sheepishly. All eyes turned to him. "Done it, or been trained to do it?"

After a pause, Cracker said, "Good point, I hadn't thought that you might be from Chicago or Detroit. I meant trained to do it. Formally." Both Dimi and Steve raised their hands. While staring at him. Dave just shrugged.

The Subsection

They did CQB in pairs, using dummy guns, and then guns—pistols and M4 carbines—which shot paintballs, until dusk. Then they ate barbeque, brought in by Cracker's wife from a local place. "It's a long day today, but you're getting your money's worth," Cracker said. After dinner they went back into the warehouse, where the plywood walls had been moved around to create different floorplans, and did CQB in low light, using weapon-mounted lights. Throughout the day they occasionally worked singly, but mostly in pairs. They switched around—at various times Dave was paired with Dimi, Steve, Cracker, Pebbles, or Don, a former Army Ranger on Cracker's staff. By the time they were done, at nine, everyone was sweaty and tired. "Breakfast is at eight tomorrow," Cracker told them. "No SEAL oh-dark-thirty wake up call for the paying customers."

The bunk house was just that, a single room with eight bunks on the walls and a common area in the center. There was an enclosed bathroom with a shower at one end. Dimi pulled the girl card and used it first. She came out with steam curling off her wet hair, in a tank top and silk boxers. Steve whistled at her. "Fuck off, Ma—" she started to say, then stopped herself. He glanced up at the ceiling, then at the two men with her. "Probably not bugged, but that's no reason to get sloppy."

"And we've got our phones here," Dave pointed out. "Even if they are burners, they're listening." He was subtle about it, but he gave her the once over.

"Right. What are you doing looking at me?" she asked him. "You break up with your porn star girlfriend?"

"I'm not blind," he said. "One can admire the beauty of a mountain range without feeling the need to climb the peaks…or explore the valleys." That got a laugh out of both of them.

"Porn star girlfriend?" Steve asked.

"Just a joke," Dave told him.

Steve headed toward the bathroom. "You're last, new guy," he said, over his shoulder, and slammed the door.

Dave looked at the door, then at Dimi. "Steve" had not been particularly pleasant to work with. She rolled her eyes as they heard the shower start. "Boys and their dick measuring. Even among guys who've got nothing to prove. Which he doesn't. He just doesn't like that you outshot him."

"Yeah, but he knows a lot more about CQB than I do. So do you."

She grunted in assent. "That stopped him pouting, at least. But don't tell him who you're dating, or it'll be even worse." She cocked her head to the side. "Would she care if you fucked somebody else? With her background…"

"No." Dave shook her head. "If it was just sex, it wouldn't bother her at all. But…it would bother me. So I don't. And she doesn't. Not guys, at least." She peered at him, trying to see if he was joking.

There was almost no hot water left by the time Dave got into the shower, which he suspected Steve did on purpose. Dave came out of the bathroom in boxers, still toweling his hair. Steve did a doubletake. "What the hell happened to you?"

Dave looked down at his body. "Which time?" He pointed. "That's a bullet wound, and that, and that. That's a burn, from a Molotov. That's grenade shrapnel, I think."

"You *think*?" Steve was frowning at him, evaluating him with new eyes. "Six a.m. PT?" he asked Dave aggressively.

"Sure. But I'll tell you right now you'll probably outrun me. Both of you. I'm still getting back into shape."

"After what?"

Dave didn't answer, he just pointed to various fresh, pink

scars. One of them clearly was a bullet wound. "Ah," Steve said, thoughtfully. "Right. Hmm. Maybe Cracker can cover ducking tomorrow. The difference between cover and concealment." Dave flipped him off, and Steve laughed, but the gesture also made him notice all the burns and skin grafts on Dave's fingers.

"I know what Black Widow over there can do, likes to do," Steve said, "and obviously you can shoot under pressure. You don't know how to duck, but what *can* you do?" He peered at Dave.

"That's not pressure," Dave said derisively. He added quickly, "As I'm sure you know. Um, I've got a lot of experience doing surveillance, and investigations. Not a cop," he added, as he could see the question forming on Steve's lips. "What about you?"

"Farm raised, but the life wasn't for me," was all Steve said. It was only later, as Dave was lying in the bunk, waiting to fall asleep, that he remembered the facility where the CIA trained their people for field operations was nicknamed "The Farm".

At six-thirty a.m. Dave was running alongside Steve on the gravel road which ran half a mile from the paved county street to Cracker's property. Dimi had started out with them, but then quickly left them behind. Steve seemed to be keeping pace with Dave, seeing what kind of shape he was in. Dave was wearing his usual fanny pack, with his Glock inside it.

Before he'd gotten brutalized and shot in the cartel attack which had terminated at the Pima Motel and given him his Pima Jack nickname, Dave had been running six miles every morning and doing a lot of bodyweight exercises. He'd struggled to get back into that kind of shape, in part because he kept getting reinjured. He ran for twenty minutes, slow, nine- or ten-minute miles, until he and Steve were on a sidewalk and getting passed by steady traffic, before he waved a hand and said, "I've got to turn around, or I'm going to be walking the whole way back." He was already feeling some twinges. He wasn't panting as hard as he expected, but the humidity had the sweat pouring off him.

"Sure, whatever, I'll follow you," Steve said.

They turned around. Dave jogged until they hit the dirt driveway, and ran down it until they were out of sight of the main road, then slowed to a walk. He put his hands on his hips, and glanced at Steve. Steve was sweating, but breathing easy, walking beside him.

"You're not fighting for air," Steve said, eyeing him.

"It's not my lungs," Dave said. He frowned a bit, concentrating. "My leg's burning a bit. Hope I didn't overdo it, tear something." He glanced at Steve. "You ever been shot?"

"No."

"I don't recommend it. Burns are better."

Steve gave him a confused look. "I thought burns were supposed to be worse."

Dave's shoulders twitched in a little shrug. "I guess they hurt more, but pain doesn't really bother me. Burns are only surface wounds, usually. Bullets go deeper, and mess things up. Structurally. I can fight through pain."

"You really should learn to fucking duck."

"Yeah, well."

"I got stabbed a little bit once."

Dave thought. "I don't think I've ever been stabbed. Unless the bolt handle of an AK counts."

"Did it break the skin?"

Dave snorted. "Oh yeah."

They walked in silence for a while. They heard a soft noise behind them and turned. Dimi was back, long fast strides, sprinting the last quarter mile to the facility. It barely looked like she'd broken a sweat, after forty minutes of running. She flew past them, flipping them a double bird.

"She does have a great ass," Steve said, staring after it wistfully. "But don't try anything, she'll kick your ass. Seriously. I'm still not sure if she's playing for the other team."

"Double agent?" Dave said it jokingly.

Steve laughed. "No, lesbian. Man, that's funny. I don't think she'd care if you called her a dyke, but shit, she'll kick your ass if you accuse her of working for the government as a double agent."

"You want to run some more, go ahead," Dave told him. "What'd we do, three miles?"

Steve checked his watch, which was GPS enabled. "Three and a half. How'd you get hooked up with the group?" He said it casually.

"If you don't know already, I don't think I'm supposed to be the one to tell you," Dave said. "I'm a bit new to this, but I've figured out that much." Steve didn't say anything, he just kept walking beside Dave. "The whole thing with a secret organization is nobody knows it exists, so I'm guessing most all of us got their attention, one way or another, and once they were sure of us, our…allegiances, I guess you could call them, they reached out." He hesitated, then stopped in the middle of the road, and held his hand out. "I'm Dave."

The other man looked from the hand to Dave's face, and only hesitated half a second before reaching out. "Max."

TWENTY-FOUR

Make-A-Wish

Aaron was installing drywall in the garage of their new house. There'd been some minor water damage down where the drywall met the concrete at the back of the garage, and the previous owners had just left it. Actually, they'd hidden it behind some shelves and boxes, and neither Aaron nor the worthless home inspector had spotted it until he and Arlene had rolled up in the U-Haul with their first load. At the closing the couple that owned the house gave him and Arlene the stinkeye, and had the balls to wonder out loud where they got the cash to buy the place outright. At the time he'd felt a little bit bad about telling them it was an insurance payout from the Special Olympics after his sister had burned to death in a freak hotel fire (Arlene had given him a hell of a kick under the table), but after finding the crumbling drywall he didn't feel bad at all. Fuckers.

He presumed there'd be other shit wrong with the house, a long list of minor stuff that would break or leak or fall apart in the first week or month, but Arlene was happy to be in an actual house, and it was nicer than the trailer, way nicer, so he kept his grumbles to himself.

There wasn't room for a whole lot of stuff in the trailer, even with it being a double-wide, so both he and Arlene had storage units. Moving into a larger place had been the kick in the ass he'd needed to sort through his stuff in the storage unit. Eighty percent of it he ended up throwing right into the dumpster. He kept a few of his mom's things, small pieces of furniture, and a few boxes of photographs and the like, but just about everything else went into the trash. Arlene wanted most of her stuff. Which didn't surprise him at all. Between her storage unit, and what they'd accumulated in the trailer, he'd thought the new house would be full of stuff. Instead, it looked almost empty. So empty Arlene was already talking about buying furniture. He kept his mouth shut, but he rolled his eyes.

Most of the boxes and odds and ends they weren't sure where to put went into the basement. He'd never had a basement before, and even though it was only under half the house he could have fit two Buicks and a family of Filipinos down there.

They spent one entire day just running the U-Haul back and forth, loading and unloading, then the next day moving boxes around and unpacking. And they still weren't done. Aaron left Arlene to it—she'd taken a few days off work for the move, and it wasn't like they needed the money—and started on the drywall.

The bottom foot or so of a couple panels of drywall were stained and crumbling. Instead of just cutting them out and patching, he decided to re-do the entire back wall of the garage, which had a lot of dents and gouges and small holes. The two-by-four studs were in good shape, which was a pleasant surprise; he'd been worried he'd have to replace them too.

Hanging sheetrock wasn't technically difficult, it could just be a pain in the ass, depending. It had been a while, but the moves came back to him. It was a beautiful day, and he had the overhead door open, letting in a nice breeze and some light, listening to some classic rock off WCSX. A black BMW SUV rolled into view, slowing down. It paused at the end of his driveway, then moved on.

Less than a minute later a shadow slid across the floor, and he looked up to see a guy in a polo shirt and khakis. "Hey," the man said, standing at the edge of the driveway. "I'm Bill Emerson, I live next door with my wife, Kelly. Welcome to the neighborhood. Saw you in here and thought I'd say hi."

"Aaron. Arlene's in the house somewhere, unpacking boxes."

"Oh, I know what that's like," Emerson said, walking into the garage. "We've been here for five years and we still haven't unpacked everything. Doing repairs already?"

"Just doctoring some drywall," Aaron said. He turned, and Emerson finally noticed the pistol on his hip.

Emerson blinked in surprise, and licked his lips. "What do you do for a living?" he asked Aaron, mostly talking to his gun. It was a Glock 20. Aaron still had his stainless Colt Delta Elite, and after collecting his spent brass and replacing his barrel there was no way to tie the gun to the murder in Arizona, and Dave had said the sheriff's department there had no leads…but it still made him nervous, having that gun on his hip. So he'd put it away, somewhere safe. The Glock 20 was ugly and soulless, and the trigger pull was shit even after Dave worked on it (at least compared to his Colt), but it was chambered in by-

God 10mm, and there were fifteen of them in the magazine.

Aaron thought up a delicious, smart-ass answer, but bit it back. He'd pissed off enough neighbors in the trailer park. And he might piss off a lot more here, unintentionally. It might be a good idea, though, not to do it deliberately. Before they'd even unpacked all their boxes. "I might be known to drive an armored car around Detroit from time to time," he told his neighbor.

"Yeah? Wow, talk about dangerous. Do you guys really carry a lot of money? Or is that just the movies?"

"If people knew how much money was in armored cars, and were willing to pull a trigger to get at it, no one would ever rob a bank again." Bill Emerson gaped at him. Aaron just shrugged. It was the truth.

Ten minutes later Arlene came out into the garage. "How's it going? Are you done already?"

"Almost. Just about done with the tape and mud, then I've got to paint." He sighed. "I figure white in here, but you've been looking at samples all week. Did you finally settle on some colors for the kitchen and the bedrooms?"

"Don't you want to…?"

Aaron shook his head. "No. I truly don't give a shit, as long as it's not something obnoxious. And I'm guessing it's not all AWFUL anti-depressant off-whites."

She frowned at him. "The what?"

"Affluent White Female Urban Liberal, the kind who drink wine, take Xanax, and paint every room in the house sad beige."

Arlene snorted. "No, no sad beiges."

Aaron coughed once, then it turned into a coughing jag.

When he was done he hawked up a big grey wad and spit it out through the open door, onto the driveway. "You okay?" Arlene asked him. "It's been hours."

"I'm fine," Aaron told her irritably.

"You should have started out walking instead of jogging."

"Fuck that. Old people walk." He'd decided that since he wasn't working, there was absolutely no reason why he couldn't start working out again. It had been years since he'd really put any serious effort into exercise. But jogging a mile, even though he'd quit cigarettes a year before, had nearly killed him. Apparently twenty years of smoking Marlboro Reds couldn't be undone with twelve months of *not*. "I talked to our neighbor."

"Yeah? Which one? What did you say?" she asked suspiciously.

"I was nice. Next door. Bill Emerson, and his wife…shit, Emily, maybe? Drives a Beemer. Looks like an accountant. A lawyer would dress nicer. And likely would have been a dick. He didn't seem too bad."

"I've seen his wife, I think. Yesterday. They've got a son, eight or ten, on crutches. Cerebral palsy, I think."

"Oh, well, shit. That sucks. But better than Downs or cancer, I guess."

She gave him a dirty look. "You."

He gave her a big smile, then cocked his head. "Think about it," he said with a big smile, warming to the subject. "The Make-A-Wish foundation is really fucking up. I mean, how much of a pain in the ass is it to get sports celebrities and actors to show up at the hospital, dressed up in their Spider-Man costumes and whatever. But these kids are terminal, they're going to die. *Die*. And not all of them are six, some of them are sixteen. You know what they'd like? Hookers."

Arlene gaped at him. "They're kids!"

Aaron nodded. "Shit, sixteen is legal in this state. And don't tell me you only get interested in sex when you turn whatever age it's legal, like the government flips a switch. I was twelve years old when I was looking at my dad's *Penthouses* and *Playboys*. Jerry Lee Lewis married a thirteen-year-old, back when it was legal. Elvis started 'dating'," he used air quotes, "Priscilla when she was fourteen. These bald cancer kids are dying. Heading to the *grave*. Dying as a virgin would suck. Sending them out with a bang, if they're interested, seems like doing God's work to me. Hookers. Hookers and blow."

"Blow? Cocaine?!"

He shrugged. "They're already dying, right? Talk about going out with a bang…"

Arlene shook her head. "I'm going inside to get the paint samples. No hookers and blow talk when we're in Home Depot, I swear to God." She glanced at his gun. "You going to cover up or go like that?" He carried openly when on the job, in uniform. This was different, but open carry was legal in the state.

Aaron shook his head. "Open carry is the short bus of self-defense. When I want someone to know I've got a gun I'll point it at them."

Picking out the various paint colors took even longer than Aaron thought it would, even though Arlene supposedly had her mind made up before they left the house. By the time they were done at Home Depot he was starving, so they stopped at Texas Roadhouse on the way home. He really enjoyed being able to eat out on a whim without having to check the balance in his checking account first. They hadn't been living paycheck-to-paycheck...but it had been close.

He didn't have the new 75-inch Samsung flat screen hooked up yet, so as the sun was setting he and Arlene were at opposite ends of the L-shaped couch in the living room, both on their phones. Peanut was in-between them, sleeping. Suddenly Arlene barked out a laugh, not one of humor but rather disbelief. He glanced over. Her face was lit up by her phone's screen.

"Can you believe these fuckers?" She shook her head violently, her hair flying around. "They should shoot all of them. Feed them into a goddamn wood chipper. Feet first."

"What are you ranting about?"

"You didn't see the story? The state police—"

"Michigan State Police?" he interrupted.

"No, not Michigan, but three, no, four different state polices arrested, today, in this big huge operation, close to a hundred people in a child porn ring. Trading and swapping it back and forth. I guess for years. And they would have gotten away with it too I guess except for one anonymous tip, it says here."

"And I'd have gotten away with it too, if it wasn't for you meddling kids!" he said, with a laugh. "*Scooby Doo*. Why would they have gotten away with it?"

"Because they're all computer nerds, probably know how to hide all that shit on their computer. But they got ratted out by someone they work with. Unbelievable. Offices all over the country. What is going on in this world, I swear. Sounds like they're planning arrests in at least a couple more states."

"What offices?"

The Subsection

"Babble," she told him. "The search engine."

"No shit?" he said, eyebrows climbing up his forehead.

"Yeah, can you believe it? I used them all the time. I guess not any more."

"What states?"

"Umm…Texas, Illinois, Ohio, Florida."

Aaron frowned. He closed out Instagram, then called Dave. His friend answered after just two rings. "What's up?" Aaron heard in his ear.

"Have you seen the news?" Aaron asked him.

"What news?"

"That big multi-state kiddie porn ring getting busted. Was that…? Did we ?" He glanced over at Arlene, but she wasn't paying attention.

There was a long pause on the other end of the call. Finally, Dave said, "I have no idea what you're talking about." His voice was flat.

Aaron blinked twice, and then a smile came over his face. "Right, right. Um, well, anyway, we're in the new house now. Still unpacking, we'll probably be unpacking for a week, and I'm fixing some shit, and then we'll be painting the hideous fucking walls, but maybe then we can have you and the pork snorkel come up here for a housewarming party."

"Just let us know where and when," Dave said.

After Aaron ended the call Arlene looked over and saw the huge smile on his face. She thought it was just because he was looking forward to seeing his friend. He looked back at her. "You know," he told her, "a house isn't a home until you've had sex in every room."

"Is that so?"

"Pretty sure it's in the Bible."

TWENTY-FIVE

A Targeted Op

CIA Director Robert MacGregor sat impatiently in his seat. He wasn't used to waiting, at least not for underlings. He checked his watch again, then looked at Dr. Mason Phillips, the Deputy Director of the CIA for Operations, sitting off to his left inside the SCIF. They'd left their phones outside in the hall, and MacGregor wondered how many texts and emails and phone calls he was missing. Then again, this shouldn't be a long meeting. And it was important. "You're sure this was a hostile action?"

Phillips made a face. "There is absolutely no chance that every single government agent embedded at every single Babble office was actively downloading and trading child porn. It is statistically impossible. As for evidence to back up that assertion," Phillips shrugged. "Don't have any. Not yet. I've talked to several sources at DHS and FBI, who have spoken to people who were on the inside of this operation, and everyone in custody has the exact same story—they're innocent, they had no idea any of that stuff was on their computers, that the evidence had to be planted."

The Subsection

"And we're not talking the borderline material, the 'jail-bait' stuff where the girls are legal but don't look it, or the Japanese cartoons…?"

Phillips shook his head. "I haven't looked at it, but from what I'm hearing there is no gray area with the material they recovered. Hundreds of sexually explicit photos and videos off of every computer involving individuals that are clearly, unequivocally children. Toddlers, even. Having sex with themselves, with adults, with other children. Even animals. The exact kind of stuff we plant when we want to remove someone from the board." The men traded a look.

The door to the SCIF opened and MacGregor's assistant Gerald came in with a sweaty, unshaven man. He was skinny and maybe thirty, and looked nervous, and MacGregor recognized the CIA's foremost expert in cyber security. Brazen, Burzen, something like that. A genius, if MacGregor had to guess, simply because of how much the man said that was completely incomprehensible, if left unchecked. He jabbed a finger at the man. "I have neither the time nor the inclination to listen to a bunch of computer technobabble from you that I will then have to make you repeat in plain English," he said very firmly. "Let's skip the middle step, shall we? Whatever you have to say, say it first in words the average idiot on the street corner would understand."

The man visibly gulped. "Yes sir. Director."

"So?"

"We've just started to…look into this, so I've got nothing like a formal report for you yet. There's a lot of…ground to cover, I guess you could say. Twenty-seven different locations, and multiple computers at each one. Dozens, maybe a hundred cell phones, although we don't have access to all of their contents yet, we've hacked in remotely to the various state police databases. But initial indications are that the material was downloaded onto those computers and cell phones, *all* the computers and cell phones, several weeks ago. All within a day or two. Which means this was not organic. Um, if all those people whose computers we're talking about were the ones doing the downloading, it would have occurred over months, or years. They find stuff they like, and trade it with other people for whatever stuff they have, and so on. There's a lot of file sharing with this crowd, but the thing is they're like addicts, they can't stop, so their download history will stretch back forever, not just pop into existence overnight. So this was clearly done to them, not done by them. But whoever did it was good—they tried to make it seem like the materials had been downloaded over a period of time, but we saw through that. And what are the chances that the only people doing the downloading in these offices were the federal agents assigned there? They were clearly targeted."

"And who alerted the state police?"

Brazen/Burzen shook his head. "Anonymous tip. Detailed, but untraceable. The same message sent out to sex crime detectives in the Ohio, Florida, and Texas state police. Although they don't call it state police in Texas. The states knew the others had been contacted, so they coordinated their investigations, and it spread to other states even before they made any arrests. I guess there was a press conference…?"

"Yes," MacGregor said drily. A joint press conference held in Dallas, attended by the attorneys general of three states, representatives from the state police of four states, and two governors. Arresting over a hundred people in six states in a multi-jurisdictional raid was big news, especially when it was for child porn. The fact that the people arrested were all federal employees was a fact so far hidden from the public, and the FBI Director (or so MacGregor had heard) had burned up a lot of the favors owed him to make that happen.

MacGregor said, "Can we…can whoever defends them in court, can the lawyers defending them, prove that it wasn't them who downloaded the kiddie porn onto their computers and phones?"

It was as yet unclear what the position would be of the Department of Homeland Security and Federal Bureau of Investigation regarding the men and women taken into custody by the various state police departments. The amount and severity of the material recovered on their computers, apparently, was part of the problem, and why the state police had shown no hesitation in putting handcuffs on people who had identified themselves as employees of federal law enforcement agencies.

Brazen/Burzen nodded. "Yes. It was done remotely. Whoever did it was good, and careful, but if you know what you're looking at, it's clear this was a targeted op. And whoever did it was located in mainland China."

MacGregor blinked at that, and traded a surprised look with Phillips. "China?"

"Yessir."

"Are you sure about that?"

"As of right now, all the…digital evidence we have tracks back to them. As you know, while they're not the black hole that North Korea is, our ability to track online activity inside China is minimal at best, their cybersecurity is excellent, so beyond saying it originated inside the borders of China I doubt I'll be able to narrow it down further. But, given how tightly controlled their digital space is, you have to assume it was a state actor who did this. Or state-sponsored."

MacGregor frowned, massaged his eyebrows, then nodded. "Okay." Which meant that, eventually, all the charges would be dropped, and this would all go away. Meanwhile, the domestic surveillance program inside Babble was completely neutralized. While it was the DHS/FBI's baby, the CIA had been skimming valuable intelligence from it as well. The DHS had similar operations in place at Google and Meta, and would likely now have to reevaluate all their cybersecurity protocols in case those were targeted next. And while it was an open secret that there were federal employees stationed at the offices of social media companies, the sheer breadth of their gatekeeping was sure to arouse a Senator or two when it came out. There'd be congressional inquiries, of that he had no doubt. "Keep working it. Anything new, of substance, that you discover, I want to know immediately. A hostile foreign nation directly harassing federal agents inside the continental U.S., deliberately compromising their ability to do their jobs, is a threat to national security."

"Yes sir."

"And the date that all this happened, that their systems were breached and this material uploaded, have you looked into that? Was anything else going on here, or in China, or at Babble?"

The man blinked. "I don't know, director. We've only been looking at the phones and hard drives."

MacGregor looked at Gerald. "Get someone on that. I want to know if something precipitated this attack." He turned his eyes back to the cyber expert. "Okay, dismissed."

They waited until he'd gone and the door had shut, and MacGregor looked at his assistant. "Gerald, schedule a call with the Director of the FBI. And the Attorney General. If we…no, not *we*, I don't want to insert the CIA into this as it's technically a domestic matter. Let's stay on the outside, feeding intel if and when. If the *federal government* has evidence that compromising material was inserted into their electronics by a hostile foreign nation, it is obligated to share that information with state law enforcement agencies. Feed it into the system through the NSA, like it came from them." Gerald nodded.

Phillips sat up. "So you believe it's China?"

MacGregor shook his head. "I don't know. It doesn't make sense, unless there's something going on here I don't know about. The White House publicly is friendly with Jinping, and privately is China's advocate and ally."

Phillips snorted. "To put it politely. I would have said giving them handjobs under the table, but…"

"That's why I'm the Director," MacGregor said with the flash of a smile. "Did somebody in the administration or on Capitol Hill do something to piss Xi off?"

"I haven't heard of anything. And if they were going to go after us, why go after our social media censors? China pioneered internet censoring. It would make more sense to plant kiddie porn on the computers of the FBI's Counterintelligence Division. Or my guys. NSA. JSOC. The people keeping an eye on *them*."

MacGregor had a look on his face like he'd eaten something rotten. "Yeah." He didn't understand it, which meant he didn't like it, not at all.

TWENTY-SIX

Homecoming

"This is nice," Eddie said, sipping at his Coors and looking around the place. Of course, standing inside the garage, the garage, driveway, and a slice of lawn were all he could see, but he'd already been through the house. Arlene was giving tours. "We moved from the east side to the west side, because things were gettin' a little spicy over there, but you got a bigger lawn."

"You know, you can move out of goddamn Detroit," Aaron told his former driver. Eddie was the first arrival Aaron cared about, everyone else who'd showed up so far was Arlene's family or coworkers. "Entire city is surrounded by suburbs with lower crime rates. Better city services. No so many packs of wild dogs roaming the streets."

"Yeah, but Detroit's my home."

Aaron shook his head. "Shit, growing up, your home was with your momma, right? But you moved out. Doesn't mean you can't still go back and visit." He eyed Eddie. "You look good. You dropped weight." Eddie had always looked a bit overinflated. Overweight, but not jiggly, just round. Under pressure. But he looked like he'd deflated a bit.

Eddie shrugged. "High blood pressure, some pre-diabetes creeping up in there, probably some heart disease too, shit, that's the number one killer of black men if you can make it out of your twenties. I decided I needed to drop a few pounds if I was going to be around for the old lady and the kids."

"You cut out the barbeque?"

Eddie laughed. "Shit no man, you take me off the meats, riding around Detroit all day in an armored car with a gun on my hip, the road rage would be legendary. They'd write fucking songs about me. Reenact it for a *Fast and Furious* movie. But I'm off the carbs."

"Yeah, I see that," Aaron said, eyeing the beer in his hands.

"Hey, you gotta have cheat days."

The speaker in the corner of the garage, which had been playing *Gimme Shelter*, moved on to a rap song. Aaron frowned a little bit—Arlene had been in charge of the playlist, and she liked a little bit of everything, which meant half of it was crap. Aaron vaguely recognized the song, and it had a good beat—but then, beat was mostly all rap songs had, beat and lyrics. He bobbed his head in time as he listened to the lyrics.

"Ball so hard, this shit crazy
Y'all don't know that shit don't faze me"

Jay-Z, and then Kanye West singing—or talking, whatever it was you did when you rapped. Then he looked at Eddie. "What's that supposed to mean? *'Ball so hard, motherfuckers want to find me.'* What, find him and kick his ass?"

Eddie shook his head, smiling and holding back a laugh. "No, *fine* him, F-I-N-E, like money." Aaron thought about it for a little while, still listening.

"I know I'm 'bout to kill it
How you know? I got that feeling
You are now watching the throne
Don't let me get into my zone
Don't let me get into my zone"

Then Aaron frowned and shook his head. "'Find' makes more sense," he said. "Rap songs are all 'bout guns and bitches and acting tough. You being so bad that somebody wants to hunt you down and take you out is more badass than getting a goddamn fine, meter maid writing you a ticket."

Eddie did laugh then, and shrugged. "Hey, man, I didn't write the song. Wish I did, half a billion plays on YouTube alone for the music video. And they're talking about hoops."

"'Ball so hard'? That's not just basketball. Or sex. Not even in the song. What's the title of it, anyway? Ball So Hard?"

"*Niggas in Paris*," Eddie told him.

"Seriously? I can't even request the song without throwing out the N-word? Type it into a search engine? I'm already on enough goddamn watchlists."

Eddie smiled, and got a wicked look in his eye. "Look, speaking 'a that, you know any cops feel like beatin' up a black man? I could use a payout like you got…"

Aaron laughed. "That's why you need to move out to the suburbs. Cops beat up everybody in Detroit, and nobody gets paid. You got your ass kicked like I did in lily-white West Bloomfield, they'd have thrown an extra mil at you just to prove they wasn't racist."

Eddie laughed so hard he spilled a little of his beer. As he was wiping it off his hand he saw a car pull up and park on the street outside. Two people got out. "Holy shit, look who it is," he said.

"Yeah, he said he'd be stopping by," Aaron said. And Dave always did what he promised, even if it meant flying most of the way across the country just for a housewarming party.

"Is that?" Eddie said, squinting at the person with him. "Sheeit, you weren't lying."

"I told you."

"Yeah, but you're so full of shit I never know when you're shining me on. Damn, she looks good. Put on a few curves. Always had great tits, but she was too skinny back when she was slingin' dick."

"A black guy liking a white chick with a dumptruck ass? That's so weird."

"Fuck you," Eddie said, laughing. He couldn't take his eyes off Lori as they walked up the driveway.

"I'll introduce you," Aaron told him, as Eddie took a sip of beer. "You get nervous talking to her, just try imagining her with her clothes off."

Eddie laughed so hard he sprayed beer all over his face, and Aaron stepped back to avoid the foam, bent over laughing as well. Then he turned and looked at the speaker in disbelief. *Niggas in Paris* had ended and Celine Dion's *My Heart Will Go On* was playing. "What the fuck is this playlist?" he demanded. "Arlene!" he roared.

"You don't look so bad. You done being a punching bag?" Gary said. He had a big strawberry margarita in his hand, with big rocks of salt around the rim—Aaron could make a hell of a frozen margarita—and it was half gone.

"What?" Dave said.

They were standing in a circle inside the garage. Dave, Aaron, Eddie, Gary, Jeff, they'd all worked together at Absolute Armored. And the four of them traded a look. "Couple years ago, it seemed like Aaron was running down to Arizona every other week because you were on the news for pissing off the cartel or whatever. Your house in Arizona was on TV in Michigan, man. I watched it burn. We all did. Bodies in the street. Shit, they blacked out your face, but we knew it was you." They all peered at him.

"I'm staying out of trouble." He had a beer in his hand, but was only drinking one, as he was carrying.

"Yeah? Good. We don't have to worry about cartel or that mob guy showing up?" Gary and Jeff glanced out the open garage door at the sunny suburban street.

"Cartel doesn't care about me anymore. And the mob guy is dead." Dave shrugged like it was no big deal. Eddie and Jeff traded a look.

"And you white," Eddie said. "So you ain't in jail." Dave snorted.

"So what'd you tell him," Jeff said, nodding at Aaron, "that had that crooked mobbed-up cop beating on him?"

"The location of Hoffa's body," Aaron interjected. When he'd gone inside to make a pitcher of margaritas he'd straightened out the music, and now it was nothing but classic rock. He could hear Journey in the background. Before that it had been Rush.

"Nothing," Dave said.

"That's why he kept hitting me," Aaron told them.

"Shit, anyone's ever talked to you wants to kick your ass," Gary said. They all laughed. He looked from Aaron to Eddie. "They ever find that guy who tried to rob you? Who shot you in the vest?"

"If they did I never heard about it," Aaron said. He looked at Eddie, who shook his head. In the middle of the day in the parking lot of a bank on Woodward Avenue. Forty rounds fired between Aaron and the robber, spent brass rolling all over the asphalt. Just another day in Detroit.

"Shoulda had Dave along," Jeff said. "Gunfighter would have laid that bitch out." They all looked at Dave, who pretended like he hadn't heard anything, and took a sip of his Coors.

"Full-auto Glock, wouldn't mind me havin' one of those," Gary said wistfully.

"You can buy those switches everywhere online," Eddie said.

"Yeah, and it's all fedbois selling them," Aaron said. "Entrapment. Don't much care about guys like the one who came after us, they're fishing for whiter bait."

"You fish with bait, not for bait," Gary said with a frown. He did a lot of walleye fishing in Lake Erie.

"I buy fish at fucking Kroger," Aaron said. "Make a hell of an *acqua pazza*. And *pescare puttanesca*."

"Hey, where's your girlfriend?" Jeff asked Dave.

"Probably inside, talking to my neighbor," Aaron volunteered. "I think he recognized her. I don't think his wife knows why he's all smiley." There were at least a dozen people inside the house. It had been an unexpected turnout. He was in good spirits.

"What's that like, man, how do you do that?" Jeff asked Dave. "With her bodycount…?"

"I've got a body count too," Dave said, his voice reasonable. "Lot of people would argue mine's worse. She doesn't hold it against me."

Nobody said anything for a few seconds, then Aaron, staring right at Eddie, said, with just a hint of rhythm, "Ball so hard, motherfuckers want to find him." The corner of Eddie's mouth twitched up, and he gave Aaron a little nod.

Half the people, when they left, did so through the garage, and their departure was often delayed. A secondary bar was set up in there, and music was playing in the background. Bill Emerson came out from the house and spotted Dave in the middle of the garage. He wandered over, trying to look casual. His wife had headed back to their house a few minutes earlier.

"So, uh, Lori? She's your girlfriend?" he asked Dave. He didn't notice the looks he got from most of the guys in earshot, who knew.

"Yep."

"And you guys live in Arizona?"

"Yeah."

"Because she looks kind of familiar." Maybe he wasn't quite sure, and wanted to confirm. Maybe he was pretty sure, and just couldn't believe it.

Dave smiled. "Yeah. She gets that a lot. But she's retired now."

"Oh. Uh…" Emerson's voice trailed off as he realized Dave had confirmed his suspicions.

The Subsection

Aaron walked up, a funny look on his face. He was holding out his cell phone. "For you," he said, frowning.

"Excuse me," Dave told Emerson, as he backed off toward the open door. "Hello?"

"What about this? Is this as sexy?"

Dave frowned, and moved out of the garage into the driveway. "Is that Russian?" The accent was unexpected, and hard to pin down over the phone.

"Yes. I tried French, but it doesn't sound very good over the phone. But I don't know if this is as sexy as the British voice."

"I don't know. You sound like a dominatrix or something. But probably not as much as if it was a German accent." Dave glanced toward the people inside the garage, then out at the street. He pulled his phone out of his pocket, set it on the hood of Aaron's car, and walked out into the middle of the yard, away from it. "Is something up? I'm not at home."

"I know exactly where you are. And I need you to do something." Dave was impressed with how fast Murph could type. It was nearly as fast as someone would talk, with slightly longer pauses between sentences.

"Um…I'm here as me. Flew here with the girlfriend, both of us using our real IDs."

"I know. But it shouldn't matter. Just need you to check out something within driving distance of where you are. Drive in, look around. Probably see a whole lot of nothing, which is what I've seen using…um, from overhead, but you never know, so…. You're the only person we've got in the area who's available, and it should only take a day."

"I don't have anything with me other than a pistol."

"All you need are your eyes. And a brain. And a car. But

since I'm guessing you don't have your burner, you need to disable your cell phone. Do you have that Faraday bag?"

"Yeah. Just in case."

"Good. Use it. You don't need anyone tracking your movements."

"I'll be in a rental car. That I rented? In my name. That probably has GPS."

"You can't borrow a car?"

Dave glanced over at Aaron's Taurus. "I guess I could." He checked his watch. "Is it a rush, or can I do it tomorrow?"

"Tomorrow's fine."

"And it's one day?"

"Probably."

"Probably." Dave sighed. "She's going to be pissed to be flying back alone." They'd arranged to spend the night in one of Aaron's spare bedrooms and fly out in the morning. The airport was maybe a fifteen-minute drive, even in traffic. It would have been so convenient....

"Can you come up with a good excuse?"

Dave shook his head. "She knows what I do." So Lori probably wouldn't actually be pissed, just disappointed. And Aaron wouldn't ask any questions if he asked to borrow his car. Well, he would, he just wouldn't get mad when Dave didn't answer them. He nodded at Bill Emerson as the man emerged from Aaron's garage and walked across the grass toward his house.

"She does?"

"The general idea. She's been through too much with me, I couldn't keep something like this secret even if I wanted to." There was silence at the other end for a while. "How bad did I fuck up?" Dave asked. "I know I probably wasn't supposed to."

The Subsection

"No, it's not that. I'm just." There was a pause. "Thinking."

The airline charged him $150 to reschedule his ticket, just because they could. Murph had been right, the job had only taken him a day, although it had been a long day—five hours of driving each way, and nearly five hours on site. Twenty-four hours after Lori landed alone at the Phoenix airport she drove back down and picked him up in her Toyota SUV. She didn't ask any questions, just gave him a smile, then drove to the airport's cell phone lot, leaned over, and gave him an unexpected welcome home present. Apparently she was very glad to see him. Maybe she was happy about the new job he had. He was grateful for the heavy tint on his window, in part because he knew Lori really didn't care if people saw her, as long as nobody called the cops. Her attitude about and experience with sex was as much outside the human norm as his when it came to violence, and somehow they were able to make it work. Mostly by knowing what questions not to ask of each other? He still wasn't sure he understood it, or what she saw in him, but he was glad to have her. For a lot of reasons. She drove home with a big smirk on her face, like he'd been the one who'd gone down on her. He really didn't understand women. Did any guy, really?

He'd bought a fancy girly unlined notebook in one of the airport stores, and a few pens, and spent most of the flight home jotting down notes and writing his report. He finished it when he got home. Dave wasn't sure how much detail Murph wanted, so he made it as detailed as possible. Pages and pages, written longhand, which he hadn't done in a while. By the time he was done his fingers were sore and his hand was cramping. He decided he needed to put a summary at the beginning:

On the Monday indicated this operative traveled to the Thornton (Illinois) Quarry, located five miles west of the Indiana border and six miles south of the city limits of Chicago, twenty-five miles or so from downtown Chicago. This is a very heavily populated/traveled area, in what is probably considered a suburb of Chicago.

The Thornton Quarry is a privately-owned quarry first opened in 1836 that is still in operation, and public records are easy to find. It is the second-largest quarry of its type in the world, 1.5 miles long, half a mile wide for most of its length, and 450 deep at its deepest. Again, this is not a remote location, Interstate 80/90/94 crosses east/west over the middle of the quarry. Called the Tri-State Tollway, it's four lanes in each direction and there are a quarter million vehicles a day on it.

He'd actually looked that up. He'd driven on that stretch of road from time to time when living in Michigan and travelling to Illinois, and if you were driving that stretch of road anywhere near rush hour you could expect four lanes of bumper-to-bumper traffic moving as fast as possible, whether that was 35 or 75, everyone ignoring the 55 MPH signs. Lot of people who worked in Chicago lived in northwest Indiana, along the 80/90/94 corridor. He knew somewhere along that stretch of interstate, when the air was clear enough, if you looked to the north at just the right time you could see the skyscrapers in downtown Chicago.

The interstate bridge running across the quarry wasn't elevated, but it looked hugely tall simply because of how

The Subsection

deeply the quarry was cut to either side of it. The bridge ran across an unquarried ridge of grey stone.

The quarry is comprised of four basic sections, divided by the roads crossing them. It is bordered by State Street to the east, a railroad trestle and/or Halsted Street to the west, and Armory Drive on the north. It is crossed (in order, from north-to-south) by the Tri-State Tollway, Margaret Street, and 183rd street, and stretches to the south to a narrow point inside Glenwoods Woods, a nature preserve. Dozens of businesses are sited around the miles-long perimeter of the quarry, including retailers like Menards and Target, commercial establishments such as trucking warehouses, residential neighborhoods, and undeveloped/wooded areas.

Operative drove and walked around as much of the property perimeter as possible. Actual access to and visual inspection of the quarry can be difficult, as the bottom of the quarry is so deep below ground level, and there are fences all around the property to prevent trespassing and people likely falling to their deaths, as most of the sides are vertical rock walls. During the five hours this operative spent in the area, inspecting and surveilling the quarry and surrounding area, he saw nothing 'suspicious' and nothing to indicate it was anything other than a privately-owned quarry in the business of selling bulk stone and aggregate. Operative saw no reason why foreign agents or the like would have any interest in the site or the operation.

Unless you could narrow your point of interest, due to its sheer physical size, surveillance of the entire quarry would be impossible without using at least dozens of people/cameras. Operative did not see any traffic cameras along this section of interstate, but many of the businesses around the perimeter of the quarry have external security cameras; if tech support can access their feeds they might prove useful.

Details to follow in body of the report.

Dave reread his entire report twice, occasionally crossing out a word or a sentence and adding a note of correction. Then he cut the pages out of the notebook, drove to a FedEx/Kinkos store, stuffed them in an overnight envelope, and mailed them to an address in Utah Murph had given him. There wasn't an immediate rush, and if the information was never uploaded it could never be hacked, so he'd been told longhand hardcopy was fine. He hoped they were happy with the report, but knew, with this job, there was a good chance he'd never know.

TWENTY-SEVEN

The Game

Roger was behind his desk in the lobby when he looked out the front windows and saw the two men approaching. One was a black guy in a suitcoat and tie as he jogged across the street, the other a white guy in a polo shirt and khakis. Both had badges on their belts and guns on their hips. And serious looks on their faces. He didn't see exactly where they'd come from, there was no police vehicle in view.

"Good morning officers, is there a problem?"

"Not officers, agents," the one in the coat and tie said. Up close, he was big. He fished out a badge wallet and flipped it open to show an ID on one side, then flipped the blue suede divider out of the way to show the concierge the badge. "FBI Special Agents. And no, there's not a problem. Not yet." He frowned at Roger in his uniform, the threat unspoken.

"Um, how can I help you?"

The smaller man next to him spoke up. "How many exits do you have in the building?"

"Uh, excuse me?"

"Exits. Doors. That the tenants use."

"Uh, is there a problem with one of the tenants?"

The smaller man, who had thick dark hair, frowned and leaned in. "No problem. We're just three guys having a casual conversation. Exits."

Roger swallowed. And thought. "Well, um, there's the front door, there," he said, nodding behind them. "Another door on the side of the building that lets out onto the side street." The twenty-two-story building was positioned at an intersection. "A back door, directly opposite this one, but it's for emergencies only, an alarm will sound if you don't use the key, and most of the time I've got the only one. We use that for some deliveries."

"What about the other deliveries?" the big FBI agent asked.

"They come in the parking garage, down below. There's a freight elevator, and a loading dock. And the other elevators go down to the garage, so I guess those are exits? Is that what you're talking about?"

They didn't answer directly. The smaller agent said, "So, three pedestrian doors, one of which is locked and the alarm will sound, and then the parking garage. And that's it?"

"Yes, I think. What is this about?"

"And the parking garage. How many exits does it have?"

"There's the car ramp. And the door right next to it, so if you're leaving on foot you can avoid the cars."

"Do you have surveillance cameras covering all the exits?"

"Yes. Please, what's going on? Is there a problem? I mean, FBI…"

"No, no problem," the big federal agent said. "Unless you want there to be a problem?"

The Subsection

"No, but...should I call the lawyer who represents the owners?"

The smaller federal agent leaned in, looking mean. "Now why would you want to do that, when we're just standing here having a nice conversation. We're going to look around. Look at the exits. Not going to bother your tenants at all. And then we'll be on our way." They didn't wait for him to respond, they just walked down the hallway into the building. Roger stared after them, nervous. Should he have asked to see a warrant? He glanced down at his desk. He had two screens there, showing him the display from the security cameras. He watched the two men walk around the common areas of the building, checking out the exit doors. Then they rode an elevator down to the parking garage and looked around. Less than ten minutes after they'd arrived, they were walking back through the lobby.

The smaller one gave Roger a nod. "Have a nice day," he said. They went through the revolving door, turned right, and strode down the sidewalk out of sight.

Roger let out the breath he didn't know he'd been holding, and looked around. Should he tell someone? If he told the owners...they might be mad he didn't ask to see a warrant. But nothing had happened, the two agents had just looked around. You could see that on the video, clear as day. They didn't touch anything or take anything. Didn't get in the elevators, didn't even talk to any tenants. The digital video was stored for ten days on the hard drive before being written over, which was forever, so if nothing happened before then he figured he was golden.

They'd detoured through a nearby commercial building and pulled off the guns and badges when no one was in sight.

Dre took off his coat and wrapped them up, then pulled off his tie. Nobody even gave them a second look as they returned to the surveillance vehicle, a short panel truck parked at the curb with the bold logo of a well-known local commercial laundry company on the side. They entered the cab from the passenger side, then crawled through the small door into the back of the truck. The cargo area of the truck was fifteen feet long and packed with surveillance equipment, most of which was sitting idle. There were two other men back there. Fergie was at the control panel. In front of Fergie were half a dozen monitors showing him the feeds from the small cameras mounted around the truck, the lenses almost impossible to spot even if you knew to look. "Well?" he asked. Luis was in a chair near the back of the truck, a police scanner and FBI prep radio on the table before him, the volume turned down low. Fergie and Luis were members of the FBI's SSG, Special Surveillance Group. While FBI employees, the SSG were not sworn gun-carrying Special Agents. Dre was a ten-year veteran FBI Special Agent, stationed in the massive Chicago office.

"We're good," Max told him. "The front door and the side door are the only ones he can use if he leaves on foot. That and the parking garage." And they could see all of them from where they were parked. They were near the intersection, with a line of sight down both streets.

"That's not *good*," Dre said. "Asshole can get picked up, get into a car, duck down in the back seat, and we'd never know he left."

Max shook his head. "You have to be a resident to get into that garage. So unless he's hitching a ride with a neighbor, anyone picking him up is going to pull up right there." He pointed at the screen displaying the front door of the apartment building. Downtown Chicago, right outside the

The Subsection

loop, the rent for their target's place had to be insane. The skyscrapers, apartment and office buildings, towered around them, making it seem like they were at the bottom of a trench. Honking traffic filled the streets around them.

"I still wish we had eyes inside," Dre said.

"We're on his phone and laptop," Fergie said with a shrug, and a glance at Max. "He calls or texts and asks for a ride, friend, Uber, whoever, we're going to know."

"Unless he's got a burner," Dre said.

Fergie frowned at him. "You are just Mister Glass Half Empty, aren't you."

Dre set his coat on the table and unfolded it. He handed Max his gun and badge, and Max put them back on his belt. The main badge for an FBI agent was the one inside their badge wallet, but sometimes you needed to have something on display. Something more subtle than a windbreaker with 'FBI' or 'POLICE' in big letters written across the back. The gold badge on his belt had an eagle on the top, and below that FEDERAL BUREAU OF INVESTIGATION. Between that and the DEPARTMENT OF JUSTICE on the bottom of the badge was an image of blind lady justice holding a sword and scale. The badge was real, as was the badge wallet in his pocket. If you searched the FBI database for the name on his FBI ID you'd discover he was an FBI Special Agent, assigned to a department whose acronym very few people recognized.

Those who did...pretended ignorance. The men and women of that small elite unit were the FBI's black bag specialists, experts in breaking and entering, surveillance, and more shady operations the FBI would, of course, never do, officially or otherwise. Because of the sensitive nature of this investigation, Max had been tasked to assist in setting up the surveillance.

The four of them were there because a senior partner at one of Chicago's most prestigious law firms was under investigation. The FBI had received compelling evidence that the man was bribing state judges to get more favorable verdicts and sentencing—exactly the kind of case the FBI loved. It allowed them to act superior to the local and state cops who'd missed the crime, or were perhaps involved in covering it up, and going after a prominent figure always got the FBI a lot of good press.

In truth, all the evidence and allegations supplied to the FBI were mostly nonsense, exaggerations of the normal, shady way business was done in the halls of justice, but none of the men in the truck with Max knew that. What the corporate lawyer was in fact doing was acting as a middleman, a bag man, transferring technical data from one of his firm's largest clients, a defense contractor, to foreign operatives. Doing it by hand, passing flash drives in person.

Any official attempt to initiate a surveillance or investigation of the attorney for that reason would have been quashed at the highest federal levels, even though the information being passed was all ITAR-restricted from foreign transfer, or actually classified. Because the lawyer was handing off the materials at the behest of the U.S. Department of State. Exactly what motivated the State Department to want to provide restricted/classified technical data on current and next-gen U.S. military aircraft to a potentially hostile foreign power, in clear violation of federal law, was unknown, but the situation seemed perfectly suited to the Subsection's mandate.

They knew the lawyer was guilty...they just didn't quite know what to do with him. Especially since they weren't sure if he knew what he was actually passing to the Chinese. Maybe he knew but the State Department had told him

The Subsection

what he was doing was perfectly legal. He was doing it for the United States' Department of State, after all. In which case he was just the patsy. Putting the FBI in a position where they would spot the (arguable) treason and then have to do something about it was a deliciously wicked twist Max had thought of himself. It would only shut down the State Department's IP transfer program temporarily…but that was the game.

"Any idea when…?" Fergie asked, looking up at Dre. Dre had seniority, and was in charge. Max was just a visiting "subject matter expert", although Dre treated him like an equal. Because you didn't want to piss off the FBI's black bag guys, they could fuck your life up in a heartbeat. Plant coke in your bedroom, empty your bank accounts, stick kiddie porn on your computer…they'd all heard the rumors.

Dre shook his head. "Could be an hour, could be a week. Or more likely a month or three. We're in the very early, preliminary stages of this investigation, and you don't go after a lawyer on first-name terms with senators, congressmen, and the governor without having your T's crossed and your I's dotted." He glanced at Max. "How long are you with us?"

Max was the one who'd entered the target's apartment without leaving any trace and uploaded the software on the man's laptop and phone—while he slept—so they could track his digital activities in real time.

"A few days, at least," Max said. "Just to make sure everything's running right. Unless they pull me off for something else."

TWENTY-EIGHT

Bush League

She had blonde hair pulled back in a loose ponytail. She wore a blue and white plaid button-down shirt pulled up, tied around her waist, and unbuttoned in front, the sleeves rolled up nearly to her elbows, tight around her corded forearms. It showed off the white tank top underneath. Below the plaid shirt—which might have been flannel, even—were jeans, and some stylish, not-quite-cowboy boots. Overall it was a touch of cowgirl chic, but Madeleine didn't think it was a put-on, an act or a costume, the woman wore them like she dressed like that all the time. What sold it was the build, she looked like a farmer. Madeleine was halfway across the room at one of the few tables, paying a bit of attention to the conversation around her, but also eyeing the woman at the bar. The jeans were tight on her simply because she had a lot of muscle.

"Yeah, give me a second, I'm going to get another drink," she said to her companions, and stood up. She'd already had a few—two, three?—and felt a little wobbly, but it passed in a second as she made her way through the crowd to the bar. She stood next to the blonde, ostensibly waiting for the bartender to notice her, but studying the blonde out of the corner of her eye. She looked just as good up close. Young, maybe ten, fifteen years younger than Maddy, maybe even more than that, but that didn't matter. Hell, that made it better.

The blonde made a sound, then untied the plaid shirt around her waist and started to take it off. "Sorry," she said, as she almost hit Maddy with an elbow. "It's too hot in here for two layers."

That gave Maddy an excuse to look at her directly. The blonde was definitely built like a country girl. Blonde, pretty, in excellent shape, and a lot younger? She was exactly Maddy's type. Then Maddy's eyes were drawn to the ink on her shoulder. "Is that a Future Farmers of America tattoo?" she blurted. It was hard to mistake it for anything else, how many logos had an eagle clutching a shield sitting on a cross-section of a corn cob? And in the center, an owl sitting on an old-fashioned tiller. The detail in the tattoo was actually pretty impressive.

The blonde rolled her eyes and looked embarrassed. "Yeah. Don't judge. I was big into the FFA as a kid, and when I turned eighteen I decided to be rebellious and get a tattoo. But I couldn't think of anything else, so…"

"I like it."

"You're making fun of me."

"No. I was in the FFA too, way back when I was just a girl, in Nebraska."

The blonde blinked in surprise. "Really? I'm from Kearney. Well, south of Loup City, actually, but nobody knows where that is. Hell, in this town, nobody knows where Nebraska is." She made a face.

Madeleine laughed. "You're not wrong. I'm from

Lincoln, originally." She held her hand out. "Madeleine Gebbie. Maddy."

The blonde shook her hand, then a line formed between her eyes. "Why is that name familiar?"

Maddy had a hint of a smile twitch the corner of her mouth. "Senator Madeleine Gebbie, from the great state of Nebraska. Pleased to meet you." She stuck her hand out again.

"Oh, shit," the blonde said, then clapped her hand over her mouth. Then they both burst out laughing. The blonde blinked twice, then looked around. "You don't…I mean, if people see you, recognize you…?"

"You're not in Nebraska anymore, um…?"

"April."

"You're not in Nebraska anymore, April. And if you were, every one of my constituents knows I've been faithfully married to the same man for twenty-six years, with two children. So I can't be gay. So even if someone does take photos of me hanging out at a dyke bar in D.C…I'm just having a drink with some friends. And it's pride month, so…" Her eyes twinkled. "What are you doing in D.C.?"

"I do ag research at UN Omaha. We're here for a conference on future farming methods being put on, in part, by the Department of Agriculture."

"Sounds…"

"Boring?" April laughed. "A bit, but it's interesting, and important. But I had to get out of the hotel, at least for a little bit. And a quick search on my phone found me this place. Where I don't have to worry about guys hitting on me. A lesbian sports bar, who knew?" April looked around. *A League of Her Own* was in the artsy Adams Morgan neighborhood in Washington D.C., one of the most well-known lesbian bars in the D.C. area. "Do you have a security guard? I mean, you're a senator, you shouldn't just be… wandering around. You're important."

"He's out in the car. I'm among friends in here." She smiled warmly at April.

The bartender finally wandered over. The sides of her head were shaved, and she had a big ring through her septum. April had a bottle of Bud Light in front of her and Maddy ordered another for her, and a dirty martini for herself. "What makes it dirty?" April asked Maddy. "I've heard of them, but I don't know how you make them. A dirty martini is like hot yoga, they both sound vaguely… naughty." Her face colored a bit. Maddy found it delightful.

"It's made with olive juice."

"Really? That seems weird. Sounds like something somebody did by accident once, spilled the olive jar into a martini and then said, 'I meant to do that'."

Maddy laughed again. She found the young woman's… freshness? Naivete?—charming and delightful. When the drink came, Maddy nodded her head at it. "Go on, try it."

April lifted the wide-mouthed glass to her lips with two hands and took a tentative sip. Then made a face, and carefully set it down. "No, not for me. I like beer, but I haven't found any hard liquor that doesn't taste like a diesel spill on my tongue."

Maddy smiled, then said, "You look amazing. How much do you work out?" She ran her eyes up and down April, from her muscled shoulder to her curvy ass and back, and wasn't subtle about it. April saw it, and clearly didn't mind.

"Not as much as I'd like to. Too busy. But thank you."

"Come on back to the table with me," Maddy said. "I've got some people I can introduce you to."

Madeleine had served one term as a representative before being elected senator, and had been in Washington for twenty years. She had all sorts of amazing, crazy stories, and kept the young ladies around the table highly entertained. At some point she pressed her leg against April's under the table, and April didn't pull away. And she just smiled when Maddy put her hand on her thigh.

An hour and three beers later, April begged off. "I've got an early morning tomorrow. As much as I don't want to go…" She looked at the senator, frowned and shrugged apologetically. Maddy's hand kept straying back to the young woman's jean-clad thigh as they'd sat there, gradually moving higher until there was nowhere else to go. April clearly didn't mind at all. Had even spread her thighs a little bit. She seemed impressed and a bit star-struck by Maddie, an actual senator. Happened all the time.

"How long are you in town?"

"Three days. Until Friday. Do you…come here a lot?"

"Here, hand me your phone," Maddy said. April dug her phone out of her back pocket and handed it over.

Maddy typed into it, then handed it back. "There, that's my number. My personal cell phone. Tomorrow I'm busy, but maybe Thursday we can get together and talk about… dirty martinis and hot yoga." They traded a smile.

April weaved a bit as she made her way toward the door. The bar was still crowded, and outside the air was cool and heavy with humidity. A few couples were standing on the sidewalk, talking, likely waiting for Ubers. The AdMo street was well lit, and it was still early enough that there were pedestrians moving up and down the sidewalks. She stepped around two slender young women who had their hips pressed together and started down the street, in no hurry, pulling the plaid button-down back on against the

The Subsection

chill. The commercial area gave way to residential, with two- and three-story townhouses on both sides of the avenue. She took one turn, sped up, losing her slight wobble, made it halfway down the block, then jogged across the narrow street. She made another turn at the end of the block, cut through an alley at a sprint, and came out in a dark street lined with cars where the mature trees blocked half the streetlights. She paused in the shadows and watched for a minute. Finally, she moved forward, slid behind the wheel of a generic sedan, and a few seconds later the car was zipping down the asphalt. She made a turn before flicking on the headlights.

Dimi absently rubbed her shoulder. The temporary tattoo was water resistant enough that she could swim or shower with it. It would last a few days if left untouched, but as soon as she had the opportunity she'd be removing it —and all it took was a paper towel and baby oil. She carefully pulled the wig off and tossed it onto the passenger seat, then pulled the pins and clips out of her hair which had been holding it down and helping to keep the wig in place.

She glanced at the clock on the dash, then thought back to what time it had been when the senator had first approached her at the bar. And told Dimi to take a sip of her martini. So easy. She did the math in her head. It would be midnight, give or take, when Senator Madeleine Gebbie would suffer her massive heart attack. Even if the coroner knew to look for something, the drug she'd used was undetectable. The woman was in her mid-fifties, overweight and a heavy drinker, so a heart attack wouldn't arouse any undue suspicion.

The political up-and-comer likely to replace Gebbie in Washington wasn't great, but at least he wasn't actively trying to subvert the U.S.'s national security. And the CIA and NSA didn't have any dirt on him to keep him in line. Unlike Gebbie, and most of the politicians in D.C.

Dimi hummed to herself as she headed south, toward Virginia, trying to shove down the vague feeling of disappointment at how easy the mission had been.

Robin's eyes were wide, as was her mouth. Bob eased back off her, and then out of her, panting a little bit. "Sorry about that," he said. "It's been a while."

"No, don't you dare apologize," she scolded him. She carefully lowered her legs. "Oof. Wow. I think you popped an ovary loose. But sometimes that's just what a girl needs, a little mindless animal lust. It makes her feel wanted. You been stressed at work? You've hardly been home the past month."

"Frustrated, more than anything else. Running in place, and it feels like I'm not getting anything done." He rolled over to lay beside her. Stared at her naked, sweaty body. Her body would have been great on a twenty-year-old, but for someone on the high side of forty it was incredible, the result of a strict diet and exercise regimen. That seemed to be completely wasted on her husband Ted. Ted worked a boring white-collar job for the Department of Energy, and was out of town at a conference for a few days.

"I know what that's like." She eyed him back. "Do you have to go, or…?"

"I've got nowhere to be until work tomorrow morning," Bob told her. Then blinked, wondering if he should have said that. Did it sound like he wanted to sleep over? He didn't, he didn't want any complications. He didn't think Robin did, either, their relationship was purely about sex. Great sex. Incredible sex. Bob preferred married women, no emotional involvement, no strings attached, and while getting involved with his next-door neighbor was a tactical misstep, every time he looked at her naked he figured it was worth it. Toned, tanned, fully waxed or lasered or whatever it was that got women slick as seals... And she performed even better than she looked.

"Good," she said, ignoring the subtext he hadn't intended. She sat up. "How about I get us a couple of bottles of water and cut up an apple, and then we can work on my frustrations?"

He was smiling as she climbed off the bed, and he watched her perfect ass walking away. Then his phone rang.

Bob grabbed his cell phone off the bedside table, frowned at the strange number, and answered. It was his personal phone, not his work phone, so he just said, "Yeah?"

"Sorry to call from the magic school bus so late, and on your personal phone," a woman from the British Isles said in his ear, "but I needed some guidance."

Bob sat up straighter in the bed. "Go ahead."

"That group we've been interested in for the past week, heading north. That nobody else seems to care about, even when they should. They stopped in the Midwest earlier today, and haven't moved for eight hours now. That's the first time they've stopped during the day. They might have reached their final destination. Which is a small trucking company."

"Trucking? Hmm. Owned by...?"

"No one of any note, but they seem to be a...similar socio-cultural persuasion of our persons of interest. All of which could mean nothing, America is the land of opportunity, the great melting pot, but...this feels like something. I'd like to get eyes on."

"Are you asking me?" he said to Murph.

"This isn't the kind of decision I usually make."

"Yeah, but you're smart and have good instincts. Go with them. Do we have anybody in the area? Or available?"

"I might could find a few people on short notice."

"Do what you think is right. That's our whole gig, anyway, right? Let your conscience be your guide."

There were two seconds' pause, then she said, "Shit."

Bob smiled. "I think that's supposed to be 'shite', with that accent."

Robin returned a few minutes later, walking carefully, heel-to-toe, carrying a plate in one hand and two cold plastic bottles of Fiji water in the other. The plate was covered with slices of apple, banana, and cheddar cheese. He loved looking at her. And loved that she was completely unselfconscious walking around naked. "Anything going on?" she asked him casually, glancing at the cell phone, which was back on the table.

"Just a co-worker a little hesitant about making a decision."

"Oh, God, tell me about it. Everyone these days is so scared to take a stand, to take a position, or even recommend a course of action. Even the guys. Afraid they're wrong. Shit, afraid they're right, because then they're going to be put in charge. Have to make more decisions. You," she said, standing beside the bed, legs pressed tightly together, "you don't seem like you'd have problems pulling the trigger on something you know is right."

Bob smiled. "No, not so much."

She set the plate and bottles of water on the table beside his phone. Then she pushed him back onto the mattress, climbed atop him, and used her knees to pin his forearms on either side of his head. She knelt directly over his face.

"Do you like grapes? I brought you some grapes. But you're not allowed to use your hands when you eat them."

Just the way she said it… He eyed the plate again, just past her thigh. Apple, banana, and cheese. When he looked back up at her, she was smirking. She slowly spread her knees, and sank down.

Yes, next door neighbor or not, she was definitely worth the risk.

Dave sprinted the last quarter mile, then slowed, his breath harsh. Four miles, and only a mild burning in his side and leg from his most recent wounds. He wasn't that sweaty, but only because the dry Arizona air sucked the sweat off his skin almost as fast as he could make it. In Florida, he'd have been dripping. He walked a block to cool down, squinting against the setting sun, then turned up the driveway. Lori was there by the house as he walked up, her phone in hand, a funny look on her face. There was no confusing whose phone it was, Lori's phone case was bright pink and covered with glitter.

"I guess because you weren't answering…" she said, and handed him the phone.

"Hello?"

"You're booked on a flight out of Phoenix, leaves in… not quite four hours now. The ID you've been using out of state." The Russian was gone, the Brit was back.

"Um, okay. What do I need to bring?"

"Other than your work phone? Nothing, they should have something for you there."

"'Should'? What am I going to be doing?"

"Just keeping an eye out. Probably."

"'Should'. 'Probably'. Great. Do you know where I'm going? Or is it 'depends'?"

"You're hilarious," the sexy accented voice said in his ear. "Chicago O'Hare. I'll send you a number to text when you arrive, you'll get picked up at baggage claim." And then the call ended.

Dave frowned at the screen, then handed the phone back to Lori. "She sounds hot," she said, with a questioning look on her face. She'd heard most of the call.

"You'd be surprised," Dave told her.

TWENTY-NINE

Sparks in the Dark

Dave walked out of the baggage claim area and looked around. Even at two a.m. there was a solid row of cars idling at the curb, in violation of all the posted signs. Traffic was paused or moving sluggishly in the other lanes. He'd sent a text as soon as he'd landed, but it had taken him forty minutes to get from the back of the plane to the curb, and he hadn't even checked a bag. He'd received a text in return, MINIVAN, but there were a dozen minivans in his immediate area. Fifty feet back a Chicago PD SUV had its red and blue lights flashing, but for no apparent reason. Maybe to keep the traffic moving? It didn't seem to be working.

"Bucky!"

Dave frowned, squinted, and then jogged between two cars to the second lane. He bent down to look through the open passenger window of a new silver minivan. Max was behind the wheel. "Steve," he said. He wrestled the sliding door open and tossed his carryon inside, then climbed into the front passenger seat. He waited until Max rolled the window up before he took off the mask he'd been wearing since he entered the Phoenix airport—a black fabric loop mask, pretty much worthless for everything but concealing your identity. He'd had to pull it down so the TSA agent could compare him to the photo on the Henry Swanson driver license, and he'd pretended to hold his breath, subtly changing the shape of his face in case there were any cameras around with a good angle on him. Between the mask, glasses with slight tint, and New York Yankees baseball cap, he was damn near unidentifiable. Max likely recognized his build. Or just zeroed in on the one dude whose face was concealed from the security cameras everywhere.

"So what'd they tell you?" Max asked him, as he tried to get into the left lane, which was actually moving.

Dave snorted, then remembered to pull off the glasses. He stowed them in his pocket next to the mask. "Shit. Nothing. I didn't even know it was you I was texting." He'd tried to get some sleep on the plane, but was too wired.

"All right. Well, I've got all the info we've got on a tablet in back, but the short story is a Syrian suspected of being a terrorist, and on the federal terror watchlist, crossed over the southern border about a week ago. The government started tracking his cell phone as soon as he was across the border, which probably means they knew about him before he crossed the border. Maybe knew when he flew into Mexico or wherever. The FBI's been tracking him as he moved north with a number of other people, two of whom are suspected Syrian associates. He went to ground yesterday around noon at a trucking company on the west side of Indianapolis. A trucking company with Syrians and Libyans on the payroll."

"Okayyy…" Dave said. "So is the FBI doing surveillance on him?"

Max shook his head. "Monitoring the movement of his cell phone, that's all. And two hours after it stopped moving yesterday, they stopped monitoring it."

"So…they're aware a known, or suspected, terrorist is inside the country, illegally, likely with some buddies, and all they were doing was tracking his phone, and now they're not even doing that?"

"That's it."

"That's…"

"Fishy as hell? Doesn't make sense? Why do you think we're rolling out on it?"

"So what do they want us to do?"

"Get down there, and get eyes on. Tech support can't see shit on satellite. He's still tracking the phone, and says it hasn't moved."

"And if we see something?"

Max gave him a look, his face lit up by passing headlights. "Then we play it by ear. You're the surveillance guy, right? So we sit and watch. What do you have on you, what did you bring with you?"

"Nothing, they told me I wouldn't need anything so I came in clean. Don't even have a pocketknife. I've got a handheld flashlight, that's it. And three days' worth of clothes."

Max nodded. "Just checking." He accelerated up a ramp onto a freeway, and glanced over at his phone stuck in the cupholder. He had a navigation app open on it. "Looks like we've got a three-hour drive ahead of us. Should be rolling in no later than five." He tilted his head toward the back of the van. "I grabbed some stuff out of our Chicago cache—we've got caches around the country," he interrupted himself to tell Dave.

"Not just in this country," Dave said.

That got a surprised look out of Max. "Yeah? What do you know about it?"

"I used one. But if you don't know about it…"

"Yeah, yeah, then I'm not cleared for it. Anyway, look through what I grabbed and get it sorted. Probably won't need any of it, but…. I know you can shoot, but do you know anything about guns?"

Dave chuckled. "Yeah," he said, and climbed into the second row. There was a big duffel bag sitting on the floor between the second and third row seats, and Dave leaned over the seat back and unzipped it. He pulled out his flashlight, clicked it to its low setting, stuck it between his teeth, and proceeded to take items out of the bag and line them up on the back seat. When he was done he pulled the flashlight out of his mouth and gave a low whistle. "Isn't pretty much all of this stuff illegal in this state?"

"Not if you've got FBI creds," Max told him.

Dave turned in the seat. He met Max's eyes in the rearview mirror. "Are they real?" He knew what kind of resources the Subsection seemed to have.

"Yeah."

"Are you…?"

"As far as they know," he said with a smile. "Yes. And no. I work for a specialized unit that both gives me a lot of freedom and allows me to see what kind of bullshit they're up to behind the scenes."

"I thought you were CIA."

"I was. Saw the heinous shit they were up to, and got out. Disillusioned and disgusted. You probably know. Got approached by our friends, got back in where I thought I would have the most opportunities to do right…"

Dave gave a grunt, then turned back around. He held the flashlight in his hand. "Well, we've got two short-barreled rifles. ARs. Old-school Aimpoint red dots on the top. 'Patrol Rifle Optic'," he read off the side. "Are these dots zeroed?"

"Presumably," Max said.

Dave sighed and made a face…but then again the Colt he'd grabbed out of the cache in Juarez had served him well. "Look like 10.5-inch barrels, Geissele handguards, and Magpul stocks and grips. The receivers say FN, but somebody Frankengunned them. Oh, and they've got a third hole, these things are full auto if we need that. And two Glock 19s in paddle holsters." He turned back to Max. "Who do these serial numbers come back to?"

"Fuck if I know. Not us."

"Full-auto guns are tightly controlled. We start rockin' and rollin'…"

Max barked out a laugh. "Shit, if you're in a gunfight long enough to reload a *pistol* you're making the national news cycle."

"Oh, I'm well aware," Dave said. He turned back to his inventory. "Looks like three mags for each Glock, and two fifty-round boxes of Winchester nine-millimeter FMJ, which is enough to fill those mags. Ten thirty-round mags for the ARs, and they're all loaded. With…" He lifted up a magazine and shined the flashlight on the bullet of the top cartridge, then tilted the magazine the other direction so he could read the headstamp on the brass. "Winchester full metal jacket as well."

"Generic stuff, that can't be traced back to anyone or anything. So try not to get your fingerprints all over it."

"Right. And a couple of chest rigs, that still have the tags on them."

"I thought those were plate carriers."

Dave shook his head. "Nope. Just chest rigs that hold

three rifle mags apiece." He read off the tag. "VIKTOS Taculus MX." Never heard of it. They were a medium gray.

"So no armor? Shit."

Dave looked from the assembled gear to the minivan. "If we're going to be doing surveillance, two guys in two cars would be better than one."

"We didn't have time. They could be gone by the time we get there."

"Or we could be sitting on them for a week, two weeks, pissing in bottles, waiting for something to happen, and nothing ever does. Trust me, I've done this dance before. Do we have digital cameras, binoculars? Anything with magnification?"

"Camera on my phone."

"Shit."

"When I got the call I was just finishing up a day of surveillance for my other job, although technically it was for this one, they just don't know. I had time to grab dinner, take a shower, and hit the cache before it was time to pick you up at the airport. If we're doing surveillance for more than a day or two, I'm guessing they'll be able to get us more guys, or gear, but right now it's just us."

Dave turned around on the seat. "You said three hours?"

Max glanced at the GPS. "Two and a half, now."

"You want me to spell you? If not, I'll load up the Glocks, then I'd like to crash. I couldn't sleep on the plane. I can sleep in a car. Couple hours and I'll be fresh. Or do you need me to help keep you awake?"

"I once did ninety-six hours straight in Dubrovnik, I'll be fine."

The Subsection

Dave slept two hours, then grabbed the tablet and read everything Murph had provided as they rolled at speed south-southeast on I-65 through Indiana. There wasn't much in the file beyond Max's thumbnail sketch of the situation. There were several photos of who the feds thought was Ali Hassan Rafiq, and a brief background on him. Active in the Islamic State, and while there was no evidence he'd directly attacked Americans, he was implicated in a bombing in eastern Turkey and a small unit attack in Azerbaijan, both of which had targeted "non-believers". He'd repeatedly traveled to several neighboring countries unfriendly to the U.S., presumably for military training.

"So, a bad guy, but unless he's decided to hang up the AK and retire to Indiana...what's he up to?" Dave asked out loud. "We're out of Afghanistan, we're out of Iraq... does ISIS care about Ukraine?" He had no clue.

"We're still The Great Satan," Max said. "We don't follow Allah, we let our gays have parades instead of tossing them off roofs, we support Israel...all the old reasons are still there. Anyone attacking us here gets huge street cred with like-minded jihadis. And it seems like, since Nine-Eleven it's never been easier, with the border open and nobody in government seeming to give a shit. Seems like now it's not a question of if, but rather when."

"It seems like it's worse than simply not giving a shit," Dave said, thinking about how the feds had stopped monitoring Rafiq's cell phone. Hell, how they were leaving the border open to let guys like Rafiq stroll across. The Border Patrol was stopping five thousand a day. A DAY. How many made it past them? Probably more than they stopped. Nobody knew how many people were coming into the country. Had come into the country. Or why.

The trucking company was in a commercial area filled with warehouses and small machine shops. They rolled in just before five a.m., and except for security lamps and widely-spaced streetlights the area was dark and still. At least, until they turned the corner and saw Fadel Brothers Trucking. There was a small warehouse with three loading docks and a fenced yard with a dozen commercial trucks in it. And it was alive with activity. The lot was brightly lit and as Max took his foot off the gas and the minivan coasted forward they saw several men walking through the gravel lot and two others standing on the loading dock, smoking. Several of the big trucks were idling, headlights on and fumes swirling from their tailpipes.

Reflexes from several years of surveillance took over and Dave reclined the passenger seat all the way back, so it looked like Max was alone in the car, and peered out the tinted window of the sliding door, his nose just clearing the bottom of the window.

"Shit, are we late? Or do they always start this early?" Max said through clenched teeth to keep his mouth from moving. He kept looking straight ahead, using his peripheral vision.

Dave shook his head. He didn't answer. There was no way to know.

"Fuck, I don't want to go too slow," Max said. He feathered the gas pedal as they rolled past the lot, the tall chain link fence topped with rolls of razor wire. One of the men on the loading dock flicked his cigarette and it arced through the night air, shedding orange sparks. He jumped down and stomped toward one of the idling trucks, the second man following him. The other men seemed to take that as a signal, everyone moving toward the trucks. The cigarette flicker passed between the truck and the fence as the minivan rolled by, and he glanced at it reflexively, then climbed up onto the running board on the passenger side.

"That was him," Dave said. "I think that was him. Shit." The light wasn't the best, but they'd been moving slow and the man had only been a dozen feet away.

"I think you're right," Max said. He looked in the rearview mirror. Right as the minivan reached the end of the block they saw headlights swing around, and the first truck nosed out of the lot. As Max slowly turned the corner they saw the headlights turning their way.

Max shut off the minivan's lights as soon as they were out of sight, sped halfway down the block, then pulled into a parking lot next to a Dumpster and shut off the van, killing all of its lights inside and out. The two trucks rolled past them thirty seconds later, diesel engines loud in the night.

Neither Max nor Dave spoke as they followed the trucks through several turns on surface streets. Max stayed well back, not worried about losing two large and slow-moving vehicles. Then they turned onto an on-ramp and slowly accelerated as they joined the sparse traffic moving northbound on I-65.

"I was sleeping on the way down," Dave said. "Is there anything north of here?"

"Not much but farms and suburbs between Indy and Chicago. Lafayette, I guess, we rolled through that."

"What do they ship?" Dave asked, eyeing the trucks. One was a full-sized tractor trailer, what they called a semi in Michigan, with an extended cab and a full-length trailer in back. It was in the lead, and Rafiq was in that one. The trailing truck was smaller, but not by much.

"Fadel Brothers? All sorts of stuff. Nothing that stuck out, I guess."

The trucks stayed in the right or center lanes, keeping to the speed limit. Max kept the minivan behind them, not as far as he would have had to in the daylight, as before dawn all the truck drivers could see behind them was anonymous headlights. Dave nodded appreciatively—the man had obviously followed people before; he knew what he was doing.

Traffic stayed light for the first hour, then began to grow a bit thicker as dawn approached and rush hours started. Even though he kept his distance Max changed lanes from time to time, and did his best to hide the minivan behind larger vehicles. The sky behind them lit up with the dawn, the new sun hidden behind a thin haze of clouds. Dave checked his watch. Nearly seven a.m. He leaned over, looking at the dash. "How are we on gas?"

Max glanced at the gauge. "Third of a tank left. Shoulda just stayed in Chicago, waited for him to drive to us."

"No kidding. You think that's where he's headed?"

But Max didn't have an answer for him, they just stared out the window at the trucks, moving with traffic, heading… somewhere.

THIRTY

This, This I Can Do

Marek Cermak realized his forearms were aching, his knuckles white on the steering wheel. He pried his hands off the wheel and shook them as he took his foot off the brake. His truck eased forward a dozen feet and then he had to stop again. Four lanes of traffic stretched ahead of him, seemingly reaching into heaven. It was an optical illusion, of course—only hell would have traffic like this. And the roof above his head added a sense of claustrophobia. A roof on a bridge? Tunnels had roofs, not bridges—and yet, there it was.

He rolled down his window and stuck his head out. "Come on," he shouted, but there was no one to listen. Most everyone in their cars around him had their windows up and their noise of choice in their ears—music, talking heads on morning shows, podcasts, whatever. Glass walled islands of solitude.

"Ooh, that's good," he said. He steered with his knee as pulled out his phone and texted GLASS WALLED

ISLANDS OF SOLITUDE, CARS IN RUSH HOUR to himself as he made another thirty feet. He was working on the idea for a novel and had written several scenes, and sketches of some of the characters, and a very rough outline of a plot, but…that was it. He'd been putting off actually digging in and starting it. Maybe because he was afraid it would be crap. But he'd already settled on a pen name—Mack Carver. Hell, half the borderline illiterates already called him Mack or Mark, and if he was going to write an old-fashioned adventure a manly American name like Mack on the cover seemed like a smart move. But before he had a cover, before he finished the book, he had to start the fucking thing…

"What have you got to lose?" he said to himself. He kept his window open. There was a lot of noise, a wall of steady noise, the noise of civilization, but there was a bit of a breeze, too. How far were they off the water, a hundred feet? Something like that. He looked at his watch. He wasn't going to be just a little late. Maybe he'd lose his job. Quarter to, and at this rate he wouldn't even be off the bridge before eight. And he knew better. The goddamn Corps had drilled that into him, five minutes early was on time, and *late*, shit, you better well not be fucking late, you'd be doing pushups until you couldn't lift your arms. Or be on latrine duty for a week. Or both.

Of course, driving a truck for Panera Bread was a far cry from the United States Marine Corps, seemingly half of everybody working for the company was a wilting flower who cried if you just raised your voice, but still, late was late. Normally he was at work at oh-dark-thirty, running around the city before the sun came up, delivering bread and syrup for the soda machines and whatever else to all the different stores inside the city and all around the suburbs.

But Panera was trying a new mid-day route for some of the trucks, meant to avoid some of the rush hour congestion. And he'd forgotten to take the traffic into account, normally there was none when driving to work just past four a.m.

Driving a truck was easy, he'd been a heavy equipment operator and truck driver in the Corps. He'd actually done it in Iraq. Most of a year in-country, but while he'd heard combat, he'd barely had a single shot fired in his direction. Always seemed to be in the right place at the wrong time. Or right place at the right time, if you listened to his mother, who'd stayed up late every night praying for his safe return, and who was he to say that hadn't worked?

The skyscrapers of downtown Cincinnati filled most of his windshield between the roofs of the cars and the highway over his head as he neared the crest of the bridge. A double-decker bridge, which was weird to see, although when you were on the southbound top deck it just looked like a regular bridge, taking I-71 and I-75 across the Ohio River between Covington, Kentucky and Cincinnati, Ohio.

Brake lights flared again, then stayed on. He found himself clutching the steering wheel again and forced himself to relax. "Zen," he told himself. "Zen and the art of not giving a fuck. Not caring that you're going to be late."

At that thought, he realized he *knew* he was going to be late. And that it was only fair and responsible to let his supervisor know. He pulled his phone out of the cupholder and was about to dial when he heard something. There was a lot of noise, wind, honks, and the repetitive banging of something loose above him getting run over by the passing southbound traffic, but *that* wasn't *this*. He frowned, and looked out the windshield. He saw a few people climbing out of their cars, standing beside the open doors.

"What now?" he sighed. And then a few of those people

turned and ran. Between the rows of cars. Toward him. Abandoning their vehicles. "That's not good," he said, leaning forward and squinting. What the hell was going on? Then his eyes flew wide, and he physically recoiled in his seat. "What the fuck?" he shouted.

"Are you sure we don't know anything about what they're planning, where they're going?" Dave said, staring out the windshield at the trucks. He was holding the burner phone out in front of him, the speaker on.

"You know everything I do. More," the sexy Brit female voice said.

"Because they're in two big goddamn trucks, and we're, what, forty-five minutes from downtown Chicago?" Dave said, glancing at Max. They'd turned onto westbound I-94 from I-65 some time ago. Chicago seemed the likely destination. "How many guys?"

"In the trucks? Can't say for sure," Max said. "But there were at least five or six at the trucking company that we saw."

"Maybe they're just heading there to move Michael Jordan out of his penthouse," Dave said, "but until we get a look inside those trucks, there's no way for us to know."

"And you're sure the target was with them."

"We both saw him. Or a guy who looked a lot like him. That cell phone?"

"Shut off now, nothing to track," Murph said.

"Shit," Dave said. "Hey, those fertilizer bombs?"

"ANFO?" Max said.

"Yeah. How big of a truck do you need for those?"

"Not big. A regular U-Haul packed with drums would do the trick. I think that's the size of the truck that was used in Oklahoma City. They wouldn't use trucks this big for a bomb like that."

"But what if they did?" Dave said. "Either one or both of them packed full. What would that do?"

"A whole tractor trailer loaded with ANFO? Park it in the middle of a street in downtown and it would likely take down the buildings to either side. It would level most of a block, that's tens of thousands of pounds of explosive. But that's not what's going on here. These trucks aren't heavily loaded, I can tell by how they're moving and accelerating."

"You sure?" Dave scowled. "Hey, Mu—Mary Poppins. Can't we get any actual law enforcement to roll out on these trucks for a traffic stop? Instead of two dudes in a minivan playing 'What If'?"

"The federal authorities seem less than worthless for this," they heard, the accented voice calm. "Which is why you're there. But if you see something that rises to the level of criminal activity, let me know. We can call the local cops, maybe state police. They've been very helpful recently."

"You can't send in an anonymous tip that there are two trucks heading to the Windy City filled with coke or sex slaves or bombs, or whatever will get the cops rolling ASAP?"

There was a pause. "I hadn't thought of that. Not a bad idea. I'll get working on that." And the call disconnected.

"Fuck," Dave swore in frustration. He peered out the windshield. "Where the fuck is the other truck?"

"It's up there," Max said, pointing.

"They're getting pretty split." For most of two hours the trucks had been in a row, but now they were separated by several hundred yards. "If they split up, what do we do?" Dave said.

Max chewed at his lip. "Rafiq is the guy. Could be

nothing in the trucks. We're not on the trucks, we're on him."

"You might want to move up then, traffic's getting a little nasty. He takes an exit and we have this many cars between us when he makes the turn, we're fucked."

Max sighed. "Yeah, I guess." He glanced at Dave. "I don't like this. This feels like something."

"Yeah." Dave felt the same way. He thought for a few minutes, then climbed into the back seat. He quickly pulled off the plaid longsleeve shirt he was wearing as a cover garment, revealing the sterile Glock in the Safariland paddle holster on his hip. Then he pulled one of the chest rigs over his head and secured the straps around his chest. He'd pulled the tags off and adjusted it for fit before taking his nap. It was very comfortable, and surprisingly low profile. The three rifle magazines lay flat against his upper chest. He pulled the plaid shirt back on over it, open in front, and if he decided to button the shirt up it wouldn't look like he was hiding anything under there, only that he was a bit chunky.

The two short rifles were identical, near as he could tell, and he slapped a loaded magazine into the well of one and chambered a round. "Here," he said, and handed the second chest rig to Max.

They were coasting along at a steady thirty-five miles an hour, four lanes of bumper-to-bumper traffic, and Max was able to get the chest rig on and adjusted in just a few minutes, while working his way closer to the larger of the two trucks, steering with a knee and the occasional hand. Dave loaded the second rifle and wedged it into the second row seat, where Max could easily reach back and grab it. He stuck an extra rifle magazine into the cargo pocket of his pants, and handed the last one to Max, who stuffed it in his pocket. Dave climbed back into the front seat, keeping the AR below the window, and propped it up between his knees when he was in place. His hands were sweaty.

The semi was maybe ten cars ahead of them in the right lane, rolling slowly but steadily west. They passed from Indiana into Illinois. Every lane was packed with cars, people heading into Chicago for work. Dave glanced at his watch again. Just about seven-thirty, the height of rush hour. At this rate, they'd be in Chicago just after eight. Actually, looking at the traffic…maybe closer to eight-thirty.

"Hey," Dave said in sudden realization. "I know where we are."

"No shit," Max said. He was sweating.

"No, I mean, Murph just had me doing some research on a quarry right around here. Right…shit, there it is," he said, pointed, as they moved steadily forward with just a bit of stop-and-go.

"A quarry?" Max said.

"Yeah, a stone quarry," Dave said, as they rolled out onto the bridge over the Thornton Quarry. He pointed, and Max looked out the side window. He couldn't see the ground below, but the vertical gray walls almost half a mile out marked the northern boundary of the quarry. "Freeway goes right over it." He blinked twice, and his eyes opened wide. He turned to Max. "You don't think…?"

"Call him." Max looked out the windshield. The big semi containing Rafiq was still in the right lane, moving along with traffic nearing the end of the bridge. He turned his head and saw the other truck had dropped back. Quite a bit, actually, it was way back there, almost lost in traffic. "Call him!" he shouted, a quaver in his voice.

Dave had his hand on the phone when the massive semi in front of them took an abrupt left turn, hooking hard, cutting across the lines of traffic, smashing cars out of the way, crushing one, glass spraying, metal buckling. The driver of the truck powered forward until his bumper slammed into the concrete divider between the westbound and eastbound lanes. Cars rear-ended each other and swerved out of the way only to hit the vehicles in the lanes next to them, instant chaos across all four lanes. And the semi stretched from one side of the freeway to the other, blocking all four lanes and most of both shoulders.

The stunned occupants of the damaged cars spread out before the truck barely had a chance to react, one driver pushing open his door and staggering to his feet in confusion, when the men began exiting the semi. Four, five, six of them. Jumping down off the running boards onto the ground and onto the hoods of some of the damaged cars. Shouting and gesturing to one another, they spread out across all four lanes of the highway. Every single one of them had a rifle in his hands, and they started shooting. First the people inside their cars, then the ones who tried to run.

The gunfire was a distant popping sound, the scene before them unreal. Many of the people watching couldn't believe it, thinking it had to be some sort of performance. Maybe they were filming a movie? So they didn't move. Not at first. Not until they saw the blood.

Max and Dave stared out the windshield at the truck sprawled across the interstate seventy-five yards in front of them. At the men with rifles. Max whipped his head around. It was way the hell back there, maybe half a mile, but the second truck was across the road behind them, at the other end of the bridge, blocking everyone in. Max glanced to the side. He couldn't see the bottom of the quarry, but just knew it had to be so far down that jumping would be a likely death sentence. He grabbed the rifle off the seat behind him, then looked at Dave.

Dave was staring out the windshield at the men with guns, coming to kill everyone. "This," Dave said, his voice rock steady, "this I can do."

THIRTY-ONE

Quarry

They looked back and forth, heads snapping on their necks as they squinted through the windshield and out the back window of the minivan. Far back behind them, at the other truck, they could see men standing on cars. Undoubtedly they had guns as well.

"It's a shooting gallery," Max said. Both he and Dave immediately understood the situation. Stay in your car and get shot. Jump over the side and fall to your death. Run away from the gunmen in front of you...straight into the guns of the men bringing up the rear, waiting for you. A textbook terrorist attack, simple, designed to inflict the greatest number of casualties with minimal effort.

The drivers of some of the vehicles in front of them were finally starting to understand the situation. They were getting out of their cars and running away from the jackknifed semi. The rifle fire started to increase. Bullets snapped overhead. Five cars up they saw a panicked man's head come apart in a spray of red. Max and Dave ducked down behind the dash as bullets cracked past the minivan.

The Subsection

Max glanced out the back window again at the distant roadblock, then at the men ahead of them, slowly working their way down the lanes of traffic. "Those guys first," he said. They were the immediate threat.

Dave nodded, then he was out his door, across the gap in a flash, ducking behind the Subaru beside them. It was in the far right lane, and there was nothing to its right but six feet of empty concrete shoulder before the retaining wall. He crabwalked around the far side of the car and peered over it. The air was full of gunfire and screams, both getting closer. The terror was starting as people realized the situation. He could barely see the riflemen past the morning commuters popping up out of their cars in sudden panic. One gunman on a hood leaned over and fired a dozen times down the lane between two rows of cars, downing a column of fleeing people. Their screams were incredible.

Bent double behind the row of cars Dave ran forward, taking cover behind a big Ford pickup with oversize tires. One woman running in blind panic froze upon seeing the rifle in his hand. "Go, go!" he shouted at her, waving. The gunshots were echoing in every direction, bouncing off concrete and glass. A bullet snapping past her head caused her to jerk, then she was off, sprinting for her life. His world was a snapshot of images, frightened faces running by, stained concrete, a window blowing out above his head from an errant shot. Dave could hear a man cursing, the words muffled—he was hiding inside a car somewhere close. There was a meaty impact somewhere nearby, a bullet hitting flesh, and a shrill scream.

Dave moved up, putting the engine block of the truck in front of him, and popped an eye up over the hood. The terrorists were moving forward in a skirmish line, maybe forty yards away. In no hurry, having fun, laughing. Moving with purpose, but not chasing after the people who ran, they knew there was no rush—the morning commuters had nowhere to go, they were just running toward more guns.

The men all had rifles, ARs mostly, a few AKs. Lots of spare magazines visible in pockets and bandoliers. Four men across the four lanes. Two more had jumped the median dividers into the eastbound lanes. Traffic there had already slowed to a crawl, gawkers staring at the jackknifed semi, and the two men started firing at those cars. The drivers died behind the wheel, and in just a few seconds the eastbound lanes were blocked as well, right at the edge of the quarry. As the traffic kept going, in just a few seconds the eastbound lanes across the quarry were wide open. Any of the people fleeing from the congested westbound lanes, who hopped the median barrier, were gunned down as they ran down the empty opposite lanes of the interstate.

Of the two closest gunmen to Dave, one man was on the ground, walking between cars, and another was atop them, having a great time denting hoods and roofs with his boots and then hopping to the next one. He jumped up and down, and if anyone inside the bouncing car made a noise he knew to shoot down through the roof and kill them. They peered into windows and behind cars, finding people who were hiding or too terrified to flee—and shooting them where they cowered, holding up their hands, begging for their life.

Dave rose up, rifle butt against his shoulder, the Aimpoint's red dot hovering before his eye, and he placed the dot on the man walking forty feet away. The man spotted the movement out of the corner of his eye and turned to look. Dave's bullet hit him directly in the hollow underneath his nose and blew out the base of his skull. Even before he dropped Dave turned to the gunman atop

The Subsection

the hatchback farther back and started pulling the trigger, four, five shots, the blast from his short-barreled rifle loud, the dot jumping and then falling back like the blip on a heartbeat monitor. The man fell backward, firing his gun into the air, and then the other gunmen began shooting at Dave.

He ducked down behind the truck, hearing the bullet impacts in sheet metal, thunks and odd hisses. He was showered with glass. But he wasn't panicked, or scared—all his emotions had been shoved far away, into a box, that box buried somewhere dark and quiet. All that was on his mind was the problem before him—angles, speeds...opportunities.

He dove forward, using the body of a small work van for cover, and as he did he saw Max pop up, two rows over and two cars back. Max fired, stroking the trigger fast, brass flying, then he dove back down out of sight and the car window behind him disintegrated. Dave took two steps forward, gun up, found a gap between the van and the panel truck in front of it, and worked his trigger like a Telegraph operator, dumping a dozen rounds at a terrorist sprinting between two rows of cars, trying to catch Dave by surprise. The man fell, mortally wounded, and Dave ducked down, behind cover, as return fire hit all around him. The car he was leaning against lurched and dropped as one of its tires exploded with a bang.

Max popped up again, after having moved. Dave found he recognized the distinctive bark of his short-barreled rifle. Max fired, then fired again. The terrorists shouted back and forth, firing wildly. They weren't expecting a gunfight, just a slaughter.

Dave moved between two vehicles and rose up again. Shoot and move, shoot and move. He couldn't see any hostiles near him in the westbound lanes, but the two men on the opposite side of the median had responded. One saw Max darting between vehicles and started blasting, shoving his rifle out in front of him, not even aiming as he ran forward. Brass flew, windows shattered, Max disappeared, and Dave wasn't sure if he'd been hit. Dave braced against the hood of a Tacoma and shot at the running man from forty yards. The gunman stumbled, and Dave dumped ten rounds at him as fast as he could aim and pull the trigger, then dove to the ground as incoming fire filled the air around him with hot metal and spraying glass. He landed on a body, rolled off, and reloaded, kneeling in a yard-wide puddle of blood. There were only two rounds left in his magazine, but he shoved it back into the pouch on his chest, just in case.

Max's SBR was barking off to his left. Dave crouch-walked backward two cars to create distance, then came up, gun ready, looking for someone to kill. He hadn't heard any shooting for a few seconds and spun left and right for a target.

"Clear, I think we're clear," he heard Max shout past his ringing ears. He caught glimpses of Max's head near the median barrier.

Dave didn't move at first, the gun locked into his shoulder, he just scanned the scene before him, looking for something more to shoot. "Moving!" he shouted. As Cracker had taught them, 'moving' was a request.

"Move!" Max shouted back. The two of them started forward, carefully, rifles up, Dave zigzagging between cars, Max straight along the shoulder.

Dave found one of the terrorists on the pavement, the man still twitching, trying to reach the rifle he'd dropped. Dave put a bullet into the side of his head and kept moving.

The Subsection

But the rest of them were dead. He met Max in the middle of the chaos, near the semi. Max climbed up, made sure the cab was empty, then jumped down.

"Holy shit," Max said, wide eyed, looking all around. He had blood running down the side of his face from flying glass. They were surrounded by shot-up vehicles, and easily a dozen bodies just in their immediate vicinity on the pavement. They could hear people screaming and sobbing in pain. There was no telling how many people had been killed inside their cars before they even knew what was happening.

"Yeah," Dave said. They turned and looked toward the other end of the bridge, half a mile away. Four rows of cars stretched away from them, and people, hundreds of them, ducked down between the cars or were still running away from the gunfire. Toward the distant truck slewed sideways across the lanes, barely visible from that distance even if you knew what you were looking at. But they could hear the popping, so far away it sounded like fireworks. The terrorists at the other end of the bridge. Slaughtering everyone who came their way.

"Shit," Max said, then broke out in a run, for the far end of the bridge, Dave right behind him. They sprinted down the inside shoulder, past cars pocked with bullet holes, past people huddling in fear. There were no tactics, no stealth, both of them ran as fast as they could, flat out, breath harsh.

The center of the bridge still looked normal, idling cars crowded close together. No death, no destruction. Most of the people there were still in their cars, not quite sure what was happening, the music they were blasting having obscured the sound of gunfire. They stared wide-eyed at Dave and Max flying past, rifles in hand.

They began to pass people running in the other direction, some of them badly wounded, staggering, bloody. "Move! Get the fuck out of the way!" Max shouted, fighting for breath. A big man saw Max's rifle, thought he was a terrorist, and tried to tackle him. Max stiff-armed him and sidestepped, and the man went bouncing off a Chevy. "FBI!" Max shouted reflexively, and kept going.

Dave hurdled the man and kept running toward the sound of the guns, dodging people, shouting "Move! Move!" His lungs burning, the not-quite-healed bullet wound in his thigh aching, but the pain was distant, unimportant. People, some of them angry, some of them crying and bloody, tried to grab him, begging for help, and he fought the urge to stop, instead jumped and juked and kept moving. "FBI!" he shouted, following Max's lead. Errant rifle bullets occasionally snapped over their heads.

The two men reached the next bodies nearly two hundred yards from the second truck barricade, people standing between cars who'd been hit by lucky shots. Max ran another fifty feet, slipped in a puddle of blood or oil, fell, and rolled ten feet into the median barrier. On all fours he scrambled behind a sedan with two flat tires, gasping, and tried to catch his breath. His elbow was badly skinned and he didn't even feel it. Dave was kneeling next to him a second later. There were terrified people all around them, ducked down between cars, inside cars, some of them crying. Bullets whipped overhead. There were a lot of bodes on the ground even this far out.

Max stuck his head out one side of the car, Dave the other, to assess the situation. Every instinct they had was to run blindly forward, because they could hear the shooting, the screaming, knew that every second they waited more people might die, would die. But there seemed to be just as

The Subsection

many gunman at this end of the bridge. The aisles between the cars were choked with bodies, dead and flailing wounded, blood everywhere. Many of the cars were at angles, jammed tight, restricting passage. The terrorists had stacked piles of bodies before them, a barricade of corpses at the end of the bridge, and were now stalking forward, slowly, taking their time, shooting steadily at everything that moved. They didn't seem to realize their team at the other end of the bridge had been taken out of commission.

Max was panting, sweaty, and bloody, and seemed unsure what to do. Dave stared at him, gave him a two-count, then said, "Stay right, on the shoulder, and I'll go left. I'll try to get an angle on them. Surprise them. We're better shots." It was a guess, but probably true. "Try to keep your distance."

Dave only waited on Max's nod and then was off, zigzagging between bumpers, scrambling with his chest bent nearly to his knees. He reached the opposite shoulder. Bodies and puddles of blood that looked black under the sky stretched ahead of him, littering the shoulder. The quarry was a massive chasm to his left. He scooted to the concrete barrier and peeked over it, then ducked down as the street erupted in renewed gunfire. But it wasn't directed at him—Max had moved behind an SUV and opened up, downing one of the terrorists. The other men were shooting at him, shouting and pointing.

Dave took the opportunity to roll over the concrete barrier. He slid down a gravel embankment and landed on his feet on a disused dirt road. On the far side of the narrow road was ninety-foot drop-off into the quarry proper, with no guard rail. Behind him the access road ran straight as an arrow to the center of the bridge span, then disappeared, cut off as if by a knife for the channel that cut through between the north and south bays of the quarry. There was only one way for him to go—forward. He sprinted along the rocky ledge, listening to a fierce gunfight above. He heard several short bursts of full-auto fire. Probably Max. That wasn't good.

Max had graduated from the CIA's field training at the tail end of the War on Terror, and the only true combat he'd seen hadn't been that serious, at least if he'd had to judge by the reactions of the Army soldiers he was travelling with. Their convoy running through northern Afghanistan had taken small arms fire. At first Max had been scared, but the Muj were hundreds of yards away, firing their AKs on full auto, and ninety percent of their bullets weren't hitting anywhere near the up-armored Humvees. The jaded soldiers' only real concern was IEDs. Apart from that, he'd shot a few people, but most of them had never seen it coming.

That was not *this*. A flat-out fucking gunbattle in the middle of the interstate, with the bodies of the dead and screaming wounded all around. He'd nearly been killed right at the start as the terrorists up near the big semi had returned fire. Nearly turned and ran in a panic. Max felt overwhelmed, like he was going to lose it, forgetting most everything he'd been taught about tactics. But Dave was there, shooting and moving. Moving toward the guns. Calm, confident, almost like he was enjoying himself at the range and not in a goddamn gunfight. It pissed Max off so much he was able to shove the fear away. Somehow Max had killed two of the terrorists, including Ali Rafiq.

And then they needed to do it all over again.

He was gasping for breath as they reached the blockade

at the other end of the bridge. Dave darted off to the other side, then moved out of sight behind a car.

Max had always heard that jihadis, as a rule, couldn't shoot worth shit, and it wasn't accidental. That they generally didn't even try to aim, trusting to Allah that their bullets would fly true. That half-assed convoy assault in Afghanistan had borne that out, and he could only hope the assholes in front of him had the same level of faith in their god…because he and Dave were outnumbered at least six to two.

He braced against a car, got an angle on the lead terrorist walking at least fifty yards away, tried to settle his red dot on the man's chest, and pulled the trigger. The man jumped, and looked surprised, and Max fired again, and again. The man dropped from view, but then the other gunmen opened up and Max dove to the pavement as glass sprayed and car bodies rocked with bullet impacts.

Max moved, popped up, fired several shots, then ducked down again. The volume of the return fire made up for its inaccuracy. He moved and came up again. The terrorists were about forty yards from him, crouched down and running between the cars, zeroing in on him. He fired, scrambled forward a car length, figuring they might not expect that, fired twice at the fleeting glimpse of a rifleman, then fell backward as the car window in front of him exploded.

Max found himself on his ass, and looked down to see blood starting to color his shirt. From flying glass he guessed, it barely hurt, so he figured he hadn't been shot, but still. He moved, rose up in a crouch behind the hood of an Altima, and fired at the men heading his way. But they stood to fire at him, no fear in their eyes. And they kept coming.

There was no sight or sound from Dave—where the fuck was he? Fighting the fear, Max flicked his selector to full-auto and started firing bursts at the darting figures, hoping the sound of a machinegun might slow them down. Three quick bursts and he was out of ammo.

He ducked down, reloading, hearing the bullets snicking and cracking overhead as he changed positions, then he was up again, firing three-, four-, five-round bursts. They kept coming, kept shooting. Suppressive fire didn't work worth a shit against people who believed life would only get better when they died. He hit one with a long burst through the back window of a Ford Flex, then he was out of ammo again.

Dave passed his first people, either crouching below the edge of the barrier wall or lying flat on the embankment, too terrified even to move. Some had slid all the way down to the narrow road and they looked at him, first in fear, as he ran. He waved them down and put a finger to his lips for them to be quiet.

At the end of the bridge the road dead-ended in a vertical rock face. To get back up onto the interstate he would have to climb up the embankment and hop the concrete barrier. That area, the embankment, the gravel road at the base of the rock face, were littered with bodies. Several hung over the concrete barrier. Maybe thirty yards from the end of the road Dave slowed to a fast walk, raising his rifle, wondering if he could get to the end of the bridge without someone looking over the edge and spotting him. There was a furious gunfight happening seemingly right above him. He made it another ten yards when he saw the muzzle of a rifle appear above and just ahead of him. He dove against the loose dirt and gravel of the embankment.

He wasn't quite quick enough, or maybe the terrorist saw the dirt cloud that puffed up under Dave, because he leaned over the concrete barrier and squinted in his direction. Dave had landed on his elbows, gun up and ready to go, and he took a snap shot as the dot of the Aimpoint moved across the man's chest. The gunman slumped backward out of sight.

Dave was up immediately, now sprinting the remaining distance to the end of the bridge. He scrambled up the embankment, loose dirt, grass, and small shrubs giving way under his feet, and popped his head and rifle up over the concrete barrier wall.

He discovered he'd actually run past the second blockade truck. It stretched across most of four lanes, and all the shooting was on the far side of it. He was nearly underneath the State Street overpass. To his left four rows of cars stretched off into the distance. The first few had their windshields pocked with bullet impacts, the people inside dead. The occupants of most of the rest, as far as he could see, seemed to be empty of people—they'd gotten out and run away, away from the kill zone. He could see crowds of people on the grassy shoulder of the highway maybe a quarter mile to the east. A lot of the people he could see on foot were still moving, running away from the sound of gunfire. And he could hear sirens.

Dave ran to the blockading truck, bent down, and duckwalked underneath it. Just past the truck, bodies covered the pavement. He had to crawl out over them. Six cars up, a terrorist crouched behind a compact SUV, his back to Dave. He popped up to fire at Max, then ran forward, shooting wildly. Dave fired half a dozen times at his retreating form.

The man fell, bouncing off the quarter panel of a Prius, and hit the ground.

The other terrorists were shouting and shooting, pressing Max, and didn't notice the gunfire coming from behind them. It looked like there were only two terrorists still up.

Dave darted forward, posted up against the A-pillar of a Ford F-150, and fired quickly at one of the gunman as he was charging down a row of cars. He staggered as if hit but didn't go down. The man turned and started shooting toward Dave. The remaining terrorists now realized they were getting fire from two different directions and spun back and forth, firing wildly.

Dave dove behind a Honda and moved sideways, trying to get a better angle on the man he might have hit. Muzzle leading the way, he came out between the first and second row of cars. Bodies stretched before him, but some of the fallen were still alive, moving feebly, drawing Dave's attention, and so he didn't see the terrorist peeking out past a bumper until almost too late. The man opened fire. Dave jerked back, feeling a bullet just miss his face. A shattering taillight sprayed him with red plastic. He fired blindly back down the aisle, aiming high to miss the wounded, then leapt across to take cover behind a big Lincoln.

He edged out from the far side of the Lincoln's bumper, aiming down the north-side shoulder of the freeway. The terrorist was eight, maybe nine car-lengths ahead of him. Dave was patient. He braced his left forearm against the Lincoln, stock tight to his shoulder, the Aimpoint's bright red dot steady. Seconds passed. He heard more gunfire off to his left, the distinctive bark of Max's SBR and another rifle, but didn't let it distract him. Then the terrorist he'd been waiting for leaned out from behind a car and fired blindly down the shoulder, then looked to see if he'd hit anything. Dave ignored the bullets skipping past him along the concrete barrier and fired once, twice, the rifle barely twitching in his hands. He had a head, shoulder, and less than half a chest to aim at, nearly fifty yards away, but that was more than enough.

Dave knew the hits were good even before the man, a surprised look on his face, slumped backward and sat on the ground. Dave fired five more times just to be sure. The man fell sideways, lifeless, his face hitting the pavement hard.

Dave crouch-walked forward, changing position. He came up, looking left and right, scanning the rows of traffic. He didn't see anyone at first, then a terrorist rose up from behind cover twenty-five yard ahead of him, firing toward the opposite shoulder. The man then charged in that direction, shouting incomprehensibly and firing. Max returned fire over the roof of the Mercedes, a short full-auto burst, but the terrorist wasn't deterred. He ignored the incoming fire and began running straight for Max, zig-zagging between the cars, firing with every step, rifle up above his head, looking to finish the fight. Dave did his best to track him, but the man kept popping in and out of view as he passed tall vehicles, pickups and full-size SUVs and work trucks. Dave sidestepped to get a better angle, steadied himself, and fired three quick shots.

The terrorist fell with a surprised look on his face, and Dave dropped nearly as quickly. He reloaded reflexively as he'd felt his bolt lock back on an empty magazine. He waited five more seconds, but there was no more shooting.

"Are we clear?" he shouted. "Ma—Steve! Are we clear?"

"Fuck, I don't know," Max shouted from somewhere off to his left.

Dave fought back a grin. "Moving!" he shouted.

There was a one second pause, then Max shouted back, "Move!" Dave rose to his feet, gun up, scanning. He saw movement off to the side and doublechecked to make sure it was Max, rising to his feet. They surveyed the sea of cars. Dave saw movement here and there, people wounded or hiding, but nothing that seemed like a threat.

He and Max moved forward, checking every aisle, every space between bumpers, moving nearly fifty yards back down the interstate. Every man with a rifle Dave found he shot in the head, just to be sure. The fact they didn't take any incoming fire was sure sign all of the hostiles were down.

The two men met in the center of the westbound lanes. Max sagged against a Hyundai with a blown-out side window. "What the fuck?" he said in disbelief, panting, eyes wide. He was covered in sweat. Then he winced, and pulled his cover garment to the side. Underneath his chest rig, his t-shirt was wet with blood.

"Are you hit?" Dave asked him.

"Flying glass," Max said. "I think. I'm not shot. Am I? I don't think I'm shot." He pulled the shirt up. There was too much blood to see the wound, but the blood was oozing, not spurting, from Max's side. He turned a bit and pulled the shirt out farther.

"No exit wound," Dave said. "That's good, I think."

They slowly became aware of the sounds of pain and fear all around them. Sobs and moans. "Shit," Max said as he saw a young woman writhing on the ground nearby, her legs covered in blood. He moved to go help her, but Dave grabbed him by the shoulder.

"No," Dave said, shaking his head. Max fought to get free, but Dave held on. "No! We can't. We can't be here. We weren't here. We have to get the fuck out of here. Now. You hear that?" He pointed at the sky. The sound of sirens. A lot of them. Loud even past the ringing in their ears.

Max looked around at all the injured and perhaps dying people, many of them starting to look to the two men for help. And he wanted to help them, he had advanced first aid training. But he knew Dave was right. Unless they wanted to be arrested and asked a lot of questions they couldn't answer, they needed to be gone. "Goddammit," he said, his voice cracking.

"Come on," Dave said, and yanked him by his shirtfront to get him moving. Behind them, someone weakly called out, "Please, help," and it tore Max up inside, but he broke into a jog.

They fled east down the shoulder overlooking the quarry, past the rear blockade truck sideways across the road. A stadium parking lot's worth of cars stretched out in front of them, many of them still running, and Dave would have grabbed one of those, but there was nowhere to drive them. Every lane was packed bumper to bumper, and the median barrier was concrete and four feet tall.

They ran under the State Street Bridge. They could hear sirens, dozens of them, and in the distance and approaching rapidly were a crowd of police cars with flashing lights, heading westbound in the clear eastbound lanes of the Tri-State Tollway. It was the only way they could approach by vehicle, and from the size of the group, the police had decided to respond in numbers to what had undoubtedly sounded like a small war. Probably armed for bear.

"Where are we going?" Max panted.

"Up here," Dave said. They climbed the fence paralleling the interstate and clambered up a steep slope covered with bushes and small trees. They came out on a narrow gravel road, a baseball diamond incongruously before them, sitting idle.

"Where the fuck are we?" Max asked, holding his side.

They were northeast of the Thornton Quarry. Dave had spent a lot of time staring at Google maps of the area when he was researching the quarry. He didn't bother answering, he just pointed off to the right and they jogged along the gravel road. There was no one else in view.

After fifty yards they came to a double set of railroad tracks. They turned north, away from the interstate, and jogged along an overgrown gravel path that ran beside the tracks, under a treeline, for a quarter mile.

A quiet, two-lane residential street crossed the tracks, and on the opposite side of the road they saw a yellow and white house on a big lot. Past it another house sat still behind a fading wood fence. They heard crickets and, in the distance, a dog barking. The horror on the interstate seemed a distant dream. Max was flagging, holding his blood-soaked side.

"Shit, this is too quiet," Dave said, but then he heard tires approaching from the left. He was hidden from view by some bushes, and jogged out into the middle of the street at the last minute.

"Out! Out of the fucking car!" he shouted, rifle up—not because he thought he'd have to shoot, but to help block his face.

It was a fat woman in a compact SUV. She shrieked and started babbling. Dave felt bad as he pulled her out of the car, made sure there wasn't a kid or a dog in the back seat, waited for Max to fall into the passenger seat, and then took off with a squeal of tires.

For thirty seconds the car was quiet as Dave raced to put

distance between them and the scene. Then Max fought back a sob. Dave glanced over at him. "Fuck you!" Max shouted with sudden venom. There were tears running down his cheeks as he glared at Dave. "Fuck you!"

Dave nodded, and looked back at the road, hands steady on the wheel.

PART IV
ACTA NON VERBA

THIRTY-TWO

The Proper Narrative

The Director of the FBI was there, along with most of his personal staff. He'd come to the CIA's Langley campus simply because it was more secure, and away from prying eyes on Capitol Hill. The conference room was big, and still it was packed with bodies—representatives from the FBI, most of the three- and four-letter federal agencies involved in law enforcement and counterterrorism, members of the White House cabinet, and, of course, the CIA. It wasn't the largest SCIF they had, that was actually an auditorium, but any conversations held in the room would remain free from electronic eavesdropping.

There were big flat screens across two walls. Most of them were tuned to cable news networks, and all of those were showing various scenes of the incidents. The story dominated the news cycle. CIA Director Robert MacGregor had the remote, and he kept switching back and forth between feeds, unmuting whichever one he wanted to listen to in the moment, as everyone settled in. It was still a few minutes before the meeting was supposed to begin.

An attractive blonde was speaking into a microphone with a metal-spanned bridge far behind her. MacGregor hit the remote to unmute her. "...Cermak, licensed to carry a pistol, might have single-handedly saved dozens of lives yesterday morning, slowing down the terrorist advance across the bridge from Cincinnati, packed with morning rush-hour commuters."

MacGregor angrily stabbed the mute button again. "What the hell are they doing?" he said, pointing at the screen. "Why are they calling them terrorists? I thought we gave explicit instructions to the media."

"Fox News," his aide Gerald said with a shrug.

"We've had them under our thumb for a couple years," MacGregor fumed. "We made them fire Tucker. They're not allowed to touch election fraud or half a dozen other topics. They know better. These suspects are not terrorists until we say they're terrorists."

"I'll have someone make a call," Gerald said.

The view changed. The truck driver was in a hospital bed, his side under the gown puffy with bandages. There were stitches down one side of his head. HERO MARINE TRUCK DRIVER was the tagline below him. MacGregor hit the volume. Marek Cermak was shaking his head. He looked haunted. "You hear the sound...and it doesn't seem real. You see the guys with guns and you can't believe it. I shot everything I had. I did everything I could." His voice started to break. "I didn't know I was going to be in a war."

The view shifted back to the female reporter standing on the bank of the Ohio River, the I-71/I-75 Brent Spence Bridge in the background. "Exactly what happened during the similar bridge attack on Interstate 80 outside Chicago is

The Subsection

unclear. According to eyewitness accounts, several heavily-armed men shot it out with the terrorists and killed many if not most of them. There are multiple reports that they identified themselves as FBI agents, but as of right now their identity remains unclear. FBI agents or not, they have not come forward. What is clear is that they saved a lot of lives. As horrific as the attack in Illinois was, it could have been much, much worse."

The video switched to a two-shot, the woman on the right, and the anchor at the Fox News headquarters in New York, sitting behind a desk, on the left. "Neither the FBI nor any other federal law enforcement agency has issued a statement on this," the anchor said. He frowned, looking concerned. "They have not confirmed that they had personnel involved, undercover or otherwise. Whoever it was, it appears they fought off a coordinated attack of as many as ten people armed with assault rifles." The anchor gave the camera a serious look. "The questions are just starting on this. And the death toll continues to rise."

MacGregor looked at James Cornell, the Director of the FBI. Cornell shook his head. "Not my people, I've told you. We had nobody on the ground. I don't know who it was. I've checked with DEA, Marshals Service, Secret Service, everyone federal you can think of. Nobody is claiming them."

"Do we have any video?"

All eyes turned to look to the speaker. MacGregor didn't know him, a thick middle-aged guy with fading blonde hair and a shovel jaw, likely from one of the intelligence agencies. A second-tier agency, as he was standing against the wall, not sitting at the conference table.

"Right now," Cornell said, "all we've got is some blurry video from a dash cam of two individuals with rifles that we don't think were any of the suspects found dead on scene. One's got a beard, the other dark hair, but it's impossible to tell much at all from the literal half-second of video, shot through a windshield spiderwebbed with bullet holes. You can see them running by, but whether they're white or Arabic we haven't been able to determine. They're in civilian clothes. If those are the guys, it appears they made quick work of Rafiq's crew."

"Who?" someone farther down the table asked.

Cornell looked at him, then at the clock on the wall, then MacGregor. "Are we starting this?"

MacGregor checked the time as well. It was nine. "Yeah, let's start this. Close that door," he called out to one of the junior men standing by the entry. "Anyone late can wait outside." He waited for the door to be closed, and the room to be secure, before pointing at the FBI Director.

Cornell made an unhappy sound deep in his throat. "We've tentatively identified one of the deceased as Ali Hassan Rafiq, a Syrian national on the terror watchlist." He paused. "Most of the others, at both locations, seem to be... foreign born."

"That was fast." The subtle implication got the speaker a lot of dirty looks. The man quickly added, "I'm just saying, if we announced that information now, that we already know who the mastermind behind the attack was, people are going to have questions. Did we know a known terrorist was inside the country. If we did know, why didn't we arrest him prior to the attack, or at least have him under surveillance. Either way, we don't look good. Especially with witnesses saying it was FBI agents who shot it out with him on the bridge. So the questions are going to get heated. Did the U.S. intelligence community have any idea that something like these attacks were going to happen? Was the FBI watching him? Was Rafiq, or any of the others, on our radar? Are you going to release Rafiq's name, or affiliation? Because if you do, once you do, that makes the argument whether or not this was a 'terror' attack pretty much moot."

The anchor onscreen was still talking. "As yet we've received no official comment from the White House, the FBI, or the Department of Homeland Security on this. The White House has scheduled a press conference for later this afternoon, and maybe we'll get some answers then."

MacGregor muted the feed, and frowned at Cornell. "And you're sure it wasn't your guys? Or somebody else on the federal payroll? Off the clock or whatever?"

Cornell snorted. "Are you kidding me? Any of my special agents stop the biggest terror attack since Nine-Eleven, you'd know about it. Everyone would know about it." Most everyone in the room chuckled. They knew how much the FBI loved their publicity. "What cop wouldn't shout that to the sky, that's a career maker. You'd never have to buy a drink again in your life. President'd pin the Medal of Freedom on you."

"Well, these guys weren't just mall cops," MacGregor growled.

"One dude with a CCW pistol managed to kill one terrorist on the Cincinnati bridge, possibly wound two others, and slow them down enough to fuck up their whole plan," the shovel-jawed blonde said. "Anyone can look like a genius when fighting Arabs."

"Who are you?" the FBI Director said with a frown.

The man beside the blonde put a hand on his thick forearm, and answered for him. Both of them were in dark suits, as were most of the people in the room. "I'm Hansford Higgins, DIA. This is Robert Grinnand, he works for me, and he's here as a subject matter expert. He's got twenty years-plus of special operations experience. From what I've been told," Higgins glanced at Bob, then back at Cornell, "jihadis generally have poor tactics and worse aim, which is why they prefer to use IEDs. The average SWAT cop could hold his own with them. And like he said," he tilted his head toward Bob, "one overweight former Marine with no combat experience, armed with just a pistol, effected a fighting retreat on that bridge, probably saving a hundred lives. The media's going to focus on the hundred-plus dead in Ohio, but it could have easily been twice that number."

Cornell grumbled, then looked at the emissaries from the White House. They had nothing to say, yet, even though, technically, the U.S. Attorney General had called the meeting, and was in charge of it. No one questioned why the top half of the cabinet was coming to the CIA for this meeting rather than having it in the White House. The President was suffering from serious health problems, and had to be propped up during his public appearances, physically and medicinally; half the time he didn't know where he was. And the Vice President was, objectively, a moron who got the nomination simply because she checked the right demographic boxes. The policy decisions coming out of the White House were being made by a small group of power brokers that included most of the cabinet, the heads of the FBI and CIA, and a former President who wasn't nearly as retired as the country thought. The people in this room were the ones making the decisions for the country. And now they had to get on top of this crisis.

No one in the "inner circle" was clueless or naïve enough to actually come out and ask if the FBI or CIA knew about the attack ahead of time, or if they'd known Rafiq or a potential terror cell was inside the country. You didn't ask questions you didn't want to know the answer to. It was better not to have to lie if called before a congressional committee. Their only concern, at this point, was agreeing on which talking points to use, and how to take advantage of whatever political opportunities were in the situation. That was the purpose of this meeting.

The Attorney General cleared his throat. "We'll have the usual senators and congresspersons on our side making the rounds to the various news networks and talk shows, hitting the talking points that you all have in front of you, trying to leverage this politically, but a push for gun control, unfortunately, is likely to fall flat due to that fucking Marine. The one thing we hoped would be a slam dunk…" He coughed to distract from his slip-up, then rushed on. "The White House press conference this afternoon is the immediate political issue. Before someone—and we haven't decided who it's going to be, me, FBI Director Cornell, the White House Press Secretary—gets up behind that podium and starts making statements, we have to come together on a narrative. Was it a terror attack? Is the threat over? How soon do we identify Rafiq? Was Rafiq or his group on our radar? For how long? Even our allies in the media are likely to hit us with some hard questions this time. And I hate to release any statement about certain specifics of the Illinois attack until we know who these men were who killed Rafiq and his crew."

The meeting officially ended just over two hours later. MacGregor stayed in his seat as most of the attendees filed out.

"What a shitshow," he said finally, when just a few men

were left in the room. The room was a bit overheated from all the bodies that had been packed into it. There were twenty seats at the table and there'd been over fifty people in the room.

"It was the deadliest terror attack in the U.S. since Nine-Eleven," Mason Phillips pointed out. "A hundred and fifty dead between the two attacks, and just as many wounded."

MacGregor made a face, then looked at James Cornell. "If those two cells had been able to complete their attacks, what would the estimated death toll have been?"

Cornell tilted his head and pursed his lips. "Combined? Four, five hundred people. At a minimum. And they—presumably," he added, trying to make it sound like this was a theoretical, even inside a supposedly secure SCIF, "planned to slip away afterward. So people wouldn't know who was responsible, and we could bang the 'white nationalist' drum again. And then the electorate would be begging us to do something. Political opportunities galore. Those rifles they were using were all bought here, legally. Huge opportunity, there. But now…"

"The story is either conspiracy theories out of the quarry attack, or the courageous Marine who used his concealed weapon to save babies and pregnant women."

"The cell in Cincinnati screwed up their blocking truck at the rear, it was too far back. Didn't actually block the south end of the bridge. Between that, the goddamn Kentucky motorcop riding his Harley up the bridge between cars like Mad Max, and the fat fuck who should have been out driving his bread truck going all Wyatt Earp, instead of shooting fish in a barrel it was a confused mess."

"Honestly, that close to Kentucky, I'm surprised more of the commuters weren't armed," Cornell said. "Maybe they were and they just ran. That was the genius of the Illinois bridge; no one heading into Chicago for work, especially crossing state lines, is going to be carrying a gun. Legally, anyway."

MacGregor leaned forward and slapped the table with his palm. "Which brings us to the team that stopped that attack. I want to know who they are. We *need* to know who they are. Them not coming forward concerns me." He looked at Cornell. "Could they have been a couple Navy SEALs or something like that who happened to be in the right place at the right time? And are keeping their mouths shut about it, like they all used to, instead of going on a book tour? I just can't believe they were, I don't know, some random Second Amendment nutjobs."

The Director of the FBI shook his head. "Multiple witnesses have stated they had automatic weapons. You know how rare those are, outside of police and government hands. So, off-the-clock Tier 1 guys is a far more likely scenario, but I've reached out to SOCOM, JSOC, Little Creek, Fort Bragg, you name it, and they didn't have anybody in the area officially or otherwise. They fled the scene by carjacking a woman. According to her, they were two white males. Or Mexicans. Or maybe Arabs." He rolled his eyes. "Mostly what she remembers is their guns. And the blood. They had a lot of it on them. She said she could smell it. We've told her not to talk to the press, and so far she's cooperating. We recovered her car this morning."

"Fingerprints? DNA?" somebody asked.

Cornell shook his head. "Burned down to the frame. Outside Dayton, Ohio."

"Ohio?" MacGregor said. "Isn't that on the way to the other bridge? Does that mean anything?"

The Director of the FBI shrugged. "Don't have a clue. As for the interstate bridge over the quarry, it's a huge crime scene. Almost half a mile. I've got over a hundred of my people on it, processing evidence, interviewing witnesses. State and local police are doing their part. If there's anything there, we'll find it. But it could take days, or weeks."

"We have had a run of bad luck recently," Phillips admitted. "A lot of things have gone sideways." He chose his words carefully. "This terror attack. The child porn debacle at Babble. A few other things." He didn't want to mention Abu al-Tunisi by name, a few of the people in the room wouldn't understand why an ISIL terrorist getting killed in Syria was bad for American interests. "But…you miss one hundred percent of the shots you don't take, I guess."

MacGregor shook his head. The Director of the CIA was not a happy man. "I don't like it. I don't like it at all."

THIRTY-THREE

Hit and Run

Max cracked open the sliding back door of the Sprinter van and looked inside. Two pairs of eyes looked back.

"Well, look who it is," Dre said with some surprise. He had a hip leaned against one of the desks hardmounted inside the surveillance van parked at the curb in downtown Chicago.

"Yeah," Max said. Slowly and with a grunt he climbed up into the van and, very carefully, slid the door closed behind him. He didn't want to tear the stitches in his abdomen. Technically he should have been in bed, after outpatient surgery (however minor), but that might have raised questions. So he was being very deliberate and careful with all his movements, and the Percocet was helping him move around without grimacing and gasping.

"I thought you were moving on to greener pastures," Fergie said. Once again—or rather, still—he was sitting before the electronic brain of the surveillance vehicle. This was an upgrade from the previous vehicle—all the electronics were newer. The glow from the computer screens lit up his sallow face. "More exciting pastures, at least."

"Yeah, well, best laid plans and all that bullshit," Max said. He pointed at the chair just behind Dre. "Mind if…?"

"No, not a problem." Dre moved aside. Max walked to the chair and settled into it like an old man. In addition to the glass and bullet jacket the doctor had pulled out of his guts—due to a bad home improvement accident, and the doctor was too stupid or too apathetic or too overworked to care that the story didn't quite match the injuries—he had bruises all over his body he didn't remember getting. And a huge scab on one elbow. He remembered that, he'd slipped on a puddle of blood and gone skidding across the pavement. Just the thought of all the blood made him shiver. He'd been lucky, the glass slivers and fragment of copper jacket had embedded themselves in his stomach muscles and not penetrated his abdominal cavity. Quite a few stitches, but his intestines and internal organs were undamaged. He still was on a lot of antibiotics, to stave off any potential infection.

"I'm surprised you're not working the bridge," Fergie said. He looked at Dre. "Either of you."

"Not my specialty," Dre said with a shrug. "I'm white collar crime. They have so many bodies over there already…they emptied out half the crime lab at Quantico to work the scene."

"Witness statements and processing crime scenes is not what I do for the Bureau," Max said simply, staring at Fergie, who looked away.

"Yeah, I guess," Fergie said nervously. Then he looked back at Max. "You were there. You saw it."

Max frowned at him. "I wasn't there and I didn't see

shit," he said firmly. "I was driving in and stacked up in traffic half a mile away when an asshole rear-ended me. And that was before people heard on the radio there were people shooting up cars on the interstate, and started doing demolition derby to get off the road. I never made it to the scene. And I was totally blocked in, I had to walk out of there."

"Whiplash?" Fergie asked. It would explain why he was moving so slowly.

Max nodded. "Bruised ribs. Sprained neck." He grumbled. "Wasn't wearing a seatbelt."

"Airbag?" Fergie asked, pointing at his own face. Max had a healing cut across one cheek.

"One big giant pain in my ass," Max said in agreement. "Bureau's pissed that I didn't use an approved medical provider, like every hospital in the area wasn't triaging gunshot victims." He sighed, and gently cleared his throat. "I'm going to be on injured reserve for at least a week, and every office, every case is short of agents due to the bridge, *bridges*, so I'd thought I'd help here. Another set of eyes and ears. And I can do it sitting down. Better than sitting at home."

"You didn't see it at all?" Fergie asked. "I heard it was bad."

"Worse even than they're showing on the news," Dre agreed.

"The bridge?"

"Yeah."

"Hundred fucking people shot," Max snapped with sudden ferocity. "How could it not be?" He stared at nothing and frowned. He sighed, and glanced at them. "Sorry. You ever get one of those wake-up calls, life slapping you in the face? Or kicking you in the balls. Pointing out that you are not, in fact, all that?"

"Dude, it's just a car accident," Fergie said.

Dre nodded. "Whiplash sucks, though, I hear that. Got it bad in high school. Whole body hurts. Bad wreck. And the other guy just walked away without a scratch."

THIRTY-FOUR

Rough Men

"That's the quarry!"

Murph didn't move, he just held up a hand, for her to lower her voice. They were in a booth in the bar area of a Texas Roadhouse on the southwest side of Phoenix. It was Friday night and every seat at the bar was filled, the restaurant was packed, and it was so loud people were nearly shouting to be heard. And all the TVs on around the bar should provide a decent amount of electronic interference as well. He'd told Hannah to leave her phone in the car. But still, you could never be too careful. "Yeah."

She leaned forward. "That you were looking into!" Her voice was lower, but she was still animated. Understandably so. It was the first time he'd seen her, since…well, since a lot of things had happened.

"Yes."

"Because the terrorists were researching it."

Murph moved his eyes left and right. Nobody was paying them any attention. Nobody was even close enough to hear them. But still, he held up a cautioning hand again, and spoke quietly, so that she almost had to read his lips. "Correct."

She got the hint, and lowered her voice. Leaned over the table. He would have sat next to her, but the booth wasn't that wide, and he had a pretty big wingspan. "And the FBI was monitoring them."

"Tracking them," he corrected her, although it was a distinction without a real difference. "But not doing anything. Which got my program's attention. Electronically tracking known terrorists inside the country illegally, but not making any attempt to arrest them, or even put them under physical surveillance, didn't make sense. And then they stopped even tracking them."

"You don't think…"

"What?"

"That they knew."

He smiled at her. Loved her, probably, because he was an idiot. But part of what he loved about her was how happy she was. She loved life. And she still had the naivete found in so many people her age. "You know my position on conspiracy theories."

She made a face. "That they're not theories, once you know the facts. But—you know how many people died! Why would they let something like that happen?"

"I can think of a lot of reasons, none of which are good. Terrorism is violence against non-military targets to effect a political or military goal. But whose violence? Whose goal?" He sat and thought for a long while, trying to find the right words. Finally he sighed. "You still think government is your friend. And I don't want to be the guy who tells you Santa Claus isn't real."

"I can't," she said, shaking her head. "Not that.

The Subsection

Hundreds of people died! Were just murdered. For no reason."

"Hundred and sixty, between the two bridges," he said. The death toll had been inching up as a few of the most seriously wounded succumbed to their injuries. And dozens more would be maimed or crippled for the rest of their lives. Rifles didn't generally cause minor wounds.

"You knew," she said. "You could have stopped it." He could tell she didn't want to believe it.

Murph took a deep breath. He was glad she was outraged, and for the right reasons. She had a lot of color in her cheeks. It made her even prettier. "I knew they were here. Just like the FBI did. I knew they were looking at the quarry. Just like the FBI did. I tried to figure out why, and couldn't. So I do what I do, I got the information to some people."

"What does that even mean?"

He took a sip of his Diet Coke, and eyed the basket of warm rolls. They were delicious, but if he ate one he'd end up eating the whole basket, and carbs were the enemy. "What happened in Illinois?" he asked her.

"You know what happened. A terrorist attack on the bridge."

He nodded. Very calmly he asked, "And what happened to the terrorists?"

"They...they got killed." She blinked several times.

He nodded again. "By whom?" he asked slowly, enunciating the words, looking her in the eye.

She opened and closed her mouth. That was the question, wasn't it? Witnesses, survivors of the Illinois bridge massacre, said that several men armed with machine guns, who identified themselves as FBI, battled it out with the terrorists. And then...disappeared. The authorities were generally discrediting those stories...but so far had yet to provide an explanation as to exactly how the terrorists had died. It was fueling a huge number of conspiracy theories. There was rumor of a carjacking by either a terrorist fleeing the scene or one of the mysterious good guys.

"The...FBI?" she asked.

He shook his head from side to side, keeping his eyes on her.

"You?" she said, frowning.

"Not me. I'm just a computer guy. You saw me, I got sweaty and shaky just staring down a couple of meth heads. From behind bulletproof glass."

"Then who?"

"I told you, I provide information to people. Some of whom were looking into it." Bob Grinnand's longtime friend, Steve Reath, was pretty high up in the NSA, and he fed a lot of information to Murph. But sometimes Murph fed him info as well, as he'd done with the phones tied to terrorists moving across the country. If Murph'd had a contact with the CIA he'd have done the same there. Just because the FBI was deliberately ignoring the situation didn't mean every agency would. But if they did...that would be valuable data as well. But the bridge attack had happened before Reath had a chance to do anything with the data.

"If they knew, why didn't they stop it?"

"They didn't know. They didn't know what was going to happen until it did. Right in front of them."

"Fifty people died there!"

"Forty-three," he corrected her. He knew the exact number from the FBI and police reports. But he knew more than they did. Max had filed the standard after-action report...but the report had been anything but standard.

Weirdly, because it was so terse and overtly clinical, completely unlike Max's usual AARs, Murph could tell how shaken up Max was. How much effort had gone into keeping the report free of emotion. Murph couldn't even imagine what it had been like for them, on the bridge. "There were over three hundred people stuck on that bridge, trapped between a dozen maniacs with rifles. Who were killing everyone. Who would have killed everyone."

"The news said there were ten terrorists there."

"Twelve," he told her firmly, and it wasn't a guess.

He was reviewing most of the evidence collected by the FBI and Illinois State Police in real time, just in case there was something that could identify Max or Dave. So far, law enforcement had nothing but a half-second of blurred video of them running by. Murph knew who they were and even he wouldn't have been able to identify them from the video. That dash cam video was the only physical evidence of the two of them. Well, that and one partial fingerprint on an AR-15 magazine that didn't belong to any of the dead terrorists but was too small and smudged to be useful for identification. When the FBI ran it through their AFIS system it produced 382,431 possible matches. Not nearly enough points of comparison for it to be useful in any court of law. Considering Dave didn't really have fingerprints any more, the print must have belonged to Max. "It was twelve against two. I...I would have been worthless, curled up in a ball and crying. But I'm glad I know rough men." The way he said it made her frown, like she was missing something, so he hit her with the full quote. "'People sleep peaceably in their beds at night only because rough men stand ready to do violence on their behalf.' Orwell. Right, once again."

Murph, within an hour of the incident, had received one very brief, generic, vague voicemail from Dave, to one of the two dozen or so sterile phone numbers he was currently using, unbeknownst to the cell carriers. Letting him know they were clear of the scene, and still alive. Details came later, in Max's AAR. Dave was completely unharmed. Max was fine, having gotten treatment for his wounds in an ER two states over, claiming it was the result of a clumsy accident in his garage workshop. Glass shards in his abdomen…and a piece of copper bullet jacket. Fortunately the doctor hadn't recognized it for what it was.

She thought about that for a while. "And that's who you work with?"

"Most of the time, all we're doing is working puzzles. We're looking at information, and trying to figure out what it means. Internet searches, phone records, flight logs. Sitting in a coffee shop, watching people come and go, looking for a familiar face. I am the wizard, conjuring things out of thin air." He waved his hands above his head. "And passing it along, to our knights errant, or to the people and organizations that'll make the most out of it. A lot of the time they don't even know where the info comes from."

"But the other times? When it's twelve against two?"

"Then it's good to have the right people. In the right place. At the right time."

She regarded him from underneath her hair. Her eyes stayed on him as she asked the question. "And who do the people still alive have to thank for those rough men being there?"

He blinked in surprise at the question. And blinked again at the obvious answer, that she'd arrived at before him. "Me, I guess."

THIRTY-FIVE

Damn Few

Dave watched the Sheriff come through the front door of the coffee shop, in street clothes, a generically pleasant look on his face—his working face. His eyes swept the space, nodding to the few people who smiled or waved at him, and stopped on Dave. Dave was at a table at the far end of the eating area, his back to the wall, facing the door, and gave him a nod. The Sheriff stopped at the counter and ordered, then strode over to Dave's table, coffee cup in hand. He set it down on the table and sighed.

"I feel like half a man," the Sheriff said. At Dave's confused look he gestured to the drink in front of him. "Decaffeinated. I'm finally old enough that drinking coffee past six p.m. keeps me from falling asleep, even when I'm tired." He ran his eyes up and down Dave. "You look good." Physically, is what he meant. But it was clear something was bothering Dave.

"Yeah. You too." Dave meant it. Older, still physically diminished after being shot multiple times point blank with an AK, but Osterman no longer looked troubled.

"I think I'm finally getting used to the idea of retiring. That it won't be the end of the world. Although some days it still feels like it."

"Thanks for meeting me. You probably had a long day." As the Sheriff made a move to sit down Dave asked, "Do you have a cell phone on you? Can you put it in the car? Please."

Osterman blinked twice, then turned on his heel without a word and headed for the door. He was back thirty seconds later, a neutral expression on his face. He sat down next to Dave, both of them facing the door. He sipped at his coffee, and waited.

Dave opened and closed his mouth several times before managing to say, "Lori says I need to talk to you. Well, she says I need to talk to someone, and…you're the only person I know that I can talk to about this. Even if I can't…"

Osterman nodded, sipped at his neutered coffee, and waited.

Dave sighed. "I'm…I lost…" He blew out a big breath. "Some people died. Innocent people. And it's bothering me. More than I thought it would. I…" He stopped, and started again. "Normally it's just me. It's always been just me. Me against…whoever. The only people who got hurt were those who deserved it."

"Including you?" Osterman raised an eyebrow as he looked at Dave. Who sighed again.

"Yeah." He pulled a hand off his coffee cup, and looked at his broiled fingers. "I always felt like I deserved this. Deserved…all of it. But this time…not this time. I keep wondering if I screwed up. If I did everything I could have. If I could have saved more." He looked at Osterman. He wanted to tell him more, wanted to tell him everything, but didn't. Wouldn't. Not that he didn't think Osterman couldn't keep his mouth shut. Even if someone was torturing him. On that front, he could probably give Aaron a run for his money.

Osterman's head bobbed twice, very slightly, then he looked down at the cup in his hands as he spoke. "Police work, your job is to save people. Violence is a last resort, and they give you everything they can to solve the problem without bloodshed. Without using a gun. 'Less lethals', they call them now. Pepper spray. Tasers. Conversational maneuvers, defensive tactics. Hostage negotiators. If a cop has to shoot someone, it's usually assumed to be a screw-up until proven otherwise. He didn't control the scene properly, he didn't notice a dangerous suspect until too late, something like that."

Dave nodded.

"I've been in police work for over forty years. But," Osterman said, "before that I was in the military. Combat. Vietnam. You know. In the military, your job is to kill people. Kill people and break things. Kill more of them than they do of yours. Not losing any of your people is great, that's the goal, but it's unrealistic. You're going to lose people. You just are. Part of being a good officer is learning how to lose people and still function. Losing people is a part of the job. Your people, or the innocent. Bystanders, civilians…collateral damage. It's horrible, but it can be considered a part of the job. Depending on the job." He gave Dave an inquisitive look, but didn't press. After repeated problems with a Mexican drug cartel, Dave had been kidnapped in the middle of the night out of his house. And showed up two days later at a local hospital with bullet wounds and grenade shrapnel in his body. Between the time he vanished and the time he reappeared the largest single piece of combat between drug cartels and the Mexican police/military happened right over the border in Juarez. Dave hadn't said a word about where he'd been or what he'd been doing, but you didn't make it back from that, didn't get dropped off at the local hospital with your wounds professionally bandaged and morphine in your veins, unless you had government or military contacts. And since then, the young man, finally, seemed to have a purpose. Osterman could only guess...but it would be an educated guess.

Dave gave a slow nod. "Yes. I know that. In here." Dave pointed at his head. "But in here..." He pointed his thumb at his chest. "I can..." He growled, seemingly angry at himself. "I can still hear them. Crying. Screaming. Begging for help. That I couldn't give them." For a second he looked like he wanted to cry, but muscled that down. "Nightmares. I haven't had nightmares in a while. Scared the hell out of Lori." He had a hand atop the table, and squeezed it into a fist until his knuckles were white. At the time, in the middle of the fight on the bridge, he'd been too busy solving problems. Then afterward, getting Max some medical treatment. It was only after he was home, a day later, that the enormity of what had happened hit him. He got the shakes, actually fell down in the kitchen. Lori had wondered where he'd been, what he'd been doing. She'd seen him before—hell, she'd seen him in gunfights—so if he was this shook up... she figured out right quick where he must have been, and what he'd been doing. It was all over the news. After a week the nightmares were still bothering him, and Lori had told him that if he couldn't talk to her, he needed to talk to someone.

"Can you talk about it at all?" Osterman asked him

quietly. "Something other than these vague generalities. Both my phones are in the car. I presume yours is too."

"No." Dave gave a little shake of his head. "I trust you. But better for you not to know."

Osterman studied him for a while. He knew what Dave had already endured. The only thing in the news which could cause the young man this kind of trauma was one of those terrorist attacks, but he also knew just how many important, incredible things happening in the world never made the evening news.

Finally Osterman said, "Unless you're a sociopath, every man you lose, every person, haunts you. Every time you lose someone, you ask yourself, did I screw that up? Was there something I could have done that would have kept him alive? That doubt, that empty, hollow feeling, should be there. Because it should motivate you to do the best you can, for the next time. Second-guessing decisions, especially in combat, *after* combat, is human nature. But don't let it paralyze you. Don't let it stop you from doing what needs to be done. And when the shit is hitting the fan, pardon my French, doing *something* is usually better than doing nothing. Doing nothing gets you killed." He took a sip of coffee. "While you have made some choices I…I would not have made, you are a good person. I don't know exactly what you're talking about, but I know *you*. I know you're someone who tries to do the right thing. Who fights the good fight, despite the personal cost. The fact that this is bothering you proves that. You might make mistakes. You might do everything right, and still things could go horribly wrong. Mourn the lost. Try to spot any mistakes, so you don't make them again. Do your best. You still may stumble. People are imperfect, it is who and what we are. But you get up, and keep going. If you are that man. And I know you are."

Dave made a face, and looked down at the table. Osterman had a sudden thought. His eyes darted around, as he considered a few things. When Dave looked up at him, he was smiling.

"What?" Dave said.

Osterman shrugged. "You know, it's less than four months until the election, and right now the only person who has expressed an interest in running for my job is Morty Brubaker. I really don't think the President of the local Chamber of Commerce would stand much of a chance if he was running against Pima Jack."

"What?" Dave squawked, his voice cracking. "No. Hell no." He thought about the idea for a minute. It was equal parts stupid and ridiculous, and laughed. "They'd never elect me."

"Why not?" Osterman crooked an eyebrow.

"I'm too young, for one thing."

"You wouldn't even need to debate him, just run campaign ads," Osterman said confidently.

"Where I would say what?"

"Where you wouldn't need to say anything. Just play the security footage from the Pima Motel." Where Dave was covered in blood and busy having a running gun battle with cartel soldiers across a parking lot.

Dave opened and closed his mouth twice, then finally realized the Sheriff was having fun with him. He wasn't serious. Well, he was *mostly* not serious. Dave smiled, gave him a dirty look, and shook his head. "I've got a job," he said.

"Yeah? Doing what?" Osterman took a sip of coffee and tried to look innocent.

It wasn't necessarily meant as a serious question, but

Dave took it as one. "Doing right. Doing what's right," he said. "I think. I hope."

Osterman nodded, and hoisted his coffee cup. "Here's to doing what's right. Here's to us and those like us."

Dave nodded, lifted his cup, and tapped the two plastic lids together. "Damn few."

THIRTY-SIX

The Artistic Exploit

CIA Director Robert MacGregor's desk phone beeped. It was his secretary. He reached over and hit the intercom. "Yes, Nancy?"

"Director, Raphael Birzon from cybersecurity is here. He doesn't have an appointment, but he says he was working a special project for you, and that you told him if he found anything…"

Birzon, that was it, MacGregor thought. *Why am I having such a mental block on his last name?* He checked his watch. He had ten minutes before his next phone call. "Send him in."

The computer expert looked just as sweaty and harried as he had the last time MacGregor had seen him. "He used a brute force hack," Birzon said, talking rapidly. "It's fascinating. Which, you know, they normally aren't, but this one… He used a DDOS attack to trigger the automated responses, but there's a stagger delay between the various security systems in use by the airport, and he exploited—"

MacGregor frowned. "He, you're saying he. So you've got a suspect?"

Birzon blinked. "No. I'm just—crap, you're right, we had that training, I'm not supposed to assume anyone's gender now."

MacGregor sighed. "No, not—never mind. So, no suspect, just an assumption? Based on…?"

"Yes, the style of hack. Subtle, but aggressive. A bit like a work of art, actually." He was talking so fast MacGregor was having trouble following the words.

MacGregor held up a hand. "Save me the guesses about this person's identity, if you don't know, their artistic talents with code, and save me from any further cyberbabble unless those specific technical words are needed to communicate the reason why you're here. Because I already have no idea what you're talking about. You've started in the middle. Last we spoke, over a week ago, you were going to look into a few recent events, and see if you could find anything suspicious. Anything that couldn't be chalked up to blind bad luck. Starting with the Babble network infiltration. Which means I have no idea why you're talking about an airport. Perhaps you should start this conversation at the beginning." He frowned deeply at Birzon. "While it's high blood pressure that will eventually kill me, I prefer it not be this afternoon."

Birzon nodded. "Right, of course. Sorry." He took a deep breath. "So I started with the Babble incident. We already know that was an attack, the porn was planted on those computers and phones."

"By China." Birzon made a face like he'd eaten something sour. MacGregor leaned forward. "It wasn't? You said it was China."

"It came out of China," Birzon said quickly. "But it never felt right to me. The Chinese have their own way of doing things. The code they write, the way they infiltrate systems...it's pretty predictable, and easy to identify. They probably have a government training program for their hackers, and this never felt like their work. They're like a hive, like a machine. This hack was not like that at all. So it was someone, or some organization, in China...but I don't think it was the government."

"But right now that's just a hunch."

"Correct."

MacGregor nodded. "Okay, go on."

"I noticed that the first system breach was in the Cleveland offices of Babble. Babble's servers, their computers, are the same system-wide, they are no more vulnerable there than at any other office. So it got me thinking, why Cleveland? If you know anything about cyber intrusion, it's never quick or easy, you're never successful the first time. You try and try, until something works. Brute force, phishing, code exploits... Maybe you first try your luck with other corporations which have a similar structure or security. So I thought that, maybe, whoever did it was a local, and that they hacked, or tried to hack, into other systems in the Cleveland area. Or in that same building. So I went looking, see if any businesses or agencies had any problems or issued any alerts. Went poking around other sensitive computer systems in the area. If it was Washington D.C. that would have taken me a couple of years, but it's Cleveland, not a lot of national security infrastructure there. And I discovered there'd been a huge cyber breach at the Cleveland airport. That they weren't even aware of."

MacGregor frowned. "When? I mean, in relation to the Babble incident."

"It was a couple days before the porn was planted, but after the initial penetration of the Babble servers. I have the exact dates in my office."

"Okay. Now, who? Do we know who?"

"No, I—" Birzon cut himself off. "I can give you a bunch of technical reasons why, but no, I don't know who did it. Or where they were. Just that they're very, very good."

"So what did they do, when they hacked into the airport?"

"Several things. They accessed all the passenger manifests for a certain time period, about a week, and then got into the security camera footage from that same time. The cameras inside the airport."

"So they were looking for someone?"

"That's my guess."

"Who? Can you tell what video clips they were looking at?"

"I can see which files they accessed, in what order, but those files are large, each one of them contains four, eight, sometimes twelve hours of video. I checked the internet, but there were no news reports of anything happening at the airport at that time."

"Were they looking at flight logs and security footage from around the time of the Babble breach?"

Birzon shook his head. "Oh, no, it was from over a month earlier. Maybe two months? I can't remember now. But the cyber breach at the airport happened just a day or two after the first breach at Babble, so I suspect they may be connected."

"Have you watched the video? Do you know who they were looking for?"

Birzon frowned. "No, it's dozens, maybe hundreds of hours of video. Of terminal concourses and such, where hundreds of people are walking back and forth. And there's no way to know which names on which manifests they looked at."

"Put a team on that," MacGregor told him. "To watch the video files. In the order this other party watched them. Tear apart those manifests, see who was on those planes. Between the two, you should be able to figure out who they were interested in. Once we know who, maybe we can figure out why."

Birzon nodded nervously. "Yes, sir."

THIRTY-SEVEN

Greater Than Zero

"I'm heading to the range," Aaron shouted up the stairs. He got no response, then he heard Arlene moving around. She appeared at the top of the staircase.

"Again?" she said. "How much are you spending on ammo?"

"Look," he said, starting to get a little pissed, "you wanted me out of the house cuz I'm driving you nuts. I can't go to the gym again today because I'm still sore from yesterday, and I need to go somewhere and do something, so what the hell do you want me to do? I'd fly down to visit Dave except he's probably not at home, he's off saving the world or something."

"What exactly is he doing?" she asked.

"I don't exactly know. Whatever it is, it's more interesting than sitting around on my ass." The corner of his mouth twitched. "And when I get back, in celebration of pride month, I'll watch some lesbian porn. Maybe starring the Pork Snorkle herself. Although I guess she wouldn't be snorkeling any pork in those ones, would she? Just snacking on some walking tacos."

Arlene rolled her eyes at him. "Really?"

"Tuna tacos?"

"Go, for God's sake." She pointed toward the street. Smiling, Aaron headed for the garage.

Ammo would never be cheaper than it was now, Dave had told him, so Aaron had bought a case of ammunition each for all of his guns—the 10mm Glock, the shotgun, and the Bravo Company AR-15 he'd bought on Dave's recommendation. "Pistols are for shitheads," Dave had told him, "rifles are for when the shit hits the fan," and if anybody knew what he was talking about on that subject, it was Dave.

Mostly Aaron liked shooting his pistol, but 10mm ammo wasn't cheap. He still couldn't believe how much money he actually had, and didn't want to blow it like a rapper with an entourage, so to save a little money in the long run he'd spent some in the short run—he'd bought a 9mm pistol to practice with, and maybe carry. 9mm ammo was as cheap as you could find, unless you were talking .22s, and a .22 wasn't a serious cartridge. Then again, he didn't consider 9mm a serious cartridge either, not for shooting people... but then that's what Dave carried. Dave had put a fuck-ton of people in the ground with a 9mm. Aaron had only ever shot the one guy, Colman the spook sneaking around Dave's place in Arizona, and when Aaron fronted him the bastard had gone for his gun. That 10mm Black Talon had hit him dead center, punched through his heart and spine, left a golf ball-sized hole in his back, and was never seen again. Fucker was DRT, Dead Right There. Couldn't beat that performance.

He thought about that a lot. Replayed it over and over

in his head. In slow motion. The nightmares—where, usually, his gun didn't work, or he missed—had stopped, mostly, especially since the sheriff down there had shelved the investigation, officially because there was no evidence. Unofficially...Dave told him Osterman thought Dave had popped Colman, and—weird as shit, Dave had some sort of father/son relationship with the sheriff—he seemed to trust that Dave only shot people who deserved it.

Aaron hit the button on the wall for the garage door and as it rolled up, flooding the garage with light, he put his range bag in the back seat of the Taurus. In addition to two boxes of 10mm ammo for the Glock 20 on his hip, he had his new 9mm in the bag—a Wilson Combat EDC X9. The custom gun had been crazy expensive, but it was accurate as hell, looked classy, and had a single-action-only trigger system like his 10mm, so he could shoot it just as well. Maybe better. Definitely better than the Glock 10mm. It had been so expensive he was almost afraid to carry it, but he wasn't so rich he could afford to buy guns—expensive guns—he wasn't going to shoot or carry. The Wilson was smaller and lighter than his 10mm, and held six more rounds, although they were only nine millimeters.

He slid behind the wheel of the Taurus and started it up. The engine growled to life, burbling like a monster. The car had been a used police interceptor Aaron had bought for a steal from a downriver police department. He'd replaced the entire suspension—cops drove over curbs on a daily basis and beat on their cars like some dudes beat on their wives—and then started on the engine. The police engine wasn't bad at all, 365 horsepower, but it had been a bit tired out when Aaron had bought the two-year-old cruiser with 70,000 miles on it. Between the new exhaust system and the improved timing and chipset and a few other tweaks he guessed it had at least 400 HP now, maybe as much as 450. He needed to take it in and get it tested to know for sure. Shit, he had nothing else to do.

Only the fact that he kind of liked his new neighbors kept him from burning rubber out of there, but he really opened it up on I-96. He glanced into the back seat. He kept his shotgun loaded and propped up behind his bedroom door for home defense, but now his AR-15 spent most of the time in a soft case, behind the Ford's passenger seat. Unloaded—because Michigan law was stupid, even with a Concealed Pistol License you couldn't keep a loaded rifle in your vehicle. But he had five loaded thirty-round magazines in the case, just in case. The politicians kept saying there was no chance of another attack like the one two weeks earlier, that the media had coined the "Two-Bridge Terror", but they were the same incompetent assholes who'd let it happen in the first place. Close to twenty goddamn Syrian terrorists in the US, up to no fucking good—although they'd tried to bury that information. Hell, the government had done everything they could to avoid calling them terrorists. Only when every alternate news outlet was blaring their names and faces, their Al Qaeda and ISIS affiliations, did the FBI finally, grudgingly, over a week after it happened, start calling them terrorist attacks. And still they seemed to be lying, or at least hiding things—a team of dudes with ARs, according to dozens of witnesses, had killed the shit out of the terrorists on the Illinois quarry bridge, and so far nobody in the government had anything to say about that. Who they were. Why there were there. It seemed like they wanted to deny those dudes even existed, but somebody had killed the jihadis, they all hadn't just dropped dead of cancer. Some witnesses said those good guys had identified themselves as FBI. The conspiracy theorists were losing their minds. Personally, Aaron thought they were probably Delta Force guys or something like that, undercover, following the terrorists, and nobody could admit that without blowing their cover.

Aaron knew the chances were very, very low that even if there were more and similar attacks that he'd be caught in one, but very very low was still greater than zero. He wasn't going to die for lack of shooting back, hence the rifle. You didn't bring just a pistol to a party like that. And he'd driven over both those fucking bridges, more than once.

It made you think.

THIRTY-EIGHT

Rittenhoused

"Did you have a nice couple days off?" Higgins asked Bob, as Bob stood in his supervisor's doorway.

A genuine smile spread across Bob's face. "Yes, actually. Took a couple of…what's the phrase? 'Mental health' days."

"Sat around and did absolutely nothing?" Higgins couldn't even remember what that was like. Between working seventy hours a week, the wife, the kids….

Bob's easy smile grew wider. "Something like that." His first day off he'd woken up at his usual time, warmed up with half an hour of *t'ai chi ch'uan* forms, jogged ten slow ten-minute miles before dawn, spent two hours at the private range he belonged to working his carbine and pistol skills, spent three hours reading what the foreign-language newspapers around the world had to stay about current affairs, then in the afternoon went to a local boxing gym and sparred with everyone he could for a few hours. Day two, after warming up with his favorite 42-form *tai chi taolu* (form) he did a bodyweight workout in his living room—pushups, handstand pushups, pull-ups using a bar he had installed in a doorway, squats, lunges, leg lifts, and anything else he could think of for two hours. Then he did burpees until he threw up, although it was more dry heaves than anything else, as he hadn't eaten any breakfast. In the afternoon he met up with a soon-to-be divorcée he knew in Alexandria, and got in a little more cardio at the local Hampton Inn. In the evening he watched *Heat* for perhaps the thirtieth time, while eating a sirloin he grilled in his air fryer and drinking two beers. A perfect couple of days off.

"Listen, I wanted to thank you for bringing me in to the meet at Langley."

Higgins shot him a grin. "I know you like being in the field, but you're not getting any younger. You're half into management now—"

"A quarter."

Higgins laughed. "Okay, a quarter. And with your brains and your background, you could do my job easy. Hell, you'd do it better than me. You could run this section in your sleep. High-level meetings like that are where you make the contacts that make your career. You just have to remember when *not* to open your mouth in a roomful of suits. Back-handedly insult Israeli military competence…"

"I did what?"

"'Anyone can look like a genius when fighting Arabs.'"

"That's not how I meant it."

Higgins shook his head. "Room like that, they hear what you say, and then try to figure out what you really meant, as nobody at that level really says what they think."

"Yeah, well." Bob popped a few knuckles. "You hear anything new about that?"

"The terrorist attacks? No. All I know is what I see on TV. And get in the inter-agency alerts, the PDB, all the usuals, and you see those too. It's all just clean-up now. That and CYA. I thank God we weren't involved in any way. FBI smells like dogshit no matter what."

"They find anything new on the guys who stopped the Illinois attack?"

"No, which means I'm confident that they were a couple of SEALs or Delta out on an op, or doing something they weren't supposed to." He saw Bob shaking his head. "You don't think so?"

"Guys like that, who did something like that? Stopped a major terrorist attack? Dropped a dozen bodies. Even if it was never made public, people inside the community would know. They'd be made for life. Like Christian Craighead, in Nairobi. Officially he disobeyed an order when he went all *Die Hard* inside that hotel. And now he's Obi Wan Nairobi, famous, doing the right-wing podcast circuit, has his own line of gear…hell, he even wrote a book, but the UK Ministry of Defence fucked him on that, won't let him publish it. If those guys in Illinois were operators, somebody in SOCOM would know, which means I'd know. No, they were ThreePers or something like that."

"ThreePers?"

"Three Percenters. Named after the three percent of the population that fought the British in the Revolution. No? Anyway, somebody right wing, pro-Second Amendment, like that."

"But they had machineguns!"

Bob waved that away. "Machine guns are legal for private citizens to own in over forty states, including Indiana, which was only like two miles away. Only thing that makes sense is that they were private citizens who either had illegal machine guns, or they had perfectly legal guns but didn't feel like getting Rittenhoused by the justice system. If they were allowed to be there, with those guns, military or

The Subsection

law enforcement, there's no way we wouldn't know who they were."

"You think?"

"I'm positive."

"Hmm. You want to write that up as a brief for me? Position paper, whatever. I don't disagree, and I can send it up the chain. Maybe get you noticed. In a good way."

Bob shook his head and snorted. "PDB. You mentioned the Presidential Daily Brief. I knew it was bad, but I didn't think it was that bad."

"What?"

"The White House. The President. That meeting. A star chamber making up policy and taking positions for him to parrot later."

Higgins shrugged, unconcerned. "It's not like there's not precedent for it. The entire administration hid FDR's health problems from the nation. The fact that he was in a wheelchair for years."

"A wheelchair is a little different than frontotemporal dementia."

Higgins shrugged again. "No man is an island, it takes a village to raise an idiot, or whatever. Presidents have always had advisors, cabinets, all that. And we've had literal idiots in the Oval Office before, although usually they're the VP. I hear he's good and lucid half the day. But you saw the heavy hitters in that room. The adults are still in charge." He said it proudly. He glanced at his computer screen, then back at Bob. "What do you have on your plate?"

"Mission prep for that new push against ARSA in Myanmar. Staging in Thailand, with their blessing, as ARSA is getting a little sporty."

"Right. Couple of car bombs, and a few gunman attacks?"

"Yeah, so far, but the chatter is they have a lot more planned, against Thailand and the Philippines, maybe Malaysia. They're getting fresh funding from Islamists out of Saudi Arabia and have been ramping up the propaganda. Recruiting heavily. JSOC would like to stop it before it starts, and CAG—they think it'll be CAG—will be working with Task Force 90 of Thai Special Forces. Those are good guys. And know how to keep their mouths shut, as these will be black ops, cross the border. Done without the Myanmar government's knowledge. Total MACV-SOG vibes, which I dig. Provided they actually get greenlighted. I'm not convinced that will happen."

Higgins frowned. "Didn't you spend some time in Thailand?"

"In my youth." The Army had stuck him there for a year, right at the start of the war on terror, simply to keep his face away from any English-language cameras. They were doing their best to scrub the video of him beheading a CIA contractor—on the streets of Detroit—off the internet, and didn't need him making the news again. Wanted his face to fade from the national consciousness. And it was half a punishment, for getting caught on camera, not that anyone would admit that. He'd signed too many NDAs. In front of the President, in fact, as the man sat in a La-Z-Boy recliner in a safe house in Virginia. Just one of those stories he couldn't tell anyone, and that no one would believe if he did. Even the people who'd been there with him—John Phault, Jerry Phillips, Steve Reath, and Ron Kelly, all of them injured, Bob worst of all—could hardly believe it. Twenty-plus years later, it seemed like a dream.

"What was that like?"

"Hot weather, and hotter food." He smiled. "Their SF guys kept giving me spicier and spicier stuff to eat, seeing if

The Subsection

they could break me. Some of it was like eating lit gasoline. I think it took a year for my taste buds to grow back, and pepper spray still doesn't do shit to me. Oh, but gorgeous women. Damn. They really liked my blonde hair and blue eyes. And this was long enough ago I didn't have to worry about any of them being ladyboys."

"Is that really a problem now?"

Bob gave him a look. "Apparently. Thailand is a worldwide destination for people into chicks with dicks. I think they invented the term 'ladyboy'."

Higgins shook his head. "I just don't get that."

Bob shrugged his big shoulders. "You name it, there's somebody into it. I'm going to go grab a coffee, and get to work. Type up that position piece for you today or tomorrow. Probably going to be putting in a few twelve-hour days. Maybe running over to Langley or Liberty Crossing to meet with some of their people about satellite imagery. With some of their new cameras they can see through triple canopy like the trees aren't even there."

His supervisor waved a hand. "Do what you need to do."

THIRTY-NINE

Tulsa's Home for Multidimensional Computational Spaces

"It looks like a big air conditioner," Hannah said. "Like the kind that sit on the roofs of buildings." She walked around it slowly. "That somebody is repairing." It was mostly an open framework, and the interior of it was a mass of wiring and circuit boards and modules whose purpose she could only guess at.

"I guess it does," Murph said, trying not to feel disappointed at her accurate description.

"But with more wires." There were cables snaking across the floor in every direction. Hannah was having to place her feet carefully. "Am I going to be electrocuted?"

He smiled. "Most of them aren't power cables, they're data cables. It has the highest of high-speed access to the internet, hardwired, with backup satellite access. And a generator in the next room, in case the power goes out—they get tornadoes in Oklahoma. Complete violation of the building code, but in for a penny, in for a pound. There's a hundred grand in custom parts and precious metals in that, couple miles of cabling, but it doesn't use much more power than a standard server that size. Which is one of the great things about it, compared to the other junkbot quantums people have built."

"Then why is it here?" She looked around the space. Fifteen hundred square feet, a small suite in a small industrial park.

"You mean, instead of my house?" He shrugged. "More room to grow. Some people working with quantum computers think scaling is the solution to solving the errors plaguing their systems, and at first I thought they might be right, but then I realized they were looking at things all wrong. Entanglement isn't made any better by adding more qubits. They're doubling down on an approach that's, well, archaic. They need to open their minds. The real world runs on quantum physics, not zeros and ones. A quantum computer works off of multidimensional computational spaces. And the future doesn't lie in a computer that needs a super-cooled processor with parts running close to absolute zero. They should be looking at microwaves and alternative superconductors. Among other things. Their theories are all wrong. Do you know anything about chaos theory? No? Well …" He saw he was losing her, and got back on track. "Anyway, Google's quantum computer, Sycamore, recently completed a random circuit sampling test in under a minute. The conventional Frontier supercomputer would have taken nearly fifty years to do the same thing, which should give you an idea of the orders of magnitude faster a quantum computer is. And Alpha here makes Sycamore look like Jim Carrey in *Dumb and Dumber*."

Hannah was smiling at him. "And it's here…why?"

He realized he'd gone off topic. "Oh, uh, because this business doesn't come back to me, it's untraceable. I've got a backup in a secondary location, just in case something happens with this one, but Alpha here is where the magic happens."

"So is it run by AI?"

Murph frowned and crossed his arms. "I hate the term AI. Because it's not accurate. 'Artificial Intelligence' would indicate that the computer has some sort of sentience. And none of them do. They're just advanced data processing programs that simulate intelligence. And they're only as good as the people who programmed them."

"GIGO?" she said.

"Yeah, exactly." He wasn't sure how many decades the term had been around, but Garbage In, Garbage Out was a perfect description of the result you got with most "AI" programs. "And it processes so much, so fast, that it can seem alive. Conscious. How smart would you seem if you had ten years to take the SAT, and you could research the answer to every question, when everyone else just had a few hours for the entire test and couldn't look anything up? It's the same thing here. Quantum computers just simply have more time."

Hanna looked disappointed as she stared at the computer. "I was hoping for something more…"

"What?"

She shrugged. "I don't know. Scary? It looks like an HVAC unit. Does it talk?"

"Talk? No, it doesn't have a speaker. This isn't a bad sci-fi movie." Although *Wargames* was a classic, with darn-near cutting edge tech for the time period. "The speed it produces data would overrun verbal communication. Besides, I don't want to give it a voice, that would be too… creepy."

"I guess."

"Honestly, I know it doesn't look like much, but if you

knew how much work went into that...years of my life. Not just thinking and designing, I should be given an honorary masters in mechanical engineering for that build. Hell, *theoretical* mechanical engineering. Self-taught. And it wasn't easy, it's not like you can run down to the local hardware store for neodymium, tantalum...."

She looked from the quantum computer to him. "So... Tulsa?" She gave him a questioning look. "Why here?" The business park was on the northeast side of Tulsa. She'd been out of school for a couple weeks, and had agreed to go on a trip with him. He hadn't said where. He could have done the sixteen-hour drive from Phoenix to Tulsa in one day, but they'd stopped at an RV park outside Amarillo and spent the night before continuing on. Not knowing where they were going had been a tiny bit scary, but she enjoyed the mystery as well. He was a never-ending source of surprise to her, and so far every surprise had been a good one.

"The government thinks I live in Albuquerque," he told her. "I've got an apartment there. And I stop by from time to time. I've got a lot of places, in various names, most of which I never use, as I've got the RV." He took a deep breath. "But this is here, because I wanted it near my house. Where I actually live. That I'd like to show you. I mean, it doesn't look like much, it's not fancy, and I'm hardly here, there, but I..." He realized he was babbling, and shut up.

She walked back to him, and looked up into his face. "You bring a lot of girls to your house, Kelly?"

He colored, just a bit. "I've never brought anyone to my house."

She nodded. It was the answer she was expecting. "I'd like to see it," she said quietly.

He was nervous. He made faces, his mouth twisting one

way and the other. She waited. "My name's not Kelly," he said finally. "It's Daniel Michael Murphy. Murph."

"My name's not really Hannah," she told him without pause, straight-faced.

"What?" he blurted, and she burst out laughing.

"I got you," she said. "Just for a second. Murph? Murphy?" She looked him up and down. "I'm going to have to get used to that."

"Sorry."

"Guys have given fake names to girls for a lot worse reasons." She glanced back at the quantum computer, which was humming very quietly. "Well, if it's just going to sit there and not launch nukes or send robots back from the future, I guess I want to go see your house."

He was driving a ten-year-old Honda, and had she asked wouldn't have been surprised to hear him tell her it wasn't registered in his name but rather to an LLC located in Oklahoma City. The car was clean and had low mileage which, considering how much he liked to drive his giant RV, wasn't surprising. He drove out of the business park and headed north and east into Owasso, a small suburb. Hannah looked out the windows and stayed quiet as he pulled into a subdivision and drove down a narrow two-lane blacktop road, then turned into a driveway.

The house was a newer, sprawling, single-story ranch with a brick exterior, on a large lot. The house had an attached two-car garage, with an outbuilding to the rear that looked halfway between a warehouse and a barn. "I park the Landmaster in the barn," Murph said. He used a remote to open the overhead door and pulled in to the attached garage. He parked haphazardly as it was the only vehicle in the two-car garage.

Hannah followed him into the house. Murph was nervous. "I don't know if you want a tour or what," he said, as they walked in. "It's pretty much an open floor plan." They were standing in the kitchen, and past it was a high-ceilinged great room. The floors were textured concrete, stained and epoxied so they were glossy, and covered with area rugs. Hannah wandered around the kitchen, looking at the appliances. "I wanted a place far enough from the neighbors I wouldn't get questions driving in and out. And where they wouldn't know how much I was here. Or wasn't."

"How big is the lot?"

"One and a half acres. One point seven eight, actually."

Hannah moved through the great room, looking up at the walls and their high windows which let in a lot of light, and the paintings. "Did you pick these?"

"Oh God no. I mean, I like them," he said quickly, "but I don't really know art. The realtor picked them. Or I guess the decorator. I bought the house mostly furnished, and had the realtor hire a decorator to finish it off. Only ever talked to them on the phone."

She moved around, checking out the two spare bedrooms, then went into the master bedroom. "This bathroom is bigger than my dorm room," he heard her say, her voice echoing.

He followed after her and stood in the doorway to the bedroom. "Yeah, it's ridiculous," he said. "I don't need it. But the rest of the house seemed okay, so…"

She stuck her head out of the bathroom. "Okay? *Okay?* You're on two acres, you've got a huge, brand new kitchen with marble countertops and appliances that can't be more than a year or two old—how big is the house? Square feet."

"Twenty-five hundred or something like that. Too big for just me, but I like that my neighbors are way the hell over there. I didn't want to live out in the country, in the middle of nowhere, and this is a nice compromise."

She stepped out of the bathroom and put her hands on her hips. "My mom would kill for your kitchen. That Viking stove? She would straight-up contract murder someone for that. And this bathroom? Forget about it. How rich are you?"

"I'm not rich," he said quickly. It was a reflex.

She frowned. "How much money do you have?"

"I told you, I made good money working for the government, and made better money writing code for some corporations." He didn't want to lie to her. "And I might have written an algorithm that examines the stock market and works in the margins. Gaps and patterns. Which isn't illegal, but I still make sure to not make so much I get noticed. The other money I've invested, but it's Gecko that is bringing in a steady income. Daytrading on its own. Although I've throttled it, so it's really only making a fraction of what it could. So I don't get noticed."

"Gecko?"

"My program. Named after Gordon Gekko, from *Wall Street*. The movie? 'Greed is good'. No?" He sighed, and shrugged. "Fifteen, sixteen million, I guess, I haven't checked in a while. Enough that I don't have to worry about paying the bills. I don't really care about money."

"I guess not." She stared at him for a while. "I thought you lived in a trailer or something, and spent all your money on the RV. And the computer. This is a nice house. A *really* nice house." Sixteen million? Jeez.

He was glad she liked it and told her so. "Do you want pizza for dinner? I make great pizza, with homemade crust. I try to avoid carbs, but my bread's worth it. And I use all-natural ingredients, tomatoes, fresh mozzarella.... I'll have to run to the store for some ingredients, though, I've barely been here the past few months. I've got a housekeeper that comes in once a week, that's the only reason everything's not covered in dust. We could watch the movie."

"The movie?"

"*Wall Street*. I'm sure it's on Netflix or something." There was a 75-inch flatscreen in the great room. "Charlie Sheen, before he went batshit, Michael Douglas, Darryl Hannah, bunch of other people. Famous eighties movie. Won some Oscars."

"Yeah. And then I'm taking a bath in this tub. This thing's almost big as a hot tub, it's ridiculous."

"It's a jacuzzi tub," he told her. "It worked when I bought the house, but I've never used it. I've...the only person who's been in the house since I bought it is me and the interior decorator. And the maid."

"It's big enough for both of us, easy." She stared at him, her gaze steady.

"Yeah, I guess. I'm not much for baths."

She smiled and rolled her eyes. "When a girl invites you into a bathtub with her, it's not to take a bath. I'm perfectly capable of sitting on one of the jacuzzi jets myself."

His mouth opened in a small O. "Oh."

"Are you sure you're smart?"

"Only when it comes to computers. I'm not smart enough to figure girls out." She laughed out loud at that, hard. "What?" he said defensively.

"Boys are idiots," she said definitively. "Even the certified geniuses."

Murph was wide awake just after four a.m. Asleep, then fully awake, like flipping a switch. They'd gone shopping together—which was weird. It felt like they were an old married couple or something, wandering up and down the aisles of the grocery store. But he'd liked it. It felt normal. Right. Then while he made the bread she started prepping the ingredients, shredding the cheese and slicing up the pepperoni. There was more than enough room in the kitchen for the both of them.

The pizza had turned out perfect, and they'd eaten it while watching *Wall Street*, which was showing its age a bit but still a great movie. Then she'd headed into the bathroom and the giant tub, doing girl stuff. She'd called him in about twenty minutes later.

He'd never taken a bath with a girl before. Or, rather, been in a bathtub with a girl. He'd learned a few things—don't fill the tub too full, because two bodies will raise the water level quite a bit. And when you start moving…you'll splash all over the floor. Also, water tended to wash away any lube, natural or otherwise. But on the whole the experiment was a huge success. Ten out of ten stars. He would definitely recommend it.

She'd curled up beside him on the big king-size bed, smiling, and fallen right asleep. So had he, but his eyes popped wide open almost exactly at four a.m. That was nearly six hours sleep, which was all he needed. Heck, it was more than what he usually got. His brain could only sit in neutral for so long.

Hannah was a vague shape on the bed beside him, breathing softly. He listened to her for a while, then carefully eased out of bed, put on sweatpants and a t-shirt, and headed out to the kitchen. He started the coffee maker, then pulled out one of the laptops he'd basically rebuilt from the ground up, that ran on his proprietary OS, and booted it up. And his eyes widened at the alerts that flashed across the screen.

"What's going on here?" he murmured. He squinted and leaned in. Alpha had found something that it thought would be of interest to him.

And it was right. It always was.

FORTY

The Thing, In the Place, With the Guy

Aaron staggered to a near-stop at the end of his driveway, bathed in sweat. Even at nine in the morning it was hot out—over eighty, and high humidity, which was the more important aspect. Anybody who said that humidity wasn't important didn't know shit—in Arizona, if you stepped into the shade when it was eighty degrees out, you might be tempted to put on a sweatshirt. The air didn't retain any of the heat—if you were out of the sun, you were out of the heat. In high humidity, the temps would have to drop into the sixties before you'd want anything thicker than a t-shirt. He'd only done two miles, but he'd done two eight-minute miles, in high humidity—without dying or coughing up a lung. So, success.

He hocked up a big lunger and spit it on the pavement as he walked down the street, cooling off. He'd been up for over three hours, and Arlene had left for work over two hours before. He hated working out in the morning, but he'd done all the painting and home repair he could think of, all the organizing he could stand. He was going a little bit crazy, in fact, home alone all day, especially with Arlene still working. And she'd be gone all day, they had a manager's meeting at shift end at Brink's, and she wouldn't be home until seven or more likely eight. Twelve hours for him, of staring at the walls.

He walked until he no longer felt like dying or committing murder, then headed in to take a shower. Trying to think of something to do. He was done working out for the day, and didn't want to head to the range as he'd already burned up most of the ammo he'd bought, and that hadn't been cheap. He didn't feel like seeing a movie or watching anything on TV. You could only watch so much porn.

In clean clothes, hair still wet, he dropped onto the couch with a grunt. Peanut was lying on her side out on the concrete patio, in the sun. She heard him, and came in through the doggie door. With a grunt not unlike his, the aging dog jumped up onto the couch next to him, circled twice, then laid down. Aaron looked at her. "I could take you for a walk," he proposed. She lifted her head and looked at him, her ears twitching. She liked walks, although she couldn't go as far or as fast as she used to. "Let me make a call first," he told her. He pulled out his phone, and dialed. No answer, as usual. He made a sound, deep in his throat, didn't bother leaving a voicemail, and dialed a second number.

"Hey Aaron, what's up?"

"Oh, shit," he said, suddenly realizing the time where she was. He glanced at his watch, a new Timex G-Shock Mudmaster. He'd been wanting one for years, but could never justify the expense. "I didn't wake you, did I?"

Lori laughed in his ear. "No, I usually get up early. I've been bumming around the kitchen, drinking coffee."

"Okay, good. Naked? Please tell me naked."

She laughed in his ear. "Is naked better than wearing just a t-shirt that barely comes down far enough to cover my ass? You can see my nipples right through it. Guys like that, don't they?"

He could hear the smile on her face. "Ah, you're killing me, Smalls," he said, knowing there was no way to know if she was telling the truth about the t-shirt or not, but very well could be. She laughed even louder. "Is Dave around? I've been trying him for over a day, and it's going straight to voicemail. I just wanted to make sure he wasn't back in the hospital or some shit."

"No. He's, ah, out of town, and he doesn't have his phone."

Which was not unexpected information. "Is he doing what he was doing before?" Aaron asked her.

She paused, then asked, "What do you know about it?"

"What do you know about it?" he responded.

"Some. Not all the details, but…" She laughed. "You know, the thing, in the place, with the guy."

He laughed back. "I was helping him. Uh, two months ago? When he was up near here."

"You were?"

"Yeah. He didn't say? Figures. For a couple days."

"Oh. Yeah, I think he's doing that. Same place, in fact, although I actually don't know exactly where it is. Or what he was doing. Is doing. If you were there, you'd know more than me. And I don't know when he's going to be back."

"Okay, thanks. When he gets back, you have him call me." Aaron hung up, then sat, frowning at his phone. He thought for a little while. "Road trip?" he said to himself. It was a three hour trip each way, maybe a little more, but he had all fucking day. Arlene wouldn't be home for another ten hours. Peanut looked at him and cocked her head. He looked back at her. "Road trip," he said definitively, with a nod. She jumped up onto her feet. "No, not you," he said, "and maybe not the Taurus. Just in case. I'll take you for a walk, first, though. Before it gets too hot."

He'd driven a rental down to Ohio last time. Maybe it was time for another rental car. Every rental car was a four-wheel-drive truck when you got the full insurance coverage...so maybe he should get something fun. He looked at Peanut. "Something nice," he told her. "Fast. With satellite radio. Listen to some classic tunes, exceed the speed limit... and if I can't find him, shit, at least I'll be able to buy an overpriced cup of coffee and hang out with the purple-haired peacocks, do Pride Month right. Right?" Peanut cocked her head the other way, her one ear falling over, waiting to hear a word she recognized.

Aaron remembered the muscle chick working with Dave giving him grief for not doing something to disguise himself. Which still pissed him off. But maybe he could do a little something...and jogging in this heat, he'd sure noticed that he was overdue for a haircut. He pulled his phone out again, and dialed a number. Listened to it ring. "Hey, *stronzo*! It's Aaron Abruzzo. You got any openings?"

Since he hadn't made a reservation at the rental car center, his choices had been a bit limited—an EV, a Sprinter van, or a Dodge Durango with a hemi. That hadn't been any choice at all.

"Nobody wants the EV," the clerk behind the counter had said, frowning.

"No one who supports renewable energy should," Aaron told her, hitting her with his reasonable tone. "Coal-powered cars are horrible for the environment."

She'd gaped at him. "It's an electric vehicle," she said, confused.

"It's a battery-powered vehicle," he corrected her. "What do you think makes the electricity to charge the battery? Coal, or natural gas, but mostly coal. Burned in a power plant. And that giant battery in that car is nothing but toxic chemicals you can't recycle. Mined, probably, by child slaves in the Congo, just like they used to do diamonds. You seriously think a coal-powered car is better for the environment? For the world?" He tsked and shook his head. The look that came over her face had been the best thing about that conversation. It was almost worth the price of the rental, which was…well, not horrible, but still made him twitch.

The Durango had balls, but it was slow and sluggish compared to his Taurus SHO. Still, it was nice, and had satellite radio. He listened to classic rock heading down I-75 to Toledo…and then…Interstate 80. He shook his head. His wallet had been lightened more than a bit. "Toll roads, man," he muttered, shaking his head. Any state with toll roads was automatically ass in his book, whether that was Ohio or Florida. But especially Illinois.

The trip to Cleveland didn't seem to take any time at all. Aaron parked the rental on the second floor of the parking garage, got out, and stretched. The parking garage was dim and echoey, and familiar. Even though it had been a while it was, after all, the last parking garage he'd been in, now that he wasn't spending all day driving around Detroit, waiting to get robbed. He walked over to the barrier wall and looked out over 14th Street south of Euclid. Cleveland's theater district. It was early afternoon, and there wasn't much to see—cars parked at the curb, a few pedestrians going back and forth, the constant background noise of a city. The colorful banners for various plays at the theaters just up the block. But he'd stood there and watched that particular street for hours and hours when he'd been doing surveillance with Dave, and everything looked familiar. He watched for a bit, but didn't see any cars or people that he recognized. Nothing that stood out.

Aaron took the stairwell down, walked across 14th, and then up the sidewalk to the Starbucks on the corner. He'd missed the lunch rush, and there were only a few customers in the restaurant as he walked up to the counter. He didn't recognize any of the customers.

"Hi! Good afternoon! Can I help you?"

Aaron's eyes went from the pudgy young man's face to his nametag and back. "I know you."

"You do?" Mar squinted.

"I was here, with a buddy, a couple months ago. We hung out for a few days. He's tall, skinny. I had longer hair."

"And a moustache!" Mar said, in sudden recognition. He leaned back and ran his eyes over Aaron. "You've had quite the makeover. You did a Freddie Mercury, went from long hair and a shaggy moustache to short hair and clean-shaven."

"So you're saying I look gay," Aaron said. "Well, it is the right month for it."

Mar pretended to pout. "The poor man's teeth were a mess, I'll grant you that, but don't tell me he was ugly."

Aaron gave him a grudging look. "Okay, I'll take it. Freddie Mercury. I've been called a lot worse." He'd done all the spy shit he could think of. He'd swapped the plate on the Durango with one he'd grabbed off a fresh wreck in a local junkyard after his last visit to Cleveland, just in case. He'd decided to carry the custom Wilson Combat EDC X9, because why not, but he'd spent five minutes pulling all the ammo out of his carry mags, wiping off any fingerprints, then reloading the magazines using his shirtfront as a glove. And then he'd done what he could to change his appearance. His hair was long, too long, especially if he was going to be an idiot and continue jogging in this heat, so he'd told his barber to hack it all off. His hair was the shortest it had been since he'd gotten out of the Navy. And his face felt naked without a moustache, but he'd been curious what he'd look like now without one. He'd had a 'stache for ten years, maybe more. He'd pulled a baseball cap on over his head, and was wearing clear-lensed shooting glasses that, from a distance, just looked like thick-rimmed regular glasses, which were in fashion.

"You look younger. I think," Mar said. "But it's been a while."

"Yeah. And on that note, remember my buddy? Have you seen him around recently? Last day or two."

"Did you have a fight?" Mar asked, concerned.

"Our relationship is…complicated," Aaron said, deciding to have a little fun. Fuck it, wasn't he on vacation here in only-gay-for-the-stay Cleveland? Kind of? At least until he found Dave.

Mar rolled his eyes. "Oh, honey, aren't they all. Um…I think I maybe saw him earlier this morning, but we were slammed and I couldn't say for sure." He glanced past Aaron as two people entered the store and headed for the counter. "Do you want a coffee? What can I get you?"

"A hot coffee with cream. Real cream, half and half. A large."

"You mean a venti?" Mar asked.

"Are we going to start that shit again?" Aaron said, raising one eyebrow. "*Scavalcherò questo bancone e ti schiaffo da frocetto.*"

The Subsection

"I don't even know what you're saying, but anything Italian sounds so sexy," Mar said, giving him a smoldering look.

Aaron rolled his eyes. "Just the coffee. And cream from a cow, no nut juice!" Aaron said to Mar's retreating back. He heard Mar sniggering.

Large coffee in hand, Aaron stood in front of the floor-to-ceiling windows by the door and looked out over the intersection. Early afternoon was the slowest time of day, at least on a weekday in a downtown area thick with office buildings. But he watched the light traffic passing by on 14th Street and Euclid Avenue, observed the pedestrians moving up and down the sidewalks, entering the various buildings. Looking for Dave, or anything that caught his attention, because the natural ebb-and-flow of the area gradually came back to him. He'd spent a lot of hours staring out at those streets. He didn't see Dave, or the muscle chick. But maybe one or both of them was inside the U.S. Bank Centre Building across the street. Having a late lunch at the shitty Viet Cong restaurant in the lobby. Eating cat au gratin.

A new Chevy Tahoe with tinted windows pulled onto 14th from Euclid and paused at the curb in front of the U.S. Bank Centre building, partially blocking Aaron's view. He waited, but nobody exited the vehicle. And it continued to sit there, in a traffic lane. Passing cars had to go around it. The unseen driver must have shifted it into Park, as the brake lights went off, but the big vehicle didn't move. Then Aaron saw a Sprinter van with writing on the side pull to the curb up on Euclid across from the bank building, in front of the United Way building. And sit there, nobody getting in or out. He could see the vague form of the driver behind the glass. Aaron knew for a fact that was a no parking zone.

Humming to himself, Aaron pushed out the front door of the Starbucks and casually made his way across 14th Street, crossing behind the idling Tahoe. He glanced at it, like any normal person would, but there was nothing to see behind the deeply-tinted glass. Ohio plates. He kept his coffee cup up in his left hand, head down, using the cup to block his face when he looked up, pretending to take a few sips as he walked up toward the front doors of the building and entered.

The lobby was as he remembered it. He could smell the shitty food from the Vietnamese restaurant, and looked casually in that direction. He didn't see anybody he recognized, and there was hardly anyone in the lobby at the moment. Nobody who stood out, either, the few people he saw were coming or going, nobody loitering. One set of elevator doors just closing. Faint horrid music coming from hidden speakers—an all-strings version of a Taylor Swift song, dear God. While the smell of commie dumpster juice noodles filled the air. Maybe he'd actually died, and gone to Hell.

Aaron crossed the lobby, not looking at anyone or anything in particular. He glanced up and down the short hallways to either side as he neared the elevators, but didn't see anything of note. He paused just a second, then moved to the nearest elevators and hit the button. There was a car waiting right there, and the doors opened.

The car was empty. Aaron stepped in. His hand hovered over the panel, then hit the button for 7 on a hunch. The doors closed smoothly, and the elevator rose, almost silently. It wasn't until the car passed the sixth floor and began to slow that he heard anything. A sudden, loud noise, tough to make out. The elevator pinged as it reached the seventh floor and Aaron stepped out automatically, two steps, then froze.

There were three men armed for war right in front of him—suppressed submachine guns, balaclavas covering their faces, shouting down the corridor. One of them spun and stuck his muzzle right in Aaron's face, shouting "Down! Down! Get the fuck down!" The other men were shouting as well, the noise filling the corridor. From their bulk, Aaron's expert eyes told him that while they were muscled, they were also likely wearing soft body armor under their street clothes.

Aaron's hands shot up above his head, the coffee cup still in his left. "Whoa! Don't shoot! I clearly got off on the wrong fucking floor. Let me just—"

"On the fucking floor!" the man in front of him shouted again, taking half a step toward Aaron.

FORTY-ONE

So Say We All

"Okay, so I hate doing this, but we're a little pressed for time, if you want to act on this, and I'm guessing you do. I've made the connection as secure as possible, but still, avoid details as we talk." Murph was trying out a computer-generated male Russian accent this time. He sounded like a movie villain.

"What's up?" Dave heard Bob say. He had no idea where Bob might be. Dave had gotten a generic text on his personal phone which had made him drive twenty miles from home—and his personal iPhone—before pulling his work phone out of the faraday bag and making a call.

"That recent operation in the Midwest that we resolved by me planting some stuff that made me feel very dirty…"

"Yeah?" Dave said. So that was why he was on the call, they were talking about his case in Cleveland.

"If you remember, it all started with somebody having a heart attack. And with a bit of work I identified the cause of that heart attack."

Dave blinked in surprise. He couldn't remember the

The Subsection

man's name, just that he was Asian, and a high-level black CIA operative, travelling under an alias. "Right. And?"

"And I know where he's going to be in two days."

The connection hummed faintly as both Dave and Bob digested that information. "Yeah?" Bob finally said. "Where's that?"

"Right where he was before. Some sort of cleanup operation. I don't have too many details and what I do have I can't discuss here. What we did, what I did, we shut down a shitshow of an illegal government operation, but we didn't touch the guy who actually did the deed that got us into this in the first place. He's good, the guy's a ghost, even I can't figure out exactly where he's living. And I've been trying, because I know you wanted to give him a visit. But I know where he's going to be the day after tomorrow. With just one or two companions, it sounds like. Tech guys. If you're interested. Are you interested?"

"Quickdraw?" Bob said.

Dave was surprised. "There's three of us on this call, and I'm low man on the totem pole. Aren't you the group supervisor?"

"Yes, but you were the lead on this one. You ran it on the ground. Your opinion counts as much as anyone's. And decisions like this, whoever is involved, I want a unanimous decision. Like a jury. Since we are determining someone's fate." Bob went silent, waiting.

Dave thought about it. He wondered if this was some sort of test. Finally he said, "Isn't this what we do? Exactly what we do? Go after the people who are supposed to be looking out for us, but are doing very bad things? Because no one else will hold them accountable?"

"It is," Bob said. "But before you answer, just remember, if everything goes right, this won't be a heat-of-the-moment thing. A defending yourself thing. It'll be a walk up and two-to-the-back-of-the-head thing."

"I'm aware," Dave said. After a brief pause he added, "It wouldn't be my first time." He could still remember Paolo "Big Paulie" Bufonte turning, just at the last moment, as Dave flew up behind him, no headlights, fifty miles an hour on a narrow residential street, but he'd got the timing just right. Paulie's eyes went wide half a second before impact, but he'd had no time to dodge. He was a big guy and had flown up over the car, his broken legs twisting wildly. Dave had stood on the brakes, thrown it into reverse, and made sure the man who'd killed his parents was well and truly dead. He could still hear the sound the man's head had made slamming into the asphalt underneath the car. Dave'd had nightmares about doing it, and getting caught, but he'd never regretted actually doing the deed. Cold-blooded murder. One life for two seemed perfectly reasonable. "This guy murdered someone, just a regular dude doing nothing wrong, just because he might have seen the wrong person in the wrong place at the wrong time. But there's no way to prove that."

"Correct," Bob said. "And this guy's protected, at the highest levels, he'll never see the inside of a courtroom for anything, we try to go the legal route."

"I vote yes," Dave said. It wasn't a tough decision for him.

"Tech support?" Bob said.

"Christ, I hate it when you ask me," Murph typed-talked in the Russian accent. But there was hardly two seconds' pause before they heard him say "Yes".

"So say we all," Bob concluded.

"So what's next?" Dave asked.

"I've got to put together a team," Bob said. "See who's

available, short notice. And we should meet in person if at all possible, ahead of time, work out whatever kind of plan we can."

"We?" Dave said.

"I've been working sixteen-hour days for ten days straight doing mission prep for a shitshow of an overseas operation that's probably never going to happen, because the guys currently in charge over there are suddenly too busy worrying about a potential coup. Or so it seems." He sighed. "I'm due for a day off. Or two. And actually seeing some action would relieve a bit of stress from all this office work."

"We are not the same," Murph's Russian digital voice said.

Twenty-six hours later Dave drove slowly down the narrow, one-way street. He scanned the numbers on the front of the houses. The one he was looking for turned out to be a small bungalow with yellow aluminum siding and white wood trim. A narrow asphalt driveway ran up beside the house to a tall garage in back. The garage was nearly as large as the house, and looked newer. Dave drove by, scanning the passing houses and the cars parked on the street. He didn't see anything. He circled the block, parked the rental on the street six houses down, then walked up the sidewalk. As he turned up the driveway the side door of the house opened and Bob motioned him in.

"Safe house?" Dave asked, as he entered. The inside of the house was dim and cool.

"Kind of," Murph said. He was behind Bob, standing in the small kitchen. Dimi was there beside him. "An LLC that didn't exist last year rented the house four months ago, twelve months upfront. This is the first time anybody's used it. Got another fifteen or so like it around the country." And no two were rented by the same LLC, just in case one of them got compromised.

"North College Hill," Dave said. It was a tiny suburb about ten miles north of downtown Cincinnati. "Why here?"

Murph shrugged. "Central to the Midwest. From here in six hours you can drive to Michigan, Illinois, Indiana, Pennsylvania, Tennessee, Kentucky, West Virginia, western Pennsylvania, the north end of Georgia…or just stay here, out of sight, out of mind." He pointed at the refrigerator. "Anybody wants something to drink, help yourself. I went shopping. Grocery store sandwiches as well, didn't know if anybody would have had a chance to eat." Cincinnati had been an easy twelve-hour drive from Tulsa, and his RV was tucked safely inside the oversize garage out back.

It was the first time Dave had seen Dimi since Cleveland. "Hey," he said, giving her a nod. She had on a baseball cap and was in running shoes, jeans, and a man's long-sleeve button-down shirt untucked over a t-shirt. Dave saw the faint bulge of what he assumed was a pistol tucked into her waistband in front. She wasn't wearing any makeup at all, as far as he could tell. From a distance she might look like a guy, which Dave guessed was not an accident. She gave him a short nod back. Focused. All business.

"All right, should we get started?" Murph said, gesturing at the laptop on the kitchen table.

"Is this it?" Dimi asked, glancing at the side door, then back.

"This is everyone who's available," Bob told her. "Red-Moon is out of contact, undercover. Max is still recovering from his wounds. Everyone else I'd want to use for this is

The Subsection

otherwise occupied, or can't get here in time. So it's just us three."

"Max got injured?" That was news to Dimi.

"Not bad," Dave assured her. "Just a dozen stitches or so."

She frowned at him. "How do you know?"

"Because I drove him to the hospital," Dave said. He looked at Bob, apologetic. "I think he's still mad at me for pulling him out of there, but there was nothing we could do for them without getting caught. The cops barely missed us."

"You made the right call," Bob told him.

"I mean, holy shit dude, what else could you do?" Murph added. "It's only freak luck nobody got you on video, as many people are running dash cams these days. And filming everything with their damn cell phones, instead of living life."

Dimi was staring at Dave, doing the math in her head. "The terror attack? The two mystery Samaritans that chewed up the Syrians and disappeared? That was us? That was you?" She'd thought for sure it was some Tier 1 operators on a CONUS assignment that had gone sideways.

Dave didn't say anything, but Murph blurted, "Twelve against two, and he got nine of 'em!"

"Murph!" Bob growled. "You've heard the term opsec, right? Operational security? Compartmented information? Loose lips sink ships? Keeping your fucking mouth shut?"

"Oh, yeah, right, sorry," Murph said, but he didn't look or sound sorry.

Dave shook his head. "Seven or eight, maybe," he said quietly to Dimi.

"Not according to the FBI forensics reports, Gunfighter," Murph said.

"Jesus Christ, it's a kindergarten," Bob said in exasperation. "Fucking amateurs." He shook his head, then added, "Not you," looking at Dimi. She barely noticed, she was eyeing Dave, a contemplative look on her face. Bob let out a long sigh, and looked at Dave. "Anyway, since I didn't say it before, and since someone can't keep their mouth shut, that was solid work. Out-fucking-standing." He glared at Murph. "Now, can you focus?"

"Right. Okay, so this is what pinged my system," Murph said, moving to the laptop. He tapped a few keys, then pointed. "Couple of emails from the day before yesterday. One outgoing, from Dr. Mason Phillips, the Deputy Director of the CIA for Operations, to Daniel Kim. And Kim's acknowledgement. You should recognize their names."

"The same guy who originally ordered the hit on the PI, and the guy who did it," Dimi said. She leaned over and read the email. It was short.

"That's our operating assumption. From Phillips' email it sounds like they left some proprietary, classified hardware there, in that Babble office in Cleveland. That that cell of DOJ employees stationed there must have been using on site. Makes sense, they would have wanted their Big Brother work stations separate or different from the regular employees, perhaps with some sort of secure access. Babble closed that office—temporarily, officially—but meanwhile it is sitting vacant. I'm guessing they don't want any of that special government computer tech walking out the door. They're sending him there with some cyber specialists to retrieve it."

"But why Kim?" Bob said. "He's a ghost. You send him out to accident people to death, not babysit IT weenies.

The Subsection

That wasn't even the CIA's program, it was DOJ, DHS, whatever."

"Actually," Dave said slowly, "if you remember, somebody got into Blinkenschaal's computer and deleted a bunch of files, documents and videos. That could have been Kim. Probably was, he was the only person we know sent out here originally. So he might have some serious computer savvy. And we know he's familiar with the area. It wouldn't be the first op he's run there. Maybe they're just trying to keep the circle of trust tight. Or maybe there's something else there, left there accidentally, related to the government VIP visit that was caught on camera by the PI and got this whole ball rolling. One of those people was CIA." Bob thought about that and shrugged. It made some sense.

Murph went on. "As you see, there are no details in the emails, but I checked the airlines and saw that his alias James Lee is booked out of Washington Reagan tomorrow morning, to Cleveland. Landing just before noon. I don't know if he's flying with the cybertech guys or they're meeting him there, but even if he's alone and doesn't check any luggage the earliest he could get to that building is one p.m. or so. And he's booked to fly out later that same night, a 7:30 departure, so they're not expecting it to take very long. So we've got a tight window. And here he is." His fingers flew over the keys and photos of Kim filled the screen, some of them stills taken from the airport security cameras. They weren't great, but they were more than enough to make a positive ID. He looked to Bob.

Bob frowned, thinking. "So, the question is, where to take him. Or at least try. Airport's out—too many people, too many cops, too many cameras." He looked at Dave. "What's the location like?"

"I can pull it up," Murph said. His fingers flew over the keys, and photos started appearing.

Dave pointed at them. "Public entrances on three sides, not including the walkway from the parking garage on the second or third floor. So..." He thought. "The only place we know for sure he's going to be that's somewhat secluded is the Babble offices. They're on the seventh floor. Actually," he remembered, "they've got the whole seventh floor. Which is good and bad. That means the whole floor is vacant, if they closed that location. But there are a lot of offices on the floor. Going up and down the hallway, knocking on random doors, seems like a bad idea."

"I can hook into building security cameras," Murph said.

Dave shook his head. "They're only in the lobby. Actually," he corrected himself, "there are cameras in the hallway outside the Babble offices, but I think they're Babble cameras."

"Then they'll be routed into the same system I broke into last time," Murph said. "Should take me about thirteen seconds to gain access. I can monitor from here, call out what office, what door they go into. And then, I guess, you decide whether to go in after them, or wait for them to come out?" He looked at Bob.

"We're flying by the seat of our pants here," Bob said, frowning as he thought. "No time to get fancy. Looks like two to the back of the head might be the way this has to happen." The three of them, Bob, Dave, and Dimi, exchanged a look. "Okay," Bob said. "Daytime, building full of people? We go in slick, pistols and street clothes, blend in. Stage somewhere inside the building, and wait for the callout. Take him in the building, the first opportunity. Preferably as he's on his way in, less opportunity for someone to spot us."

"Three on two or three, and all but one of them a computer geek? With the element of surprise?" Dimi nodded at that. She liked those odds. "Take Kim first, because he's the target and we know he has some tactical training. And then the guys with him…?"

"We'll decide there and then," Bob said. "Depending. I hate to pop a couple of IT guys who don't know anything about anything. You set for hardware?" Bob asked, looking from Dave to Dimi and back. Dave nodded. He was carrying the sterile Glock Max had given him during their last operation.

"I'm good," Dimi said. She was wearing the same Walther PDP-F Compact she'd used during Cracker's course. It wasn't registered to her. She had a lot of guns, and none of them were registered to her.

"Okay. I'd like to be on site no later than ten a.m.," Bob said. "Give us a chance to check it out, and figure out where we're going to set up." He looked at Dave. "Unless you've got ideas?"

"Like I said, lots of ways in and out of the building, but I don't see him walking up seven floors," Dave said. "Which means keeping an eye on the elevators. Both in the lobby and on two, where he can cross over from the parking garage. There are chairs and stuff in the lobby. And the restaurant there opens at eleven. One of us in the lobby, one of us on two, hanging around the elevators, and maybe one somewhere on seven? I…" He frowned, trying to remember. "I think there's a bathroom there, right on the main corridor on seven, on every floor actually, but I don't know if you need a key or a Babble ID card to use the one on seven."

"Whatever they've got, building maintenance would need access, which means it won't be a problem getting in," Bob said confidently. He looked at Murph. "Can you set us up with earbuds for our burners, on a conference call or something like that, since we don't have tactical comms?"

"Yeah, sure, I've got a bunch of that stuff in the RV."

Bob nodded. "Shit, then, it sounds like we've got a plan."

"Actually," Murph said, "let me give you all new phones." He looked around at the three of them.

"Is there a problem?" Bob asked.

"No, but I've been working on a new digital voice modulating program."

"Aren't those available commercially?" Dave asked. "Digital voice changers?"

Murph made a rude noise. "Please. Those are kids' toys. NSA can reverse those in three seconds, get you clear as day. No, with my software, it's constantly modulating using 128-bit encryption, but all the tied-in units are synced. To us it'll sound almost like we're talking in the clear, but to anyone else it'll be completely unintelligible. Alpha would be able to straighten it out in a minute or two, which means it would take any other computer a couple of decades before they'd even be able to determine what language you're speaking."

"I'll take your word for it," Bob said. "How long of a drive is it to Cleveland?"

"Four hours, maybe," Dave said. He'd done more than a few surveillances around Ohio back in the day.

"Excellent. Okay, everybody grab something to eat or drink, and then I want you," he said this to Dave, "to walk us through the floorplan of the building, anything and everything you can remember about it, inside and out, and the immediate area. I want to be out of here tomorrow no later than oh-five-thirty."

FORTY-TWO

Aardvark and the Anthill

Murph didn't need to get up early, but he thought it only right to see them off. He stood in the kitchen, blinking sleepily, as the three of them double-checked they had everything they needed, and then drove off in two of the three cars they'd arrived in. Two cars, Bob had insisted, in case one of them had problems en route.

Murph would have liked to go back to sleep, get another couple hours of shuteye, but knew that wasn't likely to happen. He got sympathetically nervous whenever one of the teams was heading into danger, even if they were out of contact and didn't need his help. On this one he'd be providing overwatch, of a sort.

There was nothing wrong with the bathrooms or kitchen in the safe house, but he preferred his own, so he headed out the back door as the sky started to lighten. He used the side door to enter the oversize garage, locked it behind him, and then scooted around the front of his RV. He'd had the garage custom-made to house it, but still it barely fit inside. His specs for the garage had included RV hookups, so he had power and water without having to start the engine or run a generator.

Half the roof was a skylight, really brightening the inside of the garage, but that wasn't why he'd had it installed—the clear polymer panels didn't interfere with the incoming and outgoing data streams from the hidden satellite dishes on the roof of his RV.

He took a luxurious shower inside the admittedly cramped stall, ground some coffee and brewed a double espresso in his machine, then sat down in front of his monitors. He powered everything up, then spent an hour perusing the data feeds coming from Alpha, progress updates from the one other team in the field, and checking the phone numbers and email accounts he was currently using. Hannah had texted him late the night before—just an emoji, blowing him a kiss. He felt the big stupid smile stretch his face. He debated texting her back, but it was hours before dawn in Arizona, and he didn't want to wake her. So he got to work. There was always more work, and he put in over an hour on various works-in-progress before getting to the day's mission.

An hour after that he put a headset on and made a call. "Yeah?" he heard Bob say.

"Aardvark, this is tech support, confirming this number," Murph said. "I am up on this end." He checked his watch. 9:02 a.m. Then looked at the video feeds displayed in front of him. "Currently looking at live video from the Anthill, lobby and Lucky." Anthill was their code-word for the U.S. Bank Centre building, and Lucky was the seventh floor. "Lucky is empty. Lobby is full of people who don't seem to be especially happy to be going to work." Bob, Dimi, and Dave were Aardvark One, Two, and Three respectively. "Uhhh…" He wasn't used to doing surveillance, and there were a lot of people moving through the lobby, half of them probably late for work. He squinted, his eyes darting back and forth between the feed from the various cameras. "Don't see any problems. Still three hours before our guy is even supposed to land."

"Roger that. ETA to the Anthill probably thirty mikes, we've been making good time. Keep an eye out, and I'll give you a call back when we're rolling up." Bob sounded calm and relaxed. Murph was already feeling a little stressed, and he was hundreds of miles from trouble; literally all he'd be doing was watching TV.

Bob was driving a compact Nissan sedan he'd rented using one of his various IDs. Dave was in the passenger seat next to him, and Dimi was in a compact car, sometimes trailing them, sometimes in front of them, depending on the ebb and flow of traffic. By the time they were nearing Cleveland rush hour was in full swing.

They'd passed most of the trip in silence. Bob shrugged his shoulders as he drove. "Other than the fact that a successful mission likely ends with us killing a man in cold blood, this should be pretty simple," he said. "The only tricky part is spotting him, and timing it so it happens with as few witnesses as possible. And if it's not possible, knowing if and when to walk away." He glanced at Dave.

Dave shrugged back. "Only weird thing about this for me is actually working with a team." When he'd gone after Pietro Bufonte in his Las Vegas mansion he'd done it solo, coming in late at night, with very little prep. Bob nodded.

When Bob exited the freeway, Dimi was right behind them. After a few turns he activated the conference call line, connecting Dimi, Dave, and Murph. "Okay, we're rolling right in," Bob said, checking the clock on the dashboard. Just a bit after nine-thirty. "Three," he said, looking at Dave next to him in the car, "give me a bit of a narrative, if you will."

Dave watched out the windshield. The area didn't look familiar, but then Bob made another turn. "Okay," he said. "That's it, target building, last one on the left where the street ends in the T-intersection. Looks...looks like the normal amount of traffic, this time of day. It's a lot heavier before nine."

Bob rolled up 14th Street as slow as he could without drawing attention to himself. "Where should we put the cars?" Bob asked.

"There are those lots we just passed, there's on-street parking, although it looks like most of the spaces are already filled, and there's the parking garage right there." Dave pointed as they drew abreast of it. "Building opens at six a.m., and it's usually busiest around here between seven-thirty and eight-thirty. White-collar jobs."

"Hmm." Bob cruised past the U.S. Bank Centre, then turned left on Euclid and looked at it from that side. It was nothing special, just a tall office building in a downtown setting. "Tech support, you seeing anything?"

"Nothing that sticks out, just some stragglers heading into work. Again, we've got three hours before this guy is supposed to show up, at a minimum."

"Okay. Two, cruise the block, and if you don't see anything that pings your radar, park in the garage adjoining the target building. We'll find somewhere else nearby."

Bob circled the area, then ultimately parked in a lot a quarter mile northwest of the building. Before he exited the vehicle he took out a rag and wiped down every surface inside the car he might have touched. "Just in case we don't make it back here," he told Dave, then handed Dave the cloth. Dave wiped down every surface within reach on his side of the car, handed the rag back to Bob, and watched the man.

That morning, before they'd left the safe house, Bob had donned most of the disguise he'd be using. Soft body armor, which added a tiny bit of bulk. He strapped a pad around his waist, basically a small pillow mounted on an elastic band. With his thick build, if he slouched, he looked convincingly fat. In the bathroom he'd brushed at his short blonde beard, turning it gray. The coloring wasn't Hollywood grade, and would run in the rain, but it was convincing from more than six feet away, and the coloring made it look longer, thicker. He had on a long-sleeve shirt over a baggy t-shirt and loose trousers—a completely forgettable outfit. As they sat in the car he donned a snap-brim cap that had a fringe of gray hair hanging from the back. Then he stuffed some sponges into his cheeks, put on a pair of wire-rimmed glasses, and checked the results. A fat retiree looked back at him. And the gear on his belt, under his flannel shirt, made him look even bulkier.

Around his waist he had a sterile Glock 19 with an extended threaded barrel and two spare magazines. He also had a fixed-blade knife just left of his spine. He would have preferred to carry his new Acta Non Verba P250, he was really liking that knife, but just in case he had to use it, and leave it in someone, he chose a Cold Steel SRK instead, as the ANV was a new design and the purchase might be traceable. The SRK had a six-inch blade and a rubberized handle, and was issued to Navy SEALs during BUDS. It was also inexpensive had also been around for over thirty years, which meant there were tens of thousands of them in circulation—untraceable. He also had a 3D-printed polymer suppressor for his pistol, stuck in a pocket. The polymer construction was durable enough to last through more ammo than he was carrying. He didn't know if he'd end up using it—a suppressor really made a pistol unwieldy, and if they were indoors the sound of the gunshots would be contained. Knives were much quieter. But, better to have it and not need it….

"As soon as I can, I'll give you some lessons on field-expedient makeup and costuming," Bob told Dave. The sponges changed his voice slightly. He looked at Dave. "But that'll do for now." Dave had on a baseball cap with long brown hair hanging out the back, wrap-around shades, and Bob had darkened up his beard using simple cocoa powder mixed with water into a paste. It wouldn't last long, but then it didn't need to. Dimi was wearing the lesbian-ish outfit she'd been in the day before that hid her build, with the addition of a mousy brown wig that hid half her face. "Give me five minutes, then get out," Bob said. He climbed slowly out of the car, pushed the door shut, and with a lowered head and hunched, dejected walk, meandered away, a fat old man who'd been beaten down by life. The illusion was perfect.

"Wow," Dave said, watching him go. It wasn't just the outfit, he saw, it was selling it. Using the correct body language.

Dimi drove slowly through the parking garage, eyes open for anything unexpected, then parked on the third level. She took the stairs down to the second floor, then strode into the walkway between the garage and the office building. She paused, briefly, halfway across, and looked out the windows at the small courtyard below, and what she could see of 14th Street. She saw a few people walking, but that was it.

She continued into the building. She passed two people in the corridor on the way to the elevator, which she took down to the ground floor. Thinking about what Dave's friend had said about not moving right, she walked straight from the elevators, through the lobby, and across the street to the Starbucks—moving the opposite direction of most of the people at that time of morning, but someone heading determinedly toward a coffee shop at nine-thirty in the morning was unremarkable.

She got in line, ordered a coffee, then stood off to the side and while she waited dialed the party line. "Aardvark, this is Two. Walked from the garage through the building, currently at the Starbucks. Planning on hanging out here for a while, seeing as we've got some time to kill."

"Flight hasn't even left D.C. yet," Murph told them, having just checked the airline schedule.

"One copies. I'm going to walk around for a while, get a feel for the area. Tech support, any activity on Lucky?"

"Nope, it's a ghost town."

"All right, Two, Three, let's stay off Lucky for the moment."

"Three copies. I think I'll get a coffee too, then head over to the lobby."

"Three, Two—it's a little empty over there right now. You might stand out."

"I can always hang out in the bathroom," Dave told her.

XXXX

Bob walked through the lobby at a slow pace, moving like his feet hurt, took the elevator up to two, and then walked up and down the corridor twice. He wanted to check out the locks on the office doors. They were standard commercial models. If they had the same locks on the Babble offices up on seven he'd be able to get in without too much problem, using the lockpick set in one of his pockets. But he didn't think that was a likely scenario. What he hoped would happen, what he wanted to see, was someone on his crew spotting Kim as the man entered the building, and calling him out. Possibly riding up in the elevator with him. Bob, at that point, planned to be hidden somewhere on seven, and as the man headed to the Babble offices take him unawares in the corridor outside. Two, three shots into the target, decide on the spot how to handle whoever was with Kim, and then depart the building and the area in a quick but calm fashion.

After checking out the door locks he headed out to the parking garage, walked through it, went down to the first floor, then headed south on 14th Street toward the nearby parking lots, forcing himself to maintain his slow, mincing gait. There was enough foot traffic on the sidewalk that he blended right in. He glanced at his watch. Still at least an hour to kill. He didn't want to head up to seven until well after eleven a.m., just in case. Murph had eyes on, if he spotted any movement up there he'd let the team know.

XXXXX

As the time grew closer the team grew more tense. Right

before noon Bob got on the phone. "Heading to Lucky to see if I can find a spot to tuck in. Tech support?"

"I haven't seen a soul up there since I first pulled up the feeds this morning."

Bob grunted, and they kept the line open. Not much more than two minutes later they heard him quietly say, "Bathrooms up here are unlocked. I'm going to stage in a stall. Tech, you saw me go in, right?"

"Yeah."

"So when it comes time, call him out based on to my right or left, heading to a door across the hall or on the same side as me, etcetera."

"Gotcha."

"Okay, going quiet, give me a call when somebody has something."

A few minutes later Dave took a seat in the Vietnamese restaurant in the lobby, where he had a good view of the area before the elevators. He ordered a sandwich but mostly just picked at it, not feeling hungry. The thought of killing Daniel Kim didn't bother him; what bothered him was the thought of screwing up in front of his boss and his team. He didn't do well with waiting, or anticipation—he seemed to do best when in the middle of things, when he didn't have time to think or worry, just react. Just act.

"Tech support?" Bob asked in a fresh group phone call just before one p.m., nearly whispering.

"I've got nothing on the cameras," Murph said. "Flight did touch down on time, and he was listed on the manifest, so if he's coming straight from the airport he could be there any minute. If he had to go pick up people somewhere maybe you'll have a wait."

"I'm about done here," Dave announced. "Two, you want to swap out? This restaurant is a good spot."

The Subsection

"Yeah, heading in," Dimi said. She appeared thirty seconds later. As Dave was paying his bill in cash he heard her say to the hostess, in a weak mewling voice that matched her messy hair, "Oh, can I sit over here? I'm waiting for a friend, and want her to see me if she comes in." She picked the table right behind his, and never looked at him once.

Dave wandered into the lobby, in no hurry, stretched, looked around, then ambled toward the restrooms. He used a urinal, came out, looked around again, then moved to the elevators. Between Dimi and Murph on the cameras the lobby was covered, and Bob was up on seven, so he took an elevator up to the second floor and walked through the building to the walkway and then to the parking garage.

The concrete parking garage echoed with the sounds of the city. Noise filtered up from the surrounding streets and bounced around, making it impossible to tell direction. Dave walked through the second floor of the garage to the south side and peered out across Prospect Avenue. There was a fenced-in parking lot, and then an old red brick building with a five-story circular tower. He wondered exactly what the hell it was, the building looked like it dated to the Depression, or earlier. There seemed to be some decorative stone work out front.

On the west side the five-story parking garage butted up against a small commercial building. Dave had walked past it at some point, doing recon, and vaguely remembered that there was some sort of retail business on the ground floor, but that the upper floors held offices.

There was a glass-walled stairwell at the southeast corner of the parking garage and he headed up to the top floor. The fifth level of the parking garage felt like a roof, as it was empty except for three cars parked at the opposite end, nearest the bank building. The U.S. Bank Centre towered over the parking garage on the north side, all mirrored glass and modern angles. Across 14th Street the Hanna Building sat massive, the length of a long block. Dave wandered to that side and looked over the wall at the traffic going back and forth below. There was a steady stream of cars and trucks, and enough pedestrians that no one stood out. He was killing time, a little bit, but he was also watching. And thinking.

They'd made a mistake, he realized that now. Bob could cover the seventh floor, and someone could cover the lobby, but there was no real way to cover the second-floor walkway from the parking garage without looking suspicious—unless you were sitting inside a vehicle. He shouldn't be wandering around on foot, he should be hunkered down inside Dimi's rental.

Dave went back down to the second floor of the parking garage. It was nearly full of cars. Which was problematic, for his plan. It would only work if the surveillance vehicle was parked somewhere an occupant could get eyes on the entrance to the walkway. He'd gotten a good look at the vehicle Dimi was driving, and out of habit from his PI days had memorized the license plate, so he started walking up and down the aisles, looking for it. They'd rolled in late, but maybe it was close enough, or had a good angle....

He heard the hiss of car tires on concrete, but whether it was above or below him he couldn't tell. Car doors slammed in the distance. He stepped between two vehicles, then walked up the slight slope of the floor toward the north side of the garage, scanning the cars to either side of him, looking for Dimi's rental. It was a small, nondescript, silver Hyundai hatchback, which was great if you didn't want to get noticed but made it harder to spot quickly. Fifty feet

The Subsection

ahead of him two men appeared. Maybe they'd just exited a car? He wasn't sure. But they turned away from him, and headed toward the walkway. Dave stopped scanning the cars, kept his eyes on them, pulled out his phone, dialed, then stuck it back in his pocket as he started walking faster.

"It's three, got a possible, target and one other, parking garage heading toward the walkway," he muttered, just loud enough to be picked up by his ear bud. "Trying to confirm."

"One copies," Bob muttered softly.

"Standing by," Dimi said.

By the time they reached the walkway to the office building Dave was four steps behind the two men. They heard him coming as they reached the doors. Dave had his hands in his pockets and smiled blandly as the second man held the door for him. Dave took a couple quick steps so the man wouldn't be standing there too long. "Thanks," Dave said, reaching out to grab the door. He walked behind them down the second-floor hallway. He stuck his hands back in his pockets, as the position of his arms helped camouflage the bulge on his hip. His heartrate was up, but just a bit. Kim—he was pretty sure it was Kim, eighty, maybe ninety percent sure—looked bland, forgettable. Medium build, medium height, wearing a polo shirt over trousers. Dave wanted to get a better look at his face, but his back was to him as they walked. The other guy was a little bigger, and younger, also dressed business casual. And he had a leather bag slung over his shoulder, something big enough to hold a laptop.

"I'm not hearing a no," Dimi said in his ear. "Moving to intercept."

Murph was watching the feeds from the lobby cameras and called it out. "Two is heading to the elevators."

As they reached the elevators Kim hit the Up button

and glanced at Dave, then ignored him. His back was almost square to Dave. Dave was pretty sure it was Kim, but had just enough of a doubt in his mind that he didn't act, he just stood there and waited. The other man was half-turned toward Dave. Dave stared at nothing, hands in his pockets, doing his best to look nonthreatening.

The elevator car arrived, and the doors slid open to reveal Dimi. She had her phone up to her face, blocking half of it. "No, I'm in the elevator," she said. "I'm probably going to lose you. No, I'm not using that as an excuse," she said, glancing at the three men as they got on, then dismissing them. The button for the ninth floor was illuminated. The guy Dave was pretty sure was Daniel Kim reached out and hit the button for seven. Dave waited for him to move out of the way and pressed the button for twelve with his thumb. The bigger guy moved off to the side, his shoulder against the wall. Dave stepped in the opposite direction.

"I'm not having this discussion right now," Dimi said, self-consciously trying to keep her voice down. She turned toward the corner, away from everyone else. "Listen—no. No. Why does everything have to be about you?" She paused. "I am not. No."

"Umm…" Dave heard in his ear. "Should I be responding?" Murph asked.

"Do you have anything to say?" Dimi demanded. It sounded like she was fighting back tears as the elevator rose.

"Uh, is it him?"

"I should hope so," she snapped.

"Heading up to Lucky?"

"Yes!" She sounded angry and sad both, at wit's end.

"One copies," Bob said quietly.

XXXX

The six double espressos in three hours, on an empty stomach, had definitely been a bad idea, and had given Murph the jitters. And he was getting a bit sweaty, too, waiting for Certified CIA Assassin™ Daniel Kim to arrive. He still had the internal flight data from Delta up on one monitor, listing Kim as a confirmed passenger, and the feed from the cameras in the lobby and on the seventh floor filled up several more. His eyes danced back and forth as his right knee bounced uncontrollably. He checked his watch three times in three minutes and still didn't remember what time it was. Was Kim driving over straight from the airport? Murph hadn't found any rental cars reserved in his alias—did that mean he was getting picked up? He hated not knowing—he was in the business of information. He glanced at his watch a fourth time, and finally paid attention—just a few minutes before two p.m.

The phone came alive in his ear, and he automatically adjusted his headset as Dave quietly said, "Three, got a possible, target and one other, parking garage heading toward the walkway." *Figures*, Murph thought, *the one place there were no cameras*. Even as his eyes darted to the camera feeds before him. "Trying to confirm."

"One copies," Bob said.

"Standing by," Dimi said.

Murph blew out a harsh breath. His eyes roamed over the camera feeds again, but there was nothing to see. Two of his screens were filled with the usual mountain of data coming from Alpha and other sources, some of it static, some of it scrolling. Most of it had nothing to do with the current operation, so he ignored it.

"Thanks," they all heard Dave say. Murph thought he heard the sound of a door opening or closing, and cranked up the volume on his headphones. Did he hear the sound of them walking? If so, it was echoing a bit, so they had to be inside the building. But then…nothing. What were they doing?

"I'm not hearing a no," Dimi said. "Moving to intercept."

Murph could just see her sitting in the lobby restaurant near the edge of one of the lobby cameras. She tossed cash down onto the table and then was moving with a purpose across the lobby. "Two is heading to the elevators," he called out, sounding calmer than he felt. For everything he'd done for the organization, he'd never really been involved in an operation before. Even though he was hundreds of miles away, safe in a secure, armored vehicle hidden inside a garage, watching screens, his heart was racing as if he was right there.

He leaned forward and squinted, as if that would help him hear better. Was that the sound of elevator doors? Maybe. Then, nothing. Then elevator doors again.

"No, I'm in the elevator," Dimi said in Murph's ear, making him jump. "I'm probably going to lose you. No, I'm not using that as an excuse," she said.

Murph glanced up at the monitors, but of course there was nothing to see. No cameras in the elevators, or on the second floor. Who was she talking to? It sounded like she was pretending to talk to someone on the phone. And not quietly.

"I'm not having this discussion right now," Dimi said, voice a little softer and lower. The audio was different—she was in a smaller space, definitely in the elevator. The signal was still pretty good. "Listen—no." She paused. "No. Why does everything have to be about you?" She paused again. The emotion, the anguish in her voice sounded real. "I am not. No." Damn, but she could act.

"Umm…" Murph said, having a sudden realization. "Should I be responding?"

"Do you have anything to say?" Dimi demanded of him, sounding haunted. Murph reflexively felt guilty, even though that was ridiculous.

"Uh, is it him?"

"I should hope so," she snapped.

He got his mental footing, and nodded. "Heading up to Lucky?" Not asking for him, but for the others.

"Yes!" The sadness in her voice was heartbreaking. It sounded like she was barely keeping it together, on the edge of a breakdown.

"One copies," Bob said quietly.

Murph heard the elevator ping, and the very faint sound of doors opening. His eyes flicked up to the feed from the seventh floor. The cameras had been installed by Babble to cover the doors of their offices along the main corridor, and the elevators were just out of frame. Murph frowned, impatient, then his eyes were drawn to a pulsing data packet on the adjacent monitor. Pulsing meant Alpha thought it was of medium importance. But he didn't have time for that now. His eyes went back to the live video. "They're off on seven," he said, as men walked into view, heading down the hallway toward the Babble offices. "Heading to you, One." Then his eyes, for some strange reason, were drawn back to the pulsing notification.

"What?" he muttered, eyes darting from the lines of information to the video and back. He squinted at the data, then his eyes opened wide. His hands jumped forward, and started dancing over the keyboard. "No…what? That's…

hey, I think I've got a problem here," he said, but his voice was lost in the sudden wall of noise coming over the line, and he looked back at the video feed to see chaos.

Bob had been in the stall in the bathroom for fifteen minutes when the movement-sensing power-saving lights shut off, leaving him in darkness. Which was funny, and he thought about leaving them like that, but then he realized his eyes would adjust to the dark, and then when it was time to move he'd have to wait a crucial second or two. So he opened the stall door and waved an arm out into the room, and the lights clicked back on. Every fifteen minutes he had to do the same thing.

He wasn't daydreaming, although he had the urge, he was working through scenarios in his head. If you had a plan for any and every possibility, you didn't have to think about what to do in the moment, or go with your gut, hoping it was right. Of course, there was no way to predict everything, but he'd be walking up on a man or three in the hallway of a mid-America office building. There were only so many things that could happen.

As he sat and waited he could hear vague sounds from elsewhere in the building. The seventh floor was a ghost town, not a single person had walked past the bathroom door since he'd gone in, but he could hear occasional movement through the floor or ceiling, a scraped chair, a thump, the barely-audible murmurs of a voice—usually a man's voice, as they were deeper, and lower frequency sounds traveled through walls better. It was one of those random facts he knew that would likely never be of any practical value. He couldn't make out the words, or whether they were above or below him. And he only heard one voice, so he assumed the man was talking on the phone or in a group chat/online meeting.

His heart sped up as Dave called out a possible in the parking garage. He tracked them with his mind's eye, five floors below—traversing the tunnel, then the hallway to the elevators. Listened to the borderline hysterical conversation Dimi was having with herself, then with Murph. "Heading up to Lucky?" Murph asked.

"Yes!" Dimi said, half-sobbing. God was she good.

"One copies," Bob said quietly, his voice surprisingly loud in the bathroom.

The rough plan was for him to wait until Murph, watching on the video feed, called out which office Kim was heading to. But did he need to do that? If they indeed turned his way and headed down the hallway, stopped at a door to work the keypad, did he want to wait until then to rush out? Or would it be better just to step out of the bathroom when they were still on the move? Have a few more seconds to evaluate the situation. They could pass in the hallway, awkwardly and without looking each other in the eye, like everyone did in office buildings all over the world.

"They're off on seven," Murph said in his ear. "Heading to you, One."

And then Bob was off the toilet, out of the stall, heading toward the door, having made a decision. The bathroom door gave a quiet squeak as he pulled it open, and that noise was enough to remind him he was an old fat guy and needed to act like one. He paused, took a breath, then stepped out into the corridor, in no hurry. He looked left and right, then turned right and walked slowly along the hallway, head down, staring at nothing in particular, seeing Kim above the rim of his glasses, a second man beside him. Thirty feet away, then twenty. Dave and Dimi appearing in the hallway behind the two men, moving quietly.

The tall guy, not Kim, glanced briefly at Dimi as she hunched in the corner of the elevator, seemingly barely keeping it together—Dave caught the movement out of the corner of his eye. Then the elevator pinged, and the doors slid open. The men stepped out without a look back. Kim looked left and right, then pointed right, and they moved down the hallway in that direction. As soon as they were out of sight around the corner Dimi tapped Dave on the shoulder and darted out of the elevator, just on the far side of the doors. Dave moved up next to her just before the elevator doors started to close.

"They're off on seven," Murph said in their ears. "Heading to you, One."

Dimi put a hand on Dave's chest, keeping him there, as the doors slid shut behind them. Then they both leaned out, and looked down the hallway. Kim and the second man were striding down the wide corridor—and there was Bob, exiting the bathroom, between the costuming and the body language unrecognizable. Dimi and Dave started down the hallway, moving quietly. Bob would reach the targets first, he was closing distance quickly.

Kim and his partner paused at a Babble door, and looked at the keypad. Bob was six feet from them, fat, old, and worn, practically limping down the hall, staring at nothing in particular as he moved in. Dave and Dimi were four steps away from the pair in the other direction—and then doors banged open up and down the hall and the space was filled with bodies. Men with guns, shouting.

The Subsection

"Down! Down! On your knees! Don't you fucking move!"

The three of them—Dave, Dimi, and Bob—spun in surprise. The men were heavily armed, suppressed subguns in their hands. And the three of them understood immediately—it was a trap. It had all been a setup. And they'd walked right into it. Dave thought about going for his gun, but there were six armed men—three in front and three behind—their fingers on the triggers, shouting, on edge, ready to go.

He slowly sank down to his knees in the middle of the hallway, hands going up beside his head in surrender, Dimi beside him, after a long pause doing the same, looking furious.

FORTY-THREE

Acta Non Verba

Aaron froze with his hands up in the air, the muzzle of the suppressor in his face. His eyes went from the big black hole in the end of the suppressor to the gun behind it, then to the man behind that, shouting at Aaron from behind his black balaclava. But—and it was weird—his voice seemed distant. And Aaron was calm as shit, pulse just bobbing along slow and steady. Was that adrenaline, or something else? Bizarre. Aaron ignored the shouts and looked to the two men with the first. Their backs were to the elevator, to him, and they were pointing their guns down the hallway. Down a hallway filled with people. More guys with silenced subguns at the far side, and in the middle, two guys in office casual attire just standing there. But in the center of everything were three people. Three people on their knees, with their hands up. Two of them looking right at him. One of them...

"Mom?" Aaron said in utter shock.

The eyes of the man in front of Aaron widened in surprise, and he turned his head slightly, eyes sliding toward the crowded hallway. Aaron just let the coffee cup drop as his right hand chopped down, swept his work shirt out of the way, and then the Wilson was in his fist, hand coming up, the man in front of him starting to turn his head back, but it was too late, way too late, Aaron punched the pistol out in a two-handed grip at eye level, the safety already off, taking half a step to the side, just enough to get that suppressor out of his face, and he tapped the trigger three times.

The man's face was but three feet away and Aaron's shots disappeared into the black fabric of the balaclava, just as his coffee cup hit the floor. The man dropped like the coffee cup, straight down, and Aaron pivoted.

Dave was numb as he knelt on the floor, the shouting battering his ears. Trapped. Caught. Would they ever figure out where they'd gone wrong? Had someone betrayed them? Murph? He just couldn't believe that, the man didn't have a false bone in his body. But they were done, they were caught, and not by amateurs. The guy right in front of Dave had a suppressed Heckler and Koch MP7, one of the most unobtainium guns on the planet—unless you were with the government. Just one of three guys with high-end hardware filling the corridor, with more behind them.

Then Aaron stepped into view, coffee cup in hand. Haircut, moustache gone for the first time ever, wearing ugly glasses, but behind them, Dave would have known those eyes anywhere. One of the operators spun and stuck his gun right in Aaron's face. Aaron's hands, coffee cup and all, went up. Then he turned his head, and looked down the hallway. Locked eyes with Dave.

Dave knew what Aaron was going to do before he did

anything. And time didn't slow down, it damn near stopped. Aaron's mouth opened—he said something, in super-slow motion, looking at Dave. What he said didn't matter, but it distracted the man, which was the point, and he followed Aaron's gaze.

Dave saw Aaron's left hand release the coffee cup, and the right drop. He could have drawn then, he had all the time in the world, but two men with (presumably) full-auto submachine guns were just feet away, their guns trained unwaveringly on him. Aaron's hand drifted down and swept his shirt away from the grip of his pistol even as the man who was supposed to have him covered was starting to look away, now behind the curve.

Dave's vision was sharper than seemed humanly possible—he could see the texturing on the grips of Aaron's gun, see the gold Wilson Combat eagle logo medallion in the center of them before Aaron's hand closed around the pistol. The gun came out of the holster and passed the falling coffee cup in mid-air. Aaron's hands met on the grip of the pistol and as it punched out he fired. There was no noise, just the glacially-cycling slide, a smoking brass case tumbling out of the ejection port. And almost as soon as the slide closed, and the muzzle dropped, another shot.

And the two men with guns trained on Dave started to turn.

Now. Dave drew his Glock from concealment, a reflex action practiced hundreds of thousands of times. Action faster than reaction. The man in front of him, turning toward the gunfire, presented with new input, stopped, started to turn back, and Dave fired twice into his face, then lunged sideways, firing at the last man before him, Aaron shooting at him at the same time.

The Subsection

Bob, on his knees, looked calm, but his mind was racing. It was a beautifully executed ambush, and probably the only reason he wasn't already dead is because they wanted to know exactly who he and his team were. The plainclothes operators had probably been inserted into the vacant offices the day before. Just waiting. Then they popped out, three in front, three behind. Soft body armor not quite concealed under their clothes. Sure, there was a crossfire, but they couldn't risk their targets making a break for it. Overwhelm and intimidate with numbers and guns without having to fire a shot. And their timing indicated that they had eyes— yep, there was Murph, yelling in his ear that someone else had tapped into the Babble security cameras, and that he had to cut the feed and now couldn't see, *what was going on in there, what was happening?*

Kim was there, standing right in front of Bob. Sideways, still, but turning to squint down at him. A smug look on his face, but he also looked a bit confused. Bob's fat old man not what he expected to see. But there was something about Kim, something about his face… The man beside him, the supposed cyber expert, had pulled a pistol out of his computer bag and was holding it like a pro. So. Definitely a setup. A completely fabricated opportunity.

Disappointing wasn't the word.

A citizen appeared over by the elevators, Starbucks cup in hand, doing the 'Oh shit' wide-eyes dance. Providing a tiny distraction, but not enough, not with half a dozen shooters standing over them, even if it did get them looking back and forth. And then the gun came out in one of the fastest fucking draws Bob had ever seen, and the hallway rocked with gunfire. And Dave didn't draw, his pistol seemed to appear magically in his hand, more spent cases filling the air, and Bob spun on his inside knee, bending at the waist, putting all of the speed and power he could muster into his right leg as he hooked it around.

His calf slammed into the back of Kim's knees hard enough to sweep the man's feet out from under him and keep on going. Bob used the momentum, swung his arm back to his hip as he landed on his back, and grabbed hold of his pistol as Kim fell backward atop him. Bob wrapped one powerful arm around Kim's neck as he punched his pistol out one-handed, firing upside down behind him into thighs right there, groins, heads, Dimi's pistol barking now, the air in the hallway hazy with gunsmoke, everyone shooting. Kim's body atop him shuddered. Bodies fell past Bob's outstretched arm.

Then it was over.

"S'up, bitches?" Aaron said, the only man still standing in the corridor, pistol in two hands. He felt calm. His heart wasn't even racing. Was this shock? Didn't feel like shock. Whatever this was, he liked it. Calm, cool, collected, the smell of gunfire in his nose. King of the world.

"Who the fuck is this?" Bob demanded, pointing his Glock at him. But he didn't shoot, he knew the man had saved their asses.

"Don't shoot! He's with us," Dave shouted.

Dimi was on her back in the middle of the corridor, Kim's companion lying across her legs. She'd dropped him with four shots to the chest. She squinted. "Mullet man?" she said in disbelief.

"Dykeasaurus Rex," Aaron replied automatically. He blinked and shook his head. "I don't know who the fuck these guys are, but there's at least two cars waiting down-

The Subsection

stairs, full of people. Tahoe and a van. Unless they're with you?"

"No," Dimi said. The man across her legs let out a groan. She shot him in the head and then kicked him aside. One of the other operators was on his back, eyes open, twitching as his eyes darted around wildly. Dimi moved his dropped SMG away from his hand and shot him through his open mouth. She looked around, seeing if there was anyone else who needed finishing off.

"Anybody hurt? Anybody injured?" Bob called out. "Anybody? Fuck." There were bullet holes in both walls. Bob shoved Kim off him and climbed to a knee beside the man, muzzle of his pistol in his face, just in case. Kim's shirtfront was soaked with blood from a burst meant for Bob. His mouth was working but only wet gasps were coming out. Bob checked him for weapons, then any ID, and came up empty. Then he leaned close, and frowned. He reached down, pinched, and seemed to peel some skin off Kim's nose.

"Shit, really?" Dimi said, watching.

"What?" Dave said.

As the man on the floor shuddered and died, Bob grabbed a fistful of his face and pulled. A thin layer of latex peeled off the man's cheeks and around his eyes. "This guy's not even Asian," Bob said, disgusted. "He's just got the right bone structure, that's how he got the job. Shit."

"We need to get the fuck out of here," Dimi said. Murph had been shouting in their ears for a while now. "Tech. Tech support! Shut the fuck up! What do you see?"

"Guys," Murph said. "Lot of guys. In the lobby. Trying to figure out what to do, looks like. Guns. Are you okay, what happened?" They didn't bother answering.

Grumbling, Bob did a tactical reload, seeing he had only one round left in his magazine. "Check these guys for intel, ID's whatever," he barked. Then he stomped to a nearby maintenance closet. He was pretty sure one of the men had jumped out of it, and found the door unlocked. He was out five seconds later, twisting the cap off a gallon jug of bleach. "Watch out," he said, and upended the bottle over fake-Kim's face, then ran it up and down the bodies in the hallway. He wiped his prints off the plastic handle, then tossed it away. He looked left and right. "Police that coffee cup!" he said, pointing. Aaron grabbed it and stuffed it into a nearby trash can.

"I've got two wallets," Dimi said.

"Really?" Bob was surprised.

"How'd they get onto us?" Dave asked. "Tech?"

"I don't know," Murph said, sounding near tears.

"We have to assume our rides are blown," Bob said.

"I've got a rental in the parking garage," Aaron volunteered.

Bob nodded decisively. "Sounds like a plan." He grabbed one of the suppressed SMGs off the floor, a brand-new Brugger & Thomet APC9K, and pulled spare magazines for it from the dead man's chest rig. "Everybody move, move." He jogged toward the far end of the hallway and the stairwell. Dimi started after him.

Aaron bent down and picked up a suppressed HK MP7 and dug two spare magazines for it from the dead man's pockets. When he straightened up Dave was staring at him. "What?" Dave just shook his head. They ran after Dimi and Bob.

Bob was staged at the open door of the stairwell, listening. He glanced at Dave and Aaron as they came running up. "Fast and quiet," he said, then he was off, darting down the stairs, his shoes a quiet rush on the concrete steps, Dimi right behind him.

The quartet moved down the stairs, around and around, and had just passed the fourth floor when a door banged open somewhere below them, accompanied by loud men's voices. Bob stopped, aiming the SMG down the stairs, but there was nothing to see. There was no open center to the stairwell, he couldn't look down, there were just blind corners.

Dimi was at his elbow, Dave and Aaron behind her. They listened for a few seconds. Two men, probably. Hostiles, almost definitely. Not moving. Yet.

Dimi grabbed at her waist and pulled her button-down shirt, and her t-shirt, over her head, and tossed the bundle of fabric blindly behind her. Dave caught them. She hesitated, but just for a second, then pulled off her sports bra, turned, and threw it directly at Aaron. He caught it, staring wide-eyed at her. Unconcerned, the pulled off her baseball cap and threaded the back of the wig through the hole in the cap for a more attractive look. She took her pistol out of the holster at her waist and tucked it into her belt at the small of her back. Then she proceeded down the stairs, making no attempt to be quiet.

There were two men in full tactical gear on the landing of the second floor, and they stared at her openmouthed as she came into view, bouncing, topless, down the stairs. They lowered their guns as she stopped four steps up.

"What are you doing?" she demanded. "Don't you dare point those at me."

"What are *we?*—lady, get the fuck out of here," one of the men growled, talking to Dimi's chest.

She put her hands on her hips. "I will not let a man tell me what I can and cannot do with my breasts," she shouted back, defiantly. They both took half a step back in confusion and surprise. "Toplessness is perfectly legal in Ohio and you know it!" She descended two more stairs angrily, hitting her heels hard, deliberately, her breasts demonstrating the best part of jiggle physics, glaring at the men, ignoring their guns. In disbelief, they turned to look at each other, and her hand slipped behind her back and came back out holding the Walther. She shot them both twice in their heads, and when they were on the floor shot them each once more, just to be sure. Her slide locked back.

By the time she'd finished reloading Dave was there, holding out her clothes. She took the button-down shirt and pulled it on over her head. There was no time to do more. Dave dragged one of the bodies out of the way to get to the door. "When I die, that's how I want to go," Aaron told Dave, who gave him a dirty look. Dimi pulled open the door and stuck her head out. "Clear," she said quietly.

Bob covered them from the doorway as they jogged across the walkway to the parking garage. They used cars and cement columns for cover as Bob made his way across, then followed Aaron into the dim echoing parking garage. Thirty seconds later they were climbing into the rental Durango. Aaron tossed Dimi's bra in after her.

"I swapped the plates out," Aaron told Dave, who was in the passenger seat. He backed the Durango out of the space, fought the urge to smoke the tires, and made his way toward the exit on the first floor. Everyone else was scanning for threats.

The rear windows of the Durango had factory tint, and Dave leaned back, so only Aaron was visible as he nosed the Durango out of the parking garage. The Tahoe was still down there at the curb, near the end of the block, but no one was visible near it. Aaron turned the opposite direction.

The Subsection

After four turns and half a mile, everyone staring out the windows, Dave asked, "Are we good?"

"For the moment, unless they have a drone," Bob said. "Which I doubt, since this was supposed to happen indoors."

Aaron nodded, and looked at Dave with a grin. "Well, holy shit then. Man, my ears are still ringing."

Dave stared back, agog. "Dude, what the fuck are you doing here?"

Aaron shrugged. "I was bored. Lori said she thought you were back here. And even the boy who lived occasionally needs help from his idiot friend." Aaron glanced at the faces in the rearview mirror, back at Dave, then casually turned and looked over his shoulder. "So who the fuck are you guys?" he asked, looking around, including Dave in the question. And it was clear he wasn't asking their names.

FORTY-FOUR

No Such Thing As Coincidence

CIA Director Robert MacGregor sat at the head of the table, arms crossed over his chest, scowling. There were a handful of people in front of him, none of them happy. "Explain to me how this happened," he said quietly. He yelled when he was angry. He got quiet when he was furious.

"Remember, we didn't even know if we were wasting our time," Dr. Mason Phillips, Deputy Director for Operations, said. "It was a low percentage play." MacGregor glowered at him, and Phillips shrugged. It was true, even if he was doing a bit of CYA.

His cyber-specialist, Raphael Birzon, nervously cleared his throat. "Well, we can't, sir, not exactly. The enemy actor cut the video feed—"

"I know they cut the feed!" MacGregor barked. "I was watching it. How?"

"Backtrace shows the commands originated in Kuala Lumpur. He couldn't actually shut off the video directly, so he—they—initiated a reboot of the video system, which

The Subsection

interrupted the feed for…" He looked down at the paperwork in front of him. "Two hundred and twelve seconds."

"Malaysia?" Phillips said dubiously. The operation, ultimately, was his responsibility. Which meant he was responsible for its failure.

"That is the digital footprint we followed," Birzon said. Then he slumped a bit. "But we don't believe it either. We think it's a false trail. My people are trying to find the real one, but so far…" He swallowed. "We will let you know as soon as we have something."

"I don't care about the feed," MacGregor growled. "Okay, I do, but that's not what I was talking about. We had six men on them in that hallway when we lost visual. Not including Timms and…whatever his name was, the analyst we tapped to play Daniel." He tilted his head toward Daniel Kim, who was sitting at the far end of the table, and who'd been there beside MacGregor, watching the op unfold. "Eight on three. Eight more operators in the building or around it. And now ten of those sixteen men are dead, and we've got nothing?"

"Could there have been a second team in the building?" Gerald asked. He didn't know why Kim had originally gone to Cleveland, all he knew was that his movements through the airport there had been tracked, digitally, by…someone. Someone very good. And at roughly the same time the DHS's Babble operation had been compromised by a hacker inserting child porn into dozens of laptops and phones across the country. But whoever it was had gained entry into the system through the Babble offices in Cleveland. So they'd baited a hook, hoping to get a response, draw the enemy agents out into the light. They weren't sure whether anyone would take the bait. MacGregor had thought it was a likely waste of time, and been shocked when he'd seen the people moving in on the man playing Kim.

Phillips shrugged, angry that he didn't know. "There's no indication, but clearly we missed something. Maybe they ambushed our ambush. I know those three didn't do it." He nodded at the flat screens on one wall, which held still images of the three individuals, blown-up enlargements from the lobby and seventh-floor cameras. They were the best images they had of them, and still they weren't very clear, or helpful. None of them had ever looked up. "A fat old guy, a woman, and some white trash-looking guy with a mullet?"

"Those are disguises," Kim said, speaking for the first time. "Exactly the kind of things we wear in the field to prevent identification. All three of them are wearing hats indoors, to start with. Likely you're looking at three wigs, or hair extensions. And two of them in glasses, to fuck with facial recognition. We get any hits?" He looked around, and got several head shakes. "Right." He got up, moved around the table, and pointed to one of the photos. "You see this? That's muscle. That's a lot of muscle. There's a good chance that 'woman' isn't a woman. The fat guy moved like he was old, but I'm not convinced."

"Did we collect any physical evidence from the scene at all?" MacGregor asked.

"One bloody footprint in the stairwell," Gerald told him. "Men's size eleven. They've ID'ed the tread as belonging to a Brooks Glycerin GTS running shoe."

"Is that rare? Tell me that's rare."

Gerald shook his head, and read from the report in front of him. "Brooks is a well-known athletic apparel company that specializes in running shoes, and eleven is one of the most popular sizes for men in the United States."

The Subsection

Kim announced, "And by now all the clothing they were wearing has been burned, thrown in a landfill, or soaked in bleach, like they did on scene."

"Was that to prevent our collecting DNA?" MacGregor asked.

Phillips nodded. "And it worked. We got nothing out of that hallway. Well, not nothing. It appears our eight men were shot with at least four different nine-millimeter caliber weapons. Two were definitely Glock pistols. The other two couldn't be definitely identified. Over forty spent shell casings in the hallway, but no usable fingerprints were found on any of them. Two of our weapons have gone missing, presumably taken by the opfor."

"Most of our guys were taken out by headshots," Kim said. He'd read the incident report. "These guys are pros." Phillips gave him a dirty look.

"So, four?" MacGregor said. "Those three people, plus one other? Four entirely different people?"

Gerald shook his head, and looked back down at the report. "No way to tell. The scene was a mess. Um…" He scanned the document. "Interviews with people working in the building report they heard gunshots, so at least one of the guns used wasn't silenced. That…that's it. For the moment. That's all we've got."

MacGregor shook his head. He uncrossed his arms, and placed his palms flat on the table. "No, it's not. We've confirmed our suspicions. Done more than that. These people have demonstrated computer hacking skills at the very highest level, and now tactical skills at the very highest level. This isn't one person, this is an organization. Working in *this* country. Against *us*. The who is the question, and the who will tell us the why. Is this a foreign government? Well-funded terror group? Fucking Erik Prince resurrecting Blackwater?"

Gerald was looking at the images on the monitors. "They're white," he observed. "White-ish." He looked at Kim. "Unless you think that's makeup?" Kim shrugged.

"That doesn't narrow it down," Phillips said. "Are they Russians? Israelis? Germans? Goddamn Australians?" He looked at Daniel Kim. "Why the fuck do they care about you?"

"I wish I knew. Cleveland was a…there was nothing special about why I was originally sent there. Maybe…look into the family of the…" He looked at Gerald. He wasn't sure if the man knew the details of the Blinkenschaal hit. "Of the reason I was first there."

"And the bereaved family just happens to have Tier 1 trigger pullers on speed dial?" Phillips said derisively.

"We dangled me as a target of opportunity, and they bit," Kim said. "Exactly why…fuck, I wish I knew. Truly, I thought this'd be a waste of time."

"So we know they've repeatedly hacked systems," MacGregor said. "What are the chances this is the first time they've gotten their hands wet?"

"Based on these results, zero," Kim said. "Like I said, pros."

"So maybe we should start looking for outlying incidents that don't fit the norm, where people ended up dead," MacGregor said. "They went after the DHS at Babble, and then came after us here. Anybody else been hit the last year or two? Have we? By unknown actors?"

"Um," Phillips said, glancing at Gerald, then at Kim, neither of whom had the big picture. "We still don't know who the two good Samaritans were on the bridge in Illinois. Who said they were FBI, thereby creating a firestorm.

The Subsection

Behind doors FBI is just as clueless as they are publicly. I read a position paper that laid out the case for them most likely being private citizens in the right place at the right time, but I stopped believing in coincidence decades ago. And, if you remember, within the past six months we've been blamed for the assassination of Abu Ahmad al-Tunisi in Syria, an up-and-comer with ISIL. Physical evidence presented, supposedly tying us, America, to that hit. Which I know for a fact we didn't do. That's two right there that stand out. I bet we can find more, we start digging. Maybe none of them are related, maybe they're all separate incidents. Separate actors. But maybe not."

"We know for a fact somebody, some organization, is out there, working against us," MacGregor said. "Targeting us." He looked around the table, at their faces. "You're going to be part of a new task force. Find them."

The Fallen Republic Series By James Tarr

vinci-books.com/cascade

America is falling, one bite at a time.

When a devastating bioterror attack unleashes a zombie-like plague, the nation descends into chaos. Stranded in the neon jungle of Las Vegas, an unlikely group of strangers must band together to navigate this apocalyptic landscape. Their goal? To make it home in a world where "home" may no longer exist.

Turn the page for a free preview…

Cascade: Chapter One

JACK

Stuck in a window seat. Not as good as an aisle seat, but definitely better than being wedged between two people, one of whom would undoubtedly be fat and leaning into his space. Well, not leaning, just intruding. The talking heads all liked to say that America had an obesity epidemic, and never did he see the truth of that more than when travelling. Which he did, a lot.

Even though air travel was far more affordable than it had been for his parents' generation, by its very nature it attracted an older crowd. Which meant he was far more likely to be seated next to a tense businessman bloated on expense-account liquor or a middle-aged woman who every year kept adding to the weight she'd put on after getting pregnant than he was a stick-thin twelve-year-old. But a man could dream. This flight the man to his right was about fifty and compact, from his coloring and features Indian, or maybe Pakistani. They'd nodded at each other at the start of the flight, then never exchanged a word since. Jack had no idea whether the man was from London, England,

London, Kentucky, or if he even spoke English. The perfect seatmate.

The exception, which proved the rule. Jack enjoyed every minute, every second of it.

He stared out the window as the plane passed Manhattan, maybe ten miles off the southern tip of the island. New York. Beautiful from the air. From a distance. Like all cities. In fact, in his office and around his house he had several prints, famous photographs of famous cities, skylines or taken from the air, often at night so the lights set them ablaze like inverted chandeliers. Cities, those gorgeous, amazing monuments to the perseverance and capability of mankind. Except once you got down in there, on the streets with the people who lived there, you saw cities for what they were.

Dirty. Crowded. Smelly. Filled with callous people who thought their indifference, their literal blindness to the humans living and working around them, somehow made them tough.

No, it just made them assholes.

Jack was an expert on assholes, being a bit of a professional one himself, although some of that was an act. He could dial it up or back, depending. He was going to try to be on his best behavior this trip.

The skyscrapers sprouted from the island of Manhattan like crystals grown in a lab, somehow trained to reach skyward, from a distance so close together there seemed no space between them. Like wheat stalks in a field. New buildings built on the bones of old, as there hadn't been any unused land on Manhattan for hundreds of years. Buildings growing taller and taller through the centuries, anchored in bedrock. The few areas of Manhattan that weren't bristling with high-rises like quills on a porcupine, such as the area around Washington Square, suffered from a lack of bedrock near the surface, making it almost impossible to build tall buildings with any structural integrity. Some ingenious engineering student, some day, would find a way around that, and then look out.

Just east of Manhattan would have been the closest airport. La Guardia, in Queens. Old and cramped and dirty, at least the last time he'd been there. He'd heard they'd renovated it, but likely it amounted to putting lipstick on a pig. The locals pronounced it "La Guadier", which sounded vaguely French, although not with a New York accent. No one would ever confuse a New York with a French accent. He'd spent ten days in France, once, more than half of that in Paris, where your accent was very important. Another big city. Beautiful. Historic. Unforgettable. Also dirty. Smelly. And, unfortunately, filled with people.

Every morning the streets of gay Paree had smelled like piss, and street cleaning machines hosed down the gutters. Ride the Metro, and everyone had that European body odor thing still going strong. What the hell was it with Europeans, body odor, and body hair? He didn't quite get it. It wasn't as bad as it used to be, or so he'd been told, more and more women were shaving or going the laser hair removal route, but the American habit of bathing every day seemed to still be almost an exclusively American habit. Which, if he remembered his history right, was a result of ad campaigns from soap companies after World War II. To sell more product. That's how soap operas got their names, the daytime dramas were all sponsored by soap companies, convincing middle Americans they could never be too clean. Or maybe his recollection of that bit of Americana was a tad off. He made a note to himself on his phone, *look up soap operas*.

Jack prided himself on knowing a little bit about everything, and was always trying to learn more. One of the benefits of a classical education, as Hans Gruber liked to say, or being 'well-rounded', as his parents liked to say, was being able to intelligently discuss all sorts of topics with all sorts of people. Everything from history to pop culture, from politics to porn. Or the politics of porn. Jack of all trades, but master of only one—being able to write and talk, to communicate with people.

Which was ironic, considering how much he didn't like people. His joy came in making the language, written usually, dance to his bidding.

But back to Paris, and New York, and big cities in general. Flying across the vast expanse that was America, there were miles and miles of nearly nothing, and then you ran into these accretions of people, all piled up in one spot. Literally piled, so many on top of one another they rose up from the ground in tall buildings. It seemed unnatural. And yet, people had been accumulating together in large groups, settlements, cities, since humanity had moved out of caves. So it must be a natural inclination. To gather. Humans were social animals, after all.

Some definitely more than others.

Still, flying across great flat empty spaces, only to see cities rise up seemingly out of nowhere, lines of cars stretching in all directions, reminded him of spilled ice cream on a sidewalk at the height of summer. An hour later the ice cream would almost be invisible under a boiling mass of ants. The little tiny ants the size of poppy seeds, so small you nearly had to stick your nose in them to see the individual animals. Hordes of them led to and from the newfound sweet treasure in lines not so different from the traffic snaking in and out of every major city. No real intelligence, just blind animal instinct.

His plane landed at what the locals called Islip MacArthur, but was now technically Long Island MacArthur Airport. The airport was in the middle of Long Island and roughly two hours from Manhattan, depending. He retrieved his checked bag and found the shuttle. It was a five-minute ride to the LIRR, the Long Island Railroad, then a long train ride west across the island. Then another cab ride, the cabbie using his horn like it was an extension of his mouth.

Jack checked into his hotel and used his phone to figure out how far he was from where he needed to be. Less than half a mile. Easy walking distance, especially with the mild September weather. He made himself presentable, put on a casual sport coat and plain tie over khakis, then headed out.

Not quite halfway there he stumbled across a Barnes & Noble. He had the time, so he went in. He wanted to see if he could find his book. It was set out on a table in the nonfiction area, along with a P. J. O'Rourke compendium and Barack Obama's latest autobiography—his third or fourth, Jack had lost count. He stared at his book on display for a long time. He stood there staring for so long the store security officer wandered over, giving him a look from beneath his hairpiece and his cheap, dandruff-coated blazer. Seeing the book sitting there, his name on the cover, in a Manhattan bookstore, was a bit surreal. He'd been writing articles forever, but a book was, somehow, different.

The publisher's headquarters was on Broadway, less than a quarter mile from the World Trade Center. Or the hole in Manhattan that had been the WTC. Jack gave the name of the PR rep to the guard in the lobby and the man called up. A few minutes later Michelle Henskamp arrived in the elevator. He'd only ever talked to her on the phone, and weirdly enough she looked just like he'd envisioned—skinny, pretty, blonde, and dressed in the traditional Manhattan business uniform for women, a silk blouse and tight black skirt, both of which he assumed were very expensive, but that was just a guess as like most straight men the only thing he knew about women's fashion was what he liked. Heels, lipstick, and minimal jewelry completed the uniform.

"So nice to meet you," she said, shaking his hand. "Flight was okay? No problems?"

"All good," he assured her.

She cocked her head, smiling. "You're younger than I thought you'd be."

"You've got my bio." In it was a lot of personal information, including a date of birth. Thirty-five didn't feel that young. Not any more. And he was older than her. She looked to be in her late twenties, maybe thirty.

Michelle smiled. In truth, she hadn't much paid attention to the DOB. She just assumed someone covering a Presidential campaign, someone who'd generated a book out of that experience, would be older. Middleaged. Fifties. She wasn't sure how to respond, so he saved her any embarrassment by saying, "I'm not fat, and I've got all my hair. Which for thirty-five shouldn't be unusual, but apparently is."

She smiled, and checked the tiny gold watch on her slender wrist, then the time on the big smartphone in her hand. "First interview is in two hours, and it's a two-minute walk. Are you hungry? We could do lunch first, and then walk over. Unless you did airport food."

"You're coming with?"

"You get the full package for this media junket, a professional escort, ready to assist or answer any questions you might have."

"A professional escort. Well. Welcome to the Big Apple."

She laughed. "I should have known to watch what I say around you, after that book. With that sarcasm, you must have been a New Yorker in a previous life."

"You read it?" He'd been afraid to ask.

"Absolutely. Hard to rep a property without understanding what it is. Although that's done all the time." She raised a hand, as if swearing on a Bible. "And I have to admit I am guilty as charged."

"Of what?"

"Of everything you accuse New Yorkers of."

He shook his head, but was smiling. "I didn't accuse anybody of anything. I just wrote down what I observed."

She jerked her head. "Come on, let's go, I know a great place."

The restaurant was simple and upscale, the small tables filled with professionally-dressed Manhattanites. Jack got a steak salad, and a Diet Coke. Michelle got a Caesar salad, then carefully picked out all the croutons and pushed them aside. "Keto," she told him apologetically. Her salad looked good, and his was excellent, but then again they ought to have been for how much they cost. Neither of them ordered so much as a beer and still the bill was almost a hundred bucks. For two salads and soft drinks.

Afterward, she walked him over to the radio studio. Not nearly as slowly as he was expecting, with her four-inch heels.

He looked around. There were dozens, probably hundreds of people on the sidewalks within rock throwing distance, and a shocking number of them were on their phones. What was surprising to him was how many people were walking while looking at the phone in their hand. They seemed to have some sort of internal radar system that kept them from bumping into other people. Meanwhile, the streets were full of traffic, bumper to bumper, taxis and delivery vehicles and the rare personal car.

He looked at Michelle. "Do you have a hundred people a day get hit by cars while on their phone?" She was confused by the question until he gestured at the moving crowd around them. She realized just how many of the pedestrians were looking down at their phones as they went about their day-to-day lives. She had hers in her hand and would probably have been doing the same if she wasn't with a client.

"I don't know. Probably not that many. But you've got to do something to separate the real New Yorkers from the rest."

He snorted. "You're not a real New Yorker until you've been hit by a taxi? Or a bike messenger?"

"Something like that."

"I'm walkin' here!" he shouted, out, with a heavy, obnoxious New York accent. It got him a few looks.

Michelle laughed in surprise, and smiled. "Exactly. That was a movie, right?"

"*Midnight Cowboy*. Dustin Hoffman slapped a taxi when he said it, and the story is the line was ad-libbed, because he was almost actually run over."

"That's New York for you."

The radio station was the local hub of a nationwide network, but because it was the New York City station it was the biggest.

"I'll be here when you're done. It's supposed to be a fifteen-minute interview," Michelle told him.

The Subsection

They brought him into the studio during a commercial break and he shook hands with the nationally-syndicated host, a tough-looking guy who had New Yorker stamped all over him. But Bill Codell was also a former New York City cop who'd spent five years as a U.S. Secret Service agent, which made him a bit unusual in the talk radio circuit. That tough guy look—and reputation—was earned, and not an act. Jack was placed in a well-padded chair, a microphone on a boom swung close in front of his mouth. He found he was sweating under his coat. Michelle was on the far side of a wall of glass, outside of the broadcast booth, and gave him a thumbs-up.

"Today we've got an interesting guest in studio," Codell said when they were back from break. His New York accent was rich and unforced. "Jack Haley, author of *Welcome to America*, which is currently sitting at number eight on the New York Times' bestseller list for non-fiction. In spite of their scathing review." That got a laugh out of Jack. "Jack, thanks for joining us."

"Glad to be here. Long time listener, first time caller."

Codell's eyes opened wide, then he burst out laughing. "Oh, folks, this is going to be fun. If you've read this book—and I have, that's why I wanted to get him on, get him in here—it's going to make you sad, and angry, and make you think, but mostly it's going to make you laugh. My stomach was sore for a day after reading it, I laughed so hard. So, Jack, tell us about *Welcome to America*. How did it happen?"

"Well, back two years ago I was given an assignment to cover the Presidential campaign. For the *Esquire* magazine website, of all things. They wanted daily coverage of the campaign. Political stuff. Which isn't exactly my specialty, but I've done a few things and one of the editors there is someone I used to write for at another title, so he asked if

I'd be interested. He thought the fact that I wasn't a political writer would make the pieces different enough to grab readers. I figured what the hell, it would be an interesting change of pace, and I could do politics. And, you know, *Esquire* pays pretty well. So that's what I gave them, the day-to-day grind of the campaign trail from the perspective of an outsider on the inside, and everyone was happy with those articles. But it was the behind-the-scenes stuff with the press that I found far more fascinating than the politics. Politicians are a known quantity. With very few exceptions they are just horrible human beings. But it was the press pool that was the big surprise to me. Watching them follow then-Senator, now President Hellar around the country, across sixteen states, was eye-opening. Astounding. Awful. Hilarious. I started taking notes about them, and those notes turned into stories that I filed away, and eventually those stories became this book."

Codell was nodding. "Which I highly recommend, folks. And it's not about politics, not really, it's more…social commentary, I guess, disguised at hilarious anecdotes? Jack Haley, explain the title, *Welcome to America*."

Jack smiled. "In the book, you'll see, I did an informal poll of the media pool covering the campaign, because I got curious. Based on their behavior and comments. Ninety percent of them were born or raised in New York City, Los Angeles, or D.C. Most of the rest were from Chicago or another big city. San Francisco. Atlanta. And watching them as they followed the campaign through middle America, they behaved as if they were visiting a foreign country. They could speak the language, but the history and culture and people were alien to them. And that's not an exaggeration, I wish it was. To the people in the mainstream media, America is a foreign country, and they don't understand much of what goes on there. Either the people who live there or what their lives are like. And they don't care to learn, which is probably, no, definitely worse. I mean, I don't know who coined it, but we've all heard the term 'fly-over country'."

Codell said, "Right. Meaning all of America, between New York and L.A. The elites only ever see it from the windows of jets. Is that where you're from, middle America?"

"Mostly I've spent my life living in suburbia. Ohio, Michigan, North Carolina. But even Midwest suburbia is a far cry from Chicago, or New York, or Boston. And then I got an English degree at the University of Alabama."

"Roll tide," Codell said, surprising Jack.

"Hell yeah, roll tide," Jack said, smiling. "I had a lot of fond memories watching the Crimson Tide on Saturdays." He opened his mouth to continue, but Codell interrupted him in one of the classic segues that had made him so famous.

"*They call Alabama the Crimson Tide,*" the man crooned, his singing voice surprisingly deep and mellow, "*call me Deacon Blues*.... Sorry about that folks," Codell said, leaning into the microphone. "Just got a little nostalgic. Okay," he said to Jack, "back to your point."

Jack couldn't help but laugh. "I wasn't expecting to hear Steely Dan in here, but now my day is complete. Okay, Tuscaloosa, where UA is, it's not tiny, but it's not exactly one of the five boroughs, you know? And after college I spent almost two years living in a very small town in North Carolina. You could count on one hand the number of cars that would pass by the house in a day. Houses and farms out there, no apartments. Most of the people worked with their hands, or had grown up doing that. It was hard to find someone who hadn't spent a summer working on a farm, or who unironically wore plaid. Everyone there would smile and wave, even if they didn't know you. But you almost had to seek them out. Go to town to see strangers. Here, in New York, in most cities, you can't get away from people. It's the exact opposite, in almost every way. And sometimes the culture shock when someone from New York City shows up is very, very funny."

"Jack, you know I'm a New Yorker. Everyone knows I'm a New Yorker. I love this town, but I've also been around the country. Around the world. I know how unlike most of America New York City is. People either love it or hate it, with absolutely no middle ground. Tell my listeners the story from the book of Hellar's press secretary, and who was it? CNN's Brian Stelter? In Indiana. Trying to figure out how to use a push lawn mower. And everything went horribly wrong."

Jack chuckled. "That's a good one. Any story that ends up in the ER is a keeper. So…"

Near the end of the interview they were laughing together. Codell asked him, "Okay, serious question now, everyday life for someone living in a brownstone in Washington Heights is far different than for someone on a farm in Iowa. But do you think the people themselves are different? Because that's the impression I got from the book."

"Absolutely."

"Why? In what way?"

"Their environment changes them. It's the number of people or, technically, population density. You can't get away from people here, they are everywhere. All the time." He shrugged, and took a beat. "Look, people are amazing. Every one of them is a unique individual, every one of them has some aspect of their life, or some story, that will astound you. But too much of anything is never good. I'm reminded of the quote by Stalin. 'One death is a tragedy. A million deaths is a statistic.' But the spooky thing is, it's the same with people when they're alive. If you only see or interact with a handful of people every day, like most of our ancestors did, or like people out in the country do right now, you appreciate them more. You smile and wave. 'Howdy neighbor, haven't seen you in a while.' But here, in New York, in Manhattan," he waved his arm, "there are so many people they simply become an annoyance. An impediment, to living your life. White noise, at best. You see anybody smiling and waving out there on the sidewalk? If you did, you'd think they were crazy. And you'd probably be right. Which is sad. There needs to be a balance." Codell was nodding sagely.

Jack went on. "This city is full of people who have never in their lives mowed a lawn, chopped wood with an axe, hunted, cooked food over an open fire, seen any animal larger than a squirrel or rabbit outside of the zoo. And that's fine, don't get me wrong, I just don't want them thinking their life experience is the only one. Or that it's somehow superior. I mean, a tree grows in Brooklyn, right? But not all trees grow in Brooklyn. This country is full of people living very different lives than what you see on the streets of New York or Chicago or L.A. And it's better for it."

Michelle was waiting for him in the lobby afterward. "That was great," she told him. "You're a natural."

He smiled in appreciation, but told her truthfully, "Oh, I hate this." His armpits were soaked. Stress sweat.

"What?"

"Talking to people. If I wanted to talk to people I wouldn't be a writer."

She smirked at him. "I've read your stuff. You talk to a lot of people for your articles."

He shrugged. "You gotta do what you gotta do. That's why it's called work. So now what?"

"So now we walk over to Fox News. You're going on during their five o'clock show, although I'm not sure exactly when during the hour. I'll find out when we get there. After that is an interview with the New York Post. But we've got some time to kill, and you probably don't want to do it at Fox. It's really cramped, you'd never know it from what you see on TV. There's a Starbucks, two blocks up."

"I don't know if more caffeine is what I need, but I do enjoy seeing the looks on their faces when I demand vegan cow milk." They started walking in that direction.

She frowned at him. "But if it's cow milk, how can it be vegan?"

"Aren't cows vegan? Wouldn't that make all cow milk vegan?"

She gave a little shake of her head, frowning. "That's not what vegan means."

"Let's let them try to tell me that," he said, with a wide smile.

When he got to the counter at Starbucks, and with a straight face ordered a "Left-handed vegan whole milk cappuccino made from gender neutral conflict-free beans," Michelle had to turn away and cough to hide her laughter. What made it funnier was Jack's pitch-perfect English accent.

The Fox News interview was short and rather disappointing. The New York Post interview was with a young reporter

The Subsection

who seemed defensive of New Yorkers and their city. Jack was friendly and charming and ultimately got the man to admit that, 1. He'd never been further abroad than Newark, and 2. The book, dammit, was funny. The Post interview went quite long, but everyone walked away happy. Afterward he and Michelle went out for a late dinner at a trendy restaurant she'd picked. He guessed it was expensive, as there were no prices on the menu. After the hundred-dollar salad lunch he couldn't imagine how much steak would cost at a place like this, so he was glad the publisher was picking up the tab.

"So if you don't normally do politics, what is your specialty?" Michelle asked him. "The articles I read, they were all over the map on subject matter."

"My specialty? Guy stuff, I guess."

She laughed. "Guy stuff?"

He smiled. "Yeah. Traditional guy stuff. Cars, guns, watches, cigars, working out. It's easier to write compellingly about stuff you're interested in, and I like all of that stereotypical guy stuff." He shrugged.

"What are you doing next? You taking any time off because of the book?"

He shook his head. "I did after I finished the book, but that was six months ago. Now, I've actually been working out a lot, trying to get into shape, for a piece, or several pieces I have been doing and am going to be doing for *Men's Health* and *Recoil*."

"*Recoil?*"

"Yeah, it's a…gun-oriented lifestyle magazine, I guess?"

She gave him a look, one eye squinted. He smiled and pointed at her. "See, that's one of those disconnects I talk about." He waved a hand around the restaurant. "For New Yorkers, because they basically banned guns in the city so long ago, the only two kinds of people who have guns, in your mind, are cops and bad guys. But you forget that for almost every other area of the country, even Long Island and upstate New York, that's not the case. That it's never been the case. There's never been more guns and gun owners in this country than right now, especially after all the panic buying due to the pandemic, lockdown, whatever. A huge chunk of those were to first-time gun buyers, and a huge chunk of *those* were minorities and women, as everyone was worried about riots and the cops getting defunded. I did an article on it for the *Wall Street Journal*," he explained.

"I suppose. So what's this article?"

"For close to a decade there's been a weird hybrid sporting event out there called The Tactical Games. It's…" He squinched his eyes, trying to decide how to explain it. "Think of the physical test you'd have to go through it you wanted to join a police SWAT team. There's shooting, but they'd also want you to be in shape too, right? That's what this event is. There's running, and a body drag, all sorts of high-energy exercises, combined with shooting."

"So it's for cops?"

He shook his head. "No, it's for everyone. You've got some cops who compete, and some soldiers, active duty and retired, but most of the competitors are men—and women—who are plumbers, accountants, whatever. But for those few days they get to run around like SWAT team guys, wearing heavy body armor, dragging weighted dummies, rope climbing with slung rifles, pushing weighted wheelbarrows…and shooting rifles and pistols."

"Okayyy…."

He laughed. "I know, not your thing at all. In my head I keep referring to it as 'Combat CrossFit', but think of it like this—it's like starring in your own action movie. While being difficult as hell. Very athletic. I mean, you've really got to get in shape if you don't want to be sucking wind or puking in the middle of an event. So that means it's not just fun, but merely finishing gives you a sense of accomplishment. Like those Tough Mudder races. Last year the event was bought out, along with another similar crazy competition called the MGM Ironman, and now it's called The Warrior Olympics. T.W.O. Got some big-name sponsors—Red Bull, Wounded Warrior Project, and maybe Wrangler? The jeans, not the car. NBC Sports is going to televise some of it, which I find weird, normally network TV does everything it can to not show private citizens using guns, so much so that a chunk of the population thinks it never happens, but I think they've got some big names competing this year—Gina Carano, I've heard, maybe Keanu Reeves, Lou Ferrigno. Seeing them running around in plate carriers, shooting guns? That's just good TV."

"Plate carriers?"

"Body armor. The bulky stuff. What you'd wear for a romantic weekend in Chicago. Anyway, I've been writing up my progress getting into shape for this for *Men's Health*, kind of a weekly blog. It's been a long road. And I'll write up the event too, the fitness part for them, and the gun stuff for *Recoil*. Both magazines have photographers assigned."

"You look like you're in decent shape." He wasn't built like a bodybuilder, but he had some muscle on him. Looked like he did a lot of cardio. Compact. Trim. She'd noticed.

"I had some health problems last year," he admitted. "I wrote most of the book while I was dealing with that. Getting back into shape, and into better shape than I was, has been quite a project. That's why *Men's Health* was interested, they liked the beating cancer aspect of the workout regimen."

That surprised her. "Cancer? Shit." Her eyes went up and down what she could see of him across the table. "But you're only…."

"Yeah. Thirty-five. Diagnosed a week before my thirty-fourth birthday. Lucky me."

No wonder he was a smart-ass. "But you beat it?"

"Yeah. Caught it early. They cut it out. Not much chemo. Still, any chemo sucks. Trust me."

"Did you have lung cancer? You mentioned cigars."

"You don't inhale with cigars, you just take the smoke into your mouth."

Admittedly she didn't know anything about cigars, but she said, "Rush Limbaugh smoked cigars all the time, and he died of lung cancer."

"And before he smoked cigars he smoked cigarettes." He made a face and stared off into the distance. "Listen, I know I brought it up, but I'd rather not…."

"Sure, no problem."

Afterward, on the sidewalk outside the restaurant, she said to him, "Look, how about I walk you to your hotel, it's only about a block and a half away. Then I can catch a cab."

"You sure? I don't want to put you out."

"Not a problem."

They started walking. He stared up at the glittering buildings towering over them, unafraid to look like the tourist that he was. He spun around in a complete circle. "It's just incredible," he admitted, talking about the massive skyscrapers stretching into the starry sky. The city had a majestic beauty to it that was no less magnificent than the Grand Canyon for being manmade. Up from the ground instead of down into it. He found urban landscapes just as beautiful as those made by Mother Nature. But only from a distance.

"Yeah? I guess I take it for granted now. You warming up to the idea of moving here?"

"What? Oh, hell no. I'd never want to live here, I'd go postal in two weeks. But it's a fascinating place to visit." The noise of the city was constant—honking horns, voices, the rush of car tires on pavement, distant sirens, the low rumble of a passenger jet in the distance. And people. People, everywhere. "You always work such long days?"

"On days like this, yeah. The city that never sleeps. You've got a red-eye, right?"

"Six a.m. With the train ride I'm considering just going now, and sleeping at the airport."

"Why'd you fly into Long Island?" She pronounced it like most New Yorkers, *Lawn Guylind*.

"Long story."

"You still good for that phone interview tomorrow night at six? With Betty Rapplethorpe from Sirius/XM."

"Absolutely."

As they reached an intersection a man approached them from the connecting street. He was scruffy and skinny, in a long-sleeve plaid shirt that looked wet or muddy or both. "Can you spare some cash?" he asked them, running his eyes up and down Michelle. His voice was thick and phlegmy.

"I can't help you," Jack said firmly. He would have kept walking, but the light changed, and they were stuck waiting at the curb unless they wanted to risk darting into traffic. At night. In Manhattan. Rhymes with suicide....

"I didn't ask for help, I asked for some cash," the man growled. "And I know you've got some." He met Jack's gaze, and very deliberately put his hand into a baggy pocket. It was sagging from the weight of something.

Jack unbuttoned his jacket and positioned his hands near his waist, squeezing them into fists so tight his knuckles turned white. "Fuck off before you get hurt," he told the man, heat and barely restrained fury in his voice. He stared at the man, unblinking.

The man's eyes went up and down Jack again, reevaluating him, then he wandered off down the sidewalk, muttering "Asshole."

Jack watched him go, until he was sure the man wasn't going to turn around and charge back at them. Then the light changed, and they crossed the street.

"You shouldn't have done that, that was dangerous," Michelle told him quietly. She'd been a little rattled by the incident. And her client's reaction. "You should have just given him a couple of bucks."

"Not going to happen," Jack said, staring straight ahead.

"You're more likely to get injured if you put up a fight," she told him. The last thing she needed was one of their up-and-coming new authors mugged and beaten on a street corner.

Jack stopped looked at her and shook his head. "No," he told her firmly, "that's actually not true. The opposite is true, according to actual FBI statistics and everyone else. Which only makes sense. Bullies don't stop if you ask them nicely. Muggers don't want a fight, they want money, and if somebody puts up a fight they'll go move on to someone who won't." He resumed walking, and forced a smile. She seemed uneasy about what had happened. "But maybe I should have given him the cash. Then I could have crossed 'mugged in New York' off my bucket list."

"You're so bad," she told him.

He thanked her and shook her hand outside the lobby of his hotel, then waved down a cab for her. He felt like he was an actor in a play, sticking his hand out for a bright yellow taxi was something he'd only ever seen in the movies or on TV.

Upstairs, in his room, he checked the time on his watch and frowned. He hated getting up early, but he was sure he'd hate sleeping in a chair at the airport even more. He just needed to make sure the LIRR was running that early in the morning.

Jack pulled his laptop out of his carry-on and opened it. While he waited for it to boot up he took off his sport coat and laid it on the bed. His dress shirt was a little stained from the stress sweat he'd generated during the various interviews. On his right hip he had a classic Colt Lightweight Commander in .45 ACP, customized by the late Jim Hoag sometime in the early 1990s. It was in a Kramer horsehide inside-the-waistband holster, with a spare 7-round magazine on his off-side hip. The pistol was why he'd flown into Long Island.

Unless you had a New York City firearms license, simply landing at La Guardia or JFK with an otherwise legal gun in your checked baggage would land you directly in jail. Mere possession of a gun anywhere inside the five boroughs was illegal if you didn't have an NYC license. Jack hadn't been sure about Newark and its airport, and hadn't wanted to drive in all the way from the Philly airport, so he'd flown into Islip, where the 1911 was legal. Kinda. Sorta.

Non-residents couldn't bring any firearms into New York, state or City, without breaking the law. However, there were a few exceptions, and one was a 48-hour exemption if you were signed up to shoot a match inside the state. So he'd signed up to shoot a pistol match on Long Island, and had the documentation to prove it. With that, the pistol and its 7-round magazines were legal in New York state, and the TSA at Islip MacArthur wouldn't care about a legal pistol in his checked bag, whether he was arriving or departing. If any TSA agents asked him why he was leaving before shooting the match, well, he figured a death in the family was as good excuse as any….

It was not lost on him that the bureaucratic hurdles he had to jump through to legally get a gun into New York state were more burdensome than when flying into some foreign countries.

Was it legal for him to carry a pistol in the city? Oh, hell no. Completely, totally illegal, according to state and local law. So it was a good thing they hadn't gone anywhere with metal detectors. If Michelle had offered to take him on a tour of the United Nations building he would have had to politely decline. But the homicide rates in big cities across the U.S. had surged 25% or more during the government lockdown in 2020, and hadn't yet come down. Didn't look likely to, with the "defund the police" movements still going strong, and the economic downturn so serious that even the politicians who'd caused it were using the term "recession", whereas some of their opponents were claiming it met the definition of depression. Either way, a lot of people were unhappy, and restless, especially in the cities.

Walking around unarmed, in New York frickin' City? The Big Apple? The City That Never Sleeps? Not going to happen. Far better to be Bernie Goetz than Paul Kersey's wife.

The fact that he was engaging in the same kind of stereotypical profiling that he'd mocked so relentlessly in *Welcome to America* was not lost on him.

Cascade: Chapter Two

MATT

The small antique table wasn't especially valuable, or even attractive; "antique" in this instance only meant old. The legs were skinny and quite delicate, and the top was too small to be of much use; one Kleenex box and there was barely enough space left for a coaster. But the hardwood—cherry, in this case—table had been made by his great-grandfather, and passed down from generation to generation in his family, transferring to whichever family member had bought a new house, so in some way that made it priceless.

The only problem was that one of the spindly carved legs on the ugly damned thing was loose. Better to fix it now, tighten it up before anything got broken, because they always did when you had small children in the house. Matt wasn't especially artistic, but he knew a few things about working with wood. He was in the garage at his workbench, the table on its side before him, the one troublesome leg detached and set nearby, digging in a drawer for the razor blade knife, when he heard a sound. Standing in the doorway to the house was his wife and son. The expression on her face, even though he couldn't read it, made him straighten up.

"Hey," he said, voice neutral. Between the tilt of her eyebrows and the set of her lips he immediately ran through his actions for the past few days, trying to remember if he'd done something to get himself a reprimand. She didn't look mad, not exactly, but she wasn't smiling either. He couldn't think of anything, but after eight years of marriage he'd learned that just because he didn't think he'd done anything wrong didn't mean a damned thing. "What's up?"

His wife blinked before speaking. "Matty and I were just in the front room, playing with his LEGOs. He was telling me how yesterday, when you were watching him and I was at work, that you got a…" she paused briefly, "…a booty call from Janelle."

Janelle was the babysitter who had helped them keep their sanity. She was sixteen and lived halfway down the block. She wasn't especially smart, or pretty, but she was great with Matty and probably had a great future in Human Resources. Matt looked at his son, who was one month shy of his fourth birthday and hugging on his mother's leg. Then he pinched his lips together and tried to kill the smile forming there.

"I sure did," he told Carli. "A big ol' booty call. Didn't last long though."

"Oh really?" His wife could tell that there was something going on she didn't quite understand.

Matt started smiling then, and looked at his son. "Matty, I don't think your mom knows what a booty call is. Why don't you tell her?'

The Subsection

The boy rolled his eyes, in disbelief that his mom couldn't know something so simple. "It's when you sit on your phone and your booty calls someone. Some people say buttdial but butt's a bad word," he explained. He looked up at his mom. "Can we have snakes for dinner?"

Matty loved crinkle-cut frozen French fries, Ore-Ida brand most of all. When you pulled a tray of them straight from the oven they were always steaming and hissing, and he'd been calling them snakes ever since he'd been riding on his mother's hip. Which he still wanted to do, but was too big and heavy.

"Again? I suppose."

"Can I go back and play LEGOs?"

"Sure honey, I'll be there in a second," Carli said. She turned back to her husband as the boy ran off. "I knew it wasn't a booty call, a real booty call, but I didn't..." she trailed off and then shrugged, slightly embarrassed. Then they both laughed.

"We were watching TV one night and I was flipping through the channels. On one of the reality shows somebody said 'booty call' and he asked what that was."

His wife nodded. "That's the problem with having a smart kid, they notice everything." They'd had that conversation several times before. She nodded at the table. "You going to be able to fix that?"

Matt looked at the small table, and frowned. "I don't know if 'fix' is the right word, but I can make it better. Tighten the leg up. If it survives Matty I'll be shocked."

"Aren't you a professional, licensed, bonded, insured, buffed, waxed, and laminated union carpenter?"

"You forget frosted." He smiled. "Framing. Lathing. Drywall. Occasional millwork. Even some concrete, back in the day. Not a cabinet maker. And none of that is quite the same as doing delicate surgery on an antique hardwood end table." He flexed his hands. They were tough and calloused from years of manual labor, his forearms thick with muscle. Nail guns and circular saws were great, but power tools would never completely replace hand tools. He was still almost skinny, but had the forearms and shoulders of a much bigger man.

"We can always put it in the attic."

He shook his head. "No. It's an heirloom, and an antique now, but it wasn't built as a museum piece. They had a small house, so Great-Great Malcolm," that's what his father had always called his grandfather, for some reason, "made a small table."

"It's ugly enough to be in a museum."

He stared at the small table, hands on his hips. She wasn't wrong. "Yeah, well. Do you want me to put it in the attic?" Happy wife, happy life, he'd learned that long ago.

"No, absolutely not. We don't have much from your family. A few photos, and awkward uncomfortable phone calls from your brother twice a year." Matt had to snort at that. She wasn't wrong. "Leave it out. Maybe it'll come back into fashion."

That made him smile, but he admitted, "I'm not sure it ever was in fashion. I think he was going for a Louis XIV look, but it's more like…" He frowned and cocked his head, looking at the table.

"Psychedelic Art Deco the Fourteenth?" his wife volunteered.

"Yeah, that."

"Don't forget you've got a meeting tonight."

"Yeah, no, I haven't forgotten, I'm just trying to cross a few things off the list before I head out of town next week."

The Subsection

He was flying out to Vegas to spend ten days with his aunt, who'd raised him. He hadn't seen her in over a year, thanks to her fears about travelling. He'd wanted to bring Carli and Matty, but his aunt seemed terrified she'd get them sick. Or they'd get her sick. Or something. A lot of seniors, post-Covid, seemed to be terrified of everything. His aunt lived alone, and while she had a small circle of friends, he was worried about her. She was getting to the age where living alone could be a death sentence if you took a bad fall.

"Like the garbage disposal?"

"Crap, I forgot about that. Put it on the list for tomorrow? I wanted to mow today. It might rain tomorrow."

"So you do remember there's a list?"

"Ha ha," he said, and got back to work on the table.

He loved his neighborhood. Modest, one- and two-story homes on quiet, tree-lined streets. North Reading was a great place to raise Matty, and any little brothers or sisters he might eventually have—they'd been working at that, so far without success, although it had been a lot of fun. The house hadn't been cheap, thanks to nearby Boston driving up the real estate prices in all the nearby suburbs, but between the chunk of cash he'd gotten from his parents' estate as a down payment, his income as a union carpenter and his wife's as a teacher, they were able to manage the payments on the modest cape cod. Not quite two thousand square feet and it was now valued at over half a million dollars, which he found incredible. And incredibly stupid. But if they ever decided to move he figured they could sell the house and buy something bigger and nicer just about anywhere in the country. And probably have cash left over.

The lawn mower was an old gasoline push model that had belonged to his father and that he had somehow kept running all these years. He drained the oil and changed the filter and spark plug every winter, which probably helped. He wheeled it out of the garage and smiled when it started up on the third pull of the cord.

The small motor of the Ahrens putted along happily as Matt worked it back and forth across the lawn, which seemed to be getting more uneven every year. He wasn't sure if that was due to growing tree roots or the ground settling or what. The year before had been quite wet, with a cool, rainy summer and a huge amount of snow over the winter, but he wasn't sure if that had anything to do with what he was seeing.

The mature maple and oak trees kept half the yard in shade, so even when the humidity peaked, doing yard work was never too miserable. The trees were great. The big forsythia bushes running along the property line, planted by the previous owner…not so much.

Well, in truth, it wasn't fair to blame anything on the bushes. The bushes were just fine, if a little messy in the spring when they started to shed their fragrant and impossibly bright yellow flowers. The problem was his neighbor, the lawyer, who before Matt was done mowing was out in his driveway, pretending to be doing something with his BMW but really just waiting for Matt to finish. "Hey, Matt," he said, before the growl of the motor's engine had even died.

"Charles."

"So," the lawyer said, sliding over, "I thought you were going to take care of those bushes."

Matt sighed, then glanced over at the three big forsythia bushes. Charles wasn't just a lawyer, he was married to one too, and his wife had made it clear to Matt and his wife that she hated the bushes. Especially hated the bright yellow flowers they sported in the spring. Which the wind tended to blow across their yard, and onto their cars. The lawyers had moved in two years earlier, and every time Matt interacted with them he wished the Robinsons hadn't retired and moved to Arizona.

"Take care of them how?"

Charles Carmichael frowned at him. "We talked about this."

Matt really did not want to get into another argument about the damn bushes. Especially with a lawyer who thought far too highly of himself, and far too little of anyone who worked with their hands, much less someone who wore Wrangler, Carhart, or Duluth Trading Company clothes to work. But at least the man was better than his wife. If ever the term 'Masshole' applied to someone, it was Carmichael and his wife. "I've got a lot of work to do," Matt said, gesturing at his house.

"You were going to cut down those bushes."

That made Matt blink. "No I wasn't."

"You made a verbal contract with me to cut them down the last time we spoke."

Matt took a deep breath. He didn't want to have friction with anyone, friends, family, coworkers, neighbors, but sometimes life conspired against him. "The hell I did. I said I'd trim them. They are getting a little scraggly."

"They are a neighborhood eyesore," the lawyer said imperiously.

"They look just fine," Matt said. "And they're on my property."

"They are not. They are over the property line."

"Only if it's moved four feet. That, that branch," Matt

said, pointing, "maybe the tip of that is on your property. Over it. But that's about it."

"You are completely in error about the property line, and if you don't take care of those bushes, I will."

Matt took a deep breath. He knew what the problem was. It wasn't Carmichael, it was his wife. He doubted the man cared at all about the bushes, but his wife had decided she hated them, and dragged her husband into the fight. And it was clear who wore the pants in the house. "If you want to hire a surveyor just to doublecheck, go for it. But I mow to the property line as I've always understood it. The previous owner of your house and I—"

"Were in error as to the property line."

Matt looked up. The oak leaves above them were fluttering in a light breeze. Beyond the leaves the sky was bright blue, with just a few wispy clouds scudding across the sky. Such a pretty day. "Like I said, if you want to hire a surveyor just to doublecheck the property line...maybe someone from the city? Your call. Seems like a waste of money to me."

"Landscaping costs will be a lot less than legal fees, if this has to go to court," Carmichael told him ominously.

Matt looked back up at the big oak tree. The rustling of the leaves was soothing. And they turned such pretty colors in the fall. He didn't want any trouble, he didn't want any conflict, he just wanted to be able to live his life. Go along to get along, that was his motto. Usually. "You have a nice day, Chuck," he said, and pushed the lawnmower across the lawn and into his garage without looking back.

The Subsection

Union meetings were as fun or as boring as you made them. Luckily, the guys Matt usually sat with at the monthly meetings knew how to have a good time. He'd worked with all of them on various jobs over the years, and knew them as well as he knew anybody outside of his family. At least half of them were regularly employed by Wilson & Associates, General Contractors, Inc., the name at the top of Matt's paycheck. He was one of the few carpenters they had on the books full time, most everyone else was a contractor.

"You look stressed," Eddie told him. They were milling around at the back of the big room, waiting for the meeting to start. Some of the union leadership was at the front of the room, under the CARPENTER'S LOCAL 239 sign. They were part of the North Atlantic States Regional Council of Carpenters (NASRCC), which was in the United Brotherhood of Carpenters (UBC). Sometimes it was tough to keep the acronyms straight. Matt nodded and waved at guys in the crowd. There were about fifty people in the room.

Eddie pulled a can of beer out of the canvas bag he was carrying and held it out. Matt shook his head. There wasn't supposed to be drinking during the meetings, but Eddie didn't care, and if anyone ever dared to say anything to him, or even give him a dirty look, his default response was a curt, "Fuck off, narc." Eddie looked like a big fat Ted Nugent, with thinning brown hair in a ponytail. He almost always wore plaid long-sleeved shirts, even in the middle of summer.

"Yeah, been a long day."

The meetings were held in the second floor of the carpenters' union pension building. It was a two-story tan building in a light industrial area in Wilmington. Most of the time it was used for bookkeeping and accounting, with some occasional training of apprentices.

"If you're looking forward to a union meeting you're doing it wrong," Allen told him. He smiled, flashing bright white teeth. His hair was cut to stubble, and his head was nearly round. His skin was the color of dark chocolate, the European kind that advertised a high cacao content. "Kid got you running ragged?" Allen, a millworker, had two young twin girls.

"No, Matty's great. Between Carli, the babysitter, and the daycare we've got it covered. Just an asshole neighbor, hassling me about bushes along the property line. He doesn't like them, so he wants me to cut them down."

Eddie frowned. "Are they on your property? Or his?"

"Mine."

"You should have told that dickhead to fuck right off."

That was Eddie's response to everything. And everyone. It had never worked well for him, but he was too old to change. "I've got to live next to him."

"So what?"

"And he's a lawyer."

"So what? Lawyers are assholes. Either he's going to sue you, or he's not. What kind of lawyer is he?"

Matt hadn't thought about that. "I have no idea."

Eddie snorted. "Then there's a good chance he's blowing smoke. One of those corporate attorneys who's never stepped foot inside a courtroom. Most lawyers never do. Fucker probably wouldn't even know how to file a case in small claims court."

"You think?" Matt wasn't so sure.

Allen gestured toward the front of the room with one of his big hands. "We get free legal with the union. Maybe before you take the advice of an alcoholic in a shit-ass white trash ponytail you should talk to one of the lawyers, make sure you're good. Maybe file a case against this clown for harassment."

Eddie hoisted a beer can. "You're only an alcoholic if you're trying to quit. I can stop any time I want. But why would I want to?" It was far from the first time he'd uttered the proclamation. Allen rolled his eyes and shared a look with Matt.

Matt shook his head slowly. "I don't wanna, you know, start anything. His wife's a lawyer too. She's the real problem."

Eddie snorted, and took another long drink of beer. "'Sup to you, but it sounds like your asshole neighbor is the one starting shit."

"People just need to relax, and be good to one other," Allen said, sitting down at the table. It looked like the meeting was about to start. He nodded his big round head. "We've got to spend all our lives with each other, seems like it only makes sense to be good to one another."

"Have you ever been anywhere? Talked to anyone?" Eddie asked him. "People are dicks."

"Sometimes. But not everyone. Not most people."

Eddie shook his head side to side sharply, and finished the beer in the can, then waved it around as he spoke, to emphasize his points. "You count on people being nice, you're going to be disappointed." He pointed at Matt. "Pretty boy's living out with the Richie-Riches and you see what he's dealing with. And the economy doesn't suck too bad, we're not at war, women still have the right to vote…" Allen snorted, and Eddie jabbed a finger at him. "Things go to shit, you'll see how everyone's just a selfish, violent asshat just waiting for an excuse to come out. Stab you in the back, steal your shit, fuck your wife."

"Gee, I just don't know why Amanda divorced you, you're so positive and upbeat," Allen said, and Matt snorted.

"Screw you guys," Eddie said, as he pulled another beer out of his bag. It was cold, and covered with condensation. "You'll see. Hopefully you won't, but probably, at some point, you'll see I'm right. Never bet on altruism. Bet on the opposite of that. Whatever the fuck that is."

Cascade: Chapter Three

WHISKEY

Whiskey was, as usual, already sitting at the table when his partner arrived for the shift briefing. Lopez sat his cup of Starbucks on the table in front of him before settling into the seat. Whiskey eyed the cup, but didn't say anything. At least, not at first.

Officers shuffled into the ready room, talking and laughing. The sergeant checked his watch and crossed his arms at the front of the room, waiting. He knew there'd be a rush of cops in the door right at the last minute.

Whiskey leaned back in his seat, which between his weight and that of all his gear creaked ominously. He crossed his arms, sighed, then finally nodded at the Starbucks cup on the table. "This going to be a regular thing?"

Paul Lopez frowned when he saw Whiskey was talking about his coffee. "What?"

"How much do you make?" Whiskey's voice was deep, but somehow also melodic.

"Money? You know how much I make. Pay scale's

public, right? Based on rank and time on. And I've been on three…three and a half years."

Whiskey nodded. "Right. Which means you don't make shit, even with overtime, when we can get it. And how much did you pay for that?"

Lopez lifted the paper cup. "Like, three bucks. I just get plain coffee, then put the cream in myself. They don't charge you for that." The Starbucks was on Cicero Avenue less half a mile from his house in Belmont Cragin. Only a quarter mile out of his way to work.

Whiskey grunted. "Three bucks. Well, hell. That's nothing at all. Three bucks a shift. That's what, just twelve or fifteen bucks a week? Barely notice that, right? In a year, that's only six, seven hundred bucks. That's only one car payment."

One of the other cops sitting nearby laughed. "Uh-oh, Mother Whiskey's in the building."

Lopez looked like he'd eaten something sour. He'd been partnered with Williams for eight months, and most of the time enjoyed working with the veteran officer. Most of the time. "Leave my coffee alone. You don't mess with a man's coffee." Especially not early in the morning, before the caffeine had a chance to kick in.

"You know how much it would cost to make your own cup of coffee?" Whiskey asked him.

"How much would it cost to get you to shut up?" Lopez asked him, taking an especially loud sip. Then he snorted. "You see that episode of *Chicago P.D.* last night?"

"You know I can't watch that crap."

"You're not going to support Jorgensen?" Lopez asked with a smile. One of the technical advisors for the TV show was a Sergeant they'd both worked with, and who had recently retired.

The Subsection

Whiskey scowled at his partner. "It upsets me when I watch it, and I've got enough stuff that upsets me. It's not the technical inaccuracies that bother me," he said, "it's just so damn stupid. How dumb are the people that they're writing the show for?"

Lopez blinked, pretending surprise. "Have you met our customers?"

"Is that what we're calling them now?"

"All right, quiet down and get your asses in the seats," Sergeant Jerome bellowed from the front of the room. He leaned his big pale hands on the podium and glared at anybody still on their feet. When everyone was sitting and all eyes were on him, he nodded.

"Good morning, ladies and gents. You'll see Pete passing out some lovely info sheets our detective brothers made up last night. One Antwan Jones, fifteen years old, decided to steal a car yesterday and drive up and down a few sidewalks. Put four people in the hospital, and it looks like one of them might not make it."

"He's fifteen?" one of the officers at the front of the room asked, holding up the paper.

The Sergeant nodded. "That photo might be a year or two old, but he's supposed to look the same."

Whiskey was passed a stack of flyers, took one, and passed the rest to Lopez. He studied the photo, which was likely obtained from the kid's mother, as it looked like a school photo. Antwan Jones was a slender light-skinned black youth who looked all of twelve.

"He lives in the 9th District, Deering, but he recently moved out there from here. Dicks are sitting on his mom's house, probably a few other addresses, but he's got a lot of friends in this area still, so keep an eye out.

"Now for the only other thing I've got for you. Some of

you might have seen the Mayor on the news this morning," and at that point the room erupted in groans, profanity, and obscene gestures. Jerome held up his hands, a thin smile on his face.

"Yes, I know how just about everyone in the department feels about our current Mayor. And I'm sure she feels the same way about you," he added quickly and quietly, with a smile. Which made the room erupt in rueful laughter. The Mayor had proven herself to be no friend to the Chicago Police Department, taking the side of just about anyone who had an issue with the officers simply trying to do their jobs. The rift had gotten so bad a huge number of officers had retired as a show of 'no confidence', putting the PD at record low numbers, and many of those still on the job were suffering from very low morale. When you knew the brass and City Hall would throw you under the bus no matter what happened, even if you were in the right, many officers had stopped trying to be proactive and were just showing up after the fact to take the reports and collect the bodies. And the criminals of Chicago knew it, which was why the murder rate was the highest in the country.

"Anyway," Jerome went on, "in case you missed it, she has announced increased foot patrols in certain areas to combat crime and provide an increased sense of security to residents and visitors." That last bit was straight from her press release. "The south side neighborhoods, which are not the bailiwick of the 18th District, but also the Magnificent Mile, which is. Apparently the stores there are still suffering from depressed sales. Tourism is still down."

"Maybe the Mayor shouldn't have let the protestors trash it, then," someone said loudly.

"Or maybe let us arrest a few of them instead of

standing around with our dicks in our hands," another officer added.

"Protestors my ass," someone else grumbled. "Millions of dollars of damage isn't a protest, it's a riot," he added, loud enough for the Sergeant to hear.

Jerome waved them quiet. "First District will be donating a few officers for this detail, taking the south end of the Mag, off the river. Officers assigned to foot patrol… smile, wave, be friendly to the tourists…try not to shoot anyone, and keep the beatings down to the bare minimum," he finished with a friendly smile. He looked down at the assignment sheet and began reading through it. Then he got to Whiskey. "Williams, Lopez, you're Thirteen Frank, and you're on foot patrol with Fifteen and Eighteen. Keep yourselves spread out, I don't want six officers on the same street corner."

Whiskey nodded at the Sergeant, but made a noise deep in his throat. Lopez looked at him. "What? The detail's not that bad." Less chance of dealing with any serious crime, especially on day shift, but also less chance of being shot at, or spit on.

Whiskey gave him a dark look. "How old are your feet?" he asked.

Grab your copy…
vinci-books.com/cascade

Author's Note

While writing this book I was wondering just how much of it was going to come true before I finished. Some gentlemen made what authorities think is a "dry run" on the base at Quantico using a panel truck when I was one month into this novel, but for some strange reason the government hid that information from the public for months. The number of known terrorists or people on the terror watch list apprehended trying to cross our southern border is staggering—not that most people care, or are paying attention. The mainstream news media isn't talking about it, which means, for most people, it isn't happening. They don't know, and they don't want to know. As for me, I can only hope this novel continues to be fiction.

Also, just when I was finishing up this novel, a gunman took a shot at former President Trump, by sheer blind luck or an act of God just nicking his ear when he turned his head. The facts and craziness and inconsistencies regarding the Secret Service actions that day would make a conspiracy theorist like Murph take to the roof to shout "I told you so!"

Author's Note

at the top of his lungs. Truth is stranger than fiction, because fiction has to make sense.

For this novel I once again have to thank Jeff Dickison of Advantage Investigations for answering my questions and educating me on current commercial surveillance tech. Back in the day I worked for him and with him in and around what I like to call the artful ruin that is modern Detroit, and as PIs go he's at the top of the heap. Jeff has been using a 3D printer to construct discreet housings for surveillance cameras since before most people even knew what a 3D printer was. It's a lot cheaper to park a hidden camera somewhere to record constantly than it is to pay a person to do surveillance, and with modern technology getting better seemingly on a daily basis those cameras are getting smaller, recording better and longer, than you'd probably want to know. In regards to that tech, there's nothing in this book that's fiction.

I also want to thank Eric. I first met Eric in college, decades ago. He was an ROTC Ranger, busy running six-minute miles while I got a nearly worthless Criminal Justice degree. After graduation we lost touch, but he reached back out to me a few years ago after finding and reading *Dogsoldiers*. Turns out in the intervening years he's stayed in the business, and if you're in the spec-ops game, the business, especially since 9/11, has been very good. He liked *Dogsoldiers* because he thought it very technically accurate, and in fact reminded him a lot of Ukraine, where he'd been working as a contractor even before the war with Russia broke out. He's still living and working in the region, and a lot of the details about Russia, Georgia, regional politics, and Baltic pipelines in this book came from him.

I'm not sure how old I was when my parents took my brother and I to Devils Tower in Wyoming. We were still

Author's Note

kids, but it was definitely after Close Encounters came out, as nobody had heard of it before the movie. We weren't there for long, but I remember being awed at this massive stone tower just thrusting up out of the ground in an otherwise mostly flat area. Just to refresh my memory I rewatched Close Encounters of the Third Kind, and the movie really holds up. It's not your typical sci-fi movie, it's damn near an art-house film. There are three versions available; the original theatrical release, the Special Edition, which adds some scenes and extends others, and then the Director's Cut, which is the Special Edition plus a few tweaks. When in doubt, ALWAYS go with the director's cut.

About the Author

James Tarr is a regular contributor to numerous firearms/outdoor publications and has appeared on or hosted numerous shows on The Sportsman Channel cable network including *Handguns and Defensive Weapons* and *Guns & Ammo TV.* He is also the author of fourteen books (and counting), including the critically-acclaimed *Dogsoldiers, Whorl, Bestiarii,* and *Carnivore* (with Dillard Johnson), which was featured on The O'Reilly Factor. He lives in Michigan with his fiancée, two sons and three dogs.